Praise for Books (

First Place fo ... iction
Goethe Awards for Historical Fiction

“A triumphant tale of love, family and courage….In this beautiful, lyrical novel, Linda Cardillo creates a fierce, strong-willed heroine, unafraid of hard work, solitude, or the judgment of her fellow islanders..” — Judith Arnold, *USA Today* Bestselling Author

“**Cardillo evokes the clapboard ports of New England with sensuous prose**. . . A sympathetic depiction of the oft-forgotten New England Native American heritage in this picturesque corner of the Vineyard.” — *Kirkus Reviews*

The Uneven Road

"A measured, riveting tale, written in a confident, impassioned voice." — *Kirkus Reviews*

"*The Uneven Road* is **a sophisticated coming-of-age novel…written with verve and intelligence**. Cardillo carefully constructs *The Uneven Road* with rich characterizations, diverging and interlocking plot elements, and fine attention to detail that explores family dynamics and the search for individual identity.” — *Chanticleer Book Reviews*

Other Books by Linda Cardillo

Dancing on Sunday Afternoons
The Valentine Gift: The Hand That Gives the Rose
A Mother's Heart: A Daughter's Journey
Across the Table
The Smallest Christmas Tree

Books One and Two in the First Light Trilogy
The Boat House Café
The Uneven Road

Island Legacy

Linda Cardillo

BOOK THREE OF
First Light

ISBN: 978-1-942209-37-9

Island Legacy

Cover photo by Stephan J. W. Platzer

BELLASTORIA PRESS
P.O. Box 60341
Longmeadow, Massachusetts 01116

For my children,
who have found home all over the world

List of Characters

The Innocenti Family

Elizabeth Todd Innocenti, a 36-year-old widow and documentary filmmaker who has been living in Florence, Italy for 15 years; widow of Antonio Innocenti and mother of Matteo Innocenti.

Antonio Innocenti, husband of Elizabeth; a crusading lawyer who died from ALS (Lou Gehrig's disease) the year before the story begins.

Matteo Innocenti, the 14-year-old son of Elizabeth and Antonio and grandson of Adriana and Massimo.

Adriana Innocenti, Antonio's mother and a former Italian Vogue fashion model.

Massimo Innocenti, Antonio's father and a successful goldsmith on the Ponte Vecchio.

The Hammond and Todd Families

Lydia Hammond, the 87-year-old matriarch of her family and the owner of Innisfree since 1961, when she purchased it from Mae Monroe.

Sam Todd, Lydia's grandson and Elizabeth's older brother, married to Debbie and father of Geoff, Kyle, Ella and Jessica.

Debbie Todd, Sam's wife and mother of Geoff, Kyle, Ella and Jessica.

Geoff, Kyle, Ella and Jessica Todd, the children of Sam and Debbie and cousins to Matteo.

Susan Hammond Todd, Elizabeth and Sam's mother.

Tom Todd, Elizabeth and Sam's father.

List of Characters (Continued)

The Monroe Family

Caleb Monroe, a 37-year-old Wampanoag, son of Josiah and Grace Monroe and grandson of Mae and Tobias Monroe; recently returned to Chappaquiddick.

Tobias Monroe, the 96-year-old sachem of the Chappaquiddick Wampanoag, father of Josiah and Izzy, grandfather of Caleb.

Josiah Monroe, the 65-year-old son of Mae and Tobias, the husband of Grace, brother of Izzy and father of Caleb; retired head of public works for the island of Martha's Vineyard.

Izzy Monroe, the 60-year-old daughter of Mae and Tobias, sister of Josiah and aunt of Caleb; a professor of American Literature at Yale, she is home for the summer on Chappaquiddick.

Grace Curtis Monroe, the 63-year-old wife of Josiah and mother of Caleb; a nurse practitioner.

Cousin Sadie, the cousin of Tobias and an elder in the Chappaquiddick Wampanoag tribe.

Members of the Chappaquiddick Wampanoag

Mariah Turner
Francine Everett
Sophie Butler

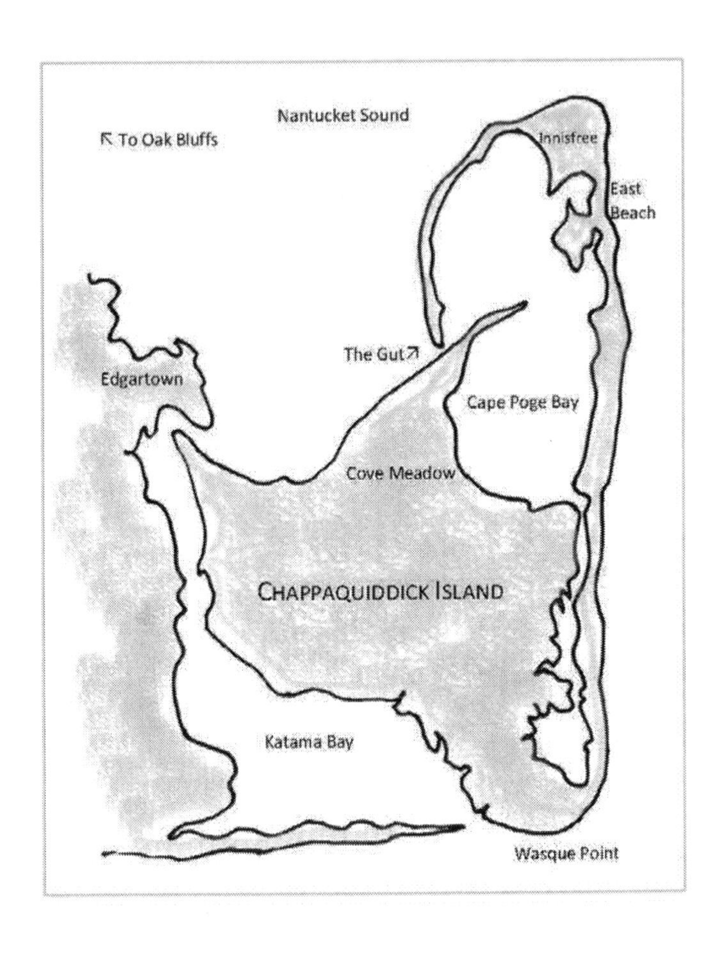

Nantucket Sound
↖ To Oak Bluffs
Innisfree
East
Beach
The Gut↗
Edgartown
Cape Poge Bay
Cove Meadow
CHAPPAQUIDDICK ISLAND
Katama Bay
Wasque Point

Chapter One

The Deep Heart's Core

"'The islanders have a saying: 'Some come here to heal; others to hide.' I don't think you need a hiding place, as far as I know, but come home to Innisfree and heal, sweetheart."

Elizabeth Innocenti read the words in her grandmother's elegant, spare hand. She had pulled the familiar, cream-colored envelope with the American postage stamp from the stack of mail that sat unread on her desk. It had been nearly a year since her husband, Antonio, had succumbed to the neurodegenerative disease that had first robbed him of his mobility and finally his life. But for Elizabeth, it could have been an hour for the sharp pain that still knifed through her when she woke every morning to the emptiness in her bed, the sheets on his side tight and flat, the pillow without his scent.

She was a widow at thirty-six, alone now with her child and her in-laws, whose loss of their only son reverberated without consolation throughout the villa in the hills above Florence where they lived together. When her mother-in-law, Adriana Innocenti, wasn't keening in grief, her wails cast out like a forlorn shepherdess seeking an echo, Adriana's deep-set eyes, rimmed in the blue-black smudge of insomnia, stared accusingly at Elizabeth for being alive.

Ever since she had first come to Italy to create the independent project that her progressive New England college required of its students to complete their degrees, Elizabeth had struggled to find acceptance in Adriana's eyes. A passionate student of history and media arts, she was determined to follow in the footsteps of her idol, Ken Burns, and become a documentary film maker.

She never anticipated that she would fall in love, either with Italy or with Antonio. She had arrived in Florence with a longing for something different and unknown, and so had been open to whatever it offered: quiet afternoons in a Uffizi gallery mesmerized by DaVinci's *Annunciation*, or a brilliant morning in the Piazza del Duomo contemplating Ghiberti's bronze doors on the Baptistery. She ate batter-fried zucchini flowers and spaghetti à la carbonara for the first time. She attended parties given by boys in silk shirts who drove Ferraris and lived in palazzos in the Oltrarno.

She met Antonio in the Laurentian Library, where they were both doing research; he for his thesis as a law student and she for the film she was planning that explored the effects of Savonarola's reign on the lives of Florentine women. Antonio, serious and contemplative, had seemed to be immersed in the ancient texts stacked around him on the table they shared without conversation for more than two weeks. A nod or an occasional "Buon giorno" was the extent of his acknowledgment of her existence. And then, one Thursday afternoon, as the discreet bell calling the monks of San Lorenzo to vespers reminded library patrons that it was time to take their leave, he unexpectedly invited her for a coffee.

That first coffee led to another, and then, when he understood why she was in Florence, he took her through the Museo dell'Antica Casa Fiorentina so that she could explore how the women of Savonarola's time had lived.

"You need more than books to understand Florentine life," he told her.

A few weeks later he offered to take her to the *Palio* in Sienna. Like all of Italy, to Elizabeth the *Palio* was both thrilling and incomprehensible—a furious horse race in the city's sloping central piazza; intense and bitter rivalries among neighborhoods vying for the championship; a riot of color as bands and flag throwers in medieval costume marched through the narrow streets and emerged into the open piazza to the roar of the crowds packed around the perimeter. Antonio held onto her in the throng, protecting her from the surge and push. They were surrounded by emotion and excitement to a degree Elizabeth had never experienced before. She absorbed it with all her senses, culminating in the moment when the race was won and Antonio kissed her, capturing in his own passion the intensity that was Italian life. The energy of the crowd and the heightened moment of victory punctuated by trumpets and the triumphant toss of the colors in an arc over them thrust her into an embrace of Italy from which she did not emerge until Antonio's death.

His love for her had been inexplicable to his mother. Despite Elizabeth's willingness to let go of all that tied her to America—family, language, even her New England sense of place and home—she had never been able to win Adriana's acceptance as her son's wife.

Elizabeth clutched her grandmother's letter and went out to the garden of the home where she and Antonio had spent their married life. The villa in the Florentine hills was where Antonio had been born and raised. When Elizabeth and Antonio married, Adriana and Massimo, his father, had converted the cinquecento building into two apartments and insisted that they live in one of them. She walked past the potted lemon trees on the terrace and down the stone steps to the sloping lawn that overlooked the city. The sun glinted on the terracotta roof of the Duomo. She had lived in Florence for fifteen years, fourteen of them as Antonio's wife. She had borne their son, Matteo, now a boy of fourteen who was thoroughly Italian, despite occasional summer visits and alternating Christmases with his American grandparents and extended family. She had been a good wife to Antonio—his confidante and advisor, his lover, his advocate and nurse as his disease had progressed and finally, the bereaved mourner at his graveside.

Adriana and Elizabeth could not comfort one another, could not acknowledge that the other's grief compared to her own.

Elizabeth reread her grandmother's letter as the sun slipped behind the hills. In it, Lydia Hammond offered her granddaughter the summer place that she and her late husband had bought decades before on the isolated barrier beach of Cape Poge on Chappaquiddick Island off the coast of Martha's Vineyard. It was a place that had once sheltered three generations of Hammond children from the day after school let out in June until Labor Day. Mae Keaney, the original owner, had called the place Innisfree, after the poem by Yeats, when it had been her home and a café that she ran for her livelihood serving fishermen on the bay. Elizabeth's grandparents kept the name, since that was how the islanders referred to the peninsula. As they had expanded the compound, they kept the connection to Yeats and continued to name additions after his poems. Lydia had called the girls' sleeping cottage "The Linnet," and decorated it with Audubon prints of finches and yellow curtains dotted with birds perched on delicate branches. The boys' cottage had been dubbed "Byzantium," and was filled with sailing gear. Even the room that housed the claw-footed tub, where hours had been spent preening, had the name "The Peacock."

When she was in high school, Elizabeth stumbled upon "The Lake Isle of Innisfree," the poem that had been Mae Keaney's inspiration, and she penned it in calligraphy for her grandparents as a Christmas gift. Lydia had framed it and hung it prominently in the living room of the main house. Enclosed in Lydia's letter was a photocopy of the poem.

I will arise and go now, and go to Innisfree,
And a small cabin build there, of clay and wattles made…
I will arise and go now, for always night and day
I hear lake water lapping with low sounds by the shore;
While I stand on the roadway, or on the pavements grey,
I hear it in the deep heart's core.

Elizabeth heard it as well, and decided to go home.

Elizabeth's announcement at dinner that she had decided to accept her grandmother's invitation was met not only with disapproval but protest. Not because Elizabeth was leaving, but because she was planning to take Matteo with her.

Adriana put down her fork. Like everything else in the villa, it was ancient, heavy with memory and tradition.

"How can you do this to us? Take away the only thing Massimo and I have left, the only joy that eases my aching heart!"

"Mama, it's only for the summer, the way we used to do before Antonio became ill. You remember that my grandmother has a cottage by the sea. It will be good for Matteo to get away from the city for a few weeks."

She did not add, good for him to get away from his nonna's unbearable sorrow; good for him to be an American child for a while, with cousins to play with and Fourth of July fireworks and baseball games to attend. She also said nothing of her own pain. That this house, Italy, held too many memories for her, too many places where she turned a corner and was brought up sharply by a vividly remembered scene—a caress, a long look across the room, a smile of gratitude and longing.

"If you must go, why can't you go alone? We can take Matteo to the sea, if you think that's so important."

Adriana sniffed, indicating that she considered it unnecessary. She herself would sit in her black dress all summer, closed in her room turning the pages of Antonio's childhood photo albums.

Elizabeth was weary. She had no desire to inflict more pain on her mother-in-law. But she also knew she yearned for the comfort and healing her grandmother had so wisely recognized Elizabeth needed. She would not find it in the villa.

She deferred that night from arguing with Adriana. But she wrote to her grandmother to let her know she and Matteo would come in June and quietly began making plans to fly to Boston as soon as school was out.

The struggle with Adriana continued. Elizabeth tried to keep the conversations away from the dinner table after the first night. Matteo was grieving in his own way and the last thing Elizabeth wanted was for him to feel torn between his mother and his nonna. Adriana's suffocating reliance on Matteo as her only hope would only deepen the boy's grief, and Elizabeth knew it was not only for herself that they needed to get away.

When Antonio had been alive—a phrase still unfamiliar and strange to her—she had always backed away from direct confrontation with her mother-in-law. It simply wasn't her nature, and she saw no point in putting Antonio in the position of having to choose. But with her son, it was different. She had no doubt that Adriana loved Matteo. But she knew in her heart that, if ever she was to have a reason to defy Adriana, Matteo's well-being was it.

The afternoon after she had booked their flights she found Adriana sitting in the loggia feeding bits of orange to her parrot. Her hair was pulled back into a severe bun, accentuating her high cheekbones. She had once been a fashion model, frequently appearing on the cover of Italian *Vogue*; and even into her sixties, she remained slender and striking, with a dramatic beauty. But since Antonio's death, she had barely eaten and Elizabeth was now struck by how skeletal her face seemed. Unaware that she was being watched, Adriana's fragility was exposed. Elizabeth was stunned by how old she looked, how vulnerable, and for a few moments her resolve waivered.

I should stay, she thought, knowing that she wouldn't leave Matteo.

And then Adriana saw her and the vulnerability hardened, sheathing her in armor. She cooed to the parrot, wiped her hands and raised her eyebrows as if to question why Elizabeth would be seeking her out.

"You've been out?"

"The marketing, some errands. I wanted to talk before Matteo gets home from school."

"Oh, Lisa, you're not going to bring up this idea again of going to America this summer!"

Antonio's family had always called her by the Italian form of her name, Elisabetta. Adriana addressed her by the diminutive, Lisa. To diminish me, Elizabeth had thought. She had never had a nickname in her family—not Liz or Beth or Betsy.

"I'm sorry, Mama. It's not an 'idea.' It's already in motion. I bought the tickets today."

"You would do this, knowing how much it hurts me!"

"Not to hurt you, Mama. But to help Matteo and me. Please understand. The pain is too fresh, the memories in this house too raw. Everywhere I turn I see Antonio's face and am reminded that he is no longer here."

"You want to run away from the memories and forget him! He's not even cold in his grave!"

"No, Mama. Not to forget. Only to find a way to continue living without him."

"You have no idea what it means to bury a child. You cannot fathom a mother's loss."

"I think I can imagine it. I am a mother. Matteo's only a boy, a boy who has lost his father, who needs his mother more than anything right now."

"Then stay here with him."

Adriana's face was taut with both anger and pleading. She was distraught, she was outraged. It was easier for Elizabeth to hold her ground against the anger, and she focused on the demand in her mother-in-law's tone. Adriana didn't want her pity, Elizabeth knew.

"No, Mama. If I am going to be strong enough for Matteo, I need to heal. We need to go."

And she left the loggia, retreating to the thick-walled room with the arched ceiling and deep-set windows that had sheltered her and Antonio throughout their marriage. She ran her fingers along the top of the dark wooden paneling that lined the lower half of the stucco walls. It was trimmed with intricately carved stone pine trees, each one linked to the next by its widespread branches. On their wedding night, Antonio had whispered to her a fantastical tale of the powers of the tree, harboring dreams and wishes within its foliage like magical fruit. It was a story told to him by his grandmother when he'd been a boy unable to sleep.

"We sleep in a bower, protected by the circle of trees. Nothing can harm us within these walls."

But the trees hadn't protected Antonio and no longer offered her the solace of sleep. Her hand snagged on a sharp branch and a splinter dug deep into her ring finger, drawing blood.

She pulled it out and sucked away the beads of red, then curled up on the window seat and wept.

Chapter Two

Almost There

The night before Elizabeth and Matteo left for Boston, Adriana said her farewell to her grandson after dinner, her sadness so palpable that Matteo went to Elizabeth afterwards with uncertainty and confusion.

Elizabeth was sorting through her closet, fingering the stylish European-cut suits that had been the staple of her wardrobe as the wife of a lawyer who had fought corruption. Nothing was appropriate for a summer at the cottage, where she remembered living in shorts and t-shirts as a girl. She pulled a few blouses, a bathing suit and a pair of pants together, realizing how little she would need on the island.

"Mom, Nonna is crying and talking like we're never coming back. We are, aren't we?"

Matteo spoke English with his mother, Italian with everyone else in his life. Elizabeth and Antonio had agreed, they wanted him fluent in both languages, and now, as a teenager, he spoke both without an accent, without hesitation. But it had been an irritant to Adriana, whose own command of English was meager, that she could not always understand what Elizabeth and Matteo said to each other. No matter that it was the usual exchanges between mother and child: How was school today? Are you hungry? Do you have any homework?

Elizabeth pulled her son close.

"Of course we're coming back! This is just a visit like we've made in the past, when you were younger, to see Grandma and Grandpa and Great-Granny Lydia. They want to see us because they know how hard it has been for us losing Babbo."

"Why can't they come here? Nonna says they are welcome."

"That's very kind of her. But it's difficult for them all to travel, especially Great-Granny, who lives in a nursing home now. They miss us, Matteo. And I miss them. Just like the villa and Firenze are home to you, Massachusetts, and especially Innisfree, are home to me."

Elizabeth was furious that Adriana would project her fears onto Matteo and plant a seed of doubt in him about his mother's intentions. She fought the urge to criticize her to Matteo and did her best to calm him. She reminded herself that in twelve hours they would be on their way.

She thought about what she had said to Matteo. Italy was home to him, and she knew she couldn't take him away from it permanently.

In the morning, Adriana remained in her rooms. Don Massimo, her husband, kissed them fervently on both cheeks and pressed a clip full of bills into his grandson's hand when the taxi arrived at the door.

"For the roller coaster and the cinema," he mumbled.

Elizabeth saw that he had gone to the trouble of getting dollars for Matteo, and even though it was far more than he could spend (and there were no roller coasters on the island), she was grateful that her father-in-law wanted the boy to have some fun.

Matteo spent the flight playing games on his laptop. Elizabeth tried to pay attention to the movie, but it was a romantic comedy and she found she couldn't bear the lighthearted predicaments that she knew only temporarily kept the lovers from finally being together. She switched it off and pulled out the photocopied list her grandmother had sent her. The original had been written in ink on lined notepaper in Lydia's precise penmanship. It was her list of provisions for the cottage for the summer—everything from sugar and flour and powdered milk to flashlight batteries, insect repellent and board games. She'd started the list in 1961, when she and Poppa Lou had bought Innisfree. Lydia stocked up on staples at the beginning of summer to keep from having to make too many trips into town. Over the years she'd adapted the list as Elizabeth's mother and her brothers grew. Propane for the stove and refrigerators and gasoline for the generator that ran the washing machine on the back porch appeared on the list in the mid-1960s. It was around that time that Lydia and Grandpa Lou added amenities to the house at Lydia's insistence after dealing with the food and laundry for three teenagers for one summer too many.

Elizabeth smiled at the water-stained notations and the memories of her frugal grandmother's meals as she scanned the list of ingredients. It had been a long time since she had sat down at the oilcloth-covered table in the cottage dining room to platters of fresh-caught bluefish and boiled potatoes.

But Elizabeth reminded herself that Lydia would not be waiting for her at Innisfree. Two years before, her heart problems had become so severe that she needed constant care, and Elizabeth's mother and uncles had convinced Lydia to move into the Shady Knoll nursing home in Edgartown. From what Elizabeth understood, Lydia's mind was as engaged as ever, but her once vigorous and athletic body had betrayed her. This was a woman who had water skied every afternoon in the bay that lapped at the western edge of the property. She had once been able to outlast all her grandchildren on the water, the tennis court and at the card table.

Elizabeth knew one of the first things she and Matteo would do after they arrived on Martha's Vineyard would be to visit Shady Knoll. She hadn't asked anyone in the family to meet them at Logan Airport. Her parents were in Asia on one of her father's business trips and were coming out to the island to see them when they returned later in the summer. Her brother Chris lived too far away in New Jersey, and she had told Sam, the brother who lived year-round in Oak Bluffs, that she'd rather rent a car and make her way to the Vineyard herself. She planned to spend the night with him before driving out to the cottage. They no longer needed a boat to get to Innisfree, but there were still no roads, just a Jeep track across the dunes that led to the narrow curved arm of sand on the northern edge of what was now the Cape Poge Wildlife Refuge.

As much as Elizabeth wanted to see her family, she knew Lydia's advice was the wisdom she needed to follow: use the peace and solitude of Innisfree to heal.

She thought she had planned well by flying mid-week, expecting traffic to be lighter than on the weekend to get to Cape Cod and the ferry at Woods Hole that would carry them to Martha's Vineyard. But by the time they got through customs, picked up the four-wheel drive Jeep she had reserved and grabbed a bite to eat, it was rush hour. She struggled with the stop-and-go traffic and the unfamiliar car, much larger than her compact Fiat. Matteo was cranky, his stomach was upset from the fast food he'd craved and she'd reluctantly agreed to, and they were both starting to feel the effects of the six-hour time difference. It was nearly midnight by their body clocks, and they'd been up since dawn in Florence to make their flight.

Up ahead she could see that traffic was at a standstill. She didn't have a cell phone that worked in the States and realized it was one thing Lydia didn't have on her list. It was the first time in years that no one knew where she was. She swallowed down the flicker of panic rising in her throat and glanced at Matteo, who did not look well.

"Take a sip of Coke and open the window."

She could see how pale he was, the beads of sweat forming above his upper lip. Not even peach fuzz there yet, she realized. She'd been so preoccupied with grief and this journey that she hadn't looked at him closely in the last month. A glimmer of relief washed over her. He was still a boy. She wasn't ready for his adolescence; had never imagined she'd have to face it without Antonio. She began making her own list now; unlike Lydia's, it wasn't one of provisions, but of the milestones she would be reaching alone.

"Mom, I really don't feel good. I think I'm going to throw…."

She put the car in park, grabbed the waxy bag the burgers had come in and thrust it in front of Matteo just in time. He'd never been much of a traveler. When he was a baby and they had to go any distance in a car she'd always brought along an extra set of clothes because he invariably spit up. Once it had been an entire jar of creamed spinach.

She was grateful now that the Southeast Expressway had turned into a parking lot. She dug into her tote bag and retrieved a small container of wipes and some chewing gum.

"Here you go, wipe your mouth and take some gum."

She wanted to wipe his face herself but she could see by his expression—embarrassment at having vomited and reluctance at being treated like a baby—that she needed to back off.

"How much longer, Mom?"

"At least a couple of hours, honey. Do you want to climb into the back seat and try to get some sleep? You look wiped."

"I'm OK. It's not like I remember," he gestured out the window. They had barely made it out of the city.

"We're still quite far from the Cape. It will start to look more familiar when we get closer. Do you want to listen to the radio?"

"Nah. Maybe I'll just turn on my iPod. I want to listen to my own songs."

Within a few minutes, his eyes were closed and he slipped into the rhythmic breathing of sleep that triggers a mother's relief.

He wasn't a toddler on the verge of a tantrum, but Elizabeth sensed Matteo's mounting disappointment. It wasn't just his physical discomfort. He'd been uprooted from the familiar and dropped down into an American landscape that even to someone like Elizabeth, who'd grown up here, was ugly and crowded and oppressive.

She had wanted this trip to be a homecoming for Matteo as well as her, but she had to admit, there was little here that would speak to him of home. She hoped it would be better when they got to the island, but she was afraid his impressions of America were already being shaped by their stressful beginning.

She drank some of her own Coke, glad she'd thought to order herself one. She needed to stay awake, get through the snarled traffic and arrive at the ferry. To keep alert she turned on the radio at a low volume and caught the end of the news. She was reminded that it was a presidential campaign year, and although the party conventions wouldn't take place until August, Barack Obama and John McCain were the presumptive nominees and were already on the campaign trail. Despite living in Italy for fifteen years, Elizabeth had voted as an expatriate in every presidential election. It would be an interesting summer to be in the midst of such a groundbreaking campaign instead of watching it from afar.

They crawled for another hour before finally getting beyond the accident that had caused the delay. She was relieved that the wreckage had been cleared, the ambulances long gone to the hospital by the time they reached the scene. Just a few flares remained, a single state trooper directing traffic around the shattered glass. She gripped the steering wheel tighter and kept her eyes straight ahead. She had been with Antonio on the night of his death, as she had been constantly after it became devastatingly clear that none of the treatments his doctors had tried was going to prolong his life.

Elizabeth realized she was holding her breath a few hundred yards past the site of the accident. When she and her brothers had been kids, they'd take a deep gulp of air at the edge of the cemetery behind the Congregational church on the green in the New England town where they lived and not let it out until their father's car had cleared the white picket fence at the end. Sam had convinced her and Chris that the dead could steal your breath and suck you down into the grave with them. The only way to save yourself was to hold your breath when you passed a cemetery. Of course, as they got older, they'd make a game of trying to tickle each other until they breathed.

Breathe, Elizabeth. You're still alive. Matteo is still alive. That accident is someone else's pain. Not yours. Once on the boat, she promised herself, *things would be better.*

By the time they arrived at the ferry dock at Woods Hole, the next-to-last ferry was boarding for Oak Bluffs and Elizabeth slipped into line. The tension in her shoulders and jaw loosened. Almost there.

The sun was setting behind them as the ferry pulled out of its berth. Nearly nine in the evening; six hours since they'd landed at Logan. She roused Matteo to come out on deck with her, hoping he'd feel that same sense of peace she did as soon as the boat reached open water, leaving behind on the mainland everything unimportant that pulled and tugged and clamored for her attention. The wind was brisk, whipping the flag on the prow, pushing back the gulls that floated above the crowd waiting for a tossed piece of bread. Her hair was wild around her face.

"I'm cold. Can't I go back to the car?"

"Put your sweatshirt on. The fresh air is better for you after being cooped up in the car all these hours. We'll be at Uncle Sam's house in less than an hour, and you can go right to bed. Take a look—around you, up at the sky."

"At what? It all just looks gray to me."

He was right. The boat had headed directly into a fog bank. Elizabeth could feel the fine mist on her face and heard the buoy bells indicating the channel. Within a minute, she couldn't see the flag.

She caved. No use forcing him to stay up on deck with her if she had any hope of his enjoying this summer.

"It's OK. Go back to the car. I'll be down as soon as I get myself a cup of coffee. You hungry? Want anything from the snack bar?"

He shook his head and held up his hands. "I've had enough American fast food today."

Elizabeth watched him weave his way back to the car deck and then sat at a gray Formica table in the nearly deserted snack bar nursing a cup of bitter coffee. She'd forgotten how different American coffee was from the cappuccino and espresso that were a daily part of her routine in Florence. Despite her conviction that Lydia was right that this sojourn at Cape Poge was necessary and right for her, she worried that she'd made a mistake in thinking it would be as healing for Matteo.

The last time he'd been at Cape Poge he'd been a toddler of two, when she and Antonio had come to the States for a family gathering at the cottage to celebrate Lydia's seventy-fifth birthday. They hadn't stayed the night, although Lydia had encouraged them to take the small sleeping cottage, which still had the wooden crib that all of Lydia's grandchildren had slept in at one time or another. Elizabeth remembered why they hadn't stayed. Antonio had found the place "*primitivo*," and worried about Matteo getting scratched or dirty or bitten by mosquitoes. They stayed at the Harbor View Hotel instead and never visited the cottage again. Since then they'd made their summer visits to her parents' home outside of Boston or at Christmas, when everyone gathered at Lydia and Lou's home in town, on Water Street in Edgartown.

Elizabeth tossed the half-finished coffee in the trash and descended to the car deck as the loudspeaker announced they were approaching the harbor, still invisible in the fog. Whatever burdens had been lifted from her as the boat left Woods Hole were resettling themselves on her shoulders as she opened the door of the Jeep and saw Matteo, connected to his iPod and scowling as the boat lurched into port.

Sam's place in Oak Bluffs was a deep green Victorian with burgundy gingerbread trim on a side street just off Ocean Park. He and his wife Debbie and their four kids spilled out of the house onto the front porch as Elizabeth and Matteo arrived. Everyone raced down the steps and enveloped them in welcome as they climbed out of the Jeep.

"You made it! We figured you'd gotten caught in the traffic on Route 3. Gran's been calling every hour. We probably shouldn't have told her you were arriving today….Come on in and collapse. Kyle, Geoff, take Aunt Elizabeth's and Matteo's bags up to the sleeping porch."

"Are you hungry? Thirsty? Or do you just want to go to bed and visit tomorrow?"

Elizabeth was surrounded by voices, helping hands, the familiar smile of her brother and the casual, dowdy comfort of a house full of kids, with flip flops scattered across the hall and boogie boards stacked on the porch.

She turned to her son, expecting him to want to be pointed in the direction of the nearest bed. But Matteo had already homed in on the neon glow of the TV screen, where a video game had been halted in progress, interrupted by their arrival. His cousins handed him a controller and the three teenage boys formed a ring on the floor. The sisters, Ella and Jessica, who at eight and six were younger than the boys by several years, were hunched over a jigsaw puzzle spread on a card table.

Elizabeth ran her fingers through her windblown hair.

"Maybe I'll have that drink…"

Chapter Three

Lydia

The next morning she left Matteo sleeping soundly on the screened-in sleeping porch and set out with Lydia's list to start gathering the paraphernalia she needed to set up housekeeping at Innisfree. Sam had told her the night before that no one had been living there since Lydia had gone to Shady Knoll.

"We occasionally go out for a day or two with the kids, but it's not like when we were young and were content to spend the whole summer entertaining ourselves with the water and the woods. Without electricity and, God forbid, internet, these wired children of ours start experiencing withdrawal symptoms. Chris used to come up for a week or two, but his kids all have summer jobs at the Jersey shore now. The cousins are so far flung that we only see them at Hammond family reunions. With Grandpa Lou gone and Granny Lydia in a nursing home, I don't know how long even those gatherings will continue."

Elizabeth shook off her disappointment that Innisfree was no longer the focal point of her family's life. She'd been away from it a long time. Everyone's circumstances had changed—children growing up and into their own lives; her own parents enjoying the freedom to travel; elders diminished or passed on.

She clutched Lydia's list, a relic of an idealized time Elizabeth hoped to rediscover, or at least recreate for herself and her son. She threw herself into the shopping as if she were organizing the Lewis and Clark expedition.

When she got back to Sam's the Jeep was packed with two months' supply of dry goods, a cooler filled with fresh produce and a canvas tote filled with books from the library, where she'd signed up for a card. Matteo was at the beach with his cousins.

Debbie made her a cup of tea and sat with her on the porch.

"Elizabeth, I want to make a suggestion, and please don't take offense. I know you planned this summer at Innisfree as a way for you and Matteo to recover from Antonio's death, and I can't think of a better place for you. For *you*. But in the brief time Matteo's been here, it seems to me what he needs is to be around kids his own age and be so busy that he can forget for a while that he's a boy who lost his father."

"I don't want him to forget Antonio."

"I don't mean for him to forget Antonio. I mean, he needs to define himself not as a fatherless boy, but as a boy who excels at Frisbee or learns how to catch a striper off the dock or beats his older cousin at the ninth level of Halo."

"You think I'm making a mistake, taking him out to Innisfree." It wasn't a question.

"No, not a mistake. Just premature. Listen, why don't you let him stay with us here in town for a week or two, while you get the place set up and give yourself some solitude?"

"I couldn't burden you with a child you barely know. I'd also feel like I'm abandoning him. That I brought him all this way only to leave him."

"Elizabeth, he's our nephew. He's blood, not a stranger. And one more child in this house actually makes it easier on me. They entertain one another. And I'll put him to work, just like my kids. Look, if you're feeling guilty about leaving him, why don't you ask him how he feels about it when the kids get back from the beach."

Elizabeth had lived long enough in Italy to understand the power Italian mothers wielded, especially over their sons, and she had vowed to herself when Matteo was born that she'd give him the confidence to leave her when the time came for him to be independent. It hadn't occurred to her that the moment would come this soon, but maybe this was an opportunity for both of them to test the waters.

She hated the thought of having him away from her. Since Antonio's death, she had worried more for his safety than when he'd been a toddler exploring every sharp-edged corner in the villa, with its marble floors and glass-topped wrought iron tables. But she admitted that she longed for even a few days to herself, with no one else's needs taking precedence. When she could be honest, and curse and wail to the heavens standing on the beach at Innisfree without concern for Matteo's fragile recovery from Antonio's death. When she could walk for hours, eat at midnight, swim in the pond naked at six a.m. She wanted to be grateful for Debbie's offer without damning herself as a terrible mother as if she were Adriana casting judgment.

Debbie seemed to read her mind.

"It's OK to want a few days to yourself, Elizabeth. You've been through a lot," she said gently, squeezing her hand. "If you think Matteo might back off from our invitation because he's worried about leaving you alone, the boys can reassure him that all mothers need a break. We have a saying in this house, 'When Mama ain't happy, ain't nobody happy.' It's the only time I allow them to use the word 'ain't'."

When the kids got back from the beach, Elizabeth watched the ease with which the cousins had absorbed Matteo into their fold. Even the rough-housing under the outdoor shower, with each of them jostling for control of the showerhead so he could spray the others, struck her with its normalcy. She knew that's what she wanted for Matteo. A normal life. Not one scarred by tragedy.

When he came upstairs to change into dry clothes, she presented him with his options.

"What do you want me to do?"

"Are you having fun here?"

"Yeah, sure. Kyle and Geoff are cool guys. Even Ella and Jessica aren't too much of a pain, like some of the girls back home."

"Then stay for a while."

"But what about you?"

"I need a few days to clean the place up, get it ready for us to inhabit. I think I'd actually enjoy having it to myself for a bit."

"You're sure? 'Cause I'll come with you now, like we planned."

"I'm sure. Have some fun with your cousins. The only thing I really want you to do for me is visit Great-Granny Lydia with me this afternoon."

"Is she going to pinch my cheeks like Nonna's mother?"

"No. Only Italian grandmothers do that. Great-Granny Lydia is English-French Canadian. She'll probably high-five you and challenge you to a game of poker."

The visit at Shady Knoll was crushing. Sam should have prepared her. Matteo got very still as they walked down a hallway lined with women nodding vacantly in their wheel chairs, their frail bodies hunched over and their blue-veined hands clutching like claws at whatever passed. Thank God, none of them was Lydia.

Lydia herself was propped up in her bed, her glasses perched on her nose as she read the latest issue of *Newsweek*. Nothing different about her grandmother's choice of reading material. But everything else about her stunned Elizabeth. The robust, tanned matriarch who had worked and played with such vigor in Elizabeth's earliest memories was a cipher, a spider-like shorthand symbol on a page that had once been paragraphs full of rounded nouns and verbs. She barely filled the navy blue tracksuit that Elizabeth remembered as Lydia's uniform in the cool evenings at Innisfree.

Lydia looked up from her reading at their knock and a toothless smile spread across her face, crazed with the deep-set lines of someone who has spent most of her life outdoors, on the sea.

"Oh, my girl! You are here at last! Sam phoned me last night after what must have been my millionth pestering call and let me know you had arrived late but safe. And this must be Matteo. Come and let your great-granny give you a proper New England greeting."

She held out her hands and clasped Matteo's, studying him. Elizabeth could see his relief that this old woman was not going to demand a kiss. She herself enveloped Lydia in an embrace, her arms encircling her grandmother's once strong, broad back. Despite Lydia's diminished size, however, her grip was still that of a woman who could haul a 15-pound striper over the side of a boat. She hugged Elizabeth fiercely.

"Welcome home, child."

Both women brushed aside tears. It was then that Lydia clasped her hand over her mouth.

"Oh, shit. I don't have my teeth in. No wonder Matteo is backing away, thinking I'm definitely not his type. Elizabeth, hand me that lavender box on the night table. Thank you, honey." She retrieved her dentures and slipped them in, flashing a smile when she was done.

"That's better, don't you think?"

They visited with Lydia for an hour after an aide delivered a wheel chair and they retreated to a corner on the porch where they could sit unobserved by the hungry stares of the other residents.

Lydia peppered Matteo with questions and challenged him to a game of chess while Elizabeth went off in search of coffee for them, a Coke for him.

She marveled at Lydia's apparent acceptance of this confined life, bounded by linoleum hallways that reeked of disinfectant and glassed-in solariums that kept the wind at bay. Once upon a time, she'd been mistress of a wild and uncontrollable place that she'd wrestled into a hospitable refuge without destroying what was most essential about its character. But she seemed content now, which eased Elizabeth's own dismay that her grandmother's life had been reduced to the ordered, bland routine of an institution.

She understood from Sam and Debbie the night before that the alternatives were limited. Lydia's diminished heart could barely sustain her, let alone allow her to live on her own or even with a member of the family. No one wanted to take her away from Martha's Vineyard, which had been her and Grandpa Lou's full-time home since he had retired from his medical practice.

Someday, not this visit, not with Matteo, Elizabeth would talk to Lydia. She wanted to understand how to accept, how to adapt to such profound change. Because she didn't know how she could continue with the pain, the anger and the hopelessness that now consumed her. Her grandmother's heart beat now in a whisper; Elizabeth's heart screamed in terror and loneliness.

When Elizabeth returned to the porch, Lydia had just checkmated Matteo, but she acknowledged he'd been one of her most formidable opponents. He promised he'd be back for a rematch, now that he understood her tactics. The aide appeared on the threshold, a medicine cup in her hand and a reminder, tapping her wristwatch, that Lydia usually napped at this time.

Elizabeth winced at the aide's tone of voice, as if she were coaxing a recalcitrant child. She was even more distressed by the docility with which Lydia acquiesced. But then she saw the dull film of exhaustion in her grandmother's eyes, the slump in her once-erect shoulders. She and Matteo said good-bye, and this time Lydia took Matteo's face in her hands and kissed him.

"Teach your mama to play chess. I never could get her to sit still long enough to learn."

They left the overheated air of Shady Knoll and emerged into the sunshine.

"Let's go get some ice cream." She felt a need to slake her parched throat, as if all the questions she had for Lydia had accumulated there, stopped by the crushing reality of her grandmother's frailty.

She had hoped to make her way to Innisfree that afternoon after her visit with Lydia. But it was nearly four by the time she and Matteo returned to Oak Bluffs. Sam and Debbie convinced her to stay another night with them and get an early start the next morning. Matteo threw on his bathing suit and raced across the park to join his cousins at the beach. Debbie handed her a vodka tonic and the two of them slipped into a companionable partnership preparing dinner—corn on the cob, grilled chicken, a salad of tomatoes and cucumbers from a local farm. Elizabeth smiled at how American the meal was, how American the ease with which she and her sister-in-law shared the kitchen.

In the villa, she and Adriana had separate kitchens and rarely prepared a meal together. Adriana's cooking, like her sense of style and her language, was "High Italian." She had help, whom she supervised with precise instructions and exacting demands. She had entertained often for Massimo's jewelry business, and the villa lent itself to the kind of sophisticated elegance that was Adriana's trademark.

Elizabeth's cooking had evolved from the roasts and pies that had been the staples of her mother's repertoire when she had been a girl learning to chop and stir at her side. One day, early in her marriage, she had tapped on the kitchen door on Adriana and Massimo's side of the villa and asked the cook in her then-halting Italian if she could watch her prepare one of Antonio's favorite dishes. Carmella had handed her an apron and proceeded in a combination of hand gestures and her Fiesole dialect to show her how to make spinach *gnocchi al olio*. She blended the riced potatoes, eggs and chopped spinach into a dough with her hands and then deftly shaped the gnocchi into dumplings with a twist of her thumb. It was the beginning of Elizabeth's culinary education.

Now with Debbie she stripped the silk from the corn and peeled and sliced cucumbers. The simplicity of the preparations, the ritual of mothers making a meal for their brood of children, reminded her of the summers at the cottage when she and her brothers and cousins would descend ravenous upon the dining table. Her mother, her aunts and Lydia would be navigating the kitchen in an effortless dance, their cheeks rosy from the heat of the ancient six-burner Champion gas stove that dominated the room and from their glasses of Merlot, each of them part of the secret society of women who summered at Innisfree. The men only came on the weekends, visitors, not true residents in the way the women were.

That night on Sam and Debbie's sleeping porch, her son was sprawled asleep, sunburned and exhausted on the cot next to her. The fresh memories of her afternoon with Lydia and the softer recollections of her childhood summers eased her into a sleep that could only partly be explained by the sea air and receding jet lag.

Chapter Four

Innisfree

The weather was overcast and threatening rain as Elizabeth repacked the Jeep with the paraphernalia and provisions she had accumulated. When it was time for her to go, Sam's entire family lined up with Matteo on the porch. The cousins had dragged him out there, explaining it was time for the ritual known as the "Hammond Wave." It was Lydia who had initiated the tradition, standing on her front porch and vigorously waving farewell whenever anyone in the family departed. As children, Elizabeth remembered that she and her brothers always rolled down the windows in their car and extended their arms out to their grandmother. They knew she didn't go back inside the house until the car was out of sight. Elizabeth was touched by Sam's family carrying on the practice and initiating Matteo. She saw his arm raised in salute as she rounded the corner and turned onto Beach Road.

Despite the dismal weather, a boisterous group of teenage boys in brilliantly hued baggy shorts was crowded onto a stone bridge spanning a channel between the marsh and the sea. One by one they did cannonballs from the railing into the water below, each one trying to outdo the others with the height of his leap and the magnitude of water displaced when he landed. A group of admiring girls in bikinis watched from the bank, screaming and stepping back from the splashes. Across from the bridge a van with a striped awning was selling hot dogs and cotton candy.

Elizabeth smiled at the tumult of the American seaside, and could even, reluctantly, imagine Matteo taking his place on the railing. Debbie had been right to encourage her to let him stay a few weeks.

When Elizabeth reached Edgartown she pulled into the Stop & Shop to pick up the last of the perishables she would need. Once she was out at the cottage she knew she wouldn't want to leave. The supermarket was a madhouse of tourists impatient to get their deli orders filled so that they could extract every precious second out of their week-long beach rentals. Elizabeth escaped from the crowded store with her purchases, packed them into the cooler in the back of her Jeep and dumped a couple of bags of ice on top of everything. It might take up to two hours to get from Edgartown to the cottage, depending on the wait for the Chappy ferry that plied across the mouth of the Edgartown harbor to Chappaquiddick Island. The ferry trip itself took less than five minutes, but it only carried three cars.

As she expected, the queue was long, extending beyond Daggett Street and back onto Simpsons Lane. She pulled behind the last car and forty minutes later arrived at the dock, the first in line for the next boat. The harbor was churning with activity—small dinghies with oversized outboard motors darting past luxury yachts, the ferry plowing nearly sideways through the current and booming a warning to smaller boats. At the pier adjacent to the ferry a trimaran that took tourists on harbor cruises announced its next sail over a loudspeaker. Everywhere Elizabeth looked, she saw the bustle of a waterfront summer resort, with vacationers frenetic in their search for the next adventure or the latest t-shirt.

As soon as the last car drove off the incoming ferry, the pilot waved her forward and Elizabeth crossed a clanging metal ramp onto the boat, a flat-bedded open craft with benches along both sides for walk-ons and room for three tightly parked vehicles.

At the Chappaquiddick side of the harbor, Elizabeth led the short caravan of vehicles behind her off the ferry and onto a narrow paved road. After she passed the small cluster of people waiting to board the returning ferry, Elizabeth saw only a couple of cyclists peddling. The cars behind her turned off onto side streets and she was on her own. The road meandered past an apple orchard, an improvised roadside stand with white plastic buckets filled with crimson peonies and dahlias for sale, and a few barely visible houses set back beyond meadows or woods. After the cacophony of Edgartown, this sparsely populated rural neighborhood seemed to belong to another time. When the road curved sharply to the right, Elizabeth slowed and, instead of following the turn, drove straight ahead onto a packed dirt road that lead directly to the Dike Bridge that linked Chappaquiddick to the narrow barrier island that was Cape Poge. When she reached the bridge, she stopped at a small sandy parking area and stood on the sloping bank of Poucha Pond, scanning a horizon that offered only sky, water and sand. She heard nothing but the gentle lap of water against the sturdy wooden pilings that supported the bridge.

Out of the glove compartment she dug a tire gauge that she'd remembered to purchase at the hardware store and lowered the air pressure in the tires the way she'd learned as a teenager. She'd checked the tides before she left Oak Bluffs and was glad she was crossing the beach at low tide this first time out on her own. There had been times in her youth when stormy weather had driven the tides high on the beach and she'd had to ford stretches where the water was over the wheel wells, or back up and resort to a narrow and overgrown trail in the middle of the island. She knew that years of erosion had more than likely altered what she remembered, but she was eager to move away from the tourists starting to fill up the parking lot in spite of the overcast weather. She wanted to get out onto the trail.

She climbed into the Jeep, backed away from the pond and crossed the bridge. She made the turn after the gatehouse and felt the car straining through the soft sand. But with a lurch, she managed to pass the first hurdle and guide the Jeep into the shallow tracks that lay ahead.

The three miles to the cottage through the Refuge took forty minutes to traverse, a constantly changing landscape punctuated by scrub pine and beach roses, undulating reeds, sea vistas through breaks in the dunes and the ever present birds. Elizabeth noted that, as in years past, there was not a single structure or sign of human presence on the whole route.

She finally pulled off the beach, stopped to open a wooden gate that marked the boundary between the Refuge and the Hammond land and steered the Jeep up the rutted drive to the house. She wound past a grove of red cedars, bent and twisted by a century of wind. On her left, sleek black cormorants preened on a sandbar in the middle of the pond. As the drive curved up a short incline, the grey-shingled cluster of buildings came into view, perched on a promontory at the junction of Shear Pen Pond and Cape Poge Bay. The image was at once heart-stopping in its familiarity—the source of idyllic childhood memories—and disturbing in the reality now seen through adult eyes that had been too long away.

In her memories and in her hunger for a place of refuge, Elizabeth had held onto Innisfree and its environs as a paradise. But in the dull, metallic light of this late June morning, Elizabeth was shocked to see the dilapidated structures, the rusting propane tanks stacked against the house, the weathered and splintering Adirondack chairs scattered on the rough and uncut grass, the scraggly shrubs struggling to gain a foothold in the sand. The house stood in stark isolation on the point, clearly battered by years of Nor'easters and bearing an aching, lonely witness to Lydia's absence.

Elizabeth sat in the car, mute with sadness at what had become of this precious place. She pulled her sweater tightly around her, but the chill she felt was not just coming off the water. She had journeyed here needing a respite, expecting Innisfree to envelop her in its magic. Instead, it struck her that it was as needy as she was.

A flash of lightning illuminated the sky across the bay, rousing her to the realization that she had a carload of stuff to unpack. She worked quickly to get everything inside the main house before the downpour that had been threatening finally descended, pounding the roof with the rat-a-tat of a snare drum. The air inside was stale, the cobwebs thick. Sam had managed to get out to the property earlier in the month when she had sent word she was coming, but he admitted to her he'd only had time to deal with the basics of opening the house for the summer—removed the plywood that protected the windows during the winter, ordered propane and hooked up a fresh tank, primed the pump and made sure she had diesel fuel for it and the generator. Elizabeth wandered through the stuffy rooms, absorbing both the familiar and the forgotten as she took stock in the murky light that struggled to make its way through clouded, dirt-spattered windows. She confirmed that the stove and the gaslights worked, which reassured her. But when she turned on the faucet in the kitchen it shuddered and spewed a thick torrent of rusty water. She left it running, hoping it would finally clear up. She was relieved she'd loaded a few gallons of bottled water into her cart when she'd gone shopping, although at the time it had seemed extravagant. When she opened the refrigerators on the porch, she was hit with a wave of nausea from the black mold climbing up the walls. The decline and desolation appalled her. How long had it been since anyone had lived here?

On the wall between the kitchen and the living room she brushed her fingers over the hundreds of notches that had recorded the growth of every generation of children who had summered at Innisfree. The first row, closest to the kitchen door, listed Elizabeth's mother, Susan, and her two brothers, Louis and Richard, marching up the wall from the time they were young children until they reached their teens. Parallel to them were Elizabeth, Chris and Sam and all their cousins, Louis and Richard's children. Her last notch was dated the summer before she left for Italy. Next to her generation were her nieces and nephews. Kneeling down close to the floor she searched for one mark she remembered making when she had last been at Innisfree. She found it. Matteo, at age two, who had wriggled in protest at being asked to stand still for a few seconds. Even then he was tall, she marveled. Like his father.

While she was crouched at this level she was able to see with dismay the accumulated layers of grime and the evidence of small inhabitants that had wintered over in the relative protection of the house. In all the years she had come to the cottage in the past, it had always been prepared for her. Plumped up pillows on the window seats had beckoned her to curl up with a book; frosty pitchers of lemonade in the fridge and fresh-baked vanilla crescent cookies had waited on the counter; starched curtains had fluttered in the steady sea breezes wafting through open windows. She leaned back against the wall, struggling to remind herself she was no longer a child. After the ease with which she and Matteo had been absorbed into the rhythm of Sam and Debbie's home in Oak Bluffs, she had assumed that she'd find the same comfort at Innisfree—even more so, given her memories. She had built up Innisfree in her mind as her salvation all through the spring. It had been her talisman against the gloom and weight of grief under which the villa had been buried. Everything would get better once she was here, she had promised herself. She had believed Lydia's words fervently, that she would heal here.

She'd made a terrible mistake in coming. The deteriorated condition of the house only added to her sorrow and her sense that all she cherished—Antonio, Lydia and now Innisfree—were irrevocably lost to her. As she sat in the middle of the house that had begun to be reclaimed by the wildness it had confronted for nearly a century, she felt rise from somewhere deep inside her a keening that was as primitive as the wind howling outside.

When she was spent, her face streaked with dirt as she wiped away her tears with dusty hands, it was late afternoon. The storm front had not moved on, but seemed to have settled itself over the bay for a long stay, battering the windows on the western side of the house with sheets of water that paralleled her own weeping. She pulled herself to her feet and lit one of the kitchen gas lamps to dispel the encroaching darkness. She supposed she ought to eat something. She was resigned to spending the night here, given the duration and strength of the storm and the knowledge that it was now fully high tide. But after that, she didn't know what she was going to do.

She couldn't function beyond the simplest tasks. She opened a can of tomato soup and sliced some bread; after she ate she pulled some sheets and a comforter from the cedar chest where Lydia had last packed them away and made the bed in Lydia's bedroom. She'd always slept in The Linnet, but, like the boys' sleeping cottage, it was separated from the main house, and getting across to it would soak her. She felt the need to cocoon herself. She remembered one of her mother's stories of riding out a hurricane at Innisfree when she was five. The lavatory was also an outbuilding, although reached by a covered walkway that was connected to the back porch. Lydia wouldn't let the children venture out of the house even to go to the bathroom for fear they'd be swept off the porch, and had improvised a chamber pot in the master bedroom closet. Elizabeth didn't think her situation was that drastic, but didn't relish needing the toilet in the middle of the night. She made a trip, brushed her teeth and returned to the house to close up for the night.

Once in bed, she drew the faded quilt up to her chin, gathering herself tightly against the chill and the damp. Despite her emotional exhaustion, she found herself acutely aware of every sound—the staccato metronome of her own pulse, the whipping of the ropes against the flagpole outside, the rattling of the loose windows and the rhythmic surge and recede of the waves against the beach below the house.

She slept finally, but woke abruptly around 3 a.m., her body aware of a dampness that was far more tangible than the moist air that had surrounded her since she'd arrived. With a moan Elizabeth realized that the bed was soaked from rain that had worked its way through the roof.

She grappled for her flashlight, threw off the soggy covers and padded in her bare feet to the kitchen to find a bucket. On the way she discovered more water where the French doors to the patio had blown open and rain had poured into the living room.

She rummaged under the sink and grabbed a dishpan for the bedroom leak. Flashes of lightning illuminated the way back. She pulled out a stack of towels from the linen closet and started mopping up after she secured the French doors and pushed the bed out of the way of the leak.

Stripping the bed as the storm howled around her reminded Elizabeth of the nights when Matteo had been a bed wetter sobbing in his parents' doorway, and she had dragged herself out of warmth and sleep to make everything right and dry for him.

She tossed the wet linens in a laundry basket on the back porch by the washing machine, too tired in the middle of the night to get the damn thing running. The mattress was too wet to remake the bed. Instead, she found more blankets in the cedar chest and curled up on the couch, exhausted, discouraged and cold.

Chapter Five

Trespassing

The sound of banging on the front door of the cottage, followed by shouts, roused her from her cramped sleep in the morning. The sun was just visible at the eastern edge of the pond as Elizabeth wrapped the blanket around herself and stumbled to the door.

Through the glass she saw a man in the khaki uniform of the Refuge rangers. His face, not much older than hers, was one that had spent a lot of time in the sun, and his thick black hair was pulled back into a long ponytail held by a thin strip of leather. Elizabeth cautiously opened the door.

"Is something wrong?" Elizabeth was still waking up. Had he come to warn her of flooding? Wild birds on the attack? What else could possibly have brought him here at such an ungodly hour?

"Ma'am, may I ask you what you are doing in this house?"

"Trying to sleep until a few minutes ago. Why?"

"As far as I can tell, you are trespassing. Unless you can show me some authorization from the Hammond family allowing you to be here, like a lease, I'm going to ask you to get into your car and vacate the island."

"I don't need a lease to be in my family's home. I'm Elizabeth Innocenti, the Hammond's granddaughter!" After she had said it, she realized the name Innocenti would mean nothing to him, had no relationship in more ways than he would understand, to Innisfree.

"May I see some ID please?"

The ranger stood firm in the doorway, his gaze sweeping over the disarray—soggy towels on the floor, the rumpled couch, and through the doorway to the bedroom, the stripped bed pushed askew. To someone just arriving on the scene, unaware of her miserable night during the storm, the house looked ransacked.

She pulled the threadbare blanket more tightly around her, feeling vulnerable in her thin nightshirt. Not only had it not kept her warm during the night, but now it offered her scant protection from the watchful eyes of the unyielding man in the doorway.

He was one more reason that she had made a mistake in coming to Innisfree and she wanted him to be gone. Realizing that the identification she had with her—her passport and her Italian driver's license—would not connect her to her grandparents, she swept her eyes over the room for some shred of evidence that would satisfy the arrogant and self-important intruder. With relief, she silently thanked Lydia for the bookshelf cluttered with family photographs. Both at her home in Edgartown and out here at Cape Poge, Lydia had amassed a collection of pictures that chronicled the family as thoroughly as the growth chart carved into the wall. Elizabeth strode across the room and grabbed a framed photo from the shelf. It had been taken the last time she'd been at Innisfree, when the entire family had gathered to celebrate Lydia's 75th birthday. She returned to the door and thrust it at the ranger.

"That's me at my grandmother's birthday about twelve years ago," she said, pointing to her younger self, her fingers grazing the image of Antonio next to her, one arm casually draped across her shoulders and the other arm holding Matteo, who was leaning back securely against his father's chest. She willed herself not to break down in front of the stranger. "Are you satisfied now that I'm not a squatter?"

The ranger took the photo from her and studied it, his eyes passing from the Elizabeth standing before him—sleep-deprived, as ravaged and unkempt as the house itself—and the polished, contented woman in the photograph surrounded by the sprawling Hammond clan in clearly happier times. Elizabeth watched with relief as his eyes registered a connection between the image and her exhausted self.

"Sorry to have bothered you," he said, handing her back the photo. "Just trying to keep an eye on the place as a favor to Mrs. Hammond. The old-timers on the ranger staff passed on the word that your family hasn't been out here much since she went into the nursing home. I won't be bothering you again. I've got more than enough to keep me busy on the Refuge without acting as a private security guard. Especially when it's not appreciated."

He left as abruptly as he'd arrived, striding across the lawn with a casual confidence and climbing into a dark green pickup truck with the Cape Poge Refuge seal. The cormorants rose up in a flurry as he shifted into gear and drove off, turning toward the northern tip of the island when he reached the end of the driveway.

Chapter Six

Native Son
Caleb

Caleb Monroe hadn't recognized Elizabeth Todd when she opened the door at Innisfree. Too thin, too pale, too agitated. She looked like the off-islanders who flocked to the Vineyard in the summer, with their designer sunglasses and stiletto sandals jaywalking across Water Street. She didn't look like the spunky little girl he remembered tagging after her brothers and him when they'd explored the island as children, nor the out-of-reach teenager he'd later only peripherally been aware of as he and Sam and Chris Todd had drifted apart. He'd heard that she had married some Italian and was living over there. What she was doing alone at Innisfree was beyond him.

It appeared that Elizabeth hadn't recognized him either, which didn't surprise him.

He had put women like Elizabeth Todd behind him a long time ago, women he'd known in New York when he'd followed many of his classmates there after college. He'd grown weary of people finding it surprising that he'd gone to Dartmouth. If you're Native American, they assume you're either an ironworker, a dealer at a casino or a drunk. But he knew he never would have gone to Dartmouth if he hadn't found the book on the shelf in the living room at Innisfree.

His grandfather Tobias used to be the caretaker for the Hammonds until he got too old to be wrestling with propane tanks and repairing the roof every spring after Nor'easters tore half the slates off. When he went out to the cottage, Tobias used to take Caleb with him. While his grandfather tinkered with the pump or replaced broken windows, Caleb and the Todd boys scrambled over the moors. As he got older, Caleb worked alongside Tobias, especially at the beginning and end of the season. The October of his senior year of high school they were closing up the place, shutting off the gas and boarding up the windows. Caleb was supposed to be doing a walk-through, making sure all the valves to the stove and the lamps were closed. He did as Tobias expected, but it was also an opportunity he couldn't pass up to explore. It had been awhile since he, Sam and Chris had hung out, especially after he had gotten a job at Cronig's Market. For many summers, he had only seen the family from a distance when he'd be motoring over to the Gut in his father's boat to fish after work.

Being inside the house instead of watching it from the water intrigued him. In the living room was a bookcase, filled with books on celestial navigation, crossword dictionaries and three rows of paperback novels that had curled from the dampness of the salt air. A book had been left out and he was going to put it back on the shelf—tidying up was part of what Tobias did at the end of the season before affixing the plywood to the windows that shut out the light and the weather. But Caleb turned it over to read the back cover and discovered that the author was a Modoc Indian and the head of Native

American Studies at Dartmouth. He stuck the book in his back pocket, promising himself he'd return it to the bookcase in the spring when they opened up the cottage.

Caleb didn't sleep that night until he'd finished the book, a story about three Native American women whose lives had nothing and everything to do with his. Then he did something he'd never done before—he wrote to the author. He didn't really know what he wanted when he did, but the author recognized something in Caleb that he hadn't discovered yet—an unsatisfied hunger to understand himself through his people, the Wampanoag—native to the island and parts of the Cape.

A year later Caleb was welcomed as a student at Dartmouth, which was intent on fulfilling its original charter to educate the "Youth of the Indian Tribes in this Land…." It was a heady adventure for a boy whose only experience off-island up till then had been as goalie on a traveling soccer team that played games in southeastern Massachusetts. The four years in Hanover, New Hampshire, were like a juggling act in a Wild West show, except that instead of keeping tomahawks in the air, he was balancing Pow Wows and Ivy League football games, computer science and Native American oral literature. When Caleb left Dartmouth for a finance job in New York, he was bifurcated—stripes of war paint on his cheeks and a green-and-silver striped tie around his neck.

New York was not a good place for an island boy who needed to feel the wind against his skin to know which way to turn. He quit his job and joined the Army, which trained him for Special Forces and sent him to Afghanistan.

He was good at it.

He had come home ten months ago after his second tour of duty was up because his mother had needed his help. It was temporary, she said. Give me a few months after all the years you've been away. Tobias was dying. Caleb's father, Josiah, had retired as head of public works for the entire island of Martha's Vineyard, and he was not adapting well to a life and an identity not defined by his work.

Caleb hadn't intended to stay. In the fall, Tobias had still been able to go out in his boat on the bay. They spent the time together with not much talk, some fishing and a couple of beers nursed over the course of the afternoon. As Tobias descended into the maw of his disease, what little he said was often only in Wampanaak, their native tongue. Caleb watched his once robust grandfather, the man who had taught him to sail and clam and hunt, to listen to the silence and recognize the most minute fragments of the world around him, shrivel into an empty pod. His breath, when Caleb bent his ear close to his grandfather's lips to decipher the sounds he was trying to make, stank of the decay that was eating him from the inside.

Whatever was keeping Josiah from finding a new equilibrium and peace, Caleb hadn't begun to understand. But the sadness and silence that had descended upon him and upon their home was palpable. Like Caleb, Josiah was a veteran. He'd fought in Vietnam. You'd have thought that would give them a bond. But it hadn't. Growing up, Caleb had always been closer to his grandfather. And now, with his mother counting on him to be a bridge to his withdrawn father, he was helpless.

He should have left. But like a lot of men around here in the off-season, Caleb drifted. There's not much call for trained soldiers on Martha's Vineyard, but he'd seen enough of war. He knew he wasn't going back into the Army. But he also didn't know what else he could do.

It was Caleb's cousin, Simon Banyard, who told him about the job at the Refuge. They beef up the ranger staff during the summer to handle the influx of tourists. Not folks who summer out at Poge—there's only a handful of houses up by the lighthouse, all owned by long-timers who love the land and the isolation and keep to themselves. It's the day trippers coming over to Chappy for the beach and the fishing who swell the population on the Refuge a hundredfold and who need to be reminded to deflate their tires and take their garbage out with them.

Caleb spent his days, or his nights, depending on his shift, patrolling the trails and the beaches. He didn't do the tours. The Refuge was his childhood backyard, long before the land got put into trust. He knew every cranny and cove, every clam bed and fox den. But he wasn't an entertainer. He left that to the crew-cut blond guys who cajoled the sunburned and the bored into noticing the sandpipers and the plovers as they drove them over the dunes or led a caravan of kayaks through the waters of Poucha Pond.

By sunset, the tourists were gone. When he went out at night to the Gut to fish, he shared the beach with only a handful of men who'd learned to cast, like he had, from their grandfathers. No one talked. The only sounds were the whip of a line and the ripple of a slow tide on the rock-strewn sand. It suited him.

Chapter Seven

Housekeeping

After she closed the door on the ranger, Elizabeth was too agitated to go back to her makeshift bed on the couch. She recognized that his arrival had unsettled her more than the early-morning intrusion into what had already been a rough night. She'd felt judged by him, his disapproval evident in his eyes even after he knew she wasn't a squatter. Elizabeth imagined that most of the women he'd encountered in his line of work were of the hardy, agile sort usually seen hanging from rock walls or paddling arctic kayaks in Patagonia catalogs. Confident, pioneering stock like Lydia, who relished the challenges of housekeeping in the midst of hurricanes. Or self-assured, accomplished women like Elizabeth had once been, a respected documentary filmmaker and an equal partner in her marriage until Antonio's diagnosis three years before had thrown their lives into turmoil. Antonio's illness had not only stilled his limbs and ultimately silenced his voice and his breath; it had also dimmed the creative light that had sustained Elizabeth in her work and battered her spirit as she coped with caring for her husband, nurturing her son and deflecting the hostility of her mother-in-law. Now, a year after Antonio's death, she was bereft and hollow, a shadow of her former buoyant self. That was who the ranger had seen this morning, and his perception had hurt and stung her.

Knowing it was useless to try to go back to sleep, she resigned herself to dealing with the mess surrounding her and so pointedly observed by the impeccable ranger, whose spit-and-polish bearing resembled the military more than the casual approach she remembered from the rangers in the past. She was determined to shrug off the discomfort of his appraisal. He was gone, and she soon would be as well.

She dumped the water bucket, collected the soaked towels, mopped the floors, pushed the bed back into place and dragged the mattress outside to dry in the sun. Elizabeth had never expected to be daunted by the prospect of running a washing machine, but the pile of soggy linen she had managed to create in just one night forced her to confront the diesel engine in the hutch outside the back porch that she knew was her only hope of generating enough juice to run the washer.

She lifted the tar-papered lid of the hutch, propped it open and stared at the massive piece of red machinery. The generator was a new one, installed well after Elizabeth had left for Italy. Dismayed by the choices available to her—choke, switches, battery connections—she was about to give up, throw everything into the Jeep and head to Edgartown, where she hoped she might find a Laundromat. But tucked inside a Ziploc bag that was tacked to the side of the hutch was what appeared to be an instruction booklet. Reading was a skill Elizabeth still possessed, and it seemed more promising than making the trek across the dunes and possibly encountering the ranger and his pickup truck.

She spent twenty minutes deciphering the awkward English translation, and after two sputtering false starts, finally got the generator running. The sound, after the natural stillness of the pond, was deafening. But it was generating electricity and Elizabeth nearly wept that *something* was working. She retraced her steps to the washing machine and loaded the soggy pile into it. The machine hummed and clicked at the appropriate button-pushing moments, but it became rapidly clear that this hulking white monster demanded more than electricity to satisfy its appetites. Water. Despite all the water she'd had to cope with the night before, she was faced this morning with nothing more than a trickle flowing into the washer and realized she'd forgotten to run the pump.

She knew what she had to do. It had been a chore all the grandchildren had mastered. In her exhaustion and self-pity the night before, she had completely ignored one of the nonnegotiables of life at Innisfree. You had to run the pump—twice a day, morning and evening.

Overhead an osprey circled, then swooped toward its prey. Successful, it flew off to a nest perched on a tall wooden platform across the water. Elizabeth watched the nestlings stretch their necks and open their beaks wide as the mother dropped morsels to them and then flew off, once again on the hunt, relentless.

She slipped on her sandals and made the trek to the pump. Deep puddles filled the ruts in the path from the night's storm. Despite the sun now higher over the pond, it was still cool and Elizabeth shivered in her nightshirt. But she got the pump started and watched the needle on the gauge move from left to right as water surged into the tank. When the tank was full she cut off the motor to the pump and returned to the house. By the time she reached the porch the washing machine was filling and starting to agitate.

She decided she'd earned herself a cup of coffee now that water—clear and drinkable—was running through the pipes. Lydia had an old percolator and Elizabeth dug it out of the cupboard. When the coffee was ready, she took her mug out to a bench on the cliff that jutted out where the bay flowed into the pond. It was a vantage point that gave her a view of the widest expanse of the landscape. She could see vehicles approaching on the beach path or boats coming through the narrow entrance to the bay called the Gut. At the moment, however, no other sign of human interference disturbed the stillness that presented itself to her. The wind lifted her hair, still uncombed and damp from the exertions of the morning. She stretched out her legs, spattered with mud from the hike to the pump. The shriek of a hawk over the pond pulled her away from examining the minutiae of her body, the daily ritual of taking stock, of measuring herself against the standards set by the circles in which Elizabeth used to move. Italy seemed a universe away.

The tug of the familiar—of ceilings that did not leak and faucets that delivered water with the twist of a knob—was still front and center in her thoughts. But as Elizabeth sipped her coffee she let her surroundings play at the edges of her consciousness. She was most aware of color—an unfiltered blue in the sky above; the pale browns of the wind-carved dunes to the east; and beyond, a sliver of blue-grey between sky and sand that marked Nantucket Sound and the Atlantic; across the pond to the south, the marsh and the pine grove shifted from pale grass to deep forest green.

If she had been a painter, it was a scene she would have captured in great horizontal swaths of pigment. But Elizabeth wasn't a painter. She had once been a filmmaker. But now, Elizabeth wasn't anything, except a mother without her child and a widow who had no idea what she was going to do.

She gathered her mug and her thoughts and returned to the house. She put off the decision she had to make for a while longer when she realized the washing machine had completed its cycle. The house had no dryer—the sun and the wind served that purpose at Innisfree. Elizabeth knew she had to take advantage of the good weather while it lasted. She filled the laundry basket and lugged it to the clothesline behind the kitchen. The wind whipped the sheets and towels as Elizabeth hung them, a good omen for them drying quickly.

As she finished, she was aware that the housekeeping rituals she had performed so far had kept her distracted from the pain that had so overwhelmed her the day before. And where she had already mopped up, the house was noticeably improved. Her labors, imperfect as they had been, had produced concrete results. Faced with having to stay at the house at least until the laundry and the mattress dried, Elizabeth decided to tackle the remaining rooms. She pulled ancient canvas drop cloths off the furniture, dusted and swept and mopped, and then attacked the mold growing in the refrigerators. She worked until late in the afternoon, stopping only for some cheese and bread midday, eaten on the stone steps of the patio protected from the wind, which continued to blow. On the other side of the Gut she could see the tops of sailboats skittering toward Edgartown harbor, their spinnakers rounded and taut like a pregnant belly. Inside Poge Bay only a few motorboats puttered by to choice fishing spots.

When she stopped cleaning at five she felt vaguely satisfied as she pulled the now dry laundry from the line. Its fragrance tugged at memory, reminding her of how she had learned as a girl from her mother to unpin the towels and shorts and t-shirts on the line before the dampness of dusk settled on them.

After she folded the sheets and towels, she walked down to the pump. When the tank was full, instead of returning to the house, she decided to stretch her legs and explore while she still had some daylight. She headed to the east and the break in the dunes that led to the beach.

It was empty as far as she could see to the north and south, a smooth, curving arch of sand. The waves, still wind-driven, pounded away at the shore. It was high tide again. The beach was strewn with a tangle of seaweed and water-polished stones tossed up by the storm. Slender-legged sandpipers picked over the detritus while gulls and terns swooped and floated overhead. On the horizon she could see fishing boats returning from the open expanse of Nantucket Sound. The water was a deep gray-blue and stretched limitlessly to the east. The unhindered view of the sea loosened some of the tightness that had bound her in Italy. This was one of the reasons she wanted Matteo to experience Innisfree. She took a deep breath and began to walk.

She headed north, carrying her sandals in her hand and allowing her toes to squish in the soft wetness at the water's edge. The water was still frigid in this last week of June. Up ahead she could see the Cape Poge lighthouse, its beacon beginning its nightly flash as dusk settled around it. The beach took a sharp turn to the west at the lighthouse, which was situated on a cliff above the water at the northernmost tip of the island. She knew from her childhood excursions she could continue walking along the beach and make her way back to the house on the bay side of the island. But she hadn't thought to take a flashlight, and if darkness arrived before she made it back, the route was longer and less clear than along the ocean side. Even if Elizabeth turned back now and retraced her steps, she realized she'd be hard-pressed to reach the house in daylight. She made an about-face and headed back in the direction from which she'd come.

She walked briskly, driven mostly by the desire not to have to enter a darkened house. Intent on finding her way, Elizabeth was startled by the sudden appearance of a battered, rusty Blazer with fishing poles mounted on the front bumper and plastered with at least ten seasons of Refuge over-sand permits.

"Are you lost?" came a voice from inside the cab. Elizabeth couldn't see the face of the driver because he was shining a flashlight on her. But the voice was only too familiar. The ranger. Apparently off-duty, if the Blazer was any indication. It certainly wasn't the Refuge pickup he'd been driving in the morning.

"No," Elizabeth answered, shielding her eyes from the glare of the flashlight.

"I thought you might be, since you've passed the path to your grandmother's place. Unless, of course, you had another destination in mind."

She could detect a note of mockery in his voice and ignored it.

"I was about to turn around," Elizabeth lied. The mistake shook her. How could she have missed the break in the dunes? Had the years of erosion changed the landscape so much that she couldn't recognize her own driveway? Whatever confidence she'd managed to acquire during the day was crumbling in the face of this error. Who knew how long she'd have wandered up the beach before realizing she'd missed the turn? Out of the corner of her eye Elizabeth caught a glimpse of something black scurrying from the water to the dunes and she flinched.

The ranger must have noticed. But instead of making light of her discomfort, he lowered the flashlight.

"Look, I can give you a lift back to the house if you'd like. I'm off duty. Without a flashlight you're going to be scrambling to find your way."

"I'm fine, thanks."

"Consider it my atonement for disrupting your morning. Please."

His tone was genuine. And without the trappings of his uniform and his official stance of disapproval, his attitude toward her appeared to have softened.

Elizabeth considered the darkness, the empty house, her own fragile loneliness, and succumbed to his peace offering.

"OK. I guess I would appreciate a ride. Thanks."

She climbed into the cab. Despite its rusted exterior, inside the Blazer was orderly and comfortable—neatly folded maps in the door pocket, a fishing tackle box on the floor at her feet, a large thermos and an insulated picnic bag on the rear seat.

"Are you heading out to the Gut to fish?" She knew that after sundown was one of the best times for blues. There had always been a parade of headlights moving toward the Gut visible at night from the patio at Innisfree. Sometimes her uncles had been out there until two or three in the morning.

"Yep. Do you fish?"

She shook her head. "I tried it a couple of times with my grandfather when I was a kid, but piercing the jaw of a helpless fish with a barbed hook didn't resonate with me."

He nodded as if he expected her answer, and added it to the growing list of characteristics he disapproved about her.

"Here you are. Do you have a flashlight to get into the house and light the lamps?"

"No. I hadn't intended to be out so long. I'll manage."

"Come on, then, before you burn the place down. I'll walk you in."

He led the way to the kitchen door, his stride as comfortable with the dark as he had been at dawn. Despite his impatience with her, Elizabeth felt grateful for his presence. And to her surprise, Elizabeth was acutely conscious of his maleness in a way she had only experienced with Antonio. Elizabeth shook off her perception as a betrayal; it made her physically uncomfortable. She questioned whether she was reacting to the trappings of outdoor life that he carried like a badge. The big, utilitarian car; the physicality of his movements; the hunter providing food for his family; the quiet confidence with which he seemed to assess and resolve the problems he encountered. He had a solidity to him that was in direct contrast to her own fragility.

She imagined that she was a problem for him—a minor irritation, but nevertheless an interruption in his otherwise ordered existence. At the end of the day, he probably wanted nothing more than a few hours at the edge of the surf with his fishing pole. Instead, he put his own needs aside to rescue a foolish woman, as if there was no question that he would do so. He reminded Elizabeth of her grandfather, and she wondered what had shaped someone of her own generation to act with such purpose and duty.

He held open the screen door and handed her his flashlight.

"If you'll direct this toward the gas lamp, I'll light it for you."

He lit the lamp in one smooth motion and it hissed and flared into a pool of light that now illuminated them. The planes of his face were as strong as the rest of his body; but despite the strength, Elizabeth thought she caught a glimpse of something hidden, something sad, as he glanced around the room with some familiarity.

"You've been here before?" Elizabeth was curious, because she was sure he was new to the ranger staff when they spoke in the morning.

"A long time ago." That was all he offered.

Chapter Eight

Restoration

Elizabeth settled into a daily routine, her mechanism for coping when the challenges facing her were overwhelming. It was Lydia who had taught her what she called "putting one foot in front of the other."

The realities of Innisfree demanded those footsteps. If she intended to stay, even for a few days, she needed to pump water, keep tabs on the propane supply and clean up the debris of the previous winter. As Lydia had learned over the years as her own mistress of Innisfree, you have to stay on top of its needs or the property will become your mistress.

Elizabeth found in the physicality of her daily chores a welcome numbness. By tackling the cleaning and minor repairs around the house she was able, at least during the day, to hold at bay the emptiness and grief that had become her constant emotional state since Antonio's death. In the last months of Antonio's life, she had been consumed both with his care and with filming him—a request he had made of her to create a record of his final days. Like her housekeeping here at Innisfree, she had found a similar respite from her emotional pain in her tasks as caregiver and cinematographer. When he was gone, she had grappled for the distraction of physical work and had found none. In the villa, a cleaning woman kept the apartment spotless; a gardener saw to the pruning and weeding; a cook put meals on the table. During Antonio's decline, their help had been a blessing. But after his death, she was left with nothing to do.

With her head in the refrigerator, her hands raw from scrubbing away the mold, Elizabeth found a certain satisfaction in making things clean again, as if it were her grief she was scouring away.

Emboldened by her success with the refrigerators, finally sparkling and humming on the back porch, she decided to tackle the leaking roof. She hauled a ladder out of the shed to the other side of the house by the master bedroom and climbed up to survey the damage wrought by the storm.

She could see the bare spot, directly above her bed, where the wind had torn away the shingles, but it was out of reach from the ladder. She considered venturing out onto the roof, but even though the cottage was only a single story, a fall—especially when she was out here alone—was not something she wanted to risk.

Reluctantly, she climbed back down. She didn't relish spending more nights on the couch in the living room, but the roof was simply beyond her reach both literally and figuratively. She hadn't wanted to venture back to civilization so soon, but she knew she'd need to find someone who could fix the leak. A part of her suspected that her reluctance to leave had more to do with her fear that once she got to Edgartown she'd keep on going and not come back to Innisfree.

She shook off that thought. She loved Innisfree, and even though it had dismayed her to find it in such a sorry state, she knew she couldn't abandon it—not just yet.

Lydia must have known Elizabeth would find it in less than its familiar blissful condition and must have also trusted that Elizabeth would set it to rights. She smiled to herself at her grandmother's subterfuge. Nothing like scrubbing a few floors to scrub your mind of the cobwebs clinging there.

Recognizing her grandmother's plan lifted Elizabeth's spirits unexpectedly. If restoring Innisfree was the healing tonic Lydia had in mind for Elizabeth, she decided to swallow it. Nothing else had been effective so far, and she had nothing to lose.

Once she decided to throw herself into the task, Elizabeth mobilized herself and made an inventory of what the house and its outbuildings needed. As long as she was traveling back to town she would make the most of the trip.

Armed with her list, she headed out across the sand in the Jeep. Up ahead in the distance she could see a vehicle approaching, and as it neared she recognized the dark green of one of the Trustees' pickup trucks. She slowed to give it the right-of-way and saw that it was the same enigmatic ranger whose path always seemed to be crossing—or interfering—with hers.

He stopped alongside her and tipped his hat.

"Not lost today, I take it."

Elizabeth bristled and wished she had a snappy retort, but she was too tired to respond.

"No, I don't need to be rescued today, thanks. Wouldn't want to keep you from your appointed rounds." She was ready to move on, but then had a thought. If he were a local, he might actually be of help to her in finding a roofer.

"I'm on my way into town to inquire about someone who can fix the hole in my roof. I don't suppose you might know of someone?"

He turned his head away and stared out the window for a few seconds, as if in thought, and then turned back to her.

"Yes, I know someone."

Elizabeth was surprised by his answer, but reached over to grab her notebook.

"Can you give me his contact info?" she asked, handing him the spiral-bound pad.

"Sure." He took the book, wrote a name and number in a scrawling hand and passed it back to her.

She glanced at the page as she took it back from him.

"Caleb Monroe," she read. The gears of recognition began to click in her brain. "But that's you," she started to say, but he had already driven off.

The name thrust her back to childhood, to a summer when she was seven, scrambling over the dunes to catch up with her brothers and their friend, Caleb. He was the grandson of the Indian all the children had called Uncle Tobias, a friend of Lydia's and Grandpa Lou's who more often than not could be found with a hammer or screwdriver in his hand tinkering with whatever was broken at Innisfree.

"Your grandfather can fix people's hearts," Elizabeth remembered her grandmother saying, "and Tobias can fix everything else."

Elizabeth had wanted so much to keep up with the boys, who always seemed to be leaving her for a great adventure. She remembered one day when they'd left her behind and she'd sat glumly on the back porch, watching Tobias and Lydia plant a butterfly bush.

When they were finished, Tobias came up and sat beside her on the step.

"Boys run off again without you?"

She nodded, continuing to braid a clutch of meadow grass she'd pulled up in frustration after the boys had disappeared.

"What you need is your own adventure. Why don't you come with me and I'll show you something they don't know about."

He took her by the hand to a thicket of beach roses that grew along the ridge above the beach. He motioned her to crouch down, pressing his finger to his lips to warn her to be quiet. Within the thicket was a tiny nest sheltering three eggs.

When they moved away again he told her, "That's a hummingbird nest. Ever summer since I can remember there's been a hummingbird family born in this thicket. Your mom and my daughter, Izzy, used to watch them, just like you and I did now."

"How did you know it was there?" Elizabeth asked in awe.

Tobias made two of his fingers into a "V" and pointed to his eyes.

"You have to observe the world carefully. Look beyond what's on the surface—the tangled leaves and flowers everyone sees from a distance—and look within. But when you look at the world, try not to disturb it. If we had pulled away the branches, the hummingbird mother would have become frightened and might even have abandoned her eggs, especially if we had touched them. The secrets of nature are all around us, but we'll learn those secrets only if we respect them."

It was a powerful lesson for a seven-year-old, but Elizabeth had absorbed it with wonder. Looking back on that moment, as she held the notebook with the familiar name that had triggered the memory, she acknowledged that Tobias' lesson in observation had been the first step in her education, her initiation into the power of seeing. It was why she became a filmmaker.

Lydia, watching the exchange between Elizabeth and Tobias and recognizing the impact Tobias' words had on her, gave Elizabeth a little Instamatic camera that summer. Every day she crept up to the thicket and took a photograph, recording the progress of the hummingbird eggs. Somewhere in the house was the album Lydia had helped her put together, her first documentary.

Elizabeth closed the notebook, put the car in gear and continued to Edgartown.

When she returned to the house later that day she found a note tacked to the back door.

"I took a look at the roof and will pick up what I need after I finish my shift. I'm assuming you want the repair done quickly so you can get back into your bed. I'll be here tomorrow. Early."

She was sure the last word was a slight dig at her bedraggled appearance the morning Caleb had so unceremoniously banged on the door at the crack of dawn. While she was relieved to know the roof would be fixed so soon, she was uneasy about Caleb's motives in offering to do it. She found it odd that he hadn't mentioned his connection to Innisfree and her family before, especially the night he'd brought her back from her wandering on the beach. She remembered the look of pain on his face when he'd lit the gas lamp for her. She wondered what memories Innisfree had stirred for him. She'd known him only as her brothers' "partner in crime." She had a vague recollection that Tobias and his wife had owned Innisfree before Lydia and Grandpa Lou, but that was long before she or Caleb had been born. His memories couldn't be related to when his own grandparents had lived there.

She pushed aside her musings as she unpacked the supplies she'd accumulated in Edgartown. Whatever had prompted Caleb to offer to fix the roof was buried somewhere in Innisfree's history. She should simply accept the fact that she'd have a dry bed tomorrow and get on with the rest of the work surrounding her. She changed into jeans and an old t-shirt and started hauling pots and china out of kitchen cabinets thick with dust and mouse droppings.

The next morning she was at the pump at six o'clock, intending to fill the tank and jump under the shower before Caleb arrived. She'd been so tired the night before that she'd quickly heated some soup and then crashed on the couch. The grime from the kitchen still clung to her skin in streaks and her hair was tangled and damp from her sweaty tossing on the lumpy cushions.

As she switched off the pump she heard the crunch of tires on the driveway and the low rumble of an engine.

"Shit," she murmured to herself. "He really did mean early."

She straightened up to greet him, defiantly refusing to smooth her hair or acknowledge that she was still in her grubby t-shirt and a pair of boxer shorts she'd found in a dresser in the boys' cabin.

"Morning," he said, as he stopped the truck next to the pump. His eyes were shielded by a pair of sunglasses, so Elizabeth couldn't tell if he was amusing himself at her expense. "Do you want a lift back up to the house, or are you on your way out for a run?"

"I'll walk back, thanks. I'll meet you there."

She knew she needed the few minutes to cool down from her irritation. She couldn't fathom why Caleb Monroe was getting under her skin. From the moment he had awakened her two days ago and perceived her as someone barely worthy of his attention, she'd been aware of his disapproval. She'd rarely cared what other people thought of her, another lesson she'd absorbed from Lydia. So why now? Once again, she felt like the seven-year-old abandoned by Caleb and her brothers. She shook off the childhood memory and reached the house. Once the roof was fixed she could forget Caleb Monroe.

He was unloading the truck near the bedroom—a roll of tar paper, a stack of shingles, a box of nails.

"Is there still a ladder in the shed?"

"I'll get it. Anything else you need from there?" She was determined to show him she was not some fragile, helpless ditz.

When she returned with the ladder he was strapping on a tool belt.

"Will you need an extra pair of hands down here, or are you all set on your own?"

"I've got this. If I need anything else, or I fall off the roof, I'll yell."

"My grandmother would not appreciate your falling off her roof. As I recall, she pulled you and my brothers down from the roof of Byzantium once."

"Lydia was not a happy granny that day. I believe she called us idiots without a complete brain among us . . . How is she, these days?" His tone changed abruptly to one of genuine concern.

"Her own brain in functioning quite well, but her heart is not." Elizabeth could not bring herself to describe to Caleb her own dismay at seeing Lydia so confined and limited in the nursing home, nor her fear that Lydia's faltering heart would not keep beating through the summer.

"Must be tough, for her and for your family."

Elizabeth nodded and then changed the subject.

"I'm going to put on a pot of coffee now that the water tank is full. Do you want a cup?"

"No thanks. Maybe later. Just show me inside where the leak is, so I can trace it to its source."

Elizabeth led him around to the front door of the cottage and through the living room to the bedroom. The bedframe stood bare of its mattress, which Elizabeth had left propped against the wall in the girls' cottage to continue to dry. She pointed to the spot above the bucket she had planted on the floor the night of the storm.

Caleb removed his sunglasses and followed her outstretched arm to the water stain.

"Looks like it's been there awhile."

"From what Sam told me, no one's been staying here since Lydia went into the nursing home. Do you think you can fix it?"

"Yeah. Might take a little longer than I anticipated, but I picked up extra materials just in case. I'll get started."

They each went their separate ways. Elizabeth put on the coffee, cut herself some cheese and bread, and sat at the dining room table staring at the bay, which had calmed considerably since the storm.

Despite the cramped work she'd done the day before, scrubbing out the kitchen cabinets, she could feel her muscles loosening as she watched the sunlight dance on the gently lapping water. Even the ripping and hammering on the roof on the opposite side of the house had a rhythm to it. It seemed that as long as Caleb wasn't in close proximity, even though she could still hear him, his presence was less intrusive.

She sipped her coffee, turning over again in her head the puzzle of why she found Caleb so disruptive to her peace of mind. He wasn't at all like Tobias, who'd been both a comfort and a spark to her since the day he'd shown her the hummingbird nest. There was no comfort in Caleb, as far as she could tell. He was all hard surfaces and hidden crevices. Impenetrable and distant.

She was convinced his willingness to repair the roof had more to do with his concern for Innisfree than with Elizabeth's well-being. No matter, she told herself. Whatever his motivation, he was still making the cottage habitable. Which is what she needed to continue doing, she reminded herself. She got up from the table, stretched and began taking down dingy curtains. The sun was shining and a brisk breeze was blowing in. A good day to do laundry at Innisfree.

Caleb finished the roof late in the afternoon. He had declined the lunch she offered him, pulling a cooler from the truck and eating by himself in the shade.

By the time Elizabeth was hauling in the curtains off the line he was packing up his tools and putting the ladder back in the shed.

Elizabeth carried the laundry basket into the house and grabbed her wallet.

"What do I owe you?"

"It's on me."

"But why? I can't accept . . ."

"Let's just say I did it for Lydia, and leave it at that."

"But Lydia would insist on paying you."

"Lydia would say, 'Thank you, Caleb'."

That stopped her.

"Thank you, Caleb," she said quietly.

"You're welcome, Elizabeth. I'm on beach patrol in about an hour, so I'm heading home for a shower."

"Where's home?"

"At Cove Meadow. My parents have a place next to my grandparents' house. I'm staying with them for a while."

"How are Tobias and Mae?" Elizabeth didn't know why she hadn't asked sooner.

"My grandmother passed away when I was in college. Tobias is still with us, although not well. It's one of the reasons I came back."

"I'm sorry about Mae."

"Thanks. She lived far longer than anyone expected. She was one of the first successful bone marrow transplants—just before I was born."

"I didn't know you'd been away."

"No reason you would. Sam and I drifted apart as teenagers. We lost touch."

"Where'd you go?"

"Dartmouth. New York. Then the military."

"You were in the army?"

He nodded, then reached for the door of his truck.

"I've got to get going. Enjoy your dry bed tonight."

"Thanks."

And then he was gone.

Chapter Nine

The Dream

That night, Elizabeth called Matteo for what was to turn into a daily ritual of hearing his voice; confirming that he was enjoying life with his cousins, aunt and uncle. Mostly she was assuring herself that he didn't appear to miss her and she'd made the right decision to come to Innisfree alone.

She slept once again in the bed under a solid roof. No wind rattled the windows or swept in roiling gusts from across the water to engulf the house in nature's moans and howls. All was still.

In the midst of the silence, Elizabeth dreamt. It was Antonio who came to her. Not the Antonio of the last year of his life, bound to his wheelchair, his voice stilled; but the Antonio of the Palio, sweeping her up into Italy. Within the dream she was freed of the aching loss that had been her constant emotional state since Antonio's death. Instead, she experienced the fullness of their love. Laughter. The taste of their first kiss. His face when Matteo was born. The dream was a kaleidoscope of their lives together, images on a reel that had been stored away. Not forgotten, but left for another time when she would be ready to look at them without sadness. She woke, surprised that a dream like that would come to her now, here.

She and Antonio had spent very little time together at Innisfree. It was not a place that held much meaning for their history as a couple. Elizabeth did not believe that the dead spoke to the living in their dreams. But the striking character of this dream—joy in the midst of her numbing despair—spoke to her nonetheless. It might not be a message *from* Antonio, but it was certainly a message *about* Antonio.

It was early, not quite 5 a.m. Through the bedroom door and out the windows across the living room she could see the line of pink limning the East Beach horizon. An unexpected energy infused her. Normally, she would have rolled over, pulled up the covers against the early morning chill and enjoyed a few more hours of sleep. Instead, she threw back the blanket and swung her legs over and onto the rag rug beside the bed.

She pulled on a pair of shorts and a t-shirt, tied on her running shoes and left the house. She jogged to the pump, filled the tank and then continued down the drive and onto the beach. It was low tide and she was able to run along the wet, packed sand around the lighthouse point and full circle back to Innisfree. She stripped off her sweat-soaked clothes under the outdoor shower and let the water run over her as she watched an osprey swoop down to the surface of the bay and snag a fish.

Dripping, she climbed up the steps of the kitchen porch and grabbed a towel from a shelf above the washing machine. As she padded back to the bedroom she breathed in the smells of a clean house—bleach and lemon and sea air. The floors and windows gleamed. Sun- and wind-dried curtains drifted in the gentle breeze. Instead of a tangle of sheets and blankets on one of the couches in the living room, the cushions were plumped and uncluttered.

Elizabeth took it all in as she made her way through the house. I did this, she thought. I created this order. Lydia was right.

After she dressed and had some breakfast she retrieved her laptop from the closet where she had stowed it. She'd charged it at Sam's house, so she knew she had enough power to get started. Started. Was she really ready? She wasn't sure. But if nothing else, the dream had reminded her that she still possessed a glimmer of energy, a pilot light like the one on the giant Champion stove in the kitchen. It had been waiting all these months to be ignited.

She set the computer on the dining room table and turned it on. Her fingers hesitated for a moment over the mouse. *If it weren't 7 o'clock in the morning I'd pour myself a double Scotch to get through this*, she thought. Then she gently touched down and directed the cursor to the folder that had been sitting on her desktop since Antonio's death. When she clicked it open, his face appeared on the screen, smiling as it had in the dream.

Elizabeth took a deep breath and began to watch the raw footage she had shot of the last months of Antonio's life. Next to the computer was a notebook, and as she watched, she made notes, tracking the timing of scenes, identifying their content, jotting down ideas and themes. It was a process she used whenever she made a documentary and the process protected her, distanced her, from the searing emotional content of what she saw.

She lost track of time as she lost herself in the images on the screen. She did not cry, as she had for months after the funeral in Italy. She remained clear-eyed, as if seeing for the first time what she had witnessed so intimately as her husband's caretaker. She worked through the day, stopping only for a cup of tea in the middle of the afternoon.

The sun was close to the horizon in the west when she finally closed down the computer and lowered the screen. She rose from the table, stretching the kinks out of her arms and legs. She left the house and the memories behind, walking briskly to the pump to clear her head.

That night she *did* pour herself a Scotch. The air had cooled significantly and she built a fire to warm the room. The crackle and hiss of the flames, the heat of the liquor and the spirit of the house enveloped her and she fell asleep knowing she'd taken one more step on the path she was supposed to follow this summer.

Elizabeth spent the next two weeks immersed in editing Antonio's story. Her decisions were challenged by two sometimes competing audiences. Her first and highest priority was Matteo. Antonio had expressed to Elizabeth his desire to leave a record of his life for his son. At first, Elizabeth had protested.

"I can't do this," she'd told him. "I'm too close, and I know how the story ends."

"But that is precisely why I want you as my biographer. You know me. You love me. The story we create together for our son will be told with tenderness. I don't want my dying to be a mystery to him, hidden from him."

"Don't you want Matteo's memories of you to be of the strong, vibrant man who fought corruption, taught him to play soccer and how to swim, and told him magical bedtime stories?"

"Are you afraid that my decline will obliterate those memories?"

"Yes. I want him to hold on to who you were."

"I will still be who I am, *cara.* This disease does not destroy my mind. Look at Stephen Hawking. I want

Matteo to understand that within my paralyzed body, my heart still beats and loves. My brain still thinks. Being a man is not about the flesh, but about the spirit."

In the end, Elizabeth had reluctantly agreed. She had filmed Antonio's story with excruciating care. Adriana, of course, had been horrified and outraged. So much so that Elizabeth sometimes feared Adriana would destroy the files, so adamant was she that no one should ever see Antonio reduced to the shell he was becoming. But it was Antonio himself who had silenced his mother, painstakingly typing his wishes so that his mother could see for herself that he was equally adamant.

But after Antonio's death, all Elizabeth could do was save the files in several locations without looking at them. Until she had arrived at Innisfree, they had remained buried and unwatched.

The second audience for the film had emerged while Antonio could still speak. He and Elizabeth had become involved in an advocacy group for ALS families and the head of the organization had approached them when she learned that Elizabeth was filming Antonio. She asked if Antonio would allow a version of the film to be used as a way of promoting awareness of the disease—especially to raise funds for research. He had agreed without reservation.

For several days Elizabeth wrestled with the problem of reconciling the two purposes of the film—a father's legacy to his son and, essentially, a political tool.

She filled pages of her notebook with possible ideas, crossing some out, capturing words in balloons with arrows shooting out to different approaches. She realized one night that making one film that would serve both purposes was a compromise that would result in mediocrity. She had to create two films. She knew she'd been fighting the realization because of the sheer magnitude of the work required.

"Don't be lazy and settle," she berated herself. The decision was ultimately freeing, and the next morning she threw herself into Matteo's film. The first film, the more difficult one, should be his.

As she worked on editing the film she savored her solitude. Unlike the aching loneliness and disappointment of her first few days at Innisfree, she found that being alone and having a purpose, responsible for no one but herself, was a revelation and a gift. Her life in Italy, in the midst of a thriving city and Antonio's love, had always fed her. The energy and vitality of Italy were what had originally drawn her there and ultimately captured her.

But the silence and beauty at Innisfree were feeding something else that she acknowledged she sorely needed.

When she finished the final cut she knew she was ready to bring Matteo to the place that meant so much to her.

Chapter Ten

Lessons in Life at Innisfree

Sam's house at Oak Bluffs was in its usual state of tumult when Elizabeth arrived the next day just before dinner. Debbie was in the kitchen hovering over a boiling pot of spaghetti, Sam was hammering in the backyard, Ella and Jessica were squabbling over whose turn it was to set the table, and the boys were nowhere in sight.

"I stopped at the farm on the way and picked up a berry pie," Elizabeth announced, depositing the cardboard box on the counter.

Debbie greeted her with a "Yum!" and then grabbed the spaghetti pot with two mitted hands and headed across the kitchen to the colander in the sink.

"Can you ring the dinner gong on the porch? Really give it a whack or the boys won't hear it."

"Sure. Where are they?"

"They headed across the street to Ocean Park with a Frisbee about an hour ago. Provided they didn't get distracted, we should see them in a few minutes."

"How have things been going between Matteo and your tribe?"

"Couldn't be better. They taught each other a few things, some of which I didn't really need to know."

"Let me guess—a few choice words in Italian."

"You got it. How was your time alone?"

"Let's just say the house taught me a few things."

"That bad? Sam said it was in a sad state when he went out to open up the cottage and take delivery of the propane. Look, if it's really more than you bargained for when you accepted Granny Lydia's invitation, you know you're welcome to stay here. We have plenty of room for both of you."

Elizabeth held up her hand.

"Thanks, Deb, but everything's fine at Innisfree. The lessons from the house were all good ones. I detected Lydia's hand in sending me out there. Cleaning up the place helped me to clear my head as well. I'll go ring the dinner bell."

As predicted, the boys tumbled in from across the grassy swath of Ocean Park and fought each other over the sink when Debbie demanded that they wash their hands.

Elizabeth watched her son from the periphery after he had hugged her with a causal embrace. She realized that it was because of his cousins that he hadn't hugged her with his usual exuberance. It had taken her aback at first, that he hadn't seemed to miss her in their time apart. But she caught herself in the guilty memory of her time alone. Matteo seemed to have grown an inch, almost all of it in the lanky legs poking out from a pair of colorful baggy shorts she knew had not been in his suitcase when they left Florence. He had inherited Antonio's olive skin, which was now burnished from two weeks in the sun. He was no longer the pale, quiet boy who had inhabited the villa, surrounded by grieving adults who had only been going through the motions of living.

During dinner, as hands passed bowls of pasta and salad up and down the long, narrow table, Elizabeth received a complete accounting of Matteo's adventures. His cousins were full of stories. Matteo's unexpected prowess on a motor scooter was no surprise to Elizabeth. He had one in Florence, a birthday present from Massimo, who had taught his grandson to ride. Matteo's talent for quahoging, however, was a new skill.

"He always seemed to zone in exactly where the clams were burrowing."

"Aunt Debbie made spaghetti *alle vongole* for us on Friday from my clams. I convinced her to add red pepper flakes, just like Carmella does, and now she says it's the only way to make them."

After her solitude, the raucous energy of her brother's house was an adjustment, but one she welcomed in small doses. It filled her with gratitude to see how Matteo thrived here. The resilience of youth, she thought, responding to sunlight and fresh air and the company of friends. The villa had been a mausoleum, and not only since Antonio's death.

Later that night, after the kids had retreated to video games and popcorn, Elizabeth sat on the front porch with Sam and Deb sipping her second vodka tonic and giving her own debriefing of her time at Innisfree.

"Do you remember Caleb Monroe?" she asked Sam. "Tobias' grandson."

"Sure! Wow, that brings back memories. We were as thick as thieves and wilder than our crew when we were kids. Is he around? Haven't seen him since we were fifteen or sixteen, about the time we all got summer jobs and started hanging out with the kids from work. What's he up to, and where did you run into him?"

"He's working as a ranger for the summer on the Trustees land. He repaired the roof for me."

"Just like Tobias. My earliest memories of Innisfree include Tobias puttering in the shed with whatever we had broken. Did Caleb say anything about Tobias?"

"Only that he's not well and that's why Caleb came back."

"Came back?"

"Did you know he'd gone to Dartmouth?"

"No. Like I said, I haven't seen him since the summer after we were sophomores in high school, and at that time, college was the last thing on our minds."

"Sometimes I think the islanders, especially the Wampanoag, were invisible to us. I remember Caleb when I was a little girl because he was always taking you away from me when I wanted to play with the boys. But I don't recall running into him in Edgartown or even on the Chappy ferry when we got older. Even though we'd been coming to the island every summer since we were babies, our lives as adolescents here seemed to gravitate to other "summer" kids like ourselves. It surprised me when he said he'd gone to Dartmouth, and that was an 'aha' moment for me," Elizabeth admitted.

"An 'aha" as in, island kids go to UMass or Cape Cod Community College, not to the Ivy League like us."

"If you recall, I didn't go to the Ivy League, but yes, I was ashamed of my reaction. Granny Lydia would not have been proud of me. I know she holds both Mae and Tobias with great respect and affection. For what it's worth, I don't think Caleb has a very high opinion of me."

"What, the Italian *principessa* who abandoned us for the glittering life of a fashionable European city?" Sam smiled.

Elizabeth threw a pillow at her brother. She knew he was teasing, but the words cut nonetheless. That was exactly who she feared Caleb saw her as, and it surprised her that she cared so much. Since Antonio's death she had felt untethered, no longer bound to the Italy that had been her home for over fifteen years. But her experience out at Innisfree and her encounter with Caleb had reminded her with painful clarity that Cape Poge was not her home either.

Despite the embracing welcome from Deb and Sam and the offer to stay with them in Oak Bluffs, Sam's teasing held truth. She had essentially abandoned her life in the States and become absorbed into another family thousands of miles away. Although she had made an effort to spend every other Christmas with her parents and brothers, and her parents had made several trips to Italy over the years, those visits couldn't compensate for the emotional distance the miles had put between Elizabeth and the life she had once lived.

She didn't know what the life she still had to live would hold for her the single mother of a teenage boy, both of them still steeped in grief and loneliness. Any clarity her time at Innisfree had instilled in her, cleaning the house and editing the film, was now dissipating, obscured by a mist of uncertainty as dense as the fogs that engulfed Innisfree with such unpredictability and intensity.

She finished her drink and rose from the cushioned wicker chair. "I'm heading up to bed. I want to make an early-morning run to Stop & Shop to stock up before I drag Matteo kicking and screaming out to Siberia."

"You can always send him back if he really hates it. He's been a peach. In fact, we'll gladly trade you for two of ours."

"Thanks, Deb. But I at least want to try to introduce him to this part of our family history."

Sam, who had gone inside to retrieve a fresh bottle of beer, returned to the porch with a look of concern on his face.

"I just listened to the weather forecast. There's a tropical storm off Bermuda that may be moving up the coast. Are you sure you want to head back out to Innisfree?"

"It will surely take a few days to get here, don't you think, even if it does turn this way? Weather forecasters seem to cry wolf every time there's even the hint of a dramatic weather event, drive everyone into a state of frenzy emptying store shelves and then have to walk it back when it turns into a drizzle. I'd rather spend a few days with Matteo enjoying Innisfree and come back into town when we know for sure the storm is coming."

"Just be mindful of how unpredictable the conditions can be out there."

"I promise I'll be cautious."

The next morning, her shopping accomplished and the perishables buried in ice in a giant Coleman cooler, Elizabeth once again set forth on the road to Chappaquiddick. This time Matteo was at her side, his sun-tanned legs stretched in front of him and a Vineyard Vines baseball cap pulled down over his eyes. With his faded green Larsen's Fish Market t-shirt and a pair of baggy shorts, he looked as if he'd grown up on the island instead of only having been there a couple of weeks.

At the Dike Bridge Elizabeth parked and gave Matteo his first lesson in life at Innisfree, teaching him how to deflate the tires. Then, even though the tide was rising, Elizabeth decided to take the beach track out to the house to give Matteo a sense of the wildness and remoteness of Innisfree. She smiled to herself as the Jeep forded one of the rivulets that filled in first with the tide.

Matteo watched wide-eyed as they splashed across the shallow stream and climbed back up to higher ground.

"That was cool. Is it always like this?"

"During stormy weather when the tides are running high, this route would be too deep even for the Jeep. Then we take the middle track, where you're likely to see more animals—mostly deer and fox."

She had Matteo hop out to open the gate at the foot of the driveway and he decided to walk up to the house.

"I'll wait for you at the pump," she said. "We need to run it if we want any water today."

She stopped the Jeep up ahead and got out to watch her son lope down the dusty drive and take in the scope of Innisfree. After his sojourn in the hubbub of Oak Bluffs, where if you stood with outstretched arms you could touch both Sam's house and his neighbor's at the same time, Elizabeth wondered how Matteo would adapt to the silence and the space. She had filled a bag with books at the library to add to the supply on the shelves in the living room—Harry Potter books and *The Lord of the Rings*—titles she was pretty sure were not in Lydia's collection. Evenings without video games were going to be the biggest hurdle, she suspected. She bit her lip waiting for Matteo to make his way to her.

Had she made the right decision, dragging him away from all that was familiar in Italy? She had thought they both needed to be free of the oppressive gloom of the villa, but maybe it was only she who needed to escape. Innisfree was in her bones and blood and muscle. She had learned to swim and waterski and sail here. She had filled countless albums with her photographs. She had even experienced her first kiss here, one starlit night on East Beach under the cliff by the lighthouse. But except for the one disastrous visit for Lydia's 75th birthday when Matteo was a toddler, he had no memories to anchor him to this place. Was she a fool to think she could create those memories for him?

He had run up to a rise above Shear Pen and stood, hands on hips surveying the pond, the dock and the expanse of the bay beyond.

She held her breath and hoped.

When he turned back to her she searched his face for a glimmer of a response—awe, curiosity, unexpected pleasure. What was she looking for? Anything but boredom or resentment she was willing to take. But her son's expression was unreadable, a mask.

Oh, God, she thought. He hates it already, but out of concern for her feelings, he's hiding it. She forced a smile and motioned toward the pump.

"Hey, Matteo, let me show you how to run the pump so I can send you out tomorrow morning while I sleep in." She was trying too hard to be light-hearted, but he generously cut her some slack and bent over the little diesel motor to watch her demonstrate.

"It's a two-cycle motor, Mom, just like my Vespa. I think I got this."

"Keep an eye on the gauge for the water pressure."

When the tank was at full pressure he cut off the motor.

"So we need to do this every day?"

Elizabeth shook her head. "Twice a day."

"This is a different world from the Italian seashore, and even from OB." He already was using the native abbreviation for Oak Bluffs.

"It is. Let's get the Jeep up to the house and then we can explore."

After parking the car and unloading the groceries, Elizabeth gave Matteo a tour of the compound.

"When my brothers and cousins and I were kids, the boys always slept in Byzantium and the girls in the Linnet, but you can choose where you want to sleep."

"Byzantium will be great. I don't think I could live it down with the cousins if they found out I chose to sleep close to the main house in a cabin decorated with birds."

"Sounds like a good choice. Especially if you want to invite them out to stay with us. Let's go over to the beach, and then we can take a walk to the lighthouse. That will give you a sense of the lay of the land if you want to wander around later on your own."

After the tour they made some sandwiches and ate them out on the back deck overlooking the bay. Throughout that first day, Elizabeth found herself studying her son, gauging his reactions to everything she showed him and trying not to overwhelm him with her memories of idyllic childhood summers. She reminded herself that she had been surrounded by siblings and cousins during those summers and had been allowed to run free, untethered to cell phones and laptops. She couldn't recreate those days for Matteo, here alone with only his mother.

In the evening, after supper and a game of Sorry that was sadly lacking in drama with only two players, Elizabeth walked Matteo over to Byzantium. The night was overcast, so she couldn't point out to him the incredible display of stars that was one of Innisfree's gifts. At the door to the cabin she handed him the small, battery-operated lantern that had lit their short path from the house.

"Great-Granny Lydia never allowed us to have gaslights in the sleeping cabins. She was convinced we'd burn them down. If you need it, you can keep the lantern on all night."

"Mom! I'm not a baby! I'll be fine in the dark."

"OK. Goodnight, honey."

Elizabeth walked back to the main house, but instead of going inside she went around to the west and sat on the stone steps of the rear deck. Across the water she could just make out the faint lights of Edgartown. She drew her sweater around her as the damp breeze picked up. She and Matteo had survived their first day together at Innisfree without any major disappointments on either side. He seemed to be tolerating the isolation and lack of electronics, and she was taking care not to reminisce about the past. So far, so good. But she truly didn't know if they could sustain the contentment of today for the rest of the summer, or even if that was the right thing to do for Matteo.

A longing rose up in her for her grandmother's wisdom. She wished Lydia were well enough to be out here with them, dishing out her sass and her jokes along with her pan-fried bluefish and apple pie—Mae Monroe's recipe, Lydia had always said. The best apple pie on the island.

I've waited too long, Elizabeth thought. Too long to experience her grandmother's infectious energy and enthusiasm for life. Too long to introduce Matteo to this special place. Too long to come home.

Chapter Eleven

Antonio's Film

When she woke up the next morning she found Matteo asleep and sprawled across the wicker sofa in the living room. She hadn't heard him come in during the night. She guessed his bravado about thc darkened cabin hadn't lasted. She gently pulled up the afghan he had thrown over his legs—when had they grown so long?—and tiptoed to the kitchen and out the back door to run the pump.

He still hadn't stirred when she got back, so she made a pot of coffee and started a batch of pancakes as an aromatic wake-up call.

It was the sizzle and smell of bacon that finally roused him. He stuck his tousled head around the corner, a sheepish grin on his face.

"Good morning!" Elizabeth greeted him, spatula in hand.

"Hi. I guess I wasn't as ready as I thought to sleep in Byzantium. You didn't warn me about the spiders."

"I'll make a confession. I never slept alone in either cabin. I always had my cousins or a friend with me. We can do a thorough airing out of Byzantium today, or we can make you up a bed on the window seat in the alcove."

"I'll think about it. At least there weren't any snakes. But I heard a lot of hooting and rustling during the night. There may not be any *people* out here, but there sure are a lot of creatures."

"What time did you come in? I'm usually a light sleeper, but I didn't hear you."

"The clock in the kitchen said 3:20. I tried to be real quiet so you wouldn't think that someone was sneaking into the house."

"Well, thank you. And I'm sorry you had a rough time out there. Can I make it up to you with pancakes and bacon?"

He took the plate from her hands and wolfed it down at the dining room table, then went back for more.

"I really like American breakfasts. Aunt Debbie makes this French toast casserole thing. You should get the recipe from her. What are we doing today?"

"Clamming while the tide is out. Then I have something to show you later today."

After breakfast they gathered up buckets and rakes from the shed and headed down to the clam flat on Shear Pen Pond. Although she hadn't clammed since she'd left Massachusetts for Italy, Elizabeth discovered the skill was like riding a bicycle—once learned it came back as if she'd been doing it all along.

They had enough for spaghetti *alle vongole* that night.

After supper Matteo asked if she was going to submit him to the torture of Sorry again.

"Not tonight. I have something special planned." She retrieved her laptop and set it up in the living room so that they could watch it together from the couch.

"You told me there were no electronics out here! What are we going to play?"

"Not play. Watch."

"A movie?"

"Do you remember that I filmed Babbo after he got sick?"

Matteo became still and wary.

"Sure I remember. And I remember fights you and Babbo had with Nonna about it."

"Babbo wanted me to film him for you. It was his wish."

"Why didn't you show me the film before, like when we were home?"

"It wasn't ready. *I* wasn't ready. I had to edit it, and when I was out here by myself I finally found the courage to open up the file."

"The courage?"

"It's not easy, to see Babbo again, to hear him."

"Then why do you want me to see him?"

"Because it was his wish."

Matteo got up from the couch and stared out the darkened window, arms folded across his chest.

"If you aren't ready, we can wait."

"But now that I know it's there, I can't ignore it. I had nearly forgotten about it, you know. Especially after all this time. I thought maybe you had finally agreed with Nonna and decided to destroy it, and I was relieved!"

"Matteo, I would *never* destroy the film. I can understand that you might not be able to watch it now. But believe me, a day will come when you will long to see your father's face and hear the words he meant for you."

Elizabeth closed the lid of the laptop, her hand shaking. She wanted to touch Matteo, to offer him a hug of understanding; but the boy with his back to her at the window appeared to be in no mood for his mother's comfort.

"You can't possibly know what I want, now or in the future. Your fucking film is not going to bring Babbo back!"

And then he left the house, slamming the door so hard that the glass threatened to fall out.

Elizabeth let him go. In the short time they'd been at Innisfree together she had seen glimpses of a Matteo who had grown away from the little boy she'd left in Oak Bluffs. She was stunned at how little she understood her son and how profoundly she'd misjudged his reaction even to the existence of the film. She had no doubt he would one day want and need to see it. But she should never have told him that. He was right. She couldn't possibly know what was in his heart. She couldn't know his grief.

What she *did* know at that moment was his anger. She reached back to her own adolescence, wishing once again for the calming hand of her grandmother but settling instead for the memory of how Lydia had handled Elizabeth's rocky moments as a teenager.

"Let him be," Lydia's voice whispered to her above the wind. "He needs to go stand on the beach and scream at the sea."

So Elizabeth stayed behind, lighting the gas lamps throughout the house, not only to give him a beacon to guide him back but also to dispel the shadows and ghosts of her own grief. She tried to read, but found herself constantly listening, watching for his return. As she kept her vigil, she became more attuned to the physical world outside the cottage, sensations that always seemed more intense in the isolation of Innisfree—a shift in the direction and strength of the wind, an oppressive heaviness to the atmosphere that seemed to have descended upon the peninsula in stealth. A glance out the window confirmed that the cottage was engulfed in mist.

No longer willing to wait for Matteo to return on his own, she grabbed a lantern and checked first to see if he had decided to sleep in Byzantium, but it was empty. As she left the cabin it began to rain, drizzle at first that became a steady, drenching downpour. The storm Sam had warned her about appeared to have rushed up the Eastern seaboard.

With mounting anxiety Elizabeth set out toward the beach, the lantern tossing an erratic circle of light on the path. When she got to the water's edge she hesitated. Would he have gone north or south? She forced herself to choose and turned toward the lighthouse, a decision that meant walking directly into the wind.

After Antonio's diagnosis, she'd realized that she'd be raising their son alone. But the realization had been abstract. Matteo was only eleven, barely out of childhood and a sweet, affectionate boy whose ebullience had not yet been stilled by his father's illness. But as she strode into the driving rain, Elizabeth understood a painful, frightening truth. Matteo was no longer that sweet boy and she was on her own in guiding him through an adolescence complicated by their grief.

She was unprepared for the sobs rising out of her constricted chest. She felt a panic rising in her, as if Matteo were a toddler who had disappeared, snatched from her in a moment of carelessness when she had looked away, let his hand slip out of hers. She began calling his name as she ran along the beach.

She almost fell over him, sitting crouched in the rain at the edge of the water. She collapsed next to him, throwing her arm around him. She could not find the words to comfort him or calm her own terrors. He stiffened at first, and she thought he was about to shrug off her embrace. But rather than lose him again, she held fast. *I'm not going to let you go,* she conveyed to him without speaking. And with a wracking sob, he turned his head and buried himself against her breast.

She rocked with him. In the enclosed gloom of the villa they'd never descended into the profound grief this night had unleashed. When they were both spent and shivering, she pulled herself up and held out her hand to him.

"It's time we went home."

It was the first time she'd referred to Innisfree as home, and it felt right.

When they reached the house she lit a fire in the hearth and warmed some milk on the stove.

"Get into dry clothes and we'll have some hot chocolate."

She saw him look at the sideboard where she'd put the laptop earlier, but she'd stowed it away out of sight. As far as she was concerned, it would remain away until he asked for it.

When he came back in a dry t-shirt and his flannel pants she handed him the mug of hot chocolate but didn't try to cuddle with him on the couch. That moment of loss and release on the beach was singular and necessary, but she knew not to push for another.

He cradled the mug in his hands and stared into the fire.

"I was jealous of my cousins. Because they have a dad who can roughhouse with them and take them fishing and sailing. Even when he yelled at them. They have no idea what it was like to have a father who could do none of those things. Who didn't have the words to tell me he loved me or was angry with me. And now I have nothing. I didn't know how much I missed him until we came to America. I wish you'd never brought me here."

Elizabeth listened, stricken. All the things she could have said failed her. She couldn't comfort him or help him see he would have been confronted with other fathers and their children in Italy as well.

"I'm sorry, Matteo. I thought Innisfree would help us because I loved it so much. I was wrong."

"You called this home when we were on the beach. Maybe it's home to you, but not to me."

The phone rang, an unfamiliar sound that jolted both of them.

Elizabeth got up to answer. It was after eleven.

It was Sam.

"I hope you're packing up and planning to return to town. That tropical storm has been upgraded to a hurricane and it's definitely on its way to the islands faster than anticipated."

"It's high tide right now and I'm not sure I can find our way off in the dark and the fog. How close is the storm? Can't we wait until morning? And what about boarding up the house?" The questions kept coming.

"It's still at least a day off, according to the weather service. You're probably fine to spend the night there, but you'll need to get to us by mid-day tomorrow to be safe. Do you think you can handle the boarding, or do you want me to come out?"

"Matteo and I can manage. Right now we need to get some sleep. We'll get an early start in the morning. Don't worry about us."

She hung up and filled in Matteo on Sam's news.

"Let's get some rest. If we're up at dawn we can board up the windows, get the outdoor furniture into one of the cabins and be on our way in a couple of hours."

Elizabeth was physically exhausted and emotionally drained. She could see it in Matteo's eyes as well. At least she could still read *something* of her son's state of mind. She made up a bed for him on the couch, locked up all the doors and windows to prevent them from blowing open in the wind, and collapsed on top of her bed.

Chapter Twelve

Hurricane

By the time dawn arrived the wind had strengthened but the rain was intermittent. Elizabeth roused herself, made a pot of coffee and woke Matteo.

"I'm going to need your help boarding up the windows."

"What do you want me to do?"

"Get the ladder, a box of nails and a couple of hammers from the shed. I'll start pulling out the boards from under the house."

Elizabeth had helped with the boarding in the past, but the heavy lifting had been done by her brothers and father. She and Matteo struggled to fit the unwieldy pieces of plywood over the large expanses of glass on the three-sided dining room. Despite the chill of the wind-driven air, sweat fell in sheets down her face and under arms.

"I need to catch my breath," she told Matteo, wiping her face on her sweatshirt.

"I think I can handle a couple of the smaller windows on the south side, Mom. Take a break."

Elizabeth surveyed the sky, trying to gauge the progress of the storm. It had taken them nearly two hours to board one room. Her estimate that they would be off the island by noon was appearing ridiculously optimistic. She knew she was going to have to make some decisions, the most important of which was when to stop trying to protect the house and get on the road to protect themselves.

Matteo came around the corner of the house.

"Mom, there's a ranger here, asking for you."

Caleb followed behind Matteo.

"I saw your Jeep was still here and came to warn you about the hurricane."

"Sam called us last night. I thought we had time to get the house battened down, but now I'm not so sure."

"I can help you get a few more windows covered, but if you don't leave in the next hour you could be stranded. NOAA is anticipating a storm tide and it will make the beach impassable. The high road is already washed out in two places."

Elizabeth accepted his help, too exhausted and worried to question or resent his presence. With the three of them working together they finished boarding up the main house but had to leave the cabins unprotected. Once they had gathered the patio furniture and grill, trash cans and hoses and clamming tools and stacked everything in Byzantium, Elizabeth threw a hastily packed duffle bag into the Jeep and she and Matteo followed Caleb in his truck. The rain had started up again in earnest, the sky was an ominous shade of yellow-green and the air was tinged with a faintly metallic odor. Normally the Refuge teemed with flocks of birds, either hunting at the shore, floating serenely on the bay or soaring above their prey. But this morning the route was unusually still, absent of any signs of wildlife. Elizabeth noted the change with increasing uneasiness. She turned up the heat to stop her shivering. They hadn't taken the time to change into dry clothes.

She hoped that they'd evacuated in time. She remembered her grandmother's story of once riding out a hurricane at Innisfree. "One of the stupidest decisions we'd ever made," Lydia had said. The water had reached the walkway that connected the house with the lavatory and the house had groaned and shaken for hours, battered by 120-miles-per-hour winds. Elizabeth gripped the steering wheel, concentrating fiercely on keeping the Jeep on the track Caleb was carving for them in the sand. The small rivulet that they had splashed through two days before was now up to the floor boards of the Jeep.

Matteo was silent, his eyes focused straight ahead on the tail lights of Caleb's truck.

When she could see the Dike Bridge through the sheets of rain, Elizabeth let out the breath she'd been holding. The first leg of their journey—and the most treacherous—had been successfully completed. They pulled to a stop by the Trustees' air station and Matteo leapt out to inflate the tires. Elizabeth allowed herself a smile. Anything to do with motor vehicles, no matter how mundane, had captured Matteo's attention since he'd been a little boy.

Caleb came back to her after he'd filled his own tires.

"I'll drive down to the ferry landing and make sure you're able to get across."

"There's really no need. I'll be fine from here…Thanks for all your help."

"Do you ever just allow yourself to accept an offer of assistance without protest? You won't be fine if the On-Time has stopped running. Where will you take shelter?"

"But I thought the On-Time always ran."

"Not in a hurricane it doesn't. Let's get going. Maybe Joe Fallon is as stubborn as you were back at Innisfree and hasn't yet accepted that Mother Nature is a lot more powerful than his ferry."

But when they arrived at the ferry slip, Caleb was right. The On-Time was secured in her berth and a sign hung from the landing that the ferry was out of service until the hurricane passed.

"Now what?" Matteo asked. "Where will we stay? Is there a hotel on Chappy?"

Elizabeth shook her head. She'd stayed too long at Innisfree trying to protect it. As stupid as Lydia's decision.

Caleb swung his truck around to her side.

"Follow me."

That was it. No explanation of where he was leading her, but also no "I told you so" in his expression.

She put the Jeep in gear and dutifully took her place behind him without a word. They headed back east on Chappaquiddick Road and then turned off on Jeffers Lane. The rutted dirt road was filled with deep puddles, twisting and turning through overhanging thickets as it climbed a gentle rise. A few scattered houses appeared occasionally on the way, but for the most part they passed through terrain almost as remote and uncultivated as Cape Poge. Elizabeth could see glimpses of water on her right and guessed that they were on the western side of Cape Poge Bay.

"Where's he taking us?" Matteo's voice held both skepticism and fear. It had been a wild night and a wilder morning, with the onset of the hurricane echoing and amplifying their emotionally fraught conversation about the film. Elizabeth sought to reassure him.

"He's an old friend of the family," she said, catching herself from saying simply, *he's a friend of mine.* "He's taking us someplace safe to shelter through the storm." As she spoke the words, Elizabeth knew she believed them. She trusted Caleb. Despite his reserve and distance and somewhat dismissive attitude toward her, he had nevertheless done nothing but help her since she arrived at Innisfree.

Ahead of her, Caleb pulled onto a gravel drive where several other cars and trucks were parked. A sprawling house was perched on a rise above the water, its shuttered windows giving the place an aura of strength like a fortified castle. Smoke puffed out of its chimney, dispersed rapidly by the wind.

Elizabeth and Matteo clambered out of the Jeep and ran through the rain to the door that was held open by a smiling woman whose face was vaguely familiar.

"Welcome to Cove Meadow. Come in and get warm and dry."

Elizabeth reached out her hand. "Thank you so much for taking us in. I'm Elizabeth Innocenti and this is my son, Matteo."

"Of course you are Elizabeth! I remember you so well as a little girl. Your mother and I spent many a summer together as children. I'm Izzy Monroe."

Elizabeth almost collapsed into Izzy's open arms. She had to bite back tears of relief, enveloped in Izzy's strong embrace. Her memories of Izzy were rich with storytelling and playacting. Whenever Izzy had come to Innisfree to visit Elizabeth's mother, Susan, she'd brought with her a satchel full of books and elaborate props. As a child, Elizabeth had thought of Izzy as her very own Mary Poppins, who entertained even the restless boys with wildly imaginative stories.

She took a step back and searched Izzy's face. It still held the sharp intelligence and twinkling humor that had made people look beyond Izzy's twisted leg, paralyzed when she'd contracted polio at the age of seven. Elizabeth's mother had recounted stories if Izzy's indomitable spirit and brilliance from the time she was a girl. Elizabeth knew Izzy had gone to Smith when she was only sixteen and had earned a doctorate at Harvard by the time she was twenty-three. She'd gone on to write several novels, all of which Elizabeth had on her bookshelves, and a couple of plays. She was on the faculty at Yale.

"What are you doing on Chappy in the middle of a hurricane?"

"Visiting Dad, helping out, getting pulled into tribal issues—we academics take the summer off and get ourselves into all kinds of mischief. But what about you? The last I heard, you were practically a *principessa* in Italy. Your mom wrote to me about your husband. I'm so sorry, Lili."

It wasn't just Izzy's offer of condolence that touched Elizabeth at that moment, but her calling her "Lili." It was a name only Izzy had used, a character she'd created for Elizabeth in one of the plays they'd staged on the lawn at Innisfree. Like Izzy's father, Tobias, Izzy had offered Elizabeth a glimmer of who she could be when she grew up. Under Izzy's intense gaze on this storm-swept day, Elizabeth wondered if she measured up to Izzy's expectations—or even her own.

Izzy led Elizabeth and Matteo into the living room at the center of the house. The room was dim, with the shutters protecting the windows keeping out the light as well as the wind. In the corner a wood stove was throwing off welcome heat. Seated around the room were a number of unfamiliar people and Izzy quickly introduced Elizabeth and Matteo. Most were elderly members of the Chappaquiddick Wampanoag.

"We got word that the community center was already without power, so Grace and Josiah have been driving around the island gathering up the elders and anyone else who didn't make it to Edgartown this morning. Come, let me show you where you can change. Were you able to bring any dry clothes with you when you evacuated or do you need anything?"

"We're fine. I had the presence of mind to pack a bag last night. Let me know what I can do to help."

Izzy squeezed her hand. "Thanks. For the moment, dry off and come have a cup of hot coffee. We'll figure out the rest as the day goes on."

By the time she and Matteo had donned dry clothes, Grace and Josiah, Caleb's parents, had returned with the last people who needed shelter. Grace embraced her warmly.

"Caleb told us you had set up housekeeping at Innisfree. Good for you! It broke our hearts when we heard Lydia was in a nursing home and no one was caring for the place."

Elizabeth knew that Innisfree held a special place in the hearts of the Monroes. It had been established by the family's matriarch, Mae Keaney Monroe, when she opened the Boat House Café back in the early 1940s. When the café was destroyed by Hurricane Donna in 1961 and the family needed money for Izzy's medical bills, especially a surgery that enabled her to walk without her braces, Mae had sold the land to Lydia and Lou Hammond.

At her 75th birthday celebration, Lydia had said to her family and the Monroes, "The Monroes consider Innisfree not only their original homestead, but sacred land. They entrusted it to me and I intend to honor that trust until the day I die." Elizabeth had been there and remembered the moment when they had all raised their glasses to both Lydia and Innisfree.

Elizabeth helped Grace and Izzy to settle the newcomers with blankets and hot coffee and then joined them in the kitchen to make dinner.

"What's on the menu?" she asked, rolling up her sleeves.

"It's turkey sobaheg. Granny Naomi taught Grace and me to make it. Mom's forte was pies, but Granny was one for food that stuck to your ribs. Most of the elders here grew up on this. It's comfort food to them."

While she chopped and stirred, Elizabeth felt as she had in Debbie's kitchen, among the company of women. Both Grace and Izzy were of her mother's generation, but they accepted her without condescension.

"Your son is a handsome young man," Grace said, "and a thoughtful one." She gestured with her head toward Matteo refilling coffee cups and bending down to answer the questions of the exhausted and bedraggled evacuees.

"He's grown up in a house of adults, with his grandparents."

"Ah, the extended Italian family. Not so different from tribal culture," Izzy smiled.

The women managed to get the stew cooked and bread baked before the loss of power threw the house into darkness. But lanterns were lit and the woodstove fed as fifteen assorted wanderers sheltering in the house gathered in the dining room. Matteo helped Josiah and Caleb push tables together and find chairs and benches to seat everyone.

After a blessing offered in Wampanaak by an elderly woman named Sadie, the group ate and reminisced about hurricanes past. Elizabeth, Matteo and even Caleb were mere listeners to the stories. Around them, the winds howled, shutters slammed and rain beat against the roof, its cadence accompanying the tales.

Elizabeth was entranced. Her cinematographer's eye took in the scene: the lined faces of the elders, their eyes sometimes closed as they spoke, lit from below by the smoky lanterns. Gnarled hands, some encircled by the purple swirls of wampum, gestured in the air to demonstrate the height of a wave swamping a boat or the girth of a tree hurled onto a roof. She wished for her camera at that moment. It was in the bottom of her duffle bag, placed there with her laptop as the most important items to remove from the house. But she knew that to disrupt these stories with her camera would destroy the quality of the experience as surely as if she had stood on the table and tap-danced.

Instead, she held onto the images in her head, mentally taking notes. Everything about the evening—the hurricane raging against the house, the solemn voices reaching back into memory for tales of triumph or disaster, and the riveted attention of the listeners—spoke to her in a powerful way.

The spell was broken by a loud crash. Josiah and Caleb rose from the table without speaking and left to investigate. Grace and Izzy took the opportunity to begin moving the now agitated elders to their makeshift beds.

Elizabeth motioned to Matteo and they began to clear the table. In the kitchen, when he had finished carrying the last of the plates, Matteo asked, "Can I go help Josiah and Caleb?"

She understood he wanted to be with the men solving major problems, not stuck in the kitchen with his mother washing dishes.

She nodded reluctantly. "Stay out of danger."

She was still at the sink when Caleb returned. Despite the rain gear he'd donned earlier, his clothes were damp and his long hair was soaked, plastered to his skull.

"Did Matteo find you? And where is he now?

"He did find us and he's been helpful. He and Dad are right behind me, just closing up the barn."

"What happened?"

"A tree limb fell across the barn roof and gouged a hole."

"Are there animals in the barn?"

"A couple of goats and some chickens. They were restless but unhurt. Matteo calmed them down while Dad and I spread a tarp over the gash…I didn't know your husband had died. I'm sorry."

Elizabeth didn't expect the sudden turn in the conversation. "There's no reason you would have known. I haven't been on Chappy for over twelve years. Who would have told you?"

"You could have told me."

"I don't feel it necessary to announce my widowhood to everyone I meet. Besides, what difference would it have made to you to know?"

"I would have been kinder."

"You have been kind. And I don't want you to be nice to me just because you feel sorry for me. Look, in small ways and large—especially today—you've rescued me. I'm grateful. Truly," she emphasized when she saw the raised eyebrows and implied skepticism in his expression.

"But…" he prompted.

"There is no 'but.' I'm glad you didn't know my husband was dead. People have a tendency to treat me differently when they know. It's almost as if I'm contagious, and they don't want to be infected with my tragedy."

"Understood. I will forget that Izzy told me and continue to treat you as I have."

"With only minimally veiled amusement and strained tolerance." She didn't know what had prompted her to blurt out what she really thought. Normally, she was far more circumspect about her feelings.

Caleb flinched as if she had slapped him. Then he shrugged and turned away.

Chapter Thirteen

The Eye of the Storm

The storm was worsening. Elizabeth had forgotten what a New England hurricane sounded like. The shrieking wind, the groaning response of the house to the buffeting and pounding, even the restless breathing of everyone gathered for shelter, heightened Elizabeth's anxiety. She felt only slightly safer at Cove Meadow than if she and Matteo had been trapped at Innisfree.

Peering out the unshuttered window over the sink, she strained to see if Matteo was on his way back to the house as Caleb had said. Then she heard his voice behind her in the mudroom off the kitchen and turned in relief. She wanted to pull him close, confirm with her touch that he was safe, but she refrained. He'd hate to be coddled like a baby in front of the men. Instead, she scanned Josiah's face for what she hoped would be reassurance, not greater concern. But what she found was wariness and exhaustion as he peeled off his dripping rain gear.

Matteo walked into the kitchen smelling of goat and tracking in a trail of must and straw.

Caleb raised his arm in a high-five to him.

"Thanks for the help, Matt. If the goats had panicked and escaped the barn we'd still be out there."

Elizabeth watched her son's face light up from Caleb's praise and silently admitted that here was one more thing she owed the ranger on this harrowing day. She tried not to think of Matteo's outburst the night before, the searing emptiness of not having a father who could offer the kind of recognition Caleb had just given him.

She should feel grateful, she told herself. But she didn't. Instead, she felt her relief in Caleb's kindness to her son was a betrayal. It should have been Antonio acknowledging Matteo. Knowing that could never be made her desperate to ensure that Antonio's film kept him alive for his son.

Her dismay must have been broadcasting itself on her face, because she caught Caleb looking at her once again as if she had slapped him.

"I've made a fresh pot of coffee," Grace called from the living room. "Does anyone want a cup?" She seemed to have sensed the tension in the kitchen and intervened to defuse it.

At the same time, Izzy came into the kitchen bearing towels and handed one to each of the men and Matteo.

Taking her cues from Izzy and Grace, who seemed to be carrying on with serene confidence, Elizabeth refrained from expressing her rising panic. Instead, she turned to Grace. "I'm exhausted. Can you point me in the direction of a place to crash? Matteo, how about you?"

Matteo rolled his eyes. "Not yet."

"You might want to wash up before you bed down for the night," Caleb suggested. "Let me show you."

Caleb led Matteo out of the kitchen, lantern in hand.

Elizabeth watched them silently, feeling once again that her son had slipped from her grasp.

Grace called to her gently. "Don't worry. He's in good hands. Let me show you where you and Matt can sleep."

Elizabeth followed her, too tired to hover over her son and realizing how ridiculous that was. He'd already been out in the storm.

"We've put the elders in the bedrooms. I hope you don't mind sleeping on the couch."

"Oh, Grace, I'm so grateful for a roof over our heads. I'm happy to sleep on the floor if someone else needs a bed."

"No need. Caleb's already claimed the floor." She pointed to what looked like an army-issue bedroll in the corner.

Elizabeth helped Grace make up the couch and an air mattress for Matteo. It unsettled her that Caleb would be sleeping nearby, but couldn't explain even to herself why.

"Josiah will be monitoring the weather on our short-wave. Try to get some rest, and don't fret about Matt staying up. Caleb will keep him from doing anything stupid. I'll leave this lantern here for you on the table."

"Good night, Grace. And thank you."

She didn't believe she could follow Grace's comforting suggestion with the house groaning around her and the rain lashing in fury on the roof and against the shutters. But her physical exhaustion and depleted emotional reserves undid her and she drifted unwillingly into a dream-ravaged sleep.

Around 3 a.m. she bolted awake, not from the crash of a limb or the boom of a churning wind, but from the silence. Except for the steady whoosh of breathing that she recognized as her son's in deep slumber on the mattress behind the couch, the house was eerily quiet. She remembered once reading about the unnatural absence of sound in the eye of a storm and the treacherous lure to the unsuspecting that the danger was past.

She got up as quietly as she could and stood for a moment watching Matteo sprawled across the mattress, his long legs hanging over the edge. She remembered how mesmerized she'd been by him when he slept as an infant, his face a reflection of milk-sated bliss. Although he was wordless, she'd learned quickly to understand his needs. She'd been a confident mother then, a "natural," Antonio had murmured to her in their bed as she'd nursed Matteo. She no longer believed she deserved that label. She shivered in the dampness that had seeped into the house. The fire in the woodstove had burned down. She pulled from the couch the woven blanket she'd burrowed under and wrapped it around herself as she carefully padded around Matteo and into the kitchen.

The pot of coffee Grace had made earlier in the evening sat on the stove. Elizabeth retrieved a clean cup from the dish drainer and found a lighter on the counter. It took her a few seconds to get a flame to light the burner, but finally a wavering blue tongue of fire spit out of the nozzle and the gas ring on the range came to life in a burst of light.

She was pouring the reheated coffee when a voice broke the storm's soundless center. She jumped and nearly dropped the cup.

"I could use a cup of that as well." It was Caleb in the doorway, his flashlight casting a pale blue light on the sharp planes of his face, exaggerating the weariness and fatigue Elizabeth assumed was a mirror image of her own.

She handed him the cup she'd just poured and took another for herself.

Caleb moved further into the kitchen, shut the door behind him and sat at the table.

"No point in waking everybody else up."

"I'm sorry if I disturbed you."

"You didn't. I was already awake."

"The silence . . ."

"Yeah. It's far more ominous than the howling. A hidden killer, teasing its victims with the deceptive belief that the danger is past."

"How close do you think we are to the wall? When will it descend again?"

"Not sure. My dad is keeping tabs on things. He'd be sounding the alarm if we were at risk."

"It's been a long time since I've been in the middle of a hurricane. I think Matteo is finding it exciting rather than threatening."

"I did, too, at his age. Look, I may be out of place saying this, but it's okay to let him be a kid."

"And you think I'm not? I didn't hold him back from going out to the barn with you tonight." Elizabeth could sense the defensiveness in her voice, her posture.

"And good for you! I mean it. You said the words that gave him permission. But you should have seen your face."

"What about my face?" But Elizabeth already knew the answer.

"The last thing you wanted was for him to leave the safety of his mama. And you especially didn't want him spending time with me."

The physical and emotional tolls of the last twenty-four hours had finally drained Elizabeth to the point where she had no inner resources left to hear Caleb's comment as anything other than an attack on her.

"Has it somehow become your summer project to deliberately antagonize me? You're right about one thing. I'm not looking for a surrogate father for Matteo. He has a family full of role models and doesn't need someone influencing him who has such a negative view of me.

Look, I brought Matteo to Innisfree to heal us both and to find a new equilibrium as a family without a husband and father. That's been hard enough. But from my first day at Cape Poge, you've treated me as an interloper, someone who doesn't belong. Why? What difference should it make to you that I've set up housekeeping at Innisfree? Your mother and Izzy seem grateful that I'm there, that the place hasn't been abandoned."

Elizabeth stood up. "Whatever is bugging you about me or Innisfree or something that has nothing to do with either, leave me out of it. And leave my son alone."

She wanted to slam a door or throw the coffee cup against the wall. But she swallowed the anger she could only attribute to sleep deprivation and the oppressive anxiety wrought by the storm. She was a guest of Caleb and his family and had absorbed lessons of how one should behave under stress from none other than her grandmother. Elizabeth knew Lydia would have been appalled to hear her outburst. Elizabeth was appalled herself. But she couldn't take back what she'd just said. Somehow, in her exhausted and raw emotional state, she'd spoken what she truly felt about the enigmatic and judgmental man still sitting at the table.

She put the coffee cup in the sink, gathered up her blanket and left the kitchen.

She went back to the couch, knowing that she was too wired to attempt sleep but trapped into waiting out the storm. She wrapped herself up and turned away from the room. If Caleb followed her, he'd be confronted with her back. She sank into her misery, engulfed by the loneliness that had been her constant state since Antonio's death. She tried to stifle the sobs rising to the surface, but at that moment nature echoed her despair as the wall of the hurricane came roaring back across the bay.

To Elizabeth, the storm seemed even more ferocious than the evening before, and she gave herself up to her own fury.

Chapter Fourteen

Izzy's Magic

Around five in the morning the storm finally abated. The wind had weakened, and although it was still raining, it was no longer falling in torrents. From various pockets of the house people were beginning to stir, and Elizabeth pulled herself up out of the cocoon in which she'd hidden. She couldn't stop herself from glancing over at the corner where Caleb had been sleeping before their conversation in the kitchen. His bedroll was gone. She had no idea when he'd returned to retrieve it or where he might have gone to grab a few more hours of sleep. She told herself she didn't care.

As she stretched and ran her fingers through her hair to untangle it, she saw Izzy heading for the kitchen. Matteo was still sleeping soundly. Adolescents, she had learned, functioned on completely different body clocks than their elders. She quietly folded up the bed linens and joined Izzy in the kitchen.

"May I help with anything?"

"Good morning, Lili! You're up early. How did you sleep?"

"Not well, I'm afraid. I thought I'd fall into oblivion, I was so exhausted. But my mind just wouldn't let go."

"You've got a lot on your plate, hon. Coping with Innisfree by yourself is no small feat."

"But your mother did it, didn't she? Granny told us Mae spent winters alone there back in the 1940s."

"My mother was indomitable, that's for sure. She loved Innisfree with such single-minded fervor. I carried around a lot of guilt for many years for being the reason she was forced to relinquish it. But seeing you take up the reins out there gives us Monroes hope that it won't be abandoned to the ravages of nature."

"I'm not sure I'm the best custodian."

"That's not what I hear from my nephew."

Elizabeth bristled at the mention of Caleb, both surprised that he would have said anything positive about her and annoyed that he was bringing any kind of report about her back to his family.

"Lili, what you are doing takes courage—finding your way again after the death of your husband, raising your son alone. And taking on the stewardship of Innisfree to boot! Don't be too hard on yourself. And ask for help! Not just with repairing a leaky roof. This island community is pretty tight. Especially when it comes to protecting its wild and precious places. No one wants to see Innisfree become derelict, or worse yet, wind up in the hands of some wealthy celebrity or Russian oligarch."

"Oh, Izzy, Granny would never sell it!"

"I know Lydia won't, but what happens after Lydia is no longer with us? How many of your cousins are willing to preserve it the way you are?"

"I can't imagine Innisfree gone."

"I know you can't. And that's why I'm so glad you came back this summer. Now, let's get some breakfast going to feed the huddling masses under our roof. There should be a big bin of oatmeal in that cupboard. If you can get that started, I'm going to brave the elements and go milk a goat."

Izzy went out to the mud room and grabbed a rain jacket and a pair of boots, leaving Elizabeth alone in the kitchen to ponder Izzy's words. She admitted that she'd felt desperately alone managing Innisfree. She'd been so long away that the idea of Chappy as a community caring for one another had eluded her. She was reminded of the storytelling from the night before. The memory rekindled the spark of creativity that not only had lain dormant since Antonio's death but also had been trampled as she had faltered and stumbled in her relationship with Matteo.

She smiled to herself at Izzy's capacity to lift her spirits. As a girl, she'd called it Izzy's "magic"—the plays, the costumes, the glitter that Elizabeth had fervently believed was fairy dust. As she stirred the oatmeal in the largest pot she could find, Elizabeth thought about how Izzy had once again sprinkled glitter on Elizabeth's challenging life. She couldn't help remarking how different Izzy was from Caleb,. Maybe Caleb took after his father, she thought. Grace, while not as effervescent as Izzy, was a warm and compassionate woman. Josiah, on the other hand, had barely spoken during the time Elizabeth had been under their roof. He seemed more at home dealing with the ravages of the storm than with the frail and frightened elders.

By the time Izzy returned with a bucket of steaming milk, Elizabeth had made a pot of coffee and was carrying a tray of bowls and cups to the dining room. Grace was shepherding the elders from bedroom to bath and then to the dining table. Elizabeth went to wake up Matteo, but found his mattress empty.

"Have you seen Matteo?" she asked Izzy when she returned to the kitchen.

Izzy was lifting the oatmeal pot from the stove.

"Can you grab a trivet so that I can put this on the sideboard in the dining room? They're in the bottom drawer. Matt was out in the barn, gathering eggs and mucking out the goats' stall."

"He really seems to be throwing himself into country life. Who knew that a kid who spent his free time either attached to the umbilical cord of his iPod or riding around Florence on a Vespa would voluntarily shovel manure?"

"He seems eager to prove himself to Caleb," Izzy said as she pushed open the door to the dining room and disappeared with a smile.

Her comment abruptly sent a chill through Elizabeth. She may have demanded of Caleb that he stay away from Matteo in the middle of the night, but she hadn't anticipated that Matteo had already been won over. He'd only met Caleb the morning before, when they'd been trying to board up the house. She could see that in Matteo's eyes, Caleb was a hero. Why she didn't herself, and why she felt such discomfort around him, was not something she was going to be able to talk out with Izzy or Grace. She could only imagine that his aunt and his mother would neither understand nor take kindly to her doubts. This was something she'd have to sort out by herself. But in the long list of items she needed to address "by herself," Caleb Monroe was at the bottom.

As she had so many times before, she threw herself into "doing" rather than thinking. Breakfast needed to be served and cleaned away; bed linens needed to be gathered up; and eventually, as the rain lessened to a drizzle and the weather service declared the hurricane downgraded to a tropical storm and then officially blown out to sea, there were several people who needed to be driven home.

"I can take a few people," she volunteered as Josiah and Grace were divvying up the passengers and sorting out routes.

"Thank you, Elizabeth! One more vehicle means we can get everyone home in one round."

"Are we sure everyone has a safe home to get back to?"

"Caleb's on his way now to assess each situation. As he calls in, we'll let the elders know."

In all the activity during the morning, Elizabeth hadn't seen Caleb and for that she was grateful. She didn't relish any awkward moments after her outburst, and it seemed he felt the same and had deliberately avoided her.

"You know that Matt has gone with him, don't you? I specifically heard Caleb tell him to ask you." It seemed Grace was at least peripherally aware of the tension between Elizabeth and Caleb.

Elizabeth shook her head. "No, Matteo seems to have avoided what he suspected might be a 'no'."

"Would you have said no? I don't mean that to question your decision. Believe me, as a mother of a male member of the human race, it's not always easy to know where to draw the line."

"Thanks, Grace. If he *had* asked, I'd have said yes. He's been contributing to the work here, as far as I can tell, and going out to survey the aftermath of the storm is work, too. But I also know it's far more exciting than doing laundry. It troubles me that he didn't ask, and when he gets back we need to have a talk."

What was equally troubling to Elizabeth was that Caleb had taken Matteo, despite the lack of any word from her. Or even worse, had Matteo lied to Caleb that she'd given her permission? She held her suspicions and dismay in check. She'd wait till Matteo and she were alone, back at Innisfree—if Innisfree were still intact.

As the morning passed, Caleb relayed information back to Cove Meadow. It appeared that all the homes on the southern end of Chappy—the most vulnerable, given the pattern of this storm—were sound and habitable for their elderly residents. Elizabeth and Josiah each took a carload as Grace and Izzy held down the fort with the others. Each of the elders carried a basket of provisions the Monroe women had put together. They knew the elders were eager to be in their own homes, and convincing them to stay for another night or even another meal, was clearly not going to happen.

As she drove her three passengers to their cabins at Wasque, Elizabeth had an opportunity to express to them how moved she'd been by their storytelling the night before.

"Are your stories, your history, written down?"

"Ours is an oral tradition," Mariah, the most talkative of the trio, explained.

"What about recordings or video?" Elizabeth pressed.

"We have some old recordings of chanting and drumming, and there's a community TV station on the island that always sends a cameraman to Pow Wow in July to get a few clips of the dancing."

"But there's no comprehensive collection of oral history?" Elizabeth couldn't keep the disbelief from her voice.

"Not yet. We're a small, scattered tribe without the kind of revenue our Mashpee or Aquinnah cousins have to fund a project like that. Just turn down this lane, sweetheart. My cottage is the last one on the left."

By the time Elizabeth had deposited each of her passengers at their homes and returned to Cove Meadow, the spark that Izzy had blown back to life was licking at the tinder her conversation with Mariah had started to accumulate. Images of the lantern-lit faces of the night before were flickering through her brain like old daguerreotype photos or slides from a 19th-century exhibition. Excitement, passion and an eagerness to plunge deeply into the subject were coursing through her like a drug. The numbness that had paralyzed her was wearing off, as if she were shedding a suffocating mask and bulky, restrictive clothing.

Chapter Fifteen

Tobias' Blessing

Elizabeth fairly danced into the house, racing up the steps and bursting into the kitchen, but she stopped abruptly when she saw Caleb and Matteo at the table making sandwiches.

"Hi, Mom," Matteo greeted her as if he had nothing to explain. "Want a turkey sandwich?"

Elizabeth held back from confronting him in Caleb's presence. She'd promised herself she'd wait till they were alone, but it took all of her reserves not to explode at him. It horrified her that he'd been deceitful and she didn't want Caleb to know.

"Thanks, Matteo, but I'm not really hungry. I'm eager to get back to Innisfree and check on the house."

"We already did! Everything was fine and Caleb and I got the plywood down from the big windows. All that's left I can handle myself."

Elizabeth looked from Matteo to Caleb.

"Wow. Thank you!" Her concern about Matteo's deliberate unwillingness to ask her permission took a nosedive as she contemplated what he and Caleb had accomplished. She still wanted an explanation and an apology from him, but he clearly hadn't gone off to do something reckless.

"That's a huge relief. I'd still like to get back before sunset, though. And I imagine the tides are still running high. Eat up while I pull together our stuff."

She left the kitchen, aware that she hadn't even nodded a greeting to Caleb, who also had not engaged in the conversation.

She found Izzy coming out of Tobias' room, a tray with the remnants of his lunch in her hands. He'd remained there throughout the ordeal of the hurricane and Elizabeth had never had the chance to see or speak with him.

"Are your charges safely delivered?" she asked.

"Everyone. Is Josiah still out?"

"He had one more trip to make, getting Cousin Sadie over to Oak Bluffs. Her son was meeting them at the ferry terminal to escort her back to Mashpee. She got caught here visiting my dad. She's almost as old as he is, and still a spitfire. She tends to stir up the family and open old wounds. Josiah barely acknowledges her presence, thanks to some ugly comments she made about his mixed heritage when he was just a kid. How are you holding up? You know you're welcome to spend another night if you're too exhausted to head back to Innisfree."

"Oh, thank you, Izzy! But I'm anxious to get home and sleep in my own bed. Matteo tells me he and Caleb have already opened up the house."

"My nephew definitely kept your boy busy today. You can be proud of Matteo, Lili."

It appeared Grace hadn't revealed Matteo's duplicity. Elizabeth nodded, keeping a smile on her face. *If you only knew*, she thought.

"Thanks, Izzy. May I ask if Tobias is up for me to stick my head in and say hello? I promise I won't overtire him. I just would love to see him, now that the excitement is over."

"I'll check to see if he's awake. He tends to doze after lunch. Please prepare yourself, though. It's been a long time since you've seen him. He's very frail and speaks almost entirely in Wampanaak now. I'm not even sure he'll know who you are."

Izzy returned from Tobias with a nod. "He's awake. I told him you're coming in."

Elizabeth entered the room quietly and bent down to greet the old man propped up on several pillows.

"Hello, Tobias."

He reached out his good hand and grasped Elizabeth's.

"Little Elizabeth," he whispered hoarsely.

She squeezed the fragile fingers gently, stunned by the transformation of the robust, stalwart patriarch who'd had such a profound influence on her life. He was 98, but it was more than age that had weakened him. Izzy had shared with her that cancer was eating away at him. She glanced at the array of medications on the bedside table and the paraphernalia of home health care equipment around the room. The scene was all too familiar to her and she could not prevent the tears that welled up in her eyes. With her free hand she brushed them away.

"I only wanted to tell you that I've returned and I'm caring for Innisfree. A hummingbird has nested in the rugosa bush, just like when I was a little girl."

A wide smile broke out on Tobias' face and he squeezed her hand as he mumbled something in his ancestor's language.

"Take care, Tobias. I'll come back to visit you again."

Izzy was standing in the doorway.

"Do you know what he said?" Elizabeth asked.

"It was a blessing. 'May you continue to see as the creator intended.' "

Elizabeth took a deep breath as she wiped the last of the tears from her eyes.

Izzy hugged her.

"Even suffering as he is, he hasn't forgotten how to give each one of us what we need in the moment we are with him."

Elizabeth nodded.

"My husband was the same. The closer he got to death, when I felt him moving farther and farther away from me on a path I couldn't follow, he communicated to me the most surprising, healing, loving words."

"I know where that wisdom and love comes from. I died when I was 23, in a horrific car accident early one morning on a rain-slicked Route 2 out in Western Mass. I have no memory of the accident itself, but what I do remember is watching my body and knowing I had left it. I was in a place of utter peace, free of pain and full of love."

"But you came back."

"I did. With great regret I came back to the messiness and complications of life."

"Do you still regret returning?"

"Oh no, Lili! I'm grateful now it wasn't my time and I've had all these years to grow and love and transform. It was a great gift to have that glimpse of death. I didn't know it at first. I plunged into a profound depression that didn't make sense to my friends and family. To them, how could I not rejoice as they did that I had survived?"

"How did you emerge from the depression? Because you had by the time I knew you."

"Time. Discovering others who had experienced the same encounter with death and who both understood and reassured me that one could go on to embrace life without losing what I had learned in death."

"I think my husband was approaching in his last days what you just described. I wish I knew how to convey that to Matteo. He has been so angry—about his own loss but also about what he believes was snatched from his father by death."

"It may be that he understood on some level the transformation his father was undergoing, even if he hasn't recognized or acknowledged it. Children perceive things that we adults sometimes believe are beyond them or too painful. Children *know*, even when we try to shield them."

"My mother-in-law didn't want Matteo to see his father in the last stages of his disease. I think because *she* didn't want to see him that way."

"I hope you didn't allow her to keep Matt away."

"It was a bitter fight, but I am Matteo's mother, and that was one argument she understood."

"Good for you! From everything I've seen of Matt in the last twenty-four hours, you've done a wonderful job of raising him. Don't worry about what he does or doesn't understand about his father's death. The anger is a necessary part of the experience. When my mother died, I raged against everything—God, cancer, the medical profession, even myself. Even with my own experience of death, I selfishly didn't want her to go. I still needed her."

"How long did it take for the anger to subside?"

"There isn't a prescribed timetable, if that is what you're seeking, Lili. Everyone faces loss in her own way. But if I had to define that time period, I'd place it at about a year."

"How did you move beyond it?"

Izzy ran her fingers through her curly hair and smiled.

"I found something else to direct my anger at. I was up for tenure and I threw my energy into completing a book on Melville. You should try it—pour yourself into creating something meaningful."

Elizabeth hugged Izzy.

"Thanks. I will," she whispered, more to herself than to Izzy.

Elizabeth and Matteo said their goodbyes and climbed into the Jeep for the journey back to Innisfree. They arrived late in the afternoon. Along the horizon to the west the sky had finally cleared, but above the thin strip of calm blue a mass of clouds still hung, the last fragments of the storm moving out.

Before she went in the house Elizabeth made a circuit through the wet grass, her hand grazing the weathered shingles. On the north side of the cottage a tattered geranium, forgotten in their hurried departure, lay tipped on its side. As she came around to the bay side, the sun had begun its drop from behind the clouds, descending rapidly through the luminous sliver of sky across the water. As it fell, its final rays reflected off the underside of the clouds.

"Matteo, look," she directed his gaze toward the deepening hues spreading across their field of vision and up into the clouds.

"Granny Lydia taught us to watch for a sky like this after a storm," she explained, with her arm around her son. They stood silently for a few moments as the sky mutated from the explosion of gold to the feathered remnants of purple and indigo.

"I used to draw pictures of sunsets like this with my crayons. When I was older, I tried to capture the image with my camera. But nothing compares to the real thing. I've missed the sky at Innisfree."

She squeezed his shoulder. "Let's get our stuff in the house and have some supper. Grace gave me some leftover sobaheg to heat up."

She didn't know if Matteo shared her awe of the sunset, but decided not to push him. Whatever he was going to take away from Innisfree and into himself could not come from her.

Chapter Sixteen

Confrontation

After they had done the supper dishes she raised the question of where he wanted to sleep.

"Here's fine for tonight, but I think I'll clean out Byzantium tomorrow."

She made no comment, and pulled sheets and a pillow from the linen closet and gave them to him to make up a bed for himself on the couch.

"I'm going to climb into my bed, which looks more than inviting after our night at the Monroes. Don't forget to turn off the gaslight before you go to sleep."

He rolled his eyes and then slipped his earphones on as he burrowed into the couch.

Elizabeth pulled closed the flowered curtain that separated her bedroom from the living room. Lydia had never put a door there, preferring both the openness to the breeze from the east and the ability to hear what was going on in the rest of the house. The villa's many rooms were all separated from one another by massive carved doors with ancient locks that needed periodic oiling. She'd been grateful for those locks at times over the years, a barrier between her and the prying, possessive eyes of Adriana.

She pummeled her pillow into a comfortable cushion and sank into the mattress, drifting quickly into an exhausted but freeing sleep.

She woke the next morning to the sound of nails being ripped from wood. She thought adolescents were supposed to be notorious late sleepers, but Matteo's biorhythms seemed to be all over the place this week. She found him on the south side of the house, a stack of plywood neatly lined up against the outer wall.

"I've only got two more windows to uncover and then I'll store everything under the house."

"Thanks, Matteo. You're awesome! I've got some bacon and a half dozen eggs that Grace put in the basket for us. Are you hungry?"

"A frittata would be great. Do you have any onions and cheese?"

"I think I can find some." She smiled at the opportunity to provide him with a meal he loved. At least he wasn't pushing away her food. Both of them were better at *doing*, keeping busy as a way of keeping at bay the feelings that threatened them, avoiding the chasm of loss that lay between them.

She plunged into activity in the kitchen, chopping onions, snipping basil and parsley from the scraggly pots of herbs she'd found at a local farm in Edgartown, whipping Grace's eggs into a frothy lemon yellow. The bacon was sizzling, the onions had caramelized and the skillet had reached the temperature when water drops beaded and danced on its cast iron surface when Matteo came into the kitchen and washed up at the sink.

"Smells good," he said.

She slid the eggs into the pan over the onions and gently shook it. Once the mixture had begun to set, she strewed the cheese and herbs over it and slipped it into the oven. When it was ready, the cheese melted and the top of the frittata a golden brown, Matteo had his plate in hand, waiting for her to slide it out of the pan. He carried the dish into the dining room and began to wolf down the frittata.

Elizabeth plucked the bacon from the frying pan, poured herself a second cup of coffee and joined her son at the table.

"What do you want to do today?"

"Caleb promised to take me fishing at the Gut."

Matteo's words elicited two reactions. The first was the same chill she'd felt the day before at Cove Meadow, the fear that Caleb was somehow stepping between her and her son. The second response was an observation, perhaps related to the first. Matteo had used the word "promised." For all his surprising her in the days since the onset of the hurricane with his unexpected maturity and physical prowess, he had reverted to the language he'd often used as a little boy in Italy when faced with a disappointment. "But you *promised*!" He would challenge her when told he couldn't do or have something because of some unanticipated obstruction. She heard in the word *promise* a little boy clinging to something he wanted desperately. Not necessarily to go fishing, but to have a man, a father, willing to take him.

Elizabeth realized in that moment that she had never had the conversation with Matteo about his failure to ask her permission to go with Caleb to check out conditions after the storm. They'd been hungry and tired when they reached the cottage yesterday, she told herself. But the truth was, she'd been avoiding the confrontation. She'd allowed herself to relish the peaceful moments of being alone with Matteo, of giving him some time and space to appreciate Innisfree as she did. But she couldn't let this go on, this growing attachment to Caleb that was effectively shutting her out.

"Were you planning to go fishing without asking permission, the way you left with Caleb yesterday at Cove Meadow without letting me know?"

"I just told you now that we're going fishing! And I couldn't find you yesterday. Caleb said it was OK."

"Caleb is not your father!"

Matteo pushed his chair back, put his hands on the table as he stood up, and leaned across at her.

"No, he's not. I don't have a father. But sometimes I feel like I don't have a mother, either. You go away in your head. Caleb's not my father, but he's my friend."

He stomped out of the dining room, walked through the kitchen and slammed the door as he left the house.

Elizabeth remained in her chair, too stunned to make sense of what had just happened between them. Her words to her son had been unspeakably cruel. Where had it come from, reminding Matteo that he was fatherless? And why was she so threatened by Caleb's presence in their lives?

She couldn't bring herself to go after Matteo at that moment, not when she didn't understand her own outburst. She took a couple of deep breaths, then stood and cleared the table. Was it only a few minutes ago that she'd been smiling to herself as she cooked one of her son's favorite meals?

She scraped the remnants of that meal from his plate into the garbage and soaked the dishes in a basin of soapy water. When she heard the rumble of a truck approaching the house, she wiped her hands on her shorts and strode outside.

Matteo already had his hand on the passenger door by the time she reached the truck. He hesitated when he saw her, a look of unrecognizable defiance on his face, and then climbed inside the cab of the truck.

"Thanks for offering to take Matteo fishing," she said to Caleb as calmly as she could contain herself, "but he's grounded."

Matteo slapped the dashboard and shouted "Why! You just want me to be as miserable as you are."

Caleb ignored his outburst and turned to Elizabeth.

"Is this about Matt or about me?"

"It's very much about Matteo, who needs to understand some limits. Even when it's with you, he can't go off without asking permission or even letting me know where he's going." She held back from saying what she truly felt—that especially when it was with Caleb, she didn't want Matteo spending time away from her.

Matteo was sputtering, "But I *did* tell you!"

"Are you talking about our riding out yesterday to check on the aftermath of the storm?" He directed his question to Elizabeth, who remained outside the truck, arms folded across her chest. She nodded.

"Matt, you told me you'd spoken to your mother. Did you lie to me?"

Caleb's tone wasn't harsh, but it conveyed a deep disappointment that Elizabeth recognized had a far more profound effect on Matteo than if Caleb had yelled at him.

She saw Matteo start to mouth the defensive excuses he'd thrown at her at the breakfast table; but then, under Caleb's unwavering gaze, her son became quiet.

Elizabeth and Caleb both waited, letting the silence build. Finally, Matteo nodded.

"Yeah. I couldn't find her, but I didn't look very hard."

"Is that because you thought she'd say no?"

Once again, Matteo nodded, his eyes focused on his feet rather than at either Caleb or Elizabeth.

"I want you to get out of the truck, apologize to your mother and spend the day doing whatever back-breaking, boring chores she gives you. Lying is what cowards do, and the young man who helped out at Cove Meadow during the hurricane was no coward. Regain your mother's forgiveness and trust, and find that courageous young man again."

Matteo climbed out of the truck and walked reluctantly around to Elizabeth.

"I'm sorry, Mom. *Mi dispiace.*"

"I think you owe Caleb an apology, too, Matteo."

He turned toward Caleb. "I'm sorry. You're right. I was a coward."

"You acted in a cowardly way, Matt. But I'm not going to brand you a coward for one offense. Just make sure you don't lie again."

"Yes, sir."

"When you mom says it's OK, we'll go fishing. But not today."

If Matteo thought his apologies might give him a reprieve from being grounded, he kept it to himself, and stood back as Caleb put the truck in gear and drove away.

Elizabeth braced herself as the dust in the drive settled, expecting resentment. But what she saw in her son's face was not anger, but sadness. He was struggling not to cry.

"I'm going to grab a broom and a mop. Let's scrub out Byzantium this morning so you can have your own place. I'll meet you there." She left him, holding back from throwing her arms around him. He needed some shred of dignity and some time to absorb the message Caleb had left with him.

She needed time as well. Caleb had surprised her both with his support for her and with the way he'd handled Matteo. As grateful as she was, she was uncomfortable with the sense of obligation that was mounting with each act of generosity he extended to her.

She retrieved the cleaning tools and supplies and spent the next few hours with Matteo swatting down cobwebs and sweeping out mouse poop and desiccated insects. They didn't speak to one another, but poured the emotional aftershocks of their confrontation into scouring the cabin.

By lunch time the curtains and blankets were hanging on the clothesline after a thorough encounter with the washing machine, the windows had been doused with Windex and polished to a gleam, and the floor had been mopped of its accumulated grime.

"How about a swim before lunch?" she suggested, surveying the streaks of sweat and muck that coated their faces and limbs. She thought he would refuse. It was one thing to do penance by cleaning out the cabin, but to participate in something that might actually break the tension still humming between them—that was probably more than he was ready to do.

"I'm going to change into my bathing suit and head over to East Beach."

She didn't see him when she emerged from the house with her beach towel, so she went alone down the drive and through the break in the dunes. But when she got to the other side, there he was, boogie board in hand, riding the waves. Despite the clear weather, the water still held the residual energy of the storm and the normally placid sea at East Beach was churning.

She threw down her towel and raced into the water, registering the shock of the cold New England ocean temperature before plunging into the waves. When she came up, she looked for Matteo, oblivious to a patch of rough water gathering momentum behind her. She heard Matteo call out a warning to her but she was too late, and the wave engulfed her in its fury before she had a chance to turn and catch it.

She was tossed and tumbled, swallowing great gulps of salt water before the wave finally released her roughly in the rock-strewn shallows. She was on her hands and knees, trying to pull herself up, when another wave crashed over her and started to suck her back into the sea. That was when she felt a hand grasp hers and pull her up and out of the water. Matteo stood in front of her, still holding on to her.

"Are you OK?" The concern in his voice was palpable. She heard a vestige of her little boy in his anxious question, not the angry teenager from a few hours before.

"You're bleeding, Mom!"

She looked down at her legs and the palms of her hands. Wherever the waves had dragged her body across the bottom, she was riddled with abrasions. Her hair was full of sand, as was the bottom of her bikini.

Matteo ran to grab her towel and wrapped it around her.

"You're shaking," he said, his words quaking almost as much as she was. "Why don't you sit down for a minute?" So she did, tossing her head to rid it of some of the sand.

Matteo took a corner of the towel and dabbed at her face. "Your nose is bleeding," he said, and showed her the bloody towel.

She finally spoke. "I'm OK. Just a little shook up. I should know better than to trust the ocean after a hurricane. Thanks for rescuing me."

She squeezed his hand, and he squeezed back with an audible sigh of relief.

"Well, I think the sand has sufficiently scoured away the grime of Byzantium. Shall we head back, or do you want to swim some more?"

"It's OK. I'm done. And I'm hungry." He grinned, perhaps a silent acknowledgment that he hadn't finished his breakfast.

"I should be able to rustle us up something to eat after I get some Band-Aids on these scrapes."

He gave her a hand as she rose and they trudged back across the sand and up to the house, each of them in their own thoughts.

As they approached the cottage, Matteo spoke.

"I know I apologized for lying this morning. But I'm also sorry for the things I said at breakfast. It's not like it's your fault I don't have a dad. And I know you're sad deep down like I am. When I saw the wave swallow you up I felt like I was losing you too, for real and not just because your head was somewhere far off and not paying attention to me."

"Oh, Matteo, I'm sorry, too, if in my sadness I've made you feel abandoned." This time she did embrace her son.

After a few minutes she stepped back. "I'm smearing you with blood." She wiped his cheek. And they walked arm-in-arm to the house.

Chapter Seventeen

Gratitude

Later that night, after Matteo had made himself a nest in Byzantium, surrounding himself with his iPod, his copy of *Lord of the Rings* and his Magic cards, Elizabeth found the Edgartown phone book in a drawer and flipped to the "M's." She ran her finger down the list until she found Josiah's number at Cove Meadow. It was around nine; she hoped not too late to call.

Grace answered.

"It's Elizabeth. First, thank you again for your generosity. I don't know what we would have done without the Monroes."

"We were happy to be here for you, Elizabeth. It's what islanders do for one another."

"So I'm learning. I hate to bother you with this, but I don't have Caleb's cell phone number. Is he there now?"

"No, hon, he's not. He headed out about an hour ago to do some night fishing at the Gut. Let me give you his number, although he may have turned off the phone. He sometimes does that when he's fishing."

"Will a ringing phone disturb the fish?"

Elizabeth heard a gentle laugh at the other end of the line.

"No, it's more that a ringing phone disturbs Caleb. He likes his peace, does my son. Here's the number, though."

Elizabeth took the number and then paced the floor, contemplating Graces' words. If Caleb truly didn't like to be summoned by the chimes of a cell phone, she was wary of intruding onto his solitude. But she didn't want to wait too long beyond the challenges of this morning without talking to him—thanking him and offering her own apology for her misgivings and misperceptions about him. He still confounded her, the contradictions of his generosity and his antipathy. But he seemed genuinely caring of Matteo and had demonstrated today that he wasn't trying to usurp her. Matteo had expressed it himself. He saw Caleb as his friend. And God knew, both Matteo and Elizabeth needed a friend.

She picked up her phone and punched in the numbers Grace had given her.

The phone went immediately to voice mail, so Grace was right in cautioning her that Caleb had likely turned it off. Elizabeth ended the call without leaving a message, not willing to express her change of heart remotely. She put down the phone, picked up a book and spent the next two hours immersed in a mystery set in Venice. Her fifteen years in Italy had not yet made her jaded, unmoved by the contradictions of the illustrious city's beauty and decay. She enjoyed reading English and American authors who used Italy as both backdrop and character in their books. She often found herself comparing her own perceptions of Italy with the impressions of these writers. As a filmmaker, her vocabulary was images and sound. It intrigued her how a novelist could conjure up her adopted country with words. To Elizabeth, her experience of the world, and of Italy especially, was intensely visual. As she read, she probed her own response to the vividly described landscape for signs of homesickness. She had never regretted her decision to settle in Italy when she married Antonio. Embracing him meant embracing his country. But for all her fascination with its complex history and cultural riches, she acknowledged to herself that it had never truly become "home."

As she meandered down narrow, twisting alleys and across arched bridges in the story, she noticed neither the deepening night nor the headlights approaching the house from the north. She'd left the front door open, enjoying both the fresh breeze and the nocturnal sounds of hunting owls and the gentle lap of high tide rising up on the banks of Shear Pen Pond. So she was startled by the voice calling to her through the screen.

"Elizabeth? I saw the light and took a chance that you were still up."

Although she couldn't see him on the darkened porch, she recognized Caleb's voice and rose to let him in.

"I saw that you'd called when I turned on my phone, and since I was passing right by the house on my way back from fishing, I decided to stop. Is anything wrong? Where's Matt?"

He looked around, but except for the gaslight over the easy chair where she'd been reading, the house was dark.

"He's settled into Byzantium. Lydia understood that kids need their own space out here. Byzantium has always been the boys' fort. First for my uncles and then my brothers. Now it's my son's. He helped clean it out today—the chore you assigned him as atonement."

"Why did you call?" His tone was bewildered, as if the only possible reason for her to call was Matt.

Elizabeth felt herself stiffen. She hadn't asked him to come, so why did he sound so put out once she'd assured him Matt was fine? Her reason for making the call earlier in the evening now seemed both foolish and futile.

"I didn't mean for you to delay your drive home."

"I thought something had happened with Matt, that he'd gone missing."

"Thanks for your concern. I would have left a message if that were the case. I wasn't calling for your help."

This conversation wasn't unfolding as she'd imagined it when she'd made the decision to speak to him, and she wasn't sure which one of them had precipitated the unraveling. But she knew she was the only one who could get it back on track. If she sent him away now without saying what she intended, she didn't think she'd find the courage again.

"Listen, I didn't leave a message because I wanted to speak directly to you, not to an inanimate device. If you have a minute, I'd like to explain."

"I have a minute. I have a lot of minutes. That's why I'm here."

She nodded in relief.

"Do you want to sit down? Can I get you anything to drink? Wine? Beer? Water?"

"A beer. Sure." He stepped away from the door and took a seat on the couch opposite the chair where her book was splayed upside down.

"I'll be right back."

When she returned with a beer for him and a glass of pinot noir for her, she found him with the book in his hand.

"I think I've read every one of the Commissario Brunetti mysteries. He's an intriguing character."

She looked surprised.

"Did you think I didn't read?" He asked.

She shook her head. "Hardly. Coming from a family like yours? I guess I thought your taste in literature would be different from mine, that's all."

"I keep a map of Venice at my fingertips when I read Donna Leon's books. I've only been there once—not enough to orient myself when Brunetti starts traipsing across the *Campo Santa Marina* and down an obscure *calle* in pursuit of truth. But I like to tell myself I grasped a sliver of the character of the landscape and its inhabitants when I was there. How about you? Have you spent much time there?"

"We went often in the early years. Antonio had a colleague in the Ministry of Justice. But I can't say I know the city well. It keeps its true self hidden. Like most of Italy."

"Have you acquired that trait of your adopted country, or have you always been 'hidden,' as you put it?"

She closed her hand tightly around the stem of her wine glass. She'd promised herself, for Matteo's sake, she would let go of the visceral reactions she had every time Caleb made an observation about her. She reminded herself of his handling of Matteo that morning and how much both Matteo and she needed him to be on their side. She took a sip of wine and plunged in to what she intended to say before she lost both the will and the desire to express her thanks.

"I'm trying not to be hidden tonight. I called to apologize and thank you. I'm sorry I've been so antagonistic toward you, especially in your own home, when you'd protected us and offered us not only shelter but an opportunity for Matteo to, well, grow up and discover something about himself. Frankly, I was a bitch."

Caleb smiled at her over his beer.

"That you were."

"What I don't understand, after I'd treated you so abominably, is why you supported me this morning when I refused to let Matteo go fishing with you."

"You're his mother, Elizabeth. I grew up in a household of strong women—my great-grandmother Naomi, my grandmother Mae, my Aunt Izzy and my mother, Grace. I have a deep-seated respect for them and learned early, 'if Mama ain't happy, ain't nobody happy.' I've had no doubt, since I met you, that you are Lydia Hammond's descendent, and I could no more step between you and your son than if I'd encountered a lioness protecting her cub on the Serengeti."

"Well, whatever motivated you this morning—fear of your grandmother or fondness for mine—I thank you."

"I did it not for them, but for you, Elizabeth. Look, I'm no psychologist, but I've seen my share of loss. You're facing the most challenging time in raising a kid, just as he hits puberty. And, you're facing it alone. You came to Chappy this summer for a reason. You knew this was a place of meaning for you, where maybe you could begin to heal, to rebuild the life that was snatched from you when your husband died. What I hope you'll understand is that this place is more than peaceful isolation and magnificent sunsets. It's a *community*. Allow us to be a part of your lives this summer, yours and Matt's. I'm not trying to replace his father—or you—but I *like* him. And I want to offer both of you my friendship."

"Thank you. That's what I realized today, and why I felt the need to extend an olive branch. Can we start over? I'll make every effort not to be defensive or feel usurped by your relationship with Matteo. Please understand that I'm only just emerging from a time when I felt under attack and isolated. When my husband was diagnosed with ALS, Lou Gehrig's disease, I understood I was going into battle for him and for our family. All my energy went into dealing with the disease, first as his advocate in seeking every hopeful bit of research and treatment, and then, when hope was no longer offered, as his caretaker. We had always been a strong team, but as he deteriorated, I had to take on the responsibility alone. I didn't have the support of a loving community—not like what I'm beginning to understand exists here. As much as Antonio's father had compassion for us, he was an old-school Italian without the capacity to step in and help. And my mother-in-law was shattered by the fear of losing her only son. She only knew how to rage against the fates, or against me for being whole and alive. Her weapon of choice was Matteo, pulling him closer as Antonio pulled away into silence and paralysis. I apologize that I felt threatened by Matteo's friendship with you. He needs a friend. We both do."

"I knew that something had happened to change you. My grandmother used to describe you as having grit and gifts. That morning when I first found you here, I thought you'd lost that spirit, had become one of the countless plastic debutantes who populate Edgartown in the summer."

"The *principessa*."

"What?"

"It's what my brother calls me when he wants to get under my skin. I was a long way from Chappy for a very long time."

"But you came back."

"I did."

"And. . ."

"I'm not sure I belong here anymore. It's changed. I've changed."

"We all have."

"But you're also back, Caleb. Why?"

"Tobias."

"But you've stayed, not just come to visit your dying grandfather."

"Let's just call it a sabbatical. I was as ready as you for a change of scenery."

"Where were you before?"

"Afghanistan."

Elizabeth was silent for a moment.

"I didn't know."

"Does that change how you see me?"

She hesitated, but then answered honestly.

"Of course it does! It fills in some of the missing pieces about you."

"Makes me less of an enigma? Allows you to slot me into a predefined box?"

"Are you implying that I'm stereotyping you? Isn't that what you did when you first met me?"

"Touché."

"Shall we agree from this point forward not to pigeonhole one another? I know we can't entirely escape where we came from before we encountered each other this summer, but as I said, let's start over again. Agreed?"

She put out her hand and he reached across the divide between them and took it.

"Agreed."

"Matteo more than made up for his behavior today. Whenever you're willing, he can go fishing with you."

"I'm on duty for the next three days, but I can take him on Thursday."

"Thanks."

"You're welcome."

He looked at his watch. "Thanks for the beer and the openness. But I need to get some sleep before I report for duty."

"What time do you have to be at the ranger station?"

"Six a.m."

"Do you want to sleep here? The other cabin still has a few cobwebs, but it's fairly habitable."

"That's OK. My uniform is at home, and I don't think Matt's quite ready to find me at the breakfast table."

Elizabeth looked up sharply at the implications of his statement. "I didn't mean it that way."

Caleb held up his hands. "And I didn't take it that way. I just meant that teenage boys tend to see life through a certain filter."

"I hear you. I'm only now getting used to the idea that my sweet little boy is a hormone-driven adolescent."

"We all come out the other side. Both parents and kids. Ask my mother."

"Were you a hellion?"

"Followed in the footsteps of my father."

"What do you mean?"

"That's a story for another night. Now I really do have to go. Thanks again."

"Thank *you,* Caleb. For everything."

She stood on the porch and watched him drive away, staying until the headlights of his truck had circled the eastern end of the pond and headed south.

The next day dawned with brilliant blue skies and a fresh breeze that blew away memories of the storm as swiftly as the winds of the hurricane itself. After breakfast Elizabeth announced that she was planning an excursion into Edgartown to stock up on groceries and do some research at the Historical Museum.

"Do you want to come?"

"Can I hang out with the cousins while you do you stuff?"

"Sure. Just give Aunt Deb and Uncle Sam a call to make sure they'll be there."

They were, and when she dropped Matteo off in Oak Bluffs she saw the enthusiasm with which the cousins greeted one another.

"We're relieved you two made it safely through the storm. Sam was a nervous wreck when he heard the ferry had shut down. He was ready to bring you across in the Whaler if you hadn't called to let us know you'd taken shelter with the Monroes." Debbie offered her a cup of coffee before she embarked on her errands.

"They took good care of us, and impressed upon me that islanders pitch in for one another."

"That we do. It's one of the reasons Sam and I decided to leave the mainland and settle here. How is Matt adjusting to life at Innisfree?"

"Fits and starts. I know I can't expect him to love it the way I do, when I have a childhood full of wonderful memories out there. He's lonely, and that is something I never experienced when we spent the summers with Granny Lydia."

"Sam talks about always having someone to play with. Are there no families with kids in the other houses near the lighthouse?"

"Not that I've seen. In fact, I think Innisfree is the only place that's inhabited right now. If anyone was planning to come, the hurricane shut down that idea pretty thoroughly. May I ask you something?"

"Of course!"

"Do you think your boys would be willing to come out and stay a while? Would you and Sam be OK with that?"

"I can't think of any objections your brother would have. He's tried in the past to entice our kids to stay at Innisfree without success. But the boys get along so well with Matt. I think they'd be willing to give it a few days, at least. We can ask them."

"Thanks. When I saw how they surrounded him this morning and dragged him off, it made me realize how much he needs that, and not a mother hovering over him."

"Let's see what they say. You go get your errands done. Take as long as you need. And plan on having supper with us!"

Elizabeth gave her sister-in-law a hug and made her way to the museum, where she'd called ahead to use their library. She spent the next several hours sifting through boxes of old photographs and documents, seeking a visual starting point for the Wampanoag project that had so fired her imagination during her stay at Cove Meadow. By the time the museum closed, she had a folder full of photocopies and several pages of notes.

She braved the post-hurricane crowds at the Stop & Shop. Large swaths of the island had lost power and people were replenishing freezers and refrigerators. She packed her groceries into a cooler, dumped several ten-pound bags of ice into it, and headed back to Sam's house after picking up a berry pie at Morning Glory Farm.

Sam and Debbie were on the porch when she arrived and greeted her with a cold beer.

"If you're up for running a summer camp, you've got two takers. The boys listened to Matt extol the virtues of Byzantium as if he were the first to discover the advantages of being out from under the watchful eyes of parents in the main house. They were sold."

"Do I have anything to worry about?"

"Nothing worse than what we got into at their ages," he smiled.

So that evening, with Matteo's cousins, their backpacks and their boogie boards sharing the back of the Jeep with him, Elizabeth negotiated the beach track back to Innisfree, guided by a full moon and the beam of the lighthouse pulling her north.

The ease with which the boys settled into the rhythm of life at Cape Poge, shuttling between Byzantium, the beach and the kitchen, left Elizabeth with uninterrupted hours to map out her plans for her film. As soon as breakfast was over, she spread out her notes and photos on the dining room table. She fed the boys lunch at the picnic table outside so she wouldn't have to clear away her work until dinner.

As promised, Caleb showed up on Thursday morning and all three boys piled into his battered truck.

"When do you think you'll be back?"

"When would you like me to bring them back? Can you make use of a full day to yourself?"

"I certainly can. Why don't you plan on returning around suppertime and stay to eat with us?" She surprised herself by extending the invitation.

"Is it OK if I take them out on my dad's boat? The blues are running, but fishing from the beach at the Gut won't bring us much, or keep them occupied."

"As long as you've got life jackets for them, I'm fine. Sam's sons have been out on the water since they were toddlers, and Matteo is a fish."

He touched the brim of his weathered baseball cap, the Special Forces insignia faded and almost invisible.

"We'll bring the fish if you can come up with enough carbs to fill what I'm sure will be three very hungry boys."

"Tell me about it. I think they're all going through growth spurts. I'll pick up some corn at Morning Glory and probably do an Italian-style three-course meal."

"Antipasto, pasta and a *prima piatto*? What, no *dolce*?" He smiled.

She noted his familiarity with the sequence of Italian dinners. "I'll think of something for you fishermen, don't worry."

Chapter Eighteen

Discoveries

After Caleb and the boys left, Elizabeth made a few phone calls, packed up her notebook, laptop and camera, and was on her way to Wasque and the home of Mariah, the talkative elder she'd met at Cove Meadow. She'd welcomed Elizabeth's call and invited her immediately to come for a chat.

The old woman beamed at Elizabeth when she opened the door.

"Come in, child. So good to see you again. I've just made a fresh pot of coffee."

Mariah led her to a sun-filled screened porch. In the corner was a folding card table over which was fanned a large swath of deerskin, part of which was decorated with colorful designs. Next to the table was a chest, with small jars of paint and a Mason jar holding brushes of various sizes arranged on top of it.

Mariah followed Elizabeth's eyes to the deerskin and explained.

"I like to work out here because of the light. I'm teaching the leatherworking to a group of young people.

It's a dying art, but a few of the quieter ones who already like to paint have been willing to listen to me."

"Have I interrupted your work?"

"I do like to take advantage of the morning light. If you don't mind, I'll get our coffee and then continue painting while we talk."

Once Mariah was settled again at the table, Elizabeth broached the idea of her camera.

"Would you mind if I filmed you while you work?"

"Why, whatever for?"

"I'm a filmmaker, Mariah. I was so inspired by all the stories told around the table during the hurricane that I'd like to capture them—create a record for the tribe of its history and culture. Your work on the deerskin is part of your culture, isn't it?"

"I told you the other day, we're not a wealthy tribe. We couldn't pay you."

"I wouldn't expect the tribe to pay. I'm going to apply for grants to fund the project. If I could film you as we talk, I'd have a sample to submit with my applications."

"I've never been in a movie before. Sometimes folks at the big summer powwow take home movies of the dancing and drumming. But I'm too old now for the dancing—my arthritis keeps me in my lawn chair when the young folks get out on the field. I miss it," she said, looking out the porch screen as if she could see her young self, clad in a deerskin tunic like the one she was painting.

Elizabeth waited, wishing she'd started the camera earlier and been able to capture Mariah's face as she spoke. Finally, she quietly asked again, pulling Mariah back into the present.

The old woman looked at Elizabeth and shook her head. At first, Elizabeth thought she was refusing, but then Mariah spoke.

"Oh, my. I guess I got lost back there. I need to shake out those cobwebs and come back to the here and now." She reached up with a slender-fingered hand and smoothed her hair.

"Of course you may film me!"

For the next hour Mariah talked about how she'd learned to paint the intricate pattern of blue, green and deep red that covered the bottom of the deerskin. She described how the original paints had been created from plants and berries.

"Now, I get them from daRosa's in Oak Bluffs." She mentioned the art supply store Elizabeth remembered seeing on Circuit Avenue.

As she spoke her hand moved delicately but confidently over the smooth leather, a fine-pointed brush leaving more of the stripes and teardrop shapes that marched across the expanse of material.

The sound of the doorbell interrupted her narration, and Elizabeth stopped the camera.

"That will be Francine with my Meals-On-Wheels," she explained, neatly capping the paint bottle in her hand and sticking the brush in a jar.

Mariah went to the door and Elizabeth heard her invite Francine in.

"I want you to meet Elizabeth," she said, and brought a middle-aged woman out to the porch and introduced her.

"Elizabeth is making a movie about us, Francine."

Francine glanced at the camera still on its tripod.

"Are you from the community TV station?"

"No, I'm an independent filmmaker. I'm here for the summer."

"Where are you from?"

"I live in Italy, but my family has had a cottage up at Cape Poge since the 1960s."

"Are your people the ones who bought the place from Mae and Tobias Monroe?"

"Yes, that was my grandparents. Did you know them?"

Francine shook her head. "My grandmother and Tobias' mother were friends." She didn't add anything else and turned to Mariah.

"Do you need anything I can bring you when I come with tomorrow's dinner?"

"Just some coffee and a pound of dried beans. I'll go get my purse."

Francine followed Mariah into the house as Elizabeth said good-bye to her back. She shrugged. Perhaps she had other meals to deliver and had no time for extended small talk. But Elizabeth was left with the distinct impression that Francine considered her an outsider. Her reference to Elizabeth's family as "your people" conveyed very clearly that they were not "our people."

Elizabeth packed up the camera while she waited for Mariah to return. The mood of the morning had been broken, and she didn't want Mariah's meal to get cold.

Mariah seemed distracted and somewhat agitated when she came back to the porch.

"Is everything OK?" Elizabeth asked.

Mariah's hands fluttered in the air in front of her.

"It's nothing. I apologize for Francine's rudeness. She has a lot of people to look after, and she worries about more than our food."

Elizabeth held off asking Mariah if Francine had expressed some concerns about her filming. She didn't want to upset the old woman any more than she appeared to be.

"I'll leave you to your dinner. Thank you for spending time with me and allowing me this wonderful glimpse into your life and your art."

Mariah smiled briefly and walked her to the door, but she didn't stay to watch as Elizabeth packed up her car. By the time she pulled out of the driveway, the front door was firmly closed.

Instead of driving back to Innisfree, Elizabeth headed toward the ferry landing. She left the Jeep in the lot on the Chappy side of the harbor and walked onto the ferry. Finding a parking space in Edgartown at the height of summer would have taken more time and energy than walking. She left the camera in the car, but had her laptop in a shoulder bag. She adjusted the strap, joined the other pedestrians filing off the ferry, and headed uphill in the direction of the public library.

Once there, she found a quiet corner with an accessible outlet. She plugged in her laptop to charge it and then signed on to the library's internet. If she were going to get the funding she'd told Mariah was available for the project, she had several hours' work ahead of her researching foundations and downloading and printing applications.

It had been many years since she'd needed to seek outside funding. She'd been able to support her creative projects by taking on contracts with businesses that engaged her to produce training videos and advertising. Her father-in-law's connections, both in Florence and in the province, had been a graciously offered resource for her at the beginning of her career, and the word-of-mouth from her satisfied clients had helped her to expand her business.

But she'd withdrawn from both her business and artistic pursuits when Antonio's condition had worsened precipitously several months before his death. Until this morning, her only work since that time had been filming her husband.

Compounding the unique experience of needing to secure financial resources was her unfamiliarity with American foundations and government agencies that might fund her. But she plunged in, typing research terms that might provide her with a wide enough pool into which she could drill down.

Rather than frustration or dread or dismay at the Sisyphean nature of her task, she found herself as energized by the hunt for funding as she was by the creative challenges of shaping the Wampanoag story.

After several hours of intense work, she finally called it a day. With a stretch of her arms, she rose from the desk, gathered together the pages of applications she'd printed, and unplugged her now fully charged laptop.

On her way out of the library she remembered the dinner she'd promised Caleb and the boys, and took a mental inventory of the cottage's two refrigerators and pantry. With a groan, she realized she needed the Jeep after all, and headed back to Chappy to pick up the car and return to the outskirts of Edgartown and groceries.

By the time she got back to Innisfree, Caleb and the boys were already there. At least, Caleb's truck was there, along with a note tacked to the kitchen door.

"Fish gutted, cleaned and in the fridge. We are washing off at East Beach."

She thanked the sea gods for the lure of the surf to teenaged boys and enjoyed the solitude of her kitchen while she chopped garlic and onions, peeled fruit, sautéed mushrooms and peppers, started water boiling for pasta and steamed asparagus.

By the time Caleb and the boys arrived from the beach she had set the table and had a cast iron frying pan ready with melted butter to sauté the bluefish waiting in the refrigerator.

The peace of her culinary retreat was shattered by adolescent energy and hunger, and she realized how much she enjoyed having them, boisterous and joking, grabbing Cokes from the fridge and spears of asparagus from the platter on the counter. Memories of summers spent in similar exuberance flooded her—Lydia stirring and frying and bearing huge platters of fish, corn and potatoes to the oilcloth-covered table; competing voices eager to recount the day's adventures; and then the silence of satisfied appetites.

She listened to all of them, but Matteo especially, with satisfaction. This was what she'd longed for. This was Innisfree as she wanted her son to know it. She remembered with gratitude how Lydia had provided a refuge to her when she was fifteen and she and her mother had been locked in battle over everything. Susan had finally thrown up her hands and sent her to Lydia on her own, giving them both some space apart. That summer, Lydia's rules—no bullshit, take responsibility for your actions, and share in the work of Innisfree—combined with her unbounded enthusiasm for Elizabeth's developing talent, provided Elizabeth with the structure and love she needed to flourish. It also cemented her relationship with her grandmother, giving her a confidant to help her navigate the turmoil of adolescence.

When dinner was over, Caleb led the boys in a clean-up marathon that left the kitchen in spotless condition within a half hour. The boys decided to haul out the Risk game board and set it up in the living room. They issued an invitation to Caleb and Elizabeth to play, but both of them threw up their hands, pleading ignorance of the complicated rules—which seemed to be the outcome the boys were hoping for.

Caleb and Elizabeth retreated to the back patio overlooking the bay and the setting sun. They settled into the white Adirondack chairs, beers in hand.

"You have a knack with them," Elizabeth smiled. "Thanks for the day off."

"I enjoy them. They're good kids. Did you have a productive day?"

"I did. Accomplished a lot." She didn't elaborate. It was part of her working style when she began a project to keep it close, especially when it had not yet taken shape. It was too early, too unformed. And she also didn't want other ideas, particularly critical or judgmental ones, trampling on this fragile, nascent seedling she was nurturing in her imagination.

"Dinner was delicious. In my travels, it was always the food of Italy that was most memorable."

"I didn't learn to cook until after I married," she admitted. "The Hammond table was strictly meat and potatoes—or fish and potatoes—when we were out here."

"My grandmother had a vegetable garden behind the Boat House, but I guess your grandmother didn't keep it up?"

"Lydia was more apt to be out on water skis than weeding a garden. But I do remember her baking. Sugar cookies and lemonade are one of those indelible summer memories I associate with summer afternoons."

"Mine is blueberry pancakes. Growing up, it was the ultimate comfort food, whipped up to soothe everything from scraped knees to broken hearts."

"Did you have many?"

"Scraped knees or broken hearts?"

"Either. Both." Elizabeth couldn't believe she was asking him such a personal question.

"Lots of bloody knees and elbows. Only one broken heart."

"I'm sorry."

"For asking, or for my broken heart?"

"Both, I guess. I shouldn't have pried."

"If I hadn't wanted to answer, I wouldn't have."

Elizabeth didn't know how to respond, so she remained silent.

Caleb took a deep swig of beer.

"Did he love you, your husband?"

Such an extraordinary question.

"Yes."

"Do you think it pained him not to be able to express his love after he became ill?"

She looked out over the water, unable to form an answer. The conversation had veered so quickly into what was for her treacherous territory. But she accepted responsibility for leading it there, however unwittingly.

"Now it's my turn to apologize for asking a sensitive question." Caleb broke the silence.

"Why did you ask it?"

"Trying to understand my own failure at love, perhaps."

"There are many ways to express love. Antonio found ways. I never doubted. Never felt unloved."

"I didn't mean to suggest that there is only one way. I'm only wondering if love unexpressed is not love at all."

"Is that what she told you?"

Caleb raised his beer in her direction.

"Yes, she did."

"Do you think men, in general, have a hard time voicing emotion? And I don't mean saying 'I love you'."

"I know what you mean. And yes, I do think we're raised to mask, if not stifle emotion. And that ultimately stunts us."

"I read something once, I don't remember where, that given the choice between being happy or being safe, we will choose safety. Not just men. All of us. Humanity."

"It takes courage to be happy, is that what you're saying?"

"Yes."

"Is that why you left Italy to come here?"

"Do you think that took courage?"

"You left your home, your life."

"Italy is not my home."

"Is Innisfree?"

Once again, she stared out over the water at the darkening sky.

"I don't know where home is at this moment in my life."

"Well, then, Elizabeth, I think you and I have found common ground beyond Matt. Because I don't know where home is either."

The boys chose that moment to pause their game and pour out of the living room onto the patio.

"Are there any snacks, Mom?"

Elizabeth rolled her eyes.

"I told you, growth spurt," she said as she rose to find more food for these growing boys.

"I think I'll take this interruption to say good night." Caleb also got up and carried his empty beer bottle into the kitchen. He rinsed it at the sink. "Where's your stash of deposit bottles?"

She pointed to a bin on the back porch and then walked him out to his truck after handing Matteo a bag of Doritos and a container of salsa.

"Thanks again for taking the boys," she said, leaning against the door after he climbed into the cab.

"Thanks for listening to my ramblings."

She shrugged. "Maybe it's this place, which prompts us to contemplate the great questions of life." She slapped the door of the truck. "Safe drive. Say hi to everyone at Cove Meadow for me."

She stayed outside long after his headlights were no longer visible, gathering up the detritus left by three boys after a day of fishing and the beach. When she came back inside, the boys were deep into their game again, the bag of chips empty and a newly discovered package of chocolate chip cookies opened in the middle of Russia.

But for the fact that there was no evidence of pot, one could have assumed that they were experiencing an attack of the munchies. "Please, God, not yet," she uttered a silent prayer. Then she plucked her book from the shelf behind the couch and retreated to her bedroom.

She thought that reading would distract her from the strange and deep direction the conversation with Caleb had led. But in retrospect, its intimacy ultimately made sense to her. Their antagonism in her early days at Innisfree now appeared to be a reflection of the intensity of emotion that seemed to bind them. They were not indifferent to one another. Something connected them. She didn't know whether it was a shared childhood, a love of this place, or simply the stage in life that found them both adrift and untethered. All she knew was that he could make her feel both anger and tenderness toward him. Feelings that elicited a sense of betrayal toward Antonio. When he died, she believed she could never love someone again the way she had loved him.

She rejected with a shudder the idea that this troubling and emotional state associated with Caleb was some nascent state of love. Gratitude and curiosity, yes. He intrigued her. But she neither wanted nor needed love.

She closed her book and turned down the gaslight above her bed. The boys eventually called a pause to their endless game and tromped off to Byzantium with a lantern. Letting go of her agitation as she listened to the call and response of waves hitting and receding from the beach, she finally slept.

Chapter Nineteen

Family, Food and Filmmaking

She spent Friday sorting through grant applications while the boys entertained themselves with kites, Frisbees and the beach. Sam called with the offer to sail their Sunfish over to Innisfree on Saturday for the boys to use. Debbie would drive over with Ella and Jessica and they could spend some family time like the old days.

"Why don't you spend the night? There's plenty of room in the Linnet."

"We'll think about it," was all he'd commit to.

In the end, they did stay. Sam spent the afternoon assuring himself that the boys, Matteo included, could safely handle the Sunfish. His instruction included taking them out to the middle of Shear Pen and deliberately capsizing the boat so that they could learn how to right it. By the end of the day, the three cousins were off into Cape Poge Bay with the admonition to be back before sunset. The little girls entertained themselves building sand castles and weaving daisy chains. Debbie and Elizabeth slipped into the ease they had found with one another, sitting on the beach while the girls played.

Dinner was another of those reminders of times past—family gathered at the table for food and then a raucous board game, with the usual accusations and antagonisms as personalities dealt with competition, losing and winning in all-too familiar ways.

By midnight the last of the colored tokens had made it home. Sam and Debbie's youngest, Jessica, was curled up asleep on the window seat. Debbie rounded up the boys to pack up the game and carry empty Coke cans into the kitchen while Sam scooped up his sleeping daughter for the short journey to the Linnet.

Within fifteen minutes, Elizabeth was alone in the house, moving from one room to the next turning down gas lamps. When she settled into her bed, she picked up the book on the night table, flipped it open to the page she'd marked with a tea-stained scrap of paper, and attempted to focus on the 19th-century prose creeping across the page in 10-point type. She fell asleep with the book splayed open on her chest and didn't wake up when it slipped and tumbled to the floor.

She did wake up shortly after dawn, and rather than linger in her bed, stretched, swung her legs over the side and planted her feet directly on the abandoned book. She grabbed it, smoothed the crushed pages and replaced it on the table, realizing in the process that she'd left the gaslight burning all night. Lydia's horror of the house going up in flames because of carelessness with the gas lights had been deeply ingrained in her grandchildren. Elizabeth was furious with herself for being so thoughtless. She was supposed to be the custodian, the watch, the guardian of Innisfree, and she'd fallen asleep on the job. She extinguished the lamp, and agitated by her lapse, decided to release her tightly wound nerves with a quick, early-morning swim. She slipped on her bathing suit, grabbed a towel and left the house by the front door.

The sun had barely risen when she arrived at East Beach, and a quick glance in both directions revealed that no hardy fishermen had yet arrived. She had the long expanse of sand and surf to herself. The sea was much calmer than it had been in the aftermath of the hurricane, and she waded into the water till it reached her shoulders. She began swimming parallel to the shore, first to the south against the current, then reversing direction, her strokes propelling her through the gentle swells. As she swam, the tension eased out of her body, swallowed up by the energy of the sea. Because her back was to the south, she didn't see the ranger truck approaching along the beach above the high-tide mark until she was climbing out of the water. It had stopped a few feet from where she had left her towel.

She reached for the towel as Caleb climbed out of the truck and came around to her.

"You're out early."

"I could say the same for you. Are you just starting or finishing a shift."

"Starting."

"Oh. I would invite you to breakfast, but if you're on duty. . ."

"I need to make the rounds and close off part of the reservation. The gulls are nesting just beyond the Elbow. Thanks," he offered, as an afterthought.

"I'll let the boys know to stay away." She wrapped the towel around her, conscious of the imbalance between Caleb in his buttoned-up uniform and she in her bikini. She'd adapted long ago to the tiny scraps of fabric Europeans—especially Italians—called bathing suits. She'd come to appreciate and share their celebration of the body and had never felt the need on American beaches to wear anything other than what she wore when swimming in the Mediterranean. But this morning she was too aware of Caleb's gaze, despite his sunglasses, and felt strangely like Eve must have felt in the Garden of Eden when she realized for the first time she was naked.

"I should get back to the house. Sam and Debbie and their daughters are here. It's like the old days," she added, expecting him to understand and take her urgency to leave as simple hospitality for her guests.

"And I need to close off that stretch of beach before the day-trippers arrive and trample the nests." He seemed as eager to be gone as she was.

She tightened the knot of the towel before waving him off and trudging back through the dunes. By the time she reached the house she'd rid herself of the early-morning dismay about the gaslight, but in its place was a discomfort and ambivalence about the encounter with Caleb that she suspected they both felt. She turned on the outdoor shower and tried to shed herself not only of salt and sand but also the sense that Caleb had seen her for the first time not as Matteo's mother or Lydia's granddaughter, but as a woman. And she truly did not know how to respond to that.

By the time she was dressed and standing at the stove flipping pancakes, she was very much Matteo's mother. Caught up in another day of family activities, she forgot about the unanticipated stirring that her encounter with Caleb had awakened.

Debbie and Sam packed up immediately after supper, preferring to get off the island before sunset. The little girls were whining, jealous that their brothers got to stay, but the promise of ice cream when they got back to OB quelled the complaints. Elizabeth and the boys lined up for the Hammond wave, the boys wildly flapping beach towels as Sam and Debbie rounded the pond and disappeared on to the trail.

"Would you boys mind taking your board games into Byzantium tonight?" Elizabeth realized that she craved an evening of silence after the hubbub that had filled the house for two days. She'd loved every minute of the visit—the energy and laughter and ease of family in the cocoon that Innisfree had always been for them.

But a piece of her was eager to get back to work, hungry for the sense of identity that her creative projects had always provided her. "Nourishment for the soul" is how she described the seed of an idea, its germination and ultimate emergence as a fully realized extension of her vision of the world.

The boys seemed more than happy to retreat to Byzantium, armed with enough snacks and soda to sustain an army on bivouac for a month.

She grabbed the book she had let fall so unceremoniously the night before and took it to the dining room, where she once again smoothed its bent pages and began taking notes.

She spent most of the next week immersed in research and roughing out an outline, as well as drawing up a multitude of lists. To the carefully compiled list of foundations she added a list of locations on the island, names of tribal members she'd met at Cove Meadow, dates of festivals, and documents she still needed to find. She recognized she was pushing herself, driven not only by her sense of finally returning to the professional life that fed her spirit, but also by the limited amount of time she had to film raw footage. The summer would come to an end, and so would her ability to capture the images of the tribe that had so inspired her.

Around her piles of notes and photographs she managed to feed the boys three meals a day and spend at least a couple of hours in the afternoons with them, either out at the beach or on the Sunfish.

When she was ready to begin filming she invited Josiah, Grace and Caleb for dinner to present her plan and enlist their support in connecting her with the other members of the tribe. Elizabeth realized Mariah had been an exception. The elder had been excited about the idea of a recorded history when she and Elizabeth had formed a bond during the hurricane, but Elizabeth was aware she needed to build trust with the tribe if she was to tell their story. After fifteen years in Italy, Elizabeth understood something about tribal loyalty. She had to have the Monroes behind her if this film was to become a reality.

She didn't tell Grace why she was inviting them. She admitted to herself that she didn't want to be shut out before she had a chance to engage them. And she knew she could only do that in person. She dealt in images. It was how she communicated best, and she didn't trust herself to convey the full power of her idea and her passion merely with words.

"I want to thank you for your hospitality during the hurricane," is how she framed the invitation.

"You know you don't have to do that," Grace assured her.

"I know. But I'd still love to cook you all an Italian meal. Is there any possibility that Tobias could come?" She asked, although she wasn't anticipating a positive reply.

"Because you saw him, I think you'll understand that he's too frail to travel, even if it's only to Innisfree. He's also too frail to leave alone, so I'm afraid we'll have to ask for a raincheck. I'm sorry."

Elizabeth was about to acquiesce, but decided to try another path.

"One of the reasons for the invitation, apart from my gratitude, is that I wanted to talk with you about something important. Are you or Josiah members of the tribal council?"

Grace was silent for a few seconds. "I am," she answered.

Elizabeth was puzzled that Josiah, the son of the sachem, was not on the council. Perhaps he and Grace rotated the responsibility.

"What's this got to do with the tribe, Elizabeth?"

"I had an idea after listening to the elders the night of the hurricane, and I wanted to run it by you."

"Does your idea have anything to do with the filming you did over at Mariah Turner's house last week?"

Elizabeth shouldn't have been surprised that news of the filming had spread. It was a small community, and even if Mariah had said nothing, Francine, the Meals-On-Wheels lady, certainly could have offered her opinion to other members of the tribe. Elizabeth felt her carefully orchestrated plan slipping away from her.

"That's part of it. I'd love the opportunity to talk to you about it. Since dinner with all of you isn't possible, do you think you'd be able to come out alone—for lunch, perhaps?"

"I can hear that this is important to you, Elizabeth, and it appears you don't want to discuss it over the phone."

"Thank you for understanding."

Elizabeth heard the riffling of paper and then Grace's voice again.

"I've just checked my calendar. I've got Wednesday open. Will that work for you?"

"Yes, yes. Wednesday would be wonderful. Thank you, Grace!"

The morning of her meeting with Grace, Elizabeth was in the kitchen chopping parsley and garlic, slicing a pound of apples, peeling asparagus stalks and pounding boneless chicken breasts to paper-thin slices. The boys had been happy to go clamming in the pond when told that the results of their labors would be *linguine alle vongole* as the pasta course for lunch.

She'd made an early-morning run to Morning Glory farm for the fruits and vegetables, relishing the aromas of herbs and ripe peaches and fresh-baked pies wafting through the barn that served as the farm's retail shop. Carmella had taught her to cook with her nose and her tongue and her hands, and she had embraced those skills with the same enthusiasm she felt for her filmmaking.

Preparing the meal eased her into a serene rhythm, moving fluidly from preparing the base for the pasta sauce to mixing the custard-like batter for an apple cake. She slid the cake into the oven to bake while she dredged the chicken slices in flour, egg and bread crumbs. She was setting out pots on top of the stove for the linguine, the clams, the chicken and the asparagus when Matteo arrived in the kitchen with a bucket full of cherrystone clams.

"Here they are, scrubbed and ready to steam, Mom. Hey, is it all right that I asked Caleb to have lunch with us? There's plenty of clams, you can see that, and you always make way more than we can eat in one meal."

She took the bucket from Matteo, its weight confirming that they had more than enough clams.

"How is it that you were able to ask Caleb?"

"He stopped to talk with us when we were down in the pond. When I described what you were cooking, he looked hungry, so I invited him. That's OK, right?"

"Sure it's OK. Granny Lydia taught me we can always set another place at the table. Is he still here?"

"No, he said he had another circuit to make out to the Gut and then he'd be back."

"So he's working today?"

"Yeah, he was in uniform. I told him we've stayed away from the gull nests. He said he'd take us fishing again on Sunday. That is, if it's OK with you."

Elizabeth smiled, acknowledging that Matteo had learned his lesson about asking permission.

"If it's fine with Caleb, it's fine with me," she assured him.

"I'll put another plate on the table," Matteo offered, reaching beyond her for the stack of dishes on an open shelf.

"Thanks, honey."

Elizabeth turned back to the stove and her cooking. Despite her assurances to Matteo about inviting Caleb, she was ambivalent about his presence—unsure about how he might react to the idea of the film but also unexpectedly pleased that he'd accepted Matteo's invitation.

At noon, Elizabeth heard the low rumble of a motor and glanced out the window overlooking the pond. The boys ran out onto the dock to catch the line and secure the boat, and Grace climbed out after handing a large basket to Matteo.

Elizabeth watched as they walked up to the house, Matteo in animated conversation with Grace, whose arm was casually draped over his shoulder as she appeared to listen to him intently. Elizabeth left the sanctuary of her kitchen to welcome Grace herself just as a dark green Refuge truck turned onto the drive from the lighthouse trail. She reached Grace and the boys at the same time Caleb emerged from the truck and gave his mother a kiss on the cheek.

"I didn't know you'd be here, too," Grace greeted her son. "You didn't mention it at breakfast."

"Because I didn't know myself. I was a late addition to the guest list, thanks to an overabundance of clams."

Elizabeth shepherded everyone into the house as she took the basket Matteo had carried up for Grace.

"I know you didn't have time to plant a vegetable garden this year, so I thought you might be able to use some of the bounty from ours," she explained. "Especially if you're feeding a house full of growing boys."

Elizabeth thanked her as she pulled zucchini, beets, Swiss chard, peppers and tomatoes from the capacious depths of the basket.

"Oh, Grace, what a treat! I can think of so many delicious ways to use all of this."

"Some of those vegetables are descendants of plants Mae grew here. She told me she'd saved seeds from each harvest, and after they moved permanently to Cove Meadow she was able to recreate a lot of what she'd grown in the garden behind the Boat House."

"Well, that makes this gift even more generous and special."

"Do you think you might plant a garden here again next spring? I'd be happy to give you some seeds from those original plants."

Elizabeth busied herself at the stove, unable to answer Grace's question with any certainty.

"I don't know, Grace. But if I do, I'll be sure to let you know. It would be an honor to revive Mae's garden." She couldn't make any promises about planting a garden when she didn't know if she'd return next year. She hadn't thought of anything beyond the summer for what life might be like for her and Matteo.

"Matt, would you get drinks for everyone while I finish the pasta?" She turned the conversation to the present, where she felt some semblance of control.

"Can I help with anything?" Caleb offered. "I can carry the pasta pot to the sink and drain it for you." He already had two potholders in his hands.

"Sure, but give me a minute to scoop out some of the pasta cooking water for the sauce."

She grabbed a ladle and spooned some of the starchy water into the clam sauce simmering in the pan next to the pasta, the cherrystones now steamed open and flecks of garlic and parsley floating in the broth.

"I've never seen that before," he observed.

"It's an old Italian housewife's trick I learned from Carmella."

"Carmella?"

She was about to say "our cook," but caught herself and said instead, "the woman who taught me how to cook."

Together, she and Caleb combined the pasta and the clams in the largest bowl Elizabeth could find and brought it to the table.

Elizabeth warned everyone that the pasta was merely the first course. There was still Chicken Milanese and asparagus, a green salad and the apple cake.

"I've eaten here before," Caleb advised his mother, "and I know what she's talking about. Enormous quantities of deliciousness."

Elizabeth beamed, not only at Caleb's compliment, but at the expressions of rapture on the faces around the table as they got their first taste of garlic-infused shellfish only an hour out of the sea. She settled back and allowed the food and the lively conversation to prepare the way for her discussion with Grace.

As soon as the last crumb of apple cake disappeared from the dessert plates and the boys had successfully cleared the table, scraped the plates and set them to soak in the sink, Elizabeth offered Grace and Caleb a second cup of coffee.

Caleb looked at his watch and shook his head with regret.

"I'd love to linger, but I've taken longer than I should have for my lunch hour. Thanks. It was even better than the bluefish. Mom, I'll see you later at home." He gave her another kiss and she squeezed his hand.

"Don't forget to go over to Edgartown and pick up Granddad's prescription at the pharmacy."

"Will do. Thanks again, Elizabeth."

And he was off. Elizabeth was actually relieved that he'd left. Although she'd eventually want Caleb's buy-in on the film, she'd started with Grace because she thought she might find an ally in her. Elizabeth's relationship with Caleb, while no longer as rocky and antagonistic as it had been when she first arrived on Chappy, was still fragile. She couldn't risk jeopardizing something as important to her as this film by exposing it to what she was sure would be Caleb's judgmental opinion. The idea was still too new, too unformed, to withstand such a critical eye.

Grace sat back in her chair and patted her belly.

"You've outdone yourself, Elizabeth! I am absolutely sated, but I don't feel stuffed. Each morsel was a burst of flavor in my mouth, but just enough not to overwhelm my taste buds. Did you invite me for this meal to tell me you're going to reestablish the Boat House Café?"

Elizabeth was struck by Grace's question. It had never occurred to her that the Monroes equated Innisfree so thoroughly with Mae's restaurant, which Lydia had torn down when it had been so severely damaged by Hurricane Gloria that Lydia felt the building couldn't be salvaged.

"Sometimes I dream about opening a restaurant," she admitted. "I love to cook—it's almost a form of meditation for me. And I love to see people around my table enjoying my food. But I think the joy I take in preparing a meal for the people I love would evaporate quickly if it were to become my livelihood. No, I brought you here and lulled you into a food-induced stupor to talk about something else."

"I'm all ears."

Elizabeth reached into the dining room cupboard where she stowed her laptop and set it up on the table in front of Grace.

"I was enthralled the night of the hurricane by the stories that were being told around the table; even the setting, with faces illuminated only by the lantern light, spoke to me deep in my core."

Grace nodded. "I know. It's quite sacred, listening to those stories. I never had that experience as a child, to be part of the tribe in such an encompassing way—the sound of their voices, the flickering light, the visions they were seeing as they recounted memories."

"I thought you were Wampanoag." Elizabeth was confused.

"I am. But my family left the island when I was a baby. Except for my grandmother, who longed to be back on Chappy, I had no connection to my tribal culture until I met Josiah and Izzy and they brought me home to meet Mae and Tobias. That first visit was a revelation. It filled up a hole in my soul that I didn't even know was there."

"Do you think there are other members of the tribe like you, who've lost touch but who long to be reconnected?"

"I'm sure there are, Elizabeth."

Elizabeth took a deep breath and turned on the computer.

"I want to bring those stories I heard that night to the screen. When Mariah told me that the tribe has no recordings beyond some home movies of drumming and ceremonial dancing at the annual gathering, I thought I might be able to help."

"How?" Grace leaned forward as she asked her question, her gaze moving between the computer screen and Elizabeth.

"Did you know I'm a documentary filmmaker?"

"I had no idea. Do you work in a particular genre?"

"Creatively, my interest is in history—which is how I got started when I was a student and why I went to Italy—to do research on the Renaissance. But to make a living, I did a variety of corporate jobs. Training videos and advertising, mostly."

Grace smiled and shook her head. "You have to forgive me for assuming you hadn't worked outside the home all those years in Italy. You had already struck me as an intelligent and empathic young woman when I met you, but now I'm even more impressed. Do you have any examples of your work on your laptop?"

"I have a few shorts. Would you like to see one?"

"I'd love to."

Elizabeth clicked on a piece she'd done on the Palio horse race for the Siena Chamber of Commerce. She then sat back to watch Grace's reaction to the three-minute film. She wasn't disappointed.

"Wow! I felt like I was there! The colors and the movement and the drumming, and then the sound of the horses' hoof beats superimposed on the drums… How did you do it? Did you put a body camera on one of the jockeys?"

Elizabeth laughed. "Almost. We had three cameras filming from different angles and I was able to combine images during the editing to create that frenetic pace. I had lots of material from which to distill those three minutes."

"And you think you can do something similar with the Wampanoag stories?"

"I'd like the opportunity to tell your history. I've worked up some ideas, if you'd like to see them. I've put together story boards in a PowerPoint slide show."

"Show me." Grace leaned her elbows on the table in front of the computer and watched and listened as Elizabeth moved through her presentation. When she reached the last slide she left the image on the screen, a still from the footage she had shot of Mariah. The old woman's face had filled the screen, an echo of an ancient heritage. A polished disk of purple and cream wampum had been nestled in the hollow of her throat.

Elizabeth waited for Grace to react.

The silence was challenging—a gaping hole Elizabeth longed to fill with questions. But she succeeded in keeping her thoughts—and her anxieties—to herself. At last, Grace spoke.

"You have a gift, Elizabeth."

"Thank you, Grace."

"I'm moved by how you see the world, and I definitely recognize something I'd call your 'signature,' even though I've only seen the Siena video and this proposal. You bring a story to life. But…" and Grace stopped for a moment, and closed her eyes as if she were rewinding and replaying part of what she'd just watched.

"… I'm not sure how *you* see us is how we see ourselves. I have a question for you. Who is the audience for this film?"

Elizabeth thought she had conveyed her intention for the film when she first introduced the idea to Grace.

"I'm doing this for the tribe, as a way to preserve the history before the elders are no longer here to tell their stories."

"It's a noble goal, and one that I think you may have strayed from as you've raced ahead to map out where you're going with the film. Have you talked to any other tribal members besides Mariah?"

"Not yet. I wanted to get your thoughts before I moved forward."

"I appreciate your trusting me with your ideas. What did Mariah say?"

"We didn't get much farther than her allowing me to film her while she worked on a piece of deerskin. Her major concern about the film seemed to be its cost and how the tribe couldn't afford me."

"She's right. Our resources are stretched as thin as that deer hide she was painting."

"I wasn't planning to charge the tribe."

"But from what I've seen here," she tapped the laptop, "the complexity and artistry of what you do requires funding."

"It does. That's why I'm planning to apply for grants to cover the costs."

"It sounds like you've not only thought this through, but have already begun to act."

"Lydia always described me as a 'doer,' plunging into something, committing early and fully. I never stuck my toe in the water to test it first as a kid. I just ran full bore into the waves."

"Elizabeth, I'm going to be frank with you, which I believe is why you asked me to hear you out. The waters you are diving into with this film are not some gentle ripples lapping at the sand on the banks of Shear Pen Pond. There are members of the tribe who have strong opinions about its history and how that history gets transmitted."

"Would one of those people be a woman named Francine?"

Grace looked up sharply. "Francine Everett? How did you meet her?"

"She delivered Mariah's dinner the day I was filming. My impression of her was that she was none too happy to find me there with a camera."

"That's Francine. She's very protective of our elders, and sees them every day because she delivers their meals and runs errands for them."

"I wasn't trying to exploit Mariah," Elizabeth protested.

Grace reached over and touched Elizabeth's hand.

"Of course you weren't. But you're a stranger to Francine. Until she knows you and accepts that you mean no harm, she's going to regard you with suspicion."

"Are there many tribal members like her? And how do I gain their trust?"

"That depends. Francine's perspective is one of protecting those she feels are vulnerable."

"Elders like Mariah."

Grace nodded. "But there are others whose viewpoint—I guess the best way to describe it—is political."

"Political?"

"They are the protectors of the tribal identity, not just of individuals, like Francine is."

Elizabeth reluctantly nodded in understanding. "And they would see my film as threatening tribal identity, even though my whole purpose is to illuminate and illustrate the tribe's identity. Is there any way to move them toward accepting me? "

"Elizabeth, you've been away a long time, immersed in a culture that is relatively homogenous compared to the United States. But think about it this way… would a Neapolitan expect a Venetian to tell an accurate story, create an honest portrait, of Naples?"

"Sometimes we need the eyes of others to see ourselves," countered Elizabeth.

"I agree with you. But not when the only portraits of my people have come from… outsiders."

Grace had hesitated over the last word. Elizabeth heard her start to say "whites," but then stop herself.

Elizabeth was silent, absorbing Grace's message. She realized she'd been naïve to expect Grace to embrace the project. Although she'd told herself initially that she was approaching Grace mainly for advice on how to gain the support of the tribe she knew was imperative, a part of her had clung to the hope that Grace would be her champion.

Elizabeth took a deep breath and acknowledged her disappointment.

"I knew at some unexpressed level I might face opposition, but I don't think I truly understood the depth of the issue. As hard as it is to hear, I'm grateful to you for being frank with me."

Grace placed her hand on top of Elizabeth's to emphasize what she was about to say.

"You are a talented artist with a unique and emotionally resonant style. But there are members of the tribe, particularly on the council, who will not be able to see beyond your status as an outsider. Believe me, I know, in a very personal way."

"What do you mean?" Elizabeth's curiosity overrode her thwarted hopes.

Grace hesitated, then spoke.

"Some people doubt Josiah's commitment to the tribe because his mother wasn't Wampanoag. They remember him abandoning his heritage and turning to his white relatives."

"But that's so…"

"Tribal?"

"This is the 21st century, not the 19th, when the government was trying to obliterate tribal identity through the guise of assimilation. Is that why Josiah isn't on the council?"

"I don't think he'd accept a position now if it were offered to him."

"It sounds like I may have walked into a complicated web," Elizabeth admitted.

Grace nodded. "It's been a relatively subdued issue, but nonetheless a constant one. The tribe is small and opinions have solidified, especially among some of the older, more vocal members."

"Is that what you meant about Cousin Sadie?"

"Yes. She said some damaging things to Josiah when he was a young boy and wounded him when he was most vulnerable, on the cusp between adolescence and adulthood, when we struggle with identity even if we aren't of mixed heritage."

"Tell me about it. I'm starting to see strains of that with Matteo."

"I know this project means a lot to you, Elizabeth, and you so clearly are putting your heart and soul into it. But I see too many obstacles—battles that will both suck your energy and deny you access to the story you want to tell. I'm sorry."

"You've given me a lot to think about. I need to tell you that I'm not quite ready to give up. Something has seized my imagination since living out here this summer, as if Chappy itself is speaking to me, whispering that its story needs to be told. It's gotten into my dreams. I don't know how else to explain how compelled I feel to make this film."

"I wish I could help you, Elizabeth. I truly do. But in addition to my heartfelt belief that the tribe's story is not yours to tell, I am so deeply consumed with caring for

Tobias as he enters this last phase of his life that I have no room for anything else that would cost me emotionally. And acknowledging that, I need to get home. Josiah is with him, but there are things only I can do for Tobias."

"You're a nurse, aren't you?"

"A nurse practitioner now, although Tobias is my only patient at the moment."

"I understand your position, and I appreciate your hearing me out. Thank you."

"You're welcome. I admire you, Elizabeth, and I applaud you for listening and being open to what this place and its history mean. You'll find a way to act on your dreams. But I'm afraid it won't be through the Wampanoag. Keep looking."

The older woman stood and embraced Elizabeth.

"Please give Tobias my love," Elizabeth said as she hugged Grace back.

By the time Grace's boat was a white spec heading across the water to Cove Meadow, Elizabeth was up to her elbows in soapy water washing the dishes from lunch and giving into the tears of disappointment that she'd managed to hold back during her conversation with Grace.

That night, Elizabeth sat in bed, notebook and pen in hand, flipping the pages that held the multiple lists she'd created at the beginning of the project and seeing how inadequate her preliminary work had been. The tears in the afternoon had released some of the pent-up energy that had been driving her toward her encounter with Grace. Moving past her initial reaction to the hard truths Grace had placed in front of her, she acknowledged her own lack of sensitivity. She'd been away from America for a long time and hadn't been a direct witness to the reclaiming of tribal identity that had been stirring among native peoples. But, she reminded herself, she was a historian! She should have recognized how entitled she must appear to the Wampanoag. She cringed with her memories of how blindly she'd plunged into the project. She hoped she hadn't completely mangled the possibility of still working with the tribe, perhaps in a collaborative way. She knew she couldn't ask any more of Grace. Elizabeth, of all people, understood how completely engulfing it was to care for a dying loved one.

But she desperately felt the need for another perspective, to help her process what she'd learned from Grace and whether there was any role at all she could play in bringing to a wider audience what she experienced that night during the hurricane.

Chapter Twenty

A Walk on the Beach

If Elizabeth had been more mindful of her own insensitivity, she probably would have turned first to Izzy, who might have schooled her, gently but firmly. But in her rush to move forward, she hadn't reached out to Izzy because she no longer lived on the island; Elizabeth had felt it vital to make her appeal in person. But she knew she needed to turn now to Izzy to guide her out of the mess she had so heedlessly made of her intentions.

The next morning Elizabeth called Izzy in New Haven and left a message on her voice mail, asking her when she'd be on the island again and could they get together.

All that day she kept her phone in her pocket, eager to answer Izzy's call directly and feeling like her teenage self, waiting anxiously for a boy's attention. She paced, she drummed her fingers on the table, she did laundry and chopped carrots and onions for a pot roast, all to keep herself from dialing Izzy's number again.

Get a grip, Innocenti, she berated herself as she jumped when the phone finally throbbed against her thigh.

"Lili? This is Izzy. How great to hear from you! I'm coming to Cove Meadow on Friday afternoon and planning to stay for a while. Grace and Jo have a wedding to go to in Providence and then were hoping to get away for a few days, so I'm coming to help with Dad."

"I'd love to see you. Can I pick you up at the ferry? What time do you get in?"

"Oh, hon, that's sweet of you to offer. I'm sure Grace would appreciate it. I'm not quite sure what boat I'll make—depends on traffic on I-95. How about if I call you when I get to Woods Hole?"

"Sounds like a plan. See you on Friday."

Elizabeth ended the call and turned to finish the pot roast, feeling the muscles in her back unwind.

When the boys gathered at the table for dinner it delighted her to see them suitably appreciative of the meal, sopping up the rich gravy with her homemade biscuits and groaning with pleasure. But Matteo surprised her with an unexpected observation.

"Great meal, Mom. It's good to hear you laugh again."

"Have I not been laughing recently?" She was struck that Matteo would be so tuned in to her mood.

"Ever since lunch yesterday you've been like the Energizer bunny, like you forgot how to relax. You didn't even go swimming."

Elizabeth shrugged, unwilling to make too much of her son's astute perception of her agitation.

"So Mom has been all work and no play, is that what you're telling me?"

"I guess. It's summer. It's vacation. Even grown-ups get some time off."

"Good advice. Why don't we leave the dishes, pile into the car and go get some ice cream in Edgartown."

"And fudge!" the cousins chimed in.

Elizabeth gave herself up to the boys' exuberance and enjoyed the outing, indulging in a double scoop of coffee ice cream with chocolate jimmies while she watched the parade of summer revelers wandering the narrow streets of Edgartown. Matteo was right, she could let go of responsibilities for a few hours. There'd be plenty of time for those when Izzy arrived on the island and she had to once again make her case for the film.

On Friday, Elizabeth brought all three boys with her to Oak Bluffs when she went to pick up Izzy. Debbie and Sam suggested all the boys spend a couple of nights in town to give her some adult time, and though she protested that she was enjoying the company, she realized what a gift it would be to have the weekend to herself.

She dropped the boys off with a quick thank you as she heard the ferry horn announce its arrival.

"Have fun," she called to her son, and then drove to the opposite side of Ocean Park and lined up with the other cars meeting the ferry.

She saw Izzy first, a burst of flamboyant color amidst the pale faces and khaki chinos of mainlanders arriving for their week in the sun. She climbed out of the car and waved to Izzy, calling her name and then crossing over to the sidewalk to relieve her of her suitcase. She noticed Izzy was using a cane, which hadn't been the case at the house in Cove Meadow.

Izzy followed Elizabeth's eyes and gestured with the stick in her hand, a wooden staff decorated with carvings all up and down its length.

"My sidekick. I can't always be sure when I travel that my muscles will hold up for the duration. I used to hate this thing when I was younger, but we've come to an understanding in my maturity."

She followed Elizabeth to the car, slid in and rolled down the window to take a deep breath.

"The air here is about ten degrees cooler than New Haven and oh-so-sweet."

"Do you miss the island?" Elizabeth asked as she put the car in gear and eased out of the line.

"Yes and no. I have a life I love on the mainland, but I'm deeply grateful that I still have a place here, a hearth to return to."

Izzy studied Elizabeth for a few moments as she maneuvered out of traffic and onto Beach Road.

"I'm not going to waste our time with small talk, Lili. Your voice in your message held a level of anxiety. I might even label it desperation. What's up?"

"Can we hold the discussion until I'm no longer driving?"

"Why don't you pull over onto the shoulder and park. We can take a walk along the beach if that will work for you. I've been sitting for several hours and the exercise would be good for me."

Elizabeth found an empty spot. The day was heading toward that moment when families gathered up their coolers and blankets and assorted toys and headed back to their cottages, sun-burned and salty and exhausted.

"Can you manage on the sand with your cane?"

"You're going to be my cane," she smiled.

As they splashed barefoot in the shallows, Elizabeth began her saga—the inspiration from the night of storytelling, the dreams that inhabited her nights, her intense desire to bring the Wampanoag history to the screen and the realization she'd faced of her insensitivity to that history, thanks to Grace's forthright response.

Izzy listened with concentration, sometimes nodding but never interrupting. When Elizabeth finished speaking Izzy stopped in the water and faced her.

"What is it you'd like from me?"

"First, tell me if I'm a fool to want to do this."

"A fool? It's not foolish to want to preserve a culture, especially through storytelling. It's what we humans have been doing for millennia."

"But?"

"The question should be, am I the right person to be telling this story?"

"That's what Grace said."

"And you don't agree with her?"

"Oh, I do. I do. But stupidly I didn't at first. And I'm deeply ashamed that I was so selfishly pursuing my own goals that I didn't stop to understand the perspective of the tribe. But a part of me is still questioning whether there is some way—any way—I can be of service to the tribe's story."

"You sound like an adolescent who didn't get the answer she wanted from Mom, so now she's trying Aunt Izzy."

"I'm sorry, Iz. You're right. I don't mean to be disingenuous. Do you think there is any possibility the tribe might accept my offer of help, possibly to collaborate with a tribal member whom they trust?"

"I may not be the best judge of that, Lili. I don't live here and I have as much Irish blood in me as Jo, who's a thorn in the side of Cousin Sadie and her purists. If it were my decision, I'd trust you to do the story with beauty and sensitivity. Don't look surprised. I know your work, both your recent stuff and your undergraduate Renaissance project."

"Thank you, Izzy."

"You're a gifted filmmaker, Lili. But I'm afraid when it comes to portraying the history of native peoples—not just here, but anywhere in the world—the white perspective is a flawed one."

Intellectually, Elizabeth grasped what both Grace, and now Izzy, had spelled out. But she still grappled emotionally with how profoundly she wanted to bring her vision of the Wampanoag stories to fruition. At the edges of her need hovered a fear she wasn't quite ready to own—that somehow she had seized on the film as a way to lift her out of her grief and bring her back to life.

But Izzy, apparently, was already there.

"Lili, I don't doubt your motive. I know your intentions for the film have the good of the tribe at their heart. But ask yourself where your intensity, your—I'll say it, obsession—is coming from. This isn't just a professional opportunity for you, is it? It seems to me that it is very personal."

"All my films are personal, Izzy. They stem from *me*, they contain a piece of me." Elizabeth pushed back defensively, still unable to examine closely why she was pursuing this particular project. But Izzy had found a chink in Elizabeth's armor.

"Of course they do. That's what makes them so wonderful. Look, I think we're both wiped. I know I am. These legs have had enough for the day and need to be stretched out in a hammock overlooking the bay. We can talk some more later in the weekend, but now I'd like you to bring me home."

Elizabeth offered her arm to Izzy as they crossed the sand back to the car. They spent the remainder of the trip to Cove Meadow on safer topics—how Matteo was adapting to life on Chappy, how Tobias was sometimes alert and present, the books Izzy was reading and either loving or hating.

When they reached the Monroe house, Grace came out to greet them.

"Elizabeth, thanks so much for being Izzy's chauffeur! Dinner's almost ready. Would you join us?"

Elizabeth recognized the conversation with Izzy had drained them both. As much as she longed for adult company, she knew the atmosphere at the Monroe dinner table would be fraught with the unspoken memories of her attempts to seek support from both Grace and Izzy. Even if Grace hadn't said anything to Josiah or Caleb about the film, it would still be there, an unwanted guest.

"Oh, Grace, you're wonderful to offer, but I'm actually relishing a quiet night to myself out at Innisfree without the kids."

"Off to the big city in OB, are they?" Grace smiled in understanding at the restlessness of teenage boys. "Enjoy your tranquility. And thanks again. It was a big help."

Elizabeth bid Izzy goodbye with a hug and slipped away.

Once back at her own house, she sat on the back deck with a glass of Malbec until the last traces of the sunset had dissolved into indigo and the stars began their light show.

Too tired to cook, she foraged in the fridge for cheese and prosciutto and a bit of fruit, then crawled into bed with a Guido Brunetti mystery. She'd explore Izzy's provocative question in the morning.

Chapter Twenty-One

Storms at Sea

Elizabeth was on her way back from her morning swim when she heard the rumble of a motor behind her. She stopped and stepped to the side of the drive as Caleb pulled up next to her. He was in his own truck, not the Refuge pickup.

"Looks like you have the day off. Maybe your mother didn't mention it, but the boys are all in OB for the weekend, if you're here to invite them fishing."

"Mom *did* let it slip that you were a free woman for the next couple of days. I thought I'd seize that opportunity and invite *you* to go fishing." He was leaning on the door, his arms folded over the open window.

Elizabeth considered his grin, his relaxed posture and the prospect of spending a few hours on a boat in the middle of Nantucket Sound instead of wrestling with the dilemma of how to move forward on her film and whether, as Izzy had implied, she had become obsessed.

"Sure," she answered, before she could change her mind. "When do you want to go?"

"I'll head back to Cove Meadow right now and pick up the boat. Can you be ready in an hour?"

She nodded and moved away from the truck as he put it in gear, drove up to a wide expanse of grass in front of the house and turned around. His hand emerged from the open window in a wave and he was gone.

By the time he was back on the Monroe boat, she'd showered, pulled on a pair of shorts and a t-shirt over a dry bathing suit, and packed a small cooler with some sandwiches and beer. She met him at the dock and climbed aboard. It wasn't a new boat, but it had been well-maintained, with gear stored neatly and ropes wound in orderly coils. It reminded her of his truck and she remembered that both he and Josiah had been in the military.

He backed the boat away from the dock, swung it in a wide arc and steered out of the pond toward the Gut.

"Where are we headed?"

"Out toward Nantucket. Not far. Although it's clear right now, I heard the weather may turn later in the afternoon, so we won't stay out long. You like cod?"

"I know how to do a few things with cod, although the Italians tend to salt and dry it. Not my favorite version."

"Baccala?"

"A staple of Italian fishwives."

"We'll catch just enough to eat fresh, then."

Until they reached the area of the sound where he assured her the cod were plentiful, they travelled in companionable silence. Both wind on the open water and the churning of the engine discouraged any meaningful conversation beyond directing her where to stow the cooler.

When they arrived at the fishing grounds she helped him drop anchor and joined him in baiting the lines. For a while, the silence of the journey extended into their fishing, a ritual as practiced as if they were worshipping at some altar of the god of the sea.

And then, Caleb spoke the words she'd been anticipating since she'd surmised the reason for his invitation—an offer he could have easily extended over the phone but had chosen instead to drive all the way to Innisfree early on a Saturday morning to ask her.

"Mom and Izzy told me about your film idea last night at dinner."

Elizabeth tightened her grip on her fishing pole, wishing that there might be a strong tug on the end of the line to distract her from engaging in the conversation. *You could have said no*, she told herself. But she had recognized after a thoughtful night under the stars that the moment had come when she had to face the roots of her obsession. The growing trust developing between her and Caleb had led her to accept his invitation, knowing that the discussion might be raw and painful, but necessary.

"And what did you think?"

"Why don't you tell me about it in your own words. I know what *they* think, but I'd like to hear directly from you what this is all about."

She looked away from the line dipping into the sea and into his eyes.

"Thanks for being willing to listen, although it's hard for me to believe your opinion hasn't been influenced by what they've told you."

"Both of them have a great deal of respect—awe even—for your talent, Elizabeth. Not to mention affection for you."

Before beginning to speak, she secured the fishing pole to one of the clamps on the side of the boat. This time, she had neither the PowerPoint presentation as she had with Grace, nor the intimacy of a shared and precious history as she had with Izzy. Like the Italians she'd lived among for so many years, she used her hands.

But instead of explaining what she wanted to do, describing her intentions for interviewing tribal members and weaving in facts from her research, she closed her eyes and began to tell a story, echoing the cadence and rhythm of the words she'd heard during the hurricane.

"It starts with the wind, roaring across the bay, whipping the waves into a frenzy and tearing the sail…" she began, and for the next twenty minutes recounted with stark images, words whispered or shouted or sung, and the beating of her palms on her thighs, on the wooden railing, even crouching down onto the deck and pounding out a soundtrack to the film she was creating before his eyes.

When she finished, she collapsed back into the webbed chair, her face pale and her hair wind-whipped into a halo, as if she were coming out of a trance.

She waited, her eyes still closed. Then she sensed him move, a disturbance in the air around her, a shadow falling across the sun on her face, before he kissed her. She opened her eyes.

"That's not how you told it to my mother and Izzy," he observed, now crouched in front of her, his hands grasping the aluminum arms of her chair, enclosing her in a circle of metal and flesh.

"No," she admitted. "But I told it to them before questioning why I felt the compelling need to tell it."

"But it seems to me now that you are questioning. Have you found the answer?"

She studied his face, now less than a foot from hers. His eyes were a deep brown, and she realized that she'd rarely seen him without sunglasses. At some point in her narration he'd taken them off. She could smell him, sweat and sea, traces of bait and diesel fuel and laundry soap.

He smelled like a man. She tried to shake off the memory of how Antonio had smelled in those final months—smells she knew appalled and shamed him. As she had when she had encountered Caleb on the beach the week before, she was overwhelmed with a sense not only of discomfort, but of betrayal.

"I thought by telling the story as I envisioned it, I might better understand where it was coming from," she announced, and made an attempt to stand up and break the circle. She wasn't sure she could continue to explore this hidden piece of herself without the barrier of her craft protecting her.

He shifted back on his haunches and let go of the chair.

She rose and turned back to the fishing rod, lifting it from the clamp and letting out more line. She was staring out at the water when she spoke again.

"What did you think? Was I telling the Wampanoag story, or my own?"

So much depended on his answer. She was troubled by what his response meant to her, entangled in her need finally to delve into why she had such a profound longing to make this film and the unwelcome desire to be seen and touched and kissed again.

He didn't answer her right away and stayed back a distance, as if he didn't trust himself to keep his hands from reaching out for her; as if he understood the ambivalence of her desire.

"You are a born storyteller," he began. "You've captured the poetry of that night during the hurricane as if you were an echo, reverberating and amplifying the words and the emotions. You brought me back to the moment with incredible clarity, listening and watching. It was very powerful."

Elizabeth remained with her back to him, not trusting his praise, waiting for the "but."

He continued.

"It was a beautiful and eloquent recreation of one moment in the life of the tribe, a moment you had the privilege to witness, and I thank you for it."

She waited for him to continue, but when he remained silent, she whispered, "Thank you." She was aware that he still hadn't approached her. She lifted one hand from the fishing rod and wiped away the tears splashed on her cheeks. Then she spoke.

"You asked me if I've found the answer to why I felt so driven to capture that moment on film. I've been struggling with this ever since my conversation with your mother. When I first spoke to her, I wasn't willing to admit that my motives were more complex than an intellectual interest in a topic that apparently hadn't yet been covered artistically. I also was willfully blind to how I'd be perceived by the tribe. If I had any illusions left about my intentions, Izzy set me straight pretty bluntly. I've spent a lot of time in the last two days trying to be honest with myself, berating myself for being so obstinate. I've come to see that night of the hurricane as a watershed moment for me, one that made me long for the connection of community. I wanted to be a part of it.

"But Izzy, especially, helped me to see that the tribe is defined by more than a romanticized evocation of ancient traditions. You're a 21st-century people trying to reconnect to your culture and restore what you've lost—land, language, history. I understand that so much of what has been taken from you is tied to the white man. As a historian I should have understood from the beginning that I wasn't the person to tell your story. And now, speaking about my tangled emotions out loud to you, I see that as someone who has experienced a profound loss, not only of my husband but also of the woman I had once been, I've been very slow to recognize that I saw creating this film as a way back to myself."

The boat, which earlier had been nearly motionless, was now rocking vigorously. She realized that the weather change Caleb had mentioned in the morning had crept up on them. The sea was reflecting her own turmoil.

"Do you understand what I am saying? I saw the film as saving my life."

Until she'd spoken the words, she hadn't admitted the truth of them. This is what Izzy had meant the day before on the beach. That Elizabeth's fascination with the Wampanoag story was something profoundly personal, preventing her from seeing with empathy any other point of view. She was finally realizing why she hadn't been able to let go of it.

"I *do* understand, Elizabeth. I, of all people, comprehend your need to reclaim your life after what you've been through. Any member of my family does. We know what it's like to accompany someone we love on their last journey. We did it with Mae, and now, here we are once again at Tobias' bedside. My mother, especially, has put aside her life to care for him; it's why I came back after half a lifetime away. You postpone, you tamp down desire, you withdraw from anything that steals your energy because you need that energy to care for another. And you do it willingly, lovingly. But when you're no longer needed, when the one you love can no longer be helped, you're bereft. Not only because they are gone, but because you are suddenly confronted with the empty hole your life has become. In caring for the dying, you've forgotten how to live."

Elizabeth listened to Caleb, stunned by his grasp of how untethered and adrift she'd become after Antonio's death.

"No one wants to thwart your finding your way back, and it makes immense sense that making a film is your path. You're a brilliant storyteller. I've already told you that. Is it so challenging for you to find another story to tell?"

"I hear you. I've been so blinded by my own needs that I charged ahead, perceiving your family's deeply felt honesty as resistance instead of the caring advice it was meant to be. I've been acting like an entitled, spoiled brat. Will you forgive me?"

He reached out and clasped her wrist, the first time he'd touched her since the kiss.

"I do. I don't want to lose your friendship. And I don't want to see you in pain or floundering."

Then he took her face in his hands and kissed her again.

The kiss caught her by surprise, not only its unexpectedness but its intensity. Thought left her, replaced by longing. The emptiness he had so accurately described began to fill with sensations too long dormant. She moved toward him, arms lifting to encircle him, lips softening to welcome him. Fragments of emotion bombarded her as her body betrayed her, rejecting any attempt by her brain to hold back or even question what was happening. She was aware only that she'd never been kissed like this before.

When they finally separated, breathless, they looked at one another. What she saw on his face she realized must be reflected on her own—disbelief, wonder, a questioning. Where had this come from?

He pulled her toward him and held her. Her head fit under his chin, and with her ear pressed against his chest she heard his heart beat, racing as if he'd just sprinted 100 meters. They stood, silent and still, for a few moments. It was Caleb who finally broke the spell.

"Shall we head back?" His voice was jagged, the unspoken part of the question pressed in the narrow space between them. For all the careful distance they'd kept from one another all morning, they now could not bear to pull apart, as if the kiss had merged their flesh and separating would tear tissue and draw blood.

She nodded her agreement, unable yet to speak. He kissed the top of her head and released his hold on her. She reluctantly let her arms drop from the solid comfort of his back.

By this time, the sea was even more turbulent and the wind had shifted. After Caleb pulled up the anchor he tossed a life jacket to her.

"Better put this on. It's going to be much rougher making our way home."

She fumbled with the straps but managed to secure herself and grab a handhold before a large wave mounted the now tilting side of the boat. Caleb had fired the ignition and the engine came to life just before the rain descended upon them, blown nearly horizontal by the northeast wind. Ahead of them, in the direction of Chappy, fog had crept across the open water.

"Change of plans. We're going to turn away from the storm for the time being. No point in trying to head directly into it." Caleb swung the wheel around and steered the boat south.

"Hold on!" He shouted, as a wave rose over the railing and crashed onto the deck.

Dripping from the wave, she was stunned and chilled, trying to hear what Caleb was shouting at her. She shook herself back into alertness, understanding at some wordless, inchoate level that they were in danger. Only once before in her life had she been so afraid at sea, when a freak storm had blown up suddenly when she was sixteen and she'd been sailing solo around Norton Point.

It had been a reckless exploit even without the storm because of the strong and unpredictable currents. But she'd been confident and fearless when she set out, as immortal as any teenager trying to defy limits and prove something. When the boat capsized she had nearly panicked as she'd gone under, swallowing great gulps of saltwater. But the lessons drilled into her by her mother, who'd taught her how to sail the lightweight Sunfish, had kicked in, and she'd managed to right the boat and steer it to a safe haven. But the memory of those frightening minutes, struggling with wind, slashing rain and the treacherous current, came surging back as she shivered on the deck.

Once he had the boat moving southward, Caleb gestured to her to attach herself to a line. Her fingers were wet and cramped and the clamp kept slipping. With one hand on the wheel, he reached down and clipped her jacket to the lifeline.

She huddled near him, knees up under her chin and arms wrapped tightly around her legs. She felt useless, but her shouted offer to help had been waved away. Her back was to the prow and she could not see what lay ahead of them, although if it resembled what was behind them, it could only be an impenetrable wall of gray mist. The boat lurched from one wave to the next, rising at an alarming angle and then slamming down, nose dipping into the water and then sending sheets of seawater washing down the deck with the next precipitous climb.

She was going to be sick. She sensed the warning signs, the muscles of her gut starting to push whatever was in her stomach up and out. There was no way she could safely make it to the railing to throw up into the sea. She twisted her body away from Caleb and heaved onto the deck, the wind tangling her hair and plastering it against her face. She tried to push it off and then felt another hand, larger, calloused, holding the heavy, wet locks away from her mouth. When it appeared her stomach was empty, she crawled back to the wheel and Caleb squeezed her shoulder.

The rain was fierce enough that it washed away most of the mess in a few minutes. She braved a look ahead and saw a sliver of light that Caleb appeared to be steering toward, but she recognized no landmarks and heard no buoys. She had no idea where they were and simply trusted that Caleb did. She wanted to close her eyes, so drained was she. But she remembered her mother's lesson from childhood about focusing on the horizon to overcome seasickness. It was a little late for that, and there was no horizon—no differentiation between sky and sea. Nevertheless, she kept her eyes open, if only to reassure herself that Caleb was still beside her, legs braced on the deck and hands gripping the wheel.

At some point—she couldn't judge how long it had been—the boat seemed to be levelling out and the sensation of riding an out-of-control rollercoaster lessened. The rain was still intense. It felt like thousands of needles pricking her bare limbs. And then she saw that the raindrops were actually tiny pellets of ice rattling against the deck. Hail. In the middle of July. She shook the ice out of her matted hair, but more took its place.

Suddenly, the sound of the motor changed and Elizabeth feared they'd stalled, the engine clogged with ice. But off to her right she saw wooden pilings emerge from the grayness that had swallowed the entire coast.

"Can you grab a line and toss it up to the dock when I pull in close?"

She scrambled unsteadily to her feet and found one of the coiled ropes coated in ice. With numb fingers she pulled it free and tossed, only to have it slide back and into the water. She hauled it up and tried again as Caleb brought the boat in. The second time she grabbed a piling and held tight as she wrapped the rope around it. Once it was in place, she climbed up onto the dock with another line in hand and secured it to a second post as Caleb shut off the engine and joined her on the slippery dock. He tightened the lines and led her away from the water.

Chapter Twenty-Two

Rescue

"Where are we?"

"Tuckernuck Island."

Nowhere near Chappy. Practically in Nantucket. Was it even inhabited? She couldn't remember. There had been no house visible when they'd tied up at the dock, but as they climbed up a shallow, overgrown hill they discovered a path hacked through the weeds and followed it. The fog was as dense on the island as it had been on the sea, so they were almost at the door of the cottage before they saw it.

Caleb knocked several times and Elizabeth peered through the windows flanking the door.

"The furniture looks draped in sheets. I don't think anyone's here."

"Makes sense, since there wasn't a boat at the dock."

"Do we walk on and try to find another house?"

Caleb studied her shivering form. Her knees were bloody where she'd scraped them getting up onto the dock.

"No. We'll stay here."

He bent down to a flat rock near the door, lifted it and retrieved a key.

"How did you know?"

"It's my cousin's house. Third or fourth—I'm not sure. His great-grandfather and my great-grandmother were brother and sister. He lives in New Haven, but comes out in August. Otherwise, the house is empty. No one on Tuckernuck rents out their cottage. Very private. Very exclusive."

He had already opened the house as he explained his connection to it.

Inside, the air was stale, but the baked-in heat had not yet seeped out through the inevitable gaps and cracks that were endemic to houses subjected to the rigors of New England maritime weather. Elizabeth absorbed the warmth that smacked her in the face as soon as she walked through the door.

"I'm going to turn on the gas and fire up the water heater so you can get out of your wet clothes and take a hot shower. Bathroom is over behind the kitchen. There's an indoor shower."

She lifted her thumbs up in gratitude. She was still buckled and zipped into the turquoise and orange life jacket. She peeled it off with trembling fingers and dropped it by the door, where it puddled onto the slate floor. She slipped off her sandals as well, which were covered in mud and weeds from their trek up from the dock.

She padded in her bare feet to the door Caleb had indicated, but not before glancing at the large open space that appeared to be both living and dining room. A woodstove was piped into a stone wall. Under the sheets she had noticed through the window were two couches flanking the stove with a low table between them holding a celestial guide, navigation charts and a stack of National Geographics from the previous year.

Behind one of the couches, centered on a braided rug, was a dining table large enough to seat twelve. Built-in cupboards and bookcases filled the walls and reminded her of a ship's cabin. Everything stowed, contained and simplified.

The kitchen was separated from the dining table by a counter. Beyond it were double refrigerators, a Champion stove like the one at Innisfree, and a large soapstone sink. The countertops were empty. Elizabeth suppressed the urge to open cabinets and instead turned the doorknob to the bathroom.

She found towels on a shelf and was uncertain how long it would take to heat a tank of water. She decided to give it a try and yanked the hot water faucet handle. A gush of rusty water spewed out of the spigot and she let it run till it was clear.

Caleb knocked. "I've found some dry clothes for you." She took them from him. "Water should be warm enough in a few minutes. Are you OK?"

"I'm a little wobbly. Nothing that a hot shower and maybe a cup of tea can't fix."

"I'll see what I can find in the kitchen. Yell if you need anything."

She stripped off her soggy clothing and threw everything into the sink. Her toe in the shower, white and wrinkled, registered a message of "warm enough" to her slightly muddled brain. Was that why Caleb's voice had sounded so uncertain about her state of being? She stepped fully into the shower, pulled closed the plastic curtain decorated with seashells, and let the water run over her still shivering body. As she expected, she found half-filled containers of shampoo and conditioner in the wire basket hanging from the shower head. She'd never known a beach cottage to be without the remnants of someone else's bathing regimen. She squeezed out a dollop of the Moroccan-oil-infused shampoo and the aroma revived her slightly. The reassuring smell of domesticity replaced the diesel fuel and metallic tang that had filled her nostrils since the storm had launched her into the nightmare from which she hadn't quite awoken.

Suddenly, as if unfrozen by the warm water now cascading over her body, she erupted into air-gulping sobs, tears mingling with the shower spray and suds from the shampoo.

Caleb found her crouched under the water in the same position she'd taken on the boat during the storm—knees pulled up, arms locked tightly around her legs.

He reached up and turned off the water and then wrapped her in the towel she'd pulled off the shelf.

"I didn't think you were fine, despite your protestations." He wiped her face with a corner of the towel and drew her gently to her feet, rubbing her briskly with the coarse terrycloth.

"I should have recognized that you were going into shock. I'm sorry. Come with me. I've got a fire going. You can dress there and I've got some soup heating."

He guided her back to the living room and a worn leather chair that he pushed closer to the woodstove. Although she'd stopped sobbing, she hadn't spoken yet. He grabbed a large afghan draped over the back of one of the couches and tucked it around her.

"I don't think you can dress yourself just yet," he murmured. His hands circled her feet, poking out from under the blanket. "Still freezing. I'm going to find you some socks."

He returned quickly with a pair of cotton tube socks and she sat numbly watching him stretch them over her feet. Then he sat on the floor in front of her and took each clad foot, one by one, and massaged it, stroking blood and life back into it.

She watched him as if he were ministering to someone else's body, not hers. She could hear his voice and feel the calloused strength of his hands, hands she knew she recognized in some remote corner of memory. She leaned back into the cushions supporting her and closed her eyes.

His voice roused her, then those hands again, this time folding her own hands around a mug filled with steaming liquid.

"Chicken soup. Campbell's. It was all I could find in the cabinet. Sip it slowly."

He didn't let go as she brought the cup to her lips. Like the shampoo, it beckoned her back to the present. You are safe, it was telling her. You are cared for.

When she'd finished half the soup, felt it warming her gut the way the fire was sending out tendrils of hcat to her limbs, she found her voice.

"Thank you," she croaked. She put the cup down on the table next to the chair and then took up his hand. She squeezed it and saw that he was still in his wet clothes, although the edges appeared to be drying in the heat from the stove.

"You haven't left me." It was an observation but also a revelation, spoken with a note of awe.

"Of course not. You…were in danger. You had drifted away as thoroughly as if you'd fallen overboard."

A flash of fear twisted her face.

"I didn't, did I?"

"No. No. You were having a delayed reaction to the peril we were in on the sea. You were freezing, wet and probably had suffered a precipitous drop in your blood sugar—all of which sent mayday signals to your brain to shut everything down and hunker in place until the danger had passed. You just needed warmth and food to bring you back."

"Speaking of warmth, I think I'm well enough for you to go shower."

"Do I smell that bad?" He smiled.

"Eau de seaweed with a hint of diesel and dead worms." She wrinkled her nose.

"You are definitely better. I hear intimations of the Elizabeth I've come to know."

He got up, stretched and left her for the shower.

While he was under the water she found the dry clothes he'd scavenged from his cousin's closet, folded neatly on the couch. She threw off the layers of afghan and towel and shook out a pair of track pants stamped "Wesleyan Cross-Country," a white t-shirt and a Boston Red Sox sweatshirt. She pulled them on, reveling in the bliss of American leisure wear and blessing the inventor of fleece. She rolled the bottoms of the pants and pushed up the sleeves of the sweatshirt so that she no longer looked like the Disney dwarf whose clothing seemed cut for someone twice his size.

She toweled her hair and braided it in a single plait down her back and then went to the windows facing the sea. It was still raining and the wind slapped against the house, sometimes causing the fire in the stove to hiss and puff. She had no idea what time it was. It was impossible to tell from the sky, which remained a mass of churning black clouds. The duration of her trance-like state of shock could have been minutes or hours.

She thought of checking her phone, but couldn't remember when she'd last seen it. Was it in the pocket of her shorts? Still on the boat? Or had it slipped into the sea during the wild ride, the memory of which was slowly returning. She had a momentary burst of fear that the memory of the storm would reignite her shock, sending her back to hovering between awareness and oblivion.

She wanted substance—the floor solid and steady under her feet; the wood snapping and flaming in the stove, its cedar aroma dispelling the stale, dead air of the closed-up cottage; the fleece against her skin, swaddling her like the soft blankets she'd wrapped around Matteo in the first months of his life. And she acknowledged, with a heat rising within her that had nothing to do with the woodstove, she wanted Caleb's calloused hands enclosing her again, protecting her.

She had no idea if his touch had meant anything more to him than what a first responder would do when encountering someone in shock. He'd saved her physically, but she also believed that her body and mind had responded to something more. Those initial moments when she'd returned to herself, it was with a sense of well-being that went beyond her pulse and glucose levels. She had felt seen, held, even loved.

She shook off that last thought. That was ridiculous, one of the effects of traumatic stress, to conflate rescue with love. It was natural that two people who'd survived a harrowing experience together might feel an intense array of emotion. *Get a grip, Innocenti.* Your adrenaline levels must still be in the stratosphere. This is a man to whom a few weeks ago you read the riot act. A man who seemed to take great pleasure in irritating you, who had once placed you in a box with all the other women he'd dismissed as superficial airheads. Despite the revelations she'd shared with him on the boat and the empathy with which he'd responded to her, she remained haunted by the still rocky nature of their friendship and her own sense of betrayal of Antonio.

She tried to hold onto that thought as Caleb emerged from the bathroom with a New England Patriots beach towel wrapped around his waist. Clearly his cousin was a diehard sports fan, her brain digressed from the lecture she'd been giving herself. She warned herself that this man standing in the doorway—strong, compassionate, a steady hand on the tiller—was as dangerous to her as the storm raging outside.

"Hey, feeling better?" He called out to her, appraising her now, on her feet and fully clothed instead of huddled in a pile of wool by the fire.

All she could do was nod.

"I'm going to borrow some more clothes from my cousin and then see if I can't find something more substantial to eat than chicken noodle soup. That is, if your stomach is up to it."

She grimaced. "I'm hungry, too. And now that I'm not lurching up and down on the ocean, I think I could manage some solid food. I'll get started hunting through cupboards."

Glad of something to do to distract her from pondering questions of the human heart, she headed for the kitchen. Whoever had closed up the cottage last season had had the good sense to pack up any dry foods in metal canisters. She found no half-eaten boxes of rice or torn bags of flour or sugar. Maybe Tuckernuck had no mice or raccoon populations. But she did find a tin stocked with dry pasta, some cans of beans, and diced tomatoes. No olive oil or fresh onions but the spice rack yielded some basil and garlic powder. It would suffice.

By the time Caleb was dressed she had a pot of salted water on to boil and a saucepan simmering with tomatoes and cannellini beans.

"What's for supper?" He lifted the lid on the tomatoes.

"Pasta Fagioli, a staple of every Southern Italian housewife."

"I bow to women who know how to create feasts from a few cans."

The meal was ready in a few minutes. Caleb knew where to find the wine, and they sat down to their repast as darkness settled on the house.

"I called Izzy when I was getting dressed and let her know we were fine and planning to sit out the storm here. I asked her to let your brother know."

"Thanks. You had your phone! At least one of us does. I don't know what happened to mine. It's probably sitting on the ocean floor or caught in some fishing trawler's nets off Menemsha. I didn't even know if there was service out here."

"It's spotty, especially in weather like this. But the cell tower on Nantucket is close enough to pick up a signal. I wasn't sure how long the battery would last, so I thought it best to get the message to Iz and then turn off the phone. Will Sam worry about you?"

"Sam, probably not. But Matteo will wonder if he doesn't hear from me. When I left him with Sam and Debbie and stayed out alone at Innisfree I made a point to talk with him every night."

"I can turn my phone back on, if you want to call him."

"Thanks. I'd like to do that. I won't talk long."

"I'll do the dishes while you call."

"That's a deal."

She kept her word and spoke only briefly to Matteo, who seemed deeply entrenched in a game of Settlers of Catan when she called. OB had lost power in the storm and the boys were playing by candlelight. She wished him goodnight and ended the call, relieved that he was having fun, but recognizing her own sense of loss in how quickly he was growing away from her.

She picked up a dish towel to dry as she put Caleb's phone on the counter.

"All's well in OB?"

"More than well, it seems. They're having their own adventure—board games, popcorn and candlelight. He hardly seems to know I'm gone."

"Isn't that a good thing—that he can start to find his own place in the world apart from his mother? He's with family, Elizabeth. It's not like he took off to hitchhike across America, which is essentially what my father did."

"Josiah? How old was he?"

"Eighteen. Just up and left one night in anger. Wound up in Vietnam and then lived on a commune writing manifestos."

"But he came back. How? Why?"

"He met my mother, who was one of Izzy's friends at Smith. He has said more than once that she saved his life."

"He's a very private guy. At least, that was the impression I got of him during the hurricane. I don't remember much about him when I was younger. It was Tobias who was out at Innisfree."

"My dad doesn't share much, that's true."

"Do you think he's happy he returned to Chappy?"

"I have no idea if my father has the capacity to be happy, either here or anywhere else in the world."

"That's a strong statement."

Caleb shrugged. "I can't solve what's eating at him. Only he can. But I don't know if he can even articulate what he needs or wants."

"They are so different, Izzy and your dad."

"Yeah. One is a master of language, in love with words, and the other one finds it actually painful to communicate. I think it's killing my mother's spirit."

"I'm sorry. You sound so frustrated."

"Because I am. I feel helpless. Almost as helpless as I am caring for my grandfather, knowing that no matter what I do, he's going to die."

Elizabeth reached out and touched his arm.

"I know that helplessness," she said quietly.

He looked at her. "Of course you do," he said. "I'm sorry. I didn't mean to magnify my problems."

"Don't be sorry. We all have challenges, and the most difficult ones have to do with the people we love."

He pulled the plug in the sink and she handed him the towel to dry his hands.

He picked up the bottle of wine still sitting on the table and held it up to a candle. "Looks like there's about a glass a piece left in here. Shall we take it to the couch and watch the fire burn down as if it were a movie?"

She smiled, grabbed their wine glasses and led the way.

They sat side by side and she tucked her feet up under her to face him. He poured, they clinked glasses and sipped. He studied the wine in his glass and then spoke.

"Can we talk about what happened on the boat just before the storm hit?"

Elizabeth stiffened. "What about it?"

"After that kiss, all I wanted to do was take you back to Innisfree and make love to you."

This was her opportunity to shut things down, stop them from crossing a line. So many ways to redirect where they were heading. She wasn't ready to consider another man in her life so soon after Antonio's death; she wanted to devote herself to raising Matteo and that didn't leave room for someone else. But none of those words formed on her lips. The danger she'd perceived earlier was still there, a presence as real as the storm outside and as vivid as the energy drawing them closer. But slipping into the room was the memory of those first moments when she was recovering from the shock and she was aware of his hands wrapped around hers as he fed her soup.

He was her safety.

She put down her glass, rose to her knees on the couch and climbed onto his lap.

"Innisfree is a long way to go when there is a bedroom down the hall."

He slipped his hands under her and lifted her up off the couch. She wound her legs around him and he carried her to bed.

The room was dark and he didn't stop to light the lantern on the dresser by the door, but found their destination as if he were a homing pigeon navigating by some instinct encoded generations before. He laid her on the mattress and she sank into its soft depths. The sheets felt like the sort of hand-me-down linens often relegated to beach houses, faded and mismatched, she imagined. But they gave off a faint trace of lavender that she found calming to her heightened state of awareness.

She felt him slide into bed next to her, his long legs stretched the length of her, and she shifted on her side to face him. Her eyes were slowly adjusting to the inky blackness of the room, but she couldn't yet see his expression or read his mood.

"I haven't been with a man in a long time," she whispered.

He placed two fingers on her lips. "Shh," he responded. "That's not important. What matters tonight is just the two us, Caleb and Elizabeth, in the present moment. No past. No future. Can you do that?"

"I feel like the Tin Man in the Wizard of Oz."

"Oh, you very definitely have a heart, Elizabeth."

"I meant stiff, rusted from standing too long exposed to the elements, alone."

"I think I saw some WD-40 under the kitchen sink. I can go get some."

"I can think of better ways to lubricate this clanking shell of tin."

"Why, Elizabeth Innocenti, I'm shocked, shocked, that you even know that word. But even more shocked that you've hidden this playful side of you."

His hands slid under the layers of her sweatshirt and t-shirt, those now familiar calloused fingertips making contact with her back and sending waves of goosebumps cascading from her shoulder blades to her waist.

"M-m-m," she murmured, and then one of those hands slid around to caress her breast, and she flinched.

She knew in some vague recess of memory that he'd already seen her naked when he'd found her huddled in the shower. But this was different. She'd been unaware of her vulnerability then, but now she was fully conscious that she was about to reveal herself to this man. Not just a body softened by motherhood and wrapped in a cloak of protection as impenetrable as the heavy, shapeless habits worn by nuns. As the wife of a man paralyzed, betrayed by his body, she had closed herself off to the pleasures and joys of physical touch. She had become as sexless as those nuns she passed everyday on the Ponte Vecchio. She had taught herself, steeled herself, to stop wanting. She had smothered desire, because to allow it to burn would have caused Antonio even more pain. Caleb's touch on her breast felt as if he had struck a match that was about to ignite a conflagration.

"Did I hurt you?" He asked, pulling away his hand.

"No. No. It's only that it's been a long time since I've been touched."

"I should have realized…"

This time it was she who touched her fingertips to his lips. "No 'shoulds' or 'shouldn'ts.' But I have one request."

"What's that?"

"Could you light the lantern? I want to see your face."

He answered by easing away from her and retreating to the dresser. Although he'd been lying next to her for only a few minutes, his absence triggered a pang of longing. It was more than the sudden chill filling the space where warmth had surrounded her.

"Hurry back," she called to him across the room. "I miss you already."

She heard the click of one of the plastic lighters that were ubiquitous in island cottages without electricity and then saw the glow of the wick fill the glass funnel of the lantern and illuminate his face.

But instead of returning to her, he stood in the pool of light and stripped off the borrowed clothes. She leaned on her elbow and watched, transfixed by the sight of this healthy, whole man, whose muscles obeyed the impulses from his brain, whose lungs gave him breath and whose vocal chords gave him speech.

"You're a miracle. Do you know that?"

"You mean, do I appreciate the miracle that is life and movement and sensation? Yes, Elizabeth, I do. I'm a survivor of a war that stole those things from too many of my friends. I am sorry they were stolen from Antonio—and from you."

He approached her, now as naked as she had been in the shower, but open to her, offering her the body she found so miraculous.

Once again he lay beside her, and this time she didn't flinch as he lifted her shirt over her head and slid the fleece warm-up pants down her legs. She turned toward him, gasping as their skin made contact, fulfilling a need so basic it began as early as an infant hungry for the scent and nourishment and comfort of its mother's skin.

Then she let go of thought and memory and regret and loneliness, and kissed this man who had offered himself to her and took him into her aching, trembling body.

She called out when she came, her voice rising above the wind and rain that battered the house, and he held her till the waves of pleasure receded.

"Thank you," he said.

"I think I am the one who is thankful. You are both a miracle and a gift."

She nestled into his shoulder as he drew his arm around her and pulled her close. She draped her arm across his chest to seal the bond between them, a layer of heat and sweat the only separation.

"I have to confess," he said to the night, and she titled her chin up to listen. "I am feeling very manly, having brought you back to life twice today."

"I much prefer the second method to the chicken soup."

"Have I earned my sleep?"

"As many hours as you wish. Except I may find myself in need of resurrection again during the night. That is, if you don't mind performing another miracle."

"With infinite joy," he murmured, and then rolled her onto her side, wrapped his protective arm around her and fit himself like a spoon against her back.

She smiled again and fell asleep.

Sometime before dawn the silence woke them. The storm had abated and slivers of light on the eastern horizon crept through the window and into their consciousness. They turned to one another without words and found another language to communicate. The pace was more languid than the night before, when their hunger for one another had driven them with an urgency heightened by the memory of the storm's menace.

Elizabeth, sated and reassured that, like riding a bicycle, she hadn't forgotten how to enjoy lovemaking, found herself encouraged as the day arrived, awakening her to the desire to offer to Caleb a bolder, more daring self. A self, she admitted only later, she'd never revealed to Antonio because she hadn't discovered it until making love with Caleb.

She was breathless with the unexpected revelation of this adventurer hidden with her.

"Who is this stranger in my bed?" Caleb exclaimed, spent and equally breathless.

"I don't know her either. I think I've been possessed by some creature of my imagination."

"A goddess. A priestess. A shaman."

"I like those word choices. They speak of power and the sacred."

He brushed the tangled hair from her face, the braid long undone and now a cloud surrounding her head.

"I chose those words because I do feel something powerful and sacred happened between us."

"Since the kiss before the storm," she said, knowing that was the moment that changed everything. The moment from which they would measure "before" and "after."

He kissed her again. She didn't understand what had happened between them, only that it was profound and had created a rift in her life, separating her from the Elizabeth who arrived on Chappy at the beginning of the summer, the Elizabeth she had always believed herself to be.

"I hate to pull us out of this bower, but there is a world out there more than likely wondering when we're going to get back and take up our responsibilities."

"To grandfathers and children. Both of whom have a legitimate claim on our time and our affections."

She sat up, stretched and swung her legs over the side of the bed.

"Does this place have a washing machine?" she asked, lifting one end of the sheet.

"There's a machine and a generator to run it in the shed. If you can get a load going, I'll check on the boat and see if it will start."

"Is there any doubt?" It hadn't occurred to her that more than the storm could strand them here.

"Not likely. But if there's a problem, I want to know about it now."

He helped her strip the bed and she gathered up the linens. Their lavender fragrance was now overlaid with a musky ripeness.

She thought better of starting the laundry without the towels and scrubbed down quickly under the shower.

"Do you want to shower before I start the wash?" He was just on the other side of the shower curtain shaving with a disposable razor he'd found in the medicine cabinet. He answered by joining her under the spray and their resolve to move toward leaving the island and heading home was temporarily set aside.

It was Elizabeth who finally pulled away from their soapy embrace.

"Laundry. Boat. Home," she sputtered. "One of us needs to keep focused." She smiled, kissed him lightly, and stepped out of the shower.

Her own clothes were still damp, so she retrieved the sweats from the bedroom. They'd just have to ship them back to the cousin.

The generator and washer were familiar to her, common enough modern additions to these remote island retreats. The noise of the motor was an assault on the peace of the morning. A flock of cormorants that had been floating on a pond near the shed rose up in a raucous flurry of black wings, and Elizabeth silently apologized for the intrusion of modern life.

As the washing machine vibrated into life, she returned to the kitchen with the slender hope she might find some coffee in one of the tins arrayed on the cupboard shelves.

She was ecstatic to find an unopened can of Lavazza, a surprising choice for this most Yankee of locations, but surmised that it had been bought in New Haven, where Italian pasticcerie and delicatessens were as numerous as in Boston's North End. She even discovered a battered Neapolitan espresso pot like the one sitting in her kitchen in Florence.

She made the coffee, but not without acknowledging the thrust back to "real life" that the coffee pot had triggered. The villa, her in-laws, Matteo's school and friends, the world she'd inhabited for the last fifteen years waited for her return at the end of the summer. The night with Caleb, even the weeks left to them if they found their way into each other's arms again, were an aberration, a deviation from the natural course of her life—and more than likely, from his as well.

Chapter Twenty-Three

Vulnerability

Elizabeth glanced around the cottage, now bright with sunshine. Its shabby comfort filled her with affection—the scene of her reawakening. No regrets, she told herself. She poured two mugs with coffee and carried them down to the dock, where she heard Caleb tapping something metallic.

It was low tide and the boat was riding several feet below the dock. She handed down the mugs and then clambered backward down a ladder that had passed a few too many winters.

Caleb took a grateful sip of coffee.

"How does it look?" she asked, casting an appraising eye at the debris-strewn deck.

"Engine started without a hitch, but there's not enough fuel to get us back to Chappy."

"I don't suppose there's a diesel station on Tuckernuck."

"No, but we can easily cruise to Nantucket and tank up. I thought I'd do that while you hang up the sheets. I can grab us some lunch as well. By the time I get back, the sheets should be dry in this wind and sun, and we can head home."

She wasn't crazy about being left alone. In the daylight she could see nothing but wetlands surrounding the house. Not a tree, not another cottage. But she wasn't looking forward to getting back on the boat, either. The wind that would dry the sheets was also whipping the sea into white caps. It was likely that by the time Caleb got back, the journey would be smoother.

"OK. When will you head out?"

He handed her back the empty mug. "Right now. Oh, and I found your phone. You put it in the cooler."

She slipped it into the pocket of her pants. He kissed her, lightly at first, but then more intently when she responded with a melting fervency.

"Hurry back," she said with a smile.

She climbed the ladder and cast off the lines that had held well during the storm.

When the boat was out of sight she returned to the shed, gathered the sheets in a basket and found the clothes line.

She was busy struggling against the blustering wind and didn't hear the approach of a vehicle or the footsteps of its driver as he came around the corner of the shed. But she heard his voice when he shouted at her above the wind and she spun around in a panic.

"I've never know thieves to do laundry, so I'm going to give you the benefit of the doubt and assume you have a right to be here."

She studied the man as she calmed herself with deep breaths. He didn't appear to have a weapon or a uniform, although she doubted an island as small as Tuckernuck had a police force. But he was big. He seemed more curious than angry. She still had a sheet in her hand and held onto it while she answered.

"I'm here with the cousin of the owner. We took shelter during the storm. Who are you?"

"A neighbor. We thought we saw lights here during the night and thought it best to check. Len doesn't usually come out till the end of August."

"That was good of you to stop by and make sure everything was OK."

"Where's the cousin?" He looked around.

Something about his tone made Elizabeth wary and reluctant to answer that Caleb was off-island. She rarely assumed menace when confronted by strangers, but she was alone on a barren stretch of a remote island, and her sense of vulnerability was amplified by the physical shock she'd experienced the day before.

"He's inside. I'll go get him." She started to move slowly but deliberately toward the house. She felt the reassuring weight of her phone in her pocket and consciously kept her hand away from it rather than alert the stranger to its presence.

As she got closer to the door she quickened her pace, aware that he was following her.

"I'll be right back," she called to him as she stepped inside and closed the door. She leaned against it, panting, and fumbled with the phone.

"Where are you?" she screamed. She couldn't modulate her voice, her fear was so palpable.

"On my way back. What's wrong?"

She described the encounter with the neighbor and her unspecific but very real fear.

"Do you know how to use a gun?"

"Antonio's uncles hunted. They invited us once and gave me an impromptu lesson."

"There's a pistol locked in the desk. Key is in the middle drawer of the dresser in the bedroom, inside an Altoid tin. Where are you?"

"I'm in the house. I locked the door. Please stay on the phone."

She found the key and the gun. A box of ammunition was in another drawer in the desk. She loaded the gun.

She could hear banging on the door, shouting, the scraping sound of a rock being lifted. She braced herself for the sound of breaking glass. But she realized he knew where Len kept the key to the house and that was what he was looking for. He muttered a curse and yelled through the door.

"You can't fool me. You're a squatter, probably a drug addict. Who brought you here? Your dealer? Your pimp? I'm calling the police. You won't be able to hide from them."

Elizabeth repeated to Caleb what she was hearing through the door.

"He sounds really unhinged. Please hurry."

"Lock yourself in the bathroom. The window there is small and high. Harder for him to get in if he decides to break a window."

"I'm already there. Can you call the Nantucket police or the Coast Guard?"

"I'm going to hang up right now and do that. I'll be there soon. I'm sorry I left you alone."

The phone was silent. She looked down and saw how low the battery level was and debated shutting down to save energy, but decided against it. Caleb would be calling back, would need to know she was still safe.

The man had stopped yelling, which made her more guarded. If she couldn't hear him she had no idea where he was, and she didn't want to look out the window and reveal where in the house she was. Once again, she found herself huddled in fear, the gun she didn't want to have to use clasped in both hands, pointed at the door.

Her sense of unreality, which earlier had been a haze of remembered passion apart from her familiar roles of mother and artist, now engulfed her with its absurdity. Idyllic rural havens weren't supposed to harbor vigilantes. Elizabeth Innocenti, more familiar with pointing a video camera at a scene of beauty or emotional resonance, shouldn't be pointing a gun.

Her phone rang, and she shifted the gun to her dominant hand and swiped with the other.

"I'm at the dock. Are you still safe in the house?"

"I am, but I don't know where he is anymore. He stopped pounding on the door and screaming. Be careful as you approach the house."

"I'm coming up over the rise now. There's an ATV parked by the side of the house but no sign of him. I'm going to approach the front door in a minute. Meet me there."

She slipped out of the bathroom with the gun leading, not sure if the stranger had managed to get into the house. Inching along the wall, she closed the distance between the bathroom and the front door with nothing distracting her except the single-minded objective of reaching Caleb and protecting him.

At the door she pressed her ear against the wood and listened.

"Elizabeth?"

"I'm here. I'm going to open the door."

She held the gun behind her, turned the lock and opened the door only enough for Caleb to slip in sideways. Once in, he put his arms around her and gently took the gun out of her hand.

"Did you see him outside?"

"He was by the shed on his phone. A police boat is on its way. I also called my cousin. He doesn't know this guy, so his claim of checking up on the house may be bogus."

"So we wait?"

"We wait. Are you OK?" He looked at her, as if searching for any visible signs of harm.

"No wounds. Surprised myself with my cold-blooded calm. I will have to thank Zio Guido for teaching me how to load and fire a gun. I will probably start shaking when I truly stop to think about what happened—is happening. But right now, I'm simply angry, furious that someone could encroach upon my well-being, threaten my safety, just because he's a big guy who assumes the worst about people. He thought I was a whore and an addict. I was doing laundry, for heaven's sake!"

Caleb smiled at her tirade. "You amaze me. I'm glad you're on my side."

A siren broke the tranquility. Once again, the cormorants screeched and ascended above the pond. Through the kitchen window they saw the stranger climb into his ATV and speed away on the path leading west away from the house.

"It appears he was not looking forward to the arrival of the police."

Two officers approached the house from the dock and Caleb's phone rang. It was one of the policemen. Caleb assured them that Elizabeth was safe in the house and he was going to open the door to them, but he also pointed out the cloud of dust that followed the intruder.

When Elizabeth had given her statement, the police said they'd had an increase in robberies on the island, apparently drug-related. But they hadn't received a call from the neighbor, as he had claimed he was doing. It was possible he wasn't a neighbor at all, but someone planning to break into the house, only to be surprised by Elizabeth's presence. By the time the police left, it was mid-afternoon. The sheets were dry. The sandwiches Caleb had picked up in Nantucket were still on the boat in the cooler. They shut off the gas, locked the shed and the house, and made their way to the dock. Elizabeth noted with relief that the sea was considerably calmer, but she buckled herself into her life jacket nonetheless.

Caleb fired up the engine, backed away from the dock and pointed the boat north in the direction of home.

They made the journey standing together at the wheel, bodies touching side-by-side. The sea was quiet enough that for most of the trip Caleb needed only one hand on the wheel and kept the other firmly around Elizabeth's waist.

"When you called me and told me you were in danger, I nearly lost it. A whole range of emotions assaulted me—guilt for leaving you alone, frustration that I couldn't be there to project you, fear for your safety."

"But you were there for me. You stayed on the line, you told me where to find the gun, you called the police. I didn't feel alone once I heard your voice."

"But I feel from the start of this trip I've put you at risk."

"They were risks I was quite willing to take. I felt—I continue to feel—safe with you, Caleb. In an exhilarating, freeing way. I think the sex is a manifestation of that, but it's more than letting go of my inhibitions in bed. I feel renewed by what has happened with you. More than renewed. I'm discovering a part of myself that has been hidden, muffled. I'm not sure the old Elizabeth could have handled the intruder with the confidence I did. You gave that to me, that opportunity to be brave, to believe in myself. So please, don't place a guilt trip on yourself. It's been a wild ride, both literally and figuratively, and I wouldn't change a minute of it."

"I've never felt as protective of someone as I do for you. This is a new experience for me, and I will be honest with you. It scares me. From the moment I found you in the shower, to racing back to Tuckernuck after you called me, my predominant mode was fear."

"What were you afraid of?"

He was silent for a moment, staring out at the horizon. Then he turned to her.

"I was afraid I was going to lose you."

So many responses rose within her, each scrambling to be expressed. She thought of her realization in the morning that her real life was in Florence; that her relationship with Caleb, despite the ineffable intimacy they had shared with one another, was a precious interlude and nothing more. A bridge between her profound grief and the acceptance of loss one needed to put one foot in front of the other and continue, as Matteo's mother, as Elizabeth the filmmaker. She didn't want to insult him by labeling their connection as a summer fling. But essentially, that was all it could be. She was returning to Italy. He was staying here to care for Tobias, but eventually he would move on, too. In truth, he *was* going to lose her. They were going to lose each other.

But she found she couldn't say any of those things. Loss was a condition she knew too well. And if she could spare both of them another loss, even for a short time, that is what she would do.

"But you didn't lose me. I'm here. Holding you, and wishing this life jacket weren't acting like a chaperone, keeping us apart." She slipped her hand beneath his jacket, his bare skin warm to her touch, familiar and inviting.

"If this boat had an autopilot I'd make love to you right now on the deck."

"Knowing that has sent a very strong message to my entire body, which thanks you and asks you to hold onto that desire until a soon-to-be-announced time and place." She smiled the smile of a woman who knows deep satisfaction from the man at her side.

As they approached the Cape Poge lighthouse, Elizabeth touched Caleb's elbow, an outward gesture that amplified what she was about to say.

"Would you mind dropping me off in OB instead of taking me back to Innisfree. I don't want to be alone just yet."

"I could stay with you."

"Don't tempt me," she smiled as she shook her head. "You need to get back to Izzy and Tobias, and I'd be wracked with guilt knowing I was keeping you from your responsibilities. It will be good for me to hug my son and surround myself with my noisy, boisterous family. It will take me out of my introspection. If I go back to Innisfree by myself I can only imagine how bereft I will feel watching you pull away from the dock and facing the prospect of an empty bed. Better for me to have a beer with my brother, eat too many apple fritters from Back Door Donuts, and lose a game of Sorry to a cut-throat crowd."

"Back to the real world." He spoke the words as if he'd been eavesdropping on her thoughts. She looked up at him, trying to mask her surprise, her guilt, but without apparent success.

"Don't look so stunned, Elizabeth. I know the past 36 hours have taken us beyond familiar waters in more ways than literally."

"There be dragons," she murmured.

"Have we gone over the edge? Is that why you're rushing back to the bosom of your family?"

"You said it yourself, it's real life awaiting us when we dock."

"Is what we've experienced together not real?"

The conversation was escaping beyond Elizabeth's intent and she did not know how to retrieve it.

"I don't want to be alone tonight. Innisfree is as isolated as Tuckernuck and I still haven't come down from my heightened sense of alertness. My hand still feels like it's clamped around the gun, for God's sake. I thought you understood that. I knew it would place a burden on your family if we were to retreat to Innisfree tonight. I want to be with you, Caleb. To answer your question, was it real? Yes. More real than I have ever known. But it was a separate reality, outside of my life as Matteo's mother, the steward of Innisfree, and a filmmaker with a burning need to make films."

Caleb lifted his hands from the wheel in supplication.

"Truce! I do understand and I shouldn't have pushed you. Tuckernuck was so simple. Two people stranded by a storm that freed us from our obligations to the ones we love. We both lead complicated, interconnected lives. But I'm telling you right now that I don't intend to allow those complications to keep us apart. I'm not a one-night stand kind of guy."

"Nor am I. You're the only man I've been with besides Antonio." She bit her lip, the confession escaping before she had a chance to stop the words from spilling out.

Caleb was silent for a moment, and she thought her revelation had surprised him.

"Then what happened last night is all the more precious. Thank you for honoring me."

She leaned over the bulk of her life jacket to kiss him. "It was you who honored me," she murmured in his ear.

Chapter Twenty-Four

Unsettled

As they neared the Oak Bluffs harbor, Elizabeth placed a call to Sam to announce their arrival and her wish to spend the night, all of which was greeted with both relief and delight.

"We're happy to hear you weathered the storm. Would Caleb like to join us for supper?"

She passed on the invitation, but he shook his head.

"Another time. He's got a family eager to see him as well."

The bustle of civilization surrounded them as they coasted into the public dock around the headland from the ferry landing. It was late Sunday afternoon and, as usual, was accompanied by the weekend arrival and departure of the big ferries. Traffic was swarming, neon-vested officers were whistling, waving and pointing to keep vehicles and pedestrians safely separated, and sun-burned tourists were juggling ice cream cones and plastic bags filled with Chappy t-shirts.

Elizabeth stood on the deck ready to toss a line over a stanchion when she heard her name—or rather, "Mom"—shouted from the dock. Matteo and his cousins came running, helped to secure the boat and grabbed both the cooler and Elizabeth's hands as she disembarked.

Caleb stayed on board. By unspoken agreement, they had abandoned any thought of revealing even the slightest sign of physical affection in front of Matteo. Once on the dock she turned to thank him, placing her back briefly to the boys. She lifted two fingers to her lips and then blew the kiss in his direction. He raised his hand in a salute and then maneuvered the boat out of the slip. She didn't stay to watch as he rounded the cove and sped off in the direction of the Gut and home.

Surrounded by the boys, she made her way through the throng of vacationers, the strollers and dogs and kite fliers and Frisbee tossers reveling in a summer afternoon in Ocean Park. By the time they reached Sam's house, a gin and tonic was waiting for her on the porch and the coals on the grill were glowing. Real life.

In the morning, after a quick stop at a shop on Circuit Avenue to pick up a skirt and blouse that fit her and finally replace the borrowed clothes, Elizabeth took Debbie's car and drove to Lydia's nursing home. She brought with her Lydia's favorite Boston Cream donuts and some coffee from Espresso Love.

They sat on the sun porch and meandered from one topic to the next—Matteo, the state of the world, the state of Innisfree. But then Lydia was apparently done with meandering. Her first donut finished, she wiped her fingers on a napkin and then honed in on the topic that was hovering between them, and the real reason behind Elizabeth's visit.

"So, you've got the house and Byzantium ship-shape, Matteo's having a blast with his cousins running wild all over Cape Poge, and you've reconnected with Izzy Monroe. And yet, despite all this positive energy and good news, I sense that something is, if not tearing at the fabric of your happiness, at the very least is nibbling at the edges, trying to unravel what I applaud you for knitting together of your unsettled life. So what is it, honey?"

"Oh, Granny! I'm hoping you can help me let go of a misguided passion and find a path to another." And Elizabeth shared with her the tale of her thwarted vision of a Wampanoag documentary.

Lydia listened with rapt attention to Elizabeth's description of the night of the hurricane and how it had inspired her to envision a film; the equally fervent redirection from the Monroes; and her final acceptance of the need to relinquish what had been pulling her out of her grief.

"It's been crushing to accept, but I have. I understand. I do. It's just that this film has been inhabiting my dreams, and I don't know where to go now. I'm floundering, where a few days ago I was driven, focused."

"Elizabeth, you're an imaginative artist and you are definitely not a one-trick pony. You've had a rich inner life since you were a girl. You'll find another vision, another dream."

"That's what Caleb said."

"Smart boy. You should listen to him," Lydia answered with a twinkle in her eye. "There's someone else you should listen to. Tobias. Ask him to guide you to what direction your passion should take."

"He's very ill."

"I know. But ask the one question and then sit and wait with him."

Elizabeth kissed her grandmother and promised she would follow her advice.

She sat in the parking lot for several minutes contemplating how to approach the Monroes and ask if she could visit with Tobias. She didn't want them to think she was going to disturb him with her entreaty and make a last-ditch effort with the sachem for permission to make the film. In the end, all she could think of was to be honest with them, and thought it best to do that in person. Summoning her courage, she put the car in gear and drove to the ferry. On a Monday morning the line was short and she was on Chappy and traveling the road to Cove Meadow before she had a chance to reconsider.

She knew that seeing Caleb again was going to set off an emotional cascade entirely separate from her anxiety about speaking to Tobias. Izzy was too astute to miss what was going on between her and Caleb. Elizabeth was a terrible actress, unable to disguise her emotional state. When she was near Caleb she felt as if she was literally crackling with energy, her hunger for him so palpable. How wise was it to reveal that to Izzy, both for her own sake and for Caleb's? They hadn't talked about whether to let anyone know the change in their relationship, although, as they had understood one another wordlessly when the boys met the boat, they weren't ready to be open. As they had realized on Sunday morning, their lovemaking had bound them profoundly, and it was a bond Elizabeth would not weaken by sharing—even with Izzy.

She pulled the car over to the side of the road near the community center and bent her head over hands on the steering wheel. *Slow down, Innocenti.*

Instead of turning off the main road to Cove Meadow, she drove down to the Dike Bridge, left the car by the pond and walked over the bridge to the beach. She kicked off her sandals and strode through the shallows heading north. Except for a lone fisherman and one birder couple with binoculars, she saw no one else and was left to her solitude. At the Jetties she stopped, realizing how far she'd come without registering her surroundings. Breathless from the frenetic pace she'd set for herself, she moved up out of the water and sat down. She berated herself for always being in a rush, for always wanting a definitive answer. She found it challenging to live with ambiguity and she knew that was why she had so quickly sought refuge in the knowledge that at the end of the summer she and Matteo would have to return to Italy. Real life. The phrase battered at her. But she remembered what Caleb had said. Their connection—sexual, emotional—was real. More real than the numbing motions of daily existence that had defined the lost and empty year since Antonio's death.

"What do you want?" she screamed to the sea, but only the birds heard her and flew off.

She rose to her feet, brushed off the sand and started back to the bridge. On an impulse, after she was back in the car, she stopped at the Refuge ticket office.

"Is Caleb Monroe around?" She asked the teenager at the counter.

"I think he's out back by the garage."

Elizabeth found her way and saw him bent over the engine of one of the dark green Refuge trucks that were used to carry tours out to the lighthouse.

"Hey," she called out when she was a few feet away.

He straightened up, wrench in hand and grinned.

"Hey, yourself. This is an unexpected brightening of my day. What brings you to this neck of the woods, or are you on your way home?"

"Not yet. I went to visit my grandmother in Edgartown and then came out here for a walk on the beach to clear my head."

"Is Lydia OK?"

"More than OK. Devouring Boston Cream donuts and dishing out advice."

"Advice you didn't want to hear?"

"No. Yes. Why did you think that?"

"Because you told me you took a walk."

"And…"

"And I've observed you taking vigorous walks when something is troubling you. You want to talk about it, since you seem to have come looking for me."

"She told me you were a smart boy and I should listen to you."

"About the film."

"Yes."

"Is that what you didn't want to hear?"

"She was my last hope. My grandmother, who loves me, refused to coddle me or soften the blow. She told me to let go of this obsession of mine and find another source of fulfillment."

"Did she actually use the word 'obsession'?"

"No. I'm the one who's labelling it. Being honest with myself. A new me seems to be inhabiting the body of the old, stuck Elizabeth."

"I like this unstuck version very much." He smiled. "If my hands weren't covered in engine grease, I'd pull you over here and kiss you."

She leaned in across the engine well and kissed him. "You don't need hands to bring me closer to you."

"So did your walk on the beach help enlighten you, or at least lessen the weight of the world you seem to carry? I'm not being flippant," he added.

"I screamed at the sea and startled a few gulls, and yes, I feel better for it."

She considered ending the conversation, leaving him to his work. But she decided to take one more step toward honesty.

"Lydia had another suggestion, and I'd like to get your opinion."

"Ah, we're getting closer to why you came looking for me."

"I had many reasons. The first and most important being simply the desire to be near you again. I lay in bed last night reliving our time together."

"I did, too. The memories are wonderful, but not as good as the real thing. I missed you…but we're digressing. What did Lydia say?"

"She thought Tobias might be able to guide me toward finding the story I *should* be telling. I don't want to tax him. That's what I need to know. May I speak with him?"

Caleb's expression became grave. Up until the moment she mentioned Tobias his tone had been light and almost playful. She waited. Everything she knew about the Monroes flowed from Tobias. They revered him, and she saw in Caleb's face a struggle to reconcile his desire to protect his grandfather with the slender bonds that now connected her to Caleb.

She reached her hand out to him, ignoring the grease.

"I understand if you say no."

"It's not my decision. It's his. I'll ask him. I think you realize, so many people want a piece of him—his wisdom, his ability to heal the torn and troubled, his hope."

"I do know. And I will abide by whatever he says."

"I appreciate that you've come to me to ask."

"It was the only way I knew. I should leave you to your work."

"I know this sounds trite, but I'll call you."

"Thank you."

She returned to Oak Bluffs and discovered the house empty. Debbie had stuck a note to the back door for her and she took its suggestion, grabbed a beer and a book and retreated to the shaded front porch to wait for everyone's return. When they arrived, pizza boxes in hand, discussion over the pepperoni, mushrooms and artichoke hearts focused on who was returning to Innisfree and when.

As much as the boys had enjoyed their sojourn on Cape Poge in the preceding weeks, it appeared that activities in OB had a stronger pull at the moment.

"Can Matt stay with us a few more days?"

Elizabeth looked to Debbie, who nodded, "Of course."

Sam offered to drive Elizabeth home whenever she was ready. She hadn't shared with Debbie and Sam her encounter with the intruder on Tuckernuck, and she felt awkward revealing her reluctance to be alone at Innisfree when she'd spent over a month there reveling it its solitude. But she wanted to get back, if only to put her life in order and start afresh on whatever was going to replace the Wampanoag film. She did some quick grocery shopping on Circuit Avenue after lunch and then found her brother to take him up on the offer of a ride home.

It became clear as they headed toward Edgartown on Beach Road that Sam saw the drive as an opportunity for more than a superficial chat.

"Are you OK?"

She turned from gazing out the passenger window at Sengekontacket Pond. "Sure. Why do you ask?"

"You've been turned inward since you got back from Tuckernuck. Less engaged than I've seen you recently. Did something happen out there?"

"You mean, besides puking my guts out on a boat being tossed around by the sea like a cat playing with a mouse, and then, when we finally found shelter, collapsing into shock?"

"Why are you just telling me this now?"

"Because you asked, and because I didn't want to scare Matteo."

"Are you sure you're recovered enough to be out at Innisfree alone? You can stay in town with us as long as you want."

"Thanks, Sam. I'm really fine. A little wiped, but the peace and quiet out there will be just what I need."

"Do you feel you made the right decision to come to the Vineyard this summer?"

"Absolutely. Gran was right. Innisfree is a place to heal."

"I've really lost touch with the place. I don't think I could do what you've done. You've put your heart and soul into bringing it back to life. I know what it looked like when I went out to hook up the propane in June and take down the winter shutters. You've worked miracles."

"Hey, thanks. I guess it was a labor of love. It also kept me from sinking into my grief any further than I'd already descended in Florence."

"I can't imagine what I'd do if I lost Deb."

"You'd put one foot in front of the other and keep moving forward for your kids."

"Is that what you're doing?"

"Some days. Other times I want to pull the covers over my head and pretend it's all a bad dream that I'll wake up from."

"Do you think you'll ever be able to love someone again?"

"Where did that come from? I don't know. I hope so, when I'm not so torn between raising Matteo and keeping his father's memory alive and the sense of betrayal I feel to that memory if I love someone else."

"Don't you think Antonio would want you to be happy?"

Elizabeth decided to deflect Sam's probing questions, which were skating too close to the thin ice of her own ambivalence about Caleb. She punched him lightly in the arm.

"What are you planning to do, big brother? Set me up on a blind date or fill out a profile for me on Match.com?"

"No. It seems to me you're doing just fine all by yourself in that department."

"What do you mean?" But she knew exactly what he meant.

"Caleb Monroe. You spend two days on a remote island with him and come back barely able to follow a conversation because your head is stuck back on Tuckernuck and whatever happened there."

She considered sputtering a denial, but realized the futility of dissembling in front of her brother.

"Am I that transparent?"

"Kiddo, you could never hide what you were feeling, even when you were a squirt."

"Do you think Matteo figured it out?"

"Would that be a problem if he did?"

"I'd rather keep it between Caleb and me for the time being. I don't know where it's going just yet. It's too new."

"Understood. But I'm glad for you, sis. You deserve some loving after what you've been through. And Caleb Monroe is a good guy."

"Yeah, he is. Gran thinks so, too."

"You told her?"

"No! We were talking about something else and I mentioned something he'd said. She told me to listen to him."

"What about?"

"Hmm?"

"What were you and Gran discussing?"

"My tendency to be seized by an idea and not let go of it even when the entire world says to drop it."

"Care to elaborate, or was this only between you and Gran."

"I don't mind telling you. I got it into my head that I could be the Ken Burns of the Chappaquiddick Wampanoag, telling their story through film. It wasn't just something I'd been thinking about. I had story boards and I'd started filming. I'd even researched opportunities for grant money."

"And…?"

"I'd missed one critical element in my grand idea. The Wampanoag want to tell their own story. It took three members of the Monroe family to educate me and help me see why I was so obsessed. I've given it up. Painfully. But I know it's the right thing for me to do."

"I had the feeling you were diving deep into something the weekend I brought the Sunfish out to Innisfree. You had that glazed look you used to get in high school when you'd pull an all-nighter working on an AP art project. I suspect the film was tied to your reclaiming your identity."

"You know me well, don't you big brother."

"And are you truly giving it up?"

"You doubt me?"

"As you said, I know you."

"Well, this time I am listening to the voices of reason. I've shelved it. At least figuratively. It's all still sitting on the dining room table at Innisfree and one of the reasons I want to go back is to pack it up. I need to start thinking about an alternative to fill what I fear will be a very large, gaping hole in a creative life that was just coming back into existence."

"I'm sorry. I know your work is part of what defines you. It can feel like a piece of you has been cut off."

"Isn't yours?"

"I'm not passionate about being a financial advisor in the way you are about being a filmmaker. I enjoy the challenges, the analysis, and, especially, finding a good fit between my clients and their investments. I'm good at it. But it doesn't nourish me. I think filmmaking for you is oxygen."

"Can't live without it," she agreed with a smile.

"Any ideas yet on what you'll do next?"

"Not a clue. I'm still in recovery from rejection, nursing my wounds. I'll take long walks on the beach and lie in the hammock at night contemplating the Milky Way. Sooner or later the muse will pay a visit." She was trying to convince herself that would be so.

They had reached the Dike Bridge and Elizabeth hopped out to let the air out of the tires. They spent the remaining forty minutes of the drive in companionable silence, until they reached Innisfree.

"I'm glad you came back this summer. It's good to be a family again. You've been missed."

"I don't think I realized how much I missed you all until I was here. Christmas visits every other year haven't given us much opportunity, have they? Especially for the kids."

"I know this may be too soon to ask, but will you stay in Italy?"

"Of course! How can you ask that! It's Matteo's home." Her response was automatic, the answer to Sam's question so clear that she didn't hesitate.

He didn't respond at first, but seemed surprised by the stridency of her answer. He put his hands up, palms out. "Whoa! You don't need to justify your decision to me. I'm not questioning your intentions. I'm genuinely interested in and care about what happens to you, wherever you decide to live your life. Just know that we'd welcome you if you should decide that home is here."

"Thanks, Sam. I didn't mean to jump all over you for asking."

"And I'm not trying to put any pressure on you to stay."

He enveloped her in a hug. "May the muse descend soon."

Chapter Twenty-Five

Mae's Box

When Sam was on his way Elizabeth wandered down to the pond and poked around for the smooth rocks she collected from beaches wherever she had traveled. Antonio used to tease her that her suitcase was always ten pounds heavier on their return trips thanks to the stones she'd selected with a curator's eye.

She gathered up a handful and rolled them around in her palm, their warmth and weight and water-smoothed edges acting like a string of worry beads to her agitation and weariness. She climbed back up to the house in time for the sunset and a glass of Pinot Noir, avoiding the stack of books and the sketchpad full of roughed out scenes that she'd left in the dining room on Saturday morning. Time enough to deal with them tomorrow.

The pizza at lunch had filled her up and she grazed on cheese and fruit for her supper. But a sudden burst of baking mania seized her—more likely a tactic for avoiding thinking about the upheaval the past few days had introduced into her life. She also figured, if she were busy in the kitchen with measuring and kneading and peeling and slicing, she'd be less focused on her solitude and isolation. She had two pounds of Italian plums and a bag of almonds. A plum tart with a ground almond and butter crust was just the thing to keep her out of trouble.

She pulverized the almonds with Lydia's marble mortar and pestle, a gift Elizabeth had brought from Italy one Christmas. With her hands, she blended the nuts with flour, sugar, nutmeg, an egg and butter, working quickly and lightly, but reveling in the tactile pleasure of turning these humble ingredients into a pastry worthy of the finest pasticceria in Florence. She put the dough in the fridge to rest while she pitted, sliced and sugared the plums. When her fingers were purple and she'd sampled more than enough fruit to insure its quality, she threw open the cupboard under the window to hunt for the battered but venerable tart pan that had been the foundation of many desserts at Innisfree. She'd pulled out every baking implement on the shelves, but the tart pan was not among them. Nor were several other pans Elizabeth remembered. She sat back on the floor and tried to imagine where Lydia might have moved them. Then she remembered something Debbie had mentioned when the discussion about moving Lydia to a nursing home had first been broached. At first, everyone thought she could manage in assisted living, and Lydia had directed the sorting and packing of some of her most beloved kitchen tools to take with her. But when her heart finally issued its warning and it was clear that anything strenuous—even baking—was no longer a possibility, the box of precious tools had been stowed in the loft.

Dusk had settled on the house, so Elizabeth lit the gas lamps and then climbed the ladder to the loft with a large flashlight. She swept the light over the piles of boxes and trunks that had accumulated during the decades her grandparents had owned Innisfree. Some were marked with their contents in Lydia's flourished handwriting—linens, beach toys, sails—and others had peeling labels with the lettering faded and barely legible. Nothing jumped out to indicate kitchenware was lurking within, and so Elizabeth resigned herself to a search box by box for the tart pan.

She'd gotten through one pile of five boxes cloaked in dust and cobwebs, their edges tattered from far too many opening and closings over the years, and rose to move on to the next pile. Her sandal caught on a floorboard that had popped up, probably from the extremes of heat and cold the cottage was subjected to over the years. She lurched forward, breaking her fall against some precariously stacked cartons. She and the boxes went sprawling. The dried-out tape sealing one split and the contents spilled out. After dusting herself off and rubbing her banged knee, she propped the flashlight on a ledge and began to retrieve the scattered items. It was an odd assortment that Elizabeth found difficult to associate with her grandmother—flannel baby clothes that looked homemade, a child-sized deerskin moccasin beaded in the pattern Elizabeth recognized from Mariah's painting, and a thick journal with water-stained cardboard covers. She put everything back in the box and turned it to look for a label. Written on the outside, in Lydia's distinctive script, were the words "Return to Mae."

Elizabeth put the box aside, wondering how long it had sat, forgotten by her usually highly organized grandmother. The existence of the box, its contents, and their owner hovered over Elizabeth's consciousness as she continued her search for the tart pan. Ten boxes later, in an unmarked but conspicuously newer carton than most in the loft, she found the object of her desire. With the tart pan and Mae's box, she retreated from the loft and extinguished the flashlight, but not her curiosity.

Back in the kitchen, she lit the oven, scrubbed the pan and assembled the tart with distracted speed. While it baked, she poured herself another glass of wine and took the box to the dining room.

She swept aside her papers and laptop and carefully unpacked the entire box. Items that hadn't fallen out in the loft were still nestled, carefully wrapped in tissue paper. The patterns on the flannel baby clothes appeared to be from the 1940s. The partner to the moccasin was still in the box, as were a silver rattle engraved with the name Josiah Liam, and some crocheted baby blankets. Mingled with the clothing and woolens were cedar chips and bundles of dried lavender, which explained why everything was still intact, not ravaged by moths or mice.

Whoever had packed the box, either Mae or Lydia, had done so with care. These were cherished things, meant to be preserved. Elizabeth felt a flash of pain for the loss the box represented. The precious memories here—and Elizabeth was convinced that was what they were—had been denied to the Monroe family. In particular, they'd been denied to Josiah.

If it hadn't been so late, she would have driven immediately to Cove Meadow, so urgent was her sense that these things belonged in Josiah's hands.

Elizabeth felt responsible for the neglect the box represented. Her family had withheld this vital piece of the Monroe family's history. She knew it was probably not deliberate on Lydia's part. The distractions of life with three children and the daily needs of this house had no doubt pushed the box further and further into the loft and out of Lydia's mind. Elizabeth always had a vague sense that the relationship between her family and the Monroes was fraught. Once again, the word "usurper" popped into her brain. The Hammonds had bought Innisfree, not confiscated it, but Elizabeth knew the sale had been filled with pain for Mae and Tobias, and by extension to their children and Caleb.

She refolded the baby clothes with care, smoothing the soft, faded flannel. It had been many years since her hands had been occupied with such a task. She'd miscarried a baby late in her pregnancy three years after Matteo was born, and it was Antonio who had packed away the baby clothes and dismantled the crib in the nursery. She didn't conceive again. At first because she wasn't ready to risk another loss as searing. With the flannel under her fingertips, she relived the night she'd been aware of the sudden stillness in her womb after she'd been feeling the baby kicking and poking; the agonizing realization that life was seeping out of her as blood streamed down her thighs and stained the sheets. When those memories had blurred enough for her to try again, Antonio was diagnosed, and bringing another child into the world when Antonio's future was so uncertain seemed like a reckless indulgence.

Elizabeth pushed the tears away. She'd not thought about those babies in years—the dead baby and the never-conceived one. She'd certainly seen baby clothes since those fragile years, but they had never elicited such an emotional, shattering response. Their connection to Josiah must have been the trigger. They reminded her that the taciturn man whose son didn't believe he knew how to be happy had worn these outfits. Outfits that someone had sewn with tiny, closely spaced stitches; washed countless times, probably well before Innisfree had a washing machine; and then stored lovingly with the intention of preserving them.

That someone had to be Mae. If Elizabeth had ever met her, she didn't remember. Mae had never come to Innisfree with Tobias, and so, in her childhood, Elizabeth's impressions of Mae were remote, almost mythical. Mae was the heroine of Innisfree's story, a woman of grit and spirit who had wrestled nature in its forms of fire and water and who had triumphed, at least for a time, well before Elizabeth's birth.

The thick journal that had tumbled out of the box in the loft still lay on the dining table. Elizabeth reached out her hand and stroked it as gently as she had the flannel pajamas. She knew she should put it back in the box, retape the worn edges of the carton, and put it in the Jeep so that she could return it to the Monroes with her apologies.

But the piercing memories the contents had evoked stirred her curiosity. How many times, she told herself, had she read the moldering journals and letters of women in the course of her research for her films. She felt a strong desire to understand the woman who had made and saved these things, who had considered them precious, and then forgotten them in the attic when she left this homestead she'd created against incredible odds.

Elizabeth picked up the journal and turned its stiff cover. The first several pages were familiar to Elizabeth the historian: lists of provisions, recipes for pies and cakes and chicken salad, dates recording weather and trips to Edgartown, counts of customers and popular menu items. But as familiar as the information was, and an interesting window into the mid-century operation of the Boat House Café, Elizabeth was disappointed. She had sought insights and found only inventories.

With her disappointment mounting, she flipped a few more pages, expecting more of the same. And then, a pressed flower fell to the table, its petals nearly translucent and the tiny bit of greenery attached to the stem just a breath away from dust. Elizabeth didn't dare touch it, convinced it would disintegrate if she did. She took two sheets of paper from her pile of notes and slid one under the flower while nudging it with the sheet. When it was safely resting, still whole, on the notepaper, she slipped the flower back into the journal. On the bottom of the page where the flower had been pressed she found a notation in Mae's handwriting.

"First flower to bloom on the rugosa bush planted by Tobias when Josiah was born."

Elizabeth knew that the beach roses grew rampant along the edge of the lawn overlooking the bay. It had never occurred to her there had once been a time when there had been none. But here was evidence that they had gotten their start at Tobias' hand. She wondered if "her" hummingbird had nested in that original bush.

After her discovery of the flower, Elizabeth held her breath and gently turned the page. She found what she'd been longing for—a record of Mae's thoughts and emotions, written as a letter to her son.

Dear Josiah,

As I write this I am sitting in the sun, listening to your gleeful screams as you fly higher and higher in the swing Daddy built for you…

Elizabeth stopped reading, interrupted by the ding of the timer she'd set for the plum tart. She placed a piece of paper into the journal to mark the start of Mae's letter and reluctantly set the book down to tend to her baking.

She slid the tart from the oven. The aromas of the buttery crust and the plums, glittering with caramelized sugar, awakened a lost memory. It surprised her that she was transplanted by her nose not to Lydia's kitchen, but to her own *cucina* in the villa. She'd learned to make the tart from her grandmother and it was one of the few things she knew how to do with confidence before she began her cooking lessons with Carmella. The first time she'd baked it for Antonio was the night she'd told him she was pregnant. He had pulled her into his lap and they'd eaten the tart from the same plate with a single fork. His kisses had been sticky with plum juice.

Was that what had prompted her to bake the tart tonight, to pull her back from Caleb to Antonio, to remind her once again that she was Matteo's mother and her place was in that kitchen in the villa?

She left the tart on top of the stove to cool and tried to shake off the waves of grief and guilt that assaulted her.

It's just a pastry, she told herself.

The mixing bowl and measuring cups were soaking in the sink and she attacked them, hoping to obliterate her discomfort with hot water and a sponge. By the time she hung up the dish towel and extinguished the gaslight over the sink, she was too tired to continue reading Mae's journal. She admitted to herself that it was more than fatigue keeping her from returning to that evocative description of a happy, energetic little boy.

She knew one of the things driving her to find Mae within the pages of the worn and forgotten book was a desire to understand more about Caleb through his grandmother. She knew Caleb had not yet been born when Mae was writing the journal, so it wasn't a search for direct information. She had hoped simply to deepen her knowledge of this complex man through his family's history and its intersection with her own. Elizabeth was acutely aware of elements of her own personality that were a reflection of Lydia. She'd assumed she'd discover Mae had exerted a similar influence on Caleb.

But now, interrupted by the memory of sharing the tart with Antonio, she questioned her motives. She recognized that what she was doing in reading the journal was an invasion of privacy. Mae's words were meant for Josiah. Elizabeth was ashamed that she'd tried to justify her search by invoking her desire to better understand her lover.

"What a crock," she muttered to herself, one of Sam's favorite phrases to describe the convoluted excuses we summon to justify our outrageous behavior.

As she placed the journal in the box, she told herself to let go of this need to know Caleb more intimately. She was leaving at the end of the summer. Why intensify the pain that was sure to accompany that departure?

She slept fitfully, a part of her brain on constant alert for unusual noises—not the sounds of wind or sea or nocturnal animals on the hunt, but footsteps, splintering glass, creaking hinges. All the signals her imagination conjured for someone breaking into the house. She pounded the pillows as a substitute for drumming into her brain the message that she was being foolish. It didn't work.

Daylight brought no relief to her agitation, and she gave up any hope of rest around five in the morning. Mae's box sat where she'd left it the night before, a blunt reminder of her confused longing. To remove its temptations, she picked it up and stowed it in the back of the Jeep.

After a swim and breakfast, she considered driving to Cove Meadow to deliver the box. Caleb had promised he'd call after speaking to Tobias, and she checked her phone obsessively, like a teenager hoping to hear from her boyfriend. But she found no messages. She didn't want to take any missteps with the Monroes and drove herself slightly crazy dithering between arriving unannounced and calling ahead. Finally she settled on telling the truth. It was Izzy who answered the phone.

"Elizabeth! How are you after your adventure on the high seas?"

"Still in recovery. I don't think I'll be going fishing on the Sound for a while. Listen, I was wondering if I could stop by briefly to drop something off for Josiah."

"For Josiah?" Izzy's tone was more skeptical than curious.

"I found a box in the loft when I was searching for something else. I believe it belongs to him."

"How odd."

"It's very old. I guess it was left by mistake and then forgotten. May I stop by today?"

"Of course. I'll be here all day."

"Then I'll come now, if that's convenient. I won't stay long."

Elizabeth ended the call with a sense of foreboding. Her few encounters with Josiah had been nearly wordless, and given what she understood from Caleb about his father, she had no idea how he might react to the discovery of the box. But the longer the box stayed in her possession the more she felt a prisoner to it, torn between wanting to shed light on the Monroe family and her need to maintain distance between Caleb and herself.

She grabbed her keys and, at the last minute, the tart. She strode out to the car, determined to be done with the task. When she pulled into the driveway at Cove Meadow she saw with dismay that Caleb's truck was there. She had counted on a short visit with clear boundaries, and Caleb's presence complicated her plans. She went around the back of the Jeep to retrieve the box and was startled by his voice behind her.

"Hey. I didn't know you were back. Thought you were still in OB at Sam's."

"He drove me home yesterday afternoon. I needed to be in my own space, get my life back in order."

She avoided commenting that he would have known where she was if he had called. Instead, she concentrated on maneuvering the box out of the car.

"I can help you with that, if you'll let me."

"I've got it. Thanks."

"What's wrong, Elizabeth? And why are you here?"

"Nothing's wrong, except another sleepless night after an evening of not hearing from you. God, I feel like I'm fourteen years old waiting for the phone to ring."

"I'm sorry. I worked a double shift yesterday. One of the other guys called in sick."

She was too exhausted and too emotionally drained to question why he couldn't have found a few minutes on his rounds to call or even stop by, as he'd often done in the past. He would have seen the lights, known she was there. Instead, she retrieved the plum tart, balanced it on top of the box and moved toward the house. She didn't want to fight with him in front of his family.

At that moment Izzy pushed open the screen door and Elizabeth forced a smile onto her face.

"Hi, Lili. Do you need help with that carton?" She asked while looking pointedly over Elizabeth's head toward Caleb.

"It's not that heavy. I'm fine. If you could just grab the tart before it slides off…" And Elizabeth stepped over the threshold into the house.

"Is Josiah here?"

"He's up the road at his and Grace's place. They just got back from their weekend away. But I called to let him know you were on your way. He should be here any minute. Can I offer you a cup of coffee? We could have a slice of this delicious-smelling tart."

"No, but thanks. I can't stay long. Please enjoy the tart yourselves."

"Are you OK, honey?"

"Sure. Just tired. I haven't slept well the past few nights."

Izzy leaned back against the kitchen counter, folded her arms and studied Elizabeth for a few minutes.

"I know I haven't spent a lot of time with you since you were a child, but I feel I've gotten to know you this summer, and there are some things about you that haven't changed."

"Like what?" Elizabeth knew, as soon as she asked, that she was giving Izzy an opening she wasn't sure she wanted Izzy to walk through.

"Like your inability to mask your feelings. Something's going on with you that has nothing to do with lack of sleep."

Elizabeth was about to protest when she heard Josiah's voice on the porch talking to Caleb, who had remained outside. She turned toward the door as both of them came into the kitchen.

"Hi. Izzy told me you'd found something of mine up at the house?" Framing his words as a question revealed his skepticism.

Elizabeth gestured at the box on the table.

"I think my grandmother intended to give it to Mae, but I'm afraid it got buried under a pile of other boxes and was forgotten. I'm so sorry."

Josiah shrugged. "It can't have been too important if Mom didn't mention it. Why did you think it was for me?"

Elizabeth felt her face redden and she stumbled over her words.

"The contents of the box spilled when I accidently knocked into the pile it was in. As I put things back it appeared that they were your baby things. Do you want to take a look?"

Josiah's face was impassive, but he approached the box and lifted the lid.

A glimmer of a smile briefly lit his face as he peeled back a layer of tissue paper and found the moccasins. He stroked them lightly with his fingertips.

"My grandmother beaded these. I remember looking for them when you were born," he turned to Caleb. "Mom was in and out of Mass General at the time, her head fogged with all the drugs. She must not have remembered leaving the box at Innisfree."

Elizabeth thought she was going to cry. The loss to Josiah and his family that her grandmother's neglect had caused was threatening to engulf her, despite Josiah's calm reaction to the discovery. She couldn't stay any longer as he unpacked the box, especially if he was going to leaf through the journal. Her presence would only be a reminder of where the box had been all these years.

"I've got to be on my way. I only wanted to deliver the box, so I'll leave you to what I hope are happy memories. Once again, I'm so sorry that it went missing for so long."

Josiah said nothing as she left. Izzy continued to watch her with concern. But Caleb followed her out to the porch and reached for her as she stepped onto the gravel driveway.

"Thank you, Elizabeth. As I've mentioned, my father is a man of few words and even fewer emotions. Whatever the contents of that carton may mean to him, I want you to know that *I* am grateful. Who knows, maybe something in there will trigger his return to us."

Elizabeth nodded, pushing away her tears.

"I think that's what I hoped when I realized Mae had saved those things for him. I hope it's not too late."

Caleb put his arm around her and she didn't try to shrug out of his embrace.

"I'm sorry I didn't call, and also sorry I offered that idiotic excuse. The truth is I was bouncing off walls wanting to be with you, but trying to rein myself in. I felt like I had jumped off a cliff into churning water expecting to find you leaping with me, only when I looked back you were crouched on the rocks, unable to make the plunge."

"I think that's a pretty accurate analogy. Since we left the bubble of Tuckernuck, I've been bouncing, too. But I can't have this conversation here in your grandfather's driveway with your father and your aunt a few feet away. Are you working today, or did your double shift earn you a few hours off?"

"I'm not on duty again till tomorrow morning."

"Then come to Innisfree for the day."

"And the night? Or are the boys back?"

"The boys are still in OB. So, yes, the night as well."

"I'll be there in a few hours. I've got a few things to take care of here."

"That's fine. I need to do some grocery shopping and return books to the library. Later then?"

"Later."

He kissed her lightly and waited till she was on the road before he turned back to his family.

Chapter Twenty-Six

Duty

When Elizabeth returned to Innisfree she dealt with the dining table, knowing that if she postponed the task, the piles of books and sketches and notes would only haunt her, a tangible reminder of her failure and disappointment. At first, she sorted and organized the stacks before packing them away, as if she might return to the material someday. But the futility of that expectation soon convinced her she was engaging in magical thinking. She retrieved the banker's box she'd picked up at da Rosa's in Oak Bluffs, placed it on a chair, and swept the entire contents of the table top into the box. It was heavier than anticipated when she lifted it. She thought about lugging it up to the loft, where it could linger as Mae's box had, hidden and forgotten until some descendant of hers—a grandchild or great-grandchild—discovered it. In the end, she stowed it on a shelf in the Linnet cottage. Perhaps she could donate some of it to the historical museum in Edgartown or even the Wampanoag museum in Aquinnah, if they would have it. She only knew she wanted it out of her sight and soon out of the house.

When the table was bare and wiped of the dust of old books and old dreams, she spread a clean tablecloth over it and set the table for two places side by side looking out over the water.

By the time she had most of dinner prepared Caleb arrived with a bouquet of Gerbera daisies and a bottle of Malbec. He put both the flowers and the wine on the table and took her wordlessly into his arms.

He held her fiercely, as if they'd been separated for two months instead of two days. The ambivalence that had kept her ricocheting between desire and duty fled the moment he embraced her. His kisses were a counterpoint to the enveloping strength in his arms—tender, tentative, exploratory, as if he were tasting some unknown substance that might just as well be poison as ambrosia. As she responded, leaning into his intensity, she gasped for air, feeling herself beginning to drown in her own need. She knew at that moment she had followed him over the cliff.

"Come to bed," she finally managed to utter, and pulled him through the house and into her room.

The sun had begun its descent and cast a swath of reddish gold light across the bed, illuminating their bodies as they celebrated one another. The push and pull of her emotions since they'd returned from Tuckernuck played out in their lovemaking. They were no longer cocooned in the storm, where the first time, sex had been about comfort and safety, and the morning after had been playful and freeing.

This time, in this house full of memories, they came to one another questioning, seeking. For Elizabeth, the questions were for herself as well as for him. The tension generated by their hunger to know one another intensified the linking of their flesh. There was no comfort or safety in this bed. They were on the edge of the world, explorers of unknown waters, and those waters were turbulent and dark, despite the piercing light of the setting sun.

Her orgasm obliterated thought and breath; his was marked by a throbbing pulse in his neck, hands locking hers above her head in an unbreakable link, and the gasps of a man engulfed.

When he collapsed at her side, they were drenched, the sheets soaked, their hair tangled and slick. He still held one of her hands. With the other hand she leaned over and stroked his neck where the pulse had slowed but was still visible, a life force pushed to extremes by desire—the desire to bond, the desire to know.

They had barely spoken ten words to one another since his arrival. And yet, crucial information had passed between them that now needed to be acknowledged.

She didn't know where to begin, and reached back to a Latin phrase that had guided her filmmaking. *In medias res.* "Into the middle of things."

"I'm afraid," she said, and he turned to face her.

"I'm afraid of the boundary we seem to have crossed this evening. Until now, I could still convince myself this was a summer fling, a welcome reawakening of my sexual self. Something I was grateful for, but from which I could return to what I have always considered to be my life."

"But now?" He still held her, his face so close to hers that his breath glanced down her cheek and into the hollow of her throat.

"I cannot go back."

"You can't go back to Italy?" She heard the glimmer of hope in his voice.

"No. I mean I can't go back to who I was before. Although that may also mean I can't go back to Florence. But I must. I'm afraid of the intensity of this." She waved her hand, gesturing between them and then, in a wider arc meant to encompass Innisfree.

"I have had so little control over my life since Antonio became ill. The decision to spend the summer here was the first step in reclaiming my life. But once again, I find myself out of control."

"I'm not trying to control you, Elizabeth. I'm not making any demands."

"It's not you. I didn't mean it in that way. It's something beyond us—this place, perhaps and what it elicits from us. Something primal. When I am with you, when we are making love, you touch a part of me that has been buried. You ignite a longing that both thrills and petrifies me. I don't know what to do with it. I don't know what to do with you and my feelings for you."

"I don't know what to do with you, either. It's why I stayed away. In the past two days I have careened between shutting down as completely as my father, and wanting to possess and be possessed by you."

"When I came just now, I felt myself dissolve. I lost the edges of myself and couldn't distinguish where I ended and you began. In the past, I've always held a piece of myself apart, an observer of Elizabeth in the arms of her lover. That didn't happen tonight."

"Whenever I touch you I surrender rational thought, caution, hesitation. I don't want anything between us—not doubt or distrust or duty."

"That's it, isn't it? We are both dutiful, and yet together, we abandon duty. But we both know that ultimately we won't shirk our responsibilities."

"We're torturing ourselves."

"This is why I go down to the sea and scream."

"We aren't going to solve this tonight. Feed me. Allow me to bask in the homecoming this evening is, inhabiting Innisfree with you. Then we can come back to bed and lose ourselves again in the oblivion of sex."

Elizabeth threw on a gauze dress she'd bought in Mykonos as a college student and retreated to the kitchen to finish cooking the simple meal she'd begun hours before.

Caleb, clad only in his jeans, poured them each a whiskey and watched her as she quickly sautéed some pounded chicken breasts and doused them with wine.

"Why did you call this evening a homecoming?"

"I think every Monroe carries a genetic marker for Innisfree, despite how long it has been since my grandmother carved it out of the wilderness. In the wintertime, Tobias and I used to hunt in the woods. When I got older I helped him open and close the cottage for your grandmother. When your family wasn't here, I pretended Innisfree was still ours."

"I remember that first night when you brought me back from my wandering on East Beach and you lit the lamp for me. I sensed that this house was familiar to you in a profound way."

"Innisfree abides with me," he said, touching his heart.

"I'm glad I've been your way back home."

Later that night, after lying wordless in the hammock mesmerized by the Perseid meteor shower, they made love again. This time with a languid tenderness rather than the raw hunger that had driven them earlier.

"Do you think that Innisfree is part of what binds us to one another?" Elizabeth asked.

"Mae and Tobias made love in this room. Your grandparents must have also. These walls have held our families at their most intimate moments. So yes, Innisfree binds us."

She lay in his arms and listened to the voices of the wind and the sea and the house that echoed Caleb's heartbeat, lulling her once again to safety, at least for a few hours.

Chapter Twenty-Seven

"Did you know that Innisfree means heaven?"

The next morning it was the rumble of an outboard motor in the pond and then human voices whooping in the yard that added another layer to the sounds of Innisfree. Caleb was in the kitchen, barefoot and shirtless, scrambling eggs. Elizabeth was making the bed and saw her phone on the night table had a message. But before she had time to listen to it, the kitchen screen door slammed and Matteo's voice called out to her.

"Hey, Mom! Uncle Sam let us take the Whaler by ourselves 'cause he had a meeting and we were bored in OB. Did you get my mess…" His voice froze as Elizabeth entered from the living room.

"Good morning, Matt," Caleb calmly greeted him, stepping in to fill the silence and defuse the anger and confusion written on Matteo's face.

"Hi, honey. Welcome back. Have you boys had breakfast?" Elizabeth took her cues from Caleb's untroubled reaction to Matteo's unexpected arrival, trying to still her agitation.

Instead of answering her, Matt turned and left, retracing his steps and probably intending to head off his cousins and keep them from entering the house and finding Caleb half-dressed in his mother's kitchen.

Elizabeth buried her head in her hands. "Shit."

Caleb kissed the top of her head.

"He was going to find out eventually."

"But not like this."

"It's messy. But not the end of the world. Matt has just learned that his mother is a human being. I suggest I put on some more clothes and we make a big batch of pancakes."

Elizabeth braided her unruly hair and put an apron on over her t-shirt and shorts, trying to appear as a facsimile of the woman Matteo had believed his mother to be.

All was quiet, both in and around the house. She got to work pulling together the pancakes while Caleb went scouting for the boys. He returned a few minutes later to report that Matt had steered them to Byzantium, where they had dumped their duffle bags.

"Why don't I take them fishing out at the Gut for a couple of hours? It will give Matt some space to cool down. And if he's angry, he can take it out on me and the bluefish."

She smiled in gratitude. "You're the best. A saint. A martyr."

"Will I have to wait for heaven to receive my reward?"

"Did you know that Innisfree means heaven?"

"I think I've heard that."

He kissed her, lingering to prolong what was probably going to be their last opportunity for a while.

"Not fair," she mumbled. "Getting me all aflutter when we can't do anything about it."

"Aflutter? Is that a word?"

"Whether it is or not, it describes accurately the leaping and flitting of my spirit, not to mention my flesh, when you touch me. I could kill my brother right now."

"I'm glad to hear you placing blame on someone other than yourself. We've done no wrong, Elizabeth, expressing our feelings by making love. No one was hurt. Not even Matt. He didn't see us in bed. He saw me in the kitchen early in the morning."

"Still, he made the assumption you hadn't just arrived."

"Trust me. He'll survive."

"And not hate us for ending his innocence? How can you be so sure?"

"Because I was once a teenage boy who had a similar experience. I'll tell you about it someday. But right now, I think we need to feed these teenage boys and get them out of here."

Elizabeth, although intrigued by Caleb's comment, agreed to postpone her curiosity and rang the bell Lydia had hung to summon generations of Innisfree children to the table.

When the boys stomped into the house like a herd of hungry buffalo, Elizabeth and Matteo avoided eye contact. Geoff, the older of the cousins, addressed Caleb.

"You're here early."

Elizabeth wanted to smack him.

Without skipping a beat, Caleb answered him. "Stopped on my way to fish at the Gut. Any of you guys interested in joining me?"

"Can we go in the Whaler instead of over sand?" Kyle had apparently not yet had enough of the motorboat.

Another reason to kill her brother, Elizabeth thought, but kept her threat to herself.

Matt remained silent, pulled out his chair with a jerk and slumped into it. His sulk was not enough to curb his hunger, however, and he piled the pancakes on his plate.

With their mouths full the boys didn't have much opportunity to ask any more questions, and Elizabeth spent most of the meal at the stove frying more bacon for the hungry horde. Within a half hour they'd consumed three dozen pancakes and were out of the house, grabbing poles and their grandfather's tackle box of lures out of the shed.

She walked down to the dock and saw them off with relief. Nothing like a noisy engine to distract a group of boys. Caleb actually looked like he was having fun as they steered out of the pond and across the bay.

She put the kitchen back in order and was about to call Sam and read him the riot act when she heard another motor approaching the house. At first she was confused by what she saw through the window. It was the boat Caleb had taken her on to Tuckernuck. But, of course, it was Josiah's boat. He was tying it off on the dock.

She waited up at the house, not at all sure he'd come to see her. Perhaps he was looking for Caleb, although he would have called his son, rather than travel all the way from Cove Meadow. Perhaps he simply wanted to spend some time at Innisfree. Her brain, between the night of sex and the morning of dismay, was mush. So she stayed in the kitchen and watched him.

He moved slowly, not like an old man but like someone listening, tracking, absorbing his surroundings. Elizabeth wondered how long it had been since he'd been here. Many years, she surmised. He stopped halfway to the house and looked back at the meadow and the cedar woods. He turned again toward the house and skimmed his hand along a bayberry bush on the side of the driveway. He came away from it with a cluster of leaves in his palm and brought them to his nose.

When he reached the yard, instead of approaching the house he walked over to the point where the pond and the bay met. The flag was whipping around the post and Elizabeth realized Matt must have hung it, the sign used by everyone at Cape Poge to indicate they were home.

Elizabeth continued her watch, reluctant to intrude upon Josiah's contemplation of his beloved home. To busy herself she started a pot of coffee.

He must have read the journal, she thought. What else could have driven him back here? She wished Caleb were here to see his father like this, because Josiah did not appear to be brooding. If Elizabeth were to describe his face, his stance, she would call it a fierce joy.

Finally, she heard her name called out.

"Elizabeth, are you home?"

She went to the front door, where Josiah was standing a few feet back, taking in the whole house.

"Hey, Josiah. Welcome." She opened the screen door and waved him in. "Would you like a cup of coffee?"

He stepped into the living room and cast his eyes around the space.

"It's been a long time since I was willing to set foot in this house."

"I'm honored, then. I'm glad you're here."

"Where's Caleb? I saw his truck outside."

"He took Mateo and my nephews fishing."

"He's good with your boy."

"Yes, he is. Would you like that cup of coffee?"

"Sure. Do you mind if I look around?"

"Of course not!"

Elizabeth retreated to the kitchen. She heard Josiah moving through the living room. She'd pulled closed the curtain separating her bedroom and wondered if he'd draw it open and look in. She'd made the bed, but she couldn't remember if Caleb had left anything of his on the bedside table. She shook her head. What were the odds that both Matt and Josiah would show up today and become witnesses to the deepening bond between her and Caleb?

She carried in the mugs of coffee and found Josiah standing by the window seats at the southern end of the room.

"This used to be my nursery," he said, gesturing at the alcove. "Dad had built a wall here to set it apart from the living room. I didn't know it had been taken down."

Elizabeth handed him the coffee.

"You must think it odd of me to show up like this."

"No. Not at all. I wish I'd thought to invite you sooner."

"I came to thank you."

Elizabeth accepted his thanks. "I only hope that you forgive us for neglecting the box for so long."

"If there's anyone to forgive, it's my mother."

"I don't understand."

"Your grandmother didn't forget about the box. My mother asked her to keep it."

"How do you know?"

"It was in the journal."

Elizabeth waited. For so many reasons she wanted to know about Mae and the journal—to better understand Caleb; to help him build a connection to his distant, estranged father; to unravel the complex, heavily laden relationship between her family and the Monroes, and between all of them and Innisfree. But she only had a way into that knowledge if Josiah would lead her there.

"Do you have time for us to talk?" Josiah asked.

She let out the breath she wasn't aware she'd been holding.

"I do. I'd love to talk. Do you want to sit outside?"

They went out through the French doors to the patio overlooking the bay. They could enjoy its beauty, but they'd also be able to see the Whaler as it returned from the Gut.

"I'm not as articulate as my son," he apologized. "Caleb took after Grace in that regard. He and I, well, we've had some tense moments over the years. Not unlike my mother and me. I was angry with him, especially, for going into the military. He had an Ivy League education, a good job. It wasn't like my situation, when I was a floundering eighteen-year-old who didn't know who he was. I knew what war does to a man, and I didn't understand why he would choose it. When I saw his truck here, I almost turned the boat around. But I thought, at least I could say thank you, if nothing else. I'm glad I found you alone. I need to speak to someone who doesn't carry the same baggage I do. I thought, because it was you who found the journal and brought it to me, that you might be willing to listen."

"I would be honored to listen to you."

"Thank you. May I ask you something first? It will make a difference in how I tell you my story."

"Ask away."

"Did you read the journal before you gave it to me?"

"I'll be honest. I wanted to. I wanted so much to know who Mae was, and I kept turning all those pages of lists, hoping to get to something meaningful. And then, when I found the opening page of her letter to you, I realized I couldn't go on. She meant those words for you. So I closed the book and packed up the box. I even put it out in the car so I wouldn't be tempted in the middle of the night. I'm a historian. Mae's journal is manna to someone like me." She distanced herself from her personal desire to understand Mae, hoping to keep her relationship with Caleb outside of this conversation. She was afraid that Josiah might retreat into his silence if he knew about the bond between Elizabeth and his son.

He was silent a moment, as if weighing her words, assessing their truthfulness.

"Thank you. For answering me honestly and for respecting the special nature of my mother's journal. I have to tell you, I don't know why I need to talk about this after all these years, but your finding the box and returning it to me—well, it's opened up wounds. But it's also opened up my heart. Maybe it will help me find a way to heal the rift with my son.

"It's been nearly twenty years since my mother passed away. That she lived as long as she did, that she overcame cancer twice, everyone called a miracle. But my mother was the miracle, a savior. She saved Innisfree, first from dereliction and then from a devastating fire; she saved my father from a murder rap; she saved me from the obsessive clutches of my Aunt Kathleen, who saw me more as an accessory than a child to love.

"My childhood was idyllic. If you read those first lines of the journal, that is what I remember from that time—screaming with glee as I soared over the grass, my mother restored to me and smiling over me, my dad showing me how to build and hunt and fish. I was loved. I was cherished.

"And then I threw all that away, in anger and guilt, because I thought losing Innisfree meant losing who we were, who I was."

Elizabeth listened as Josiah's words, at first cautious and hesitant, gathered momentum. This man, who had remained in the background, silent and watchful since her arrival on Chappy, was now revealing himself. She didn't know why he'd chosen her to be the recipient of his confession—for that is what this recitation of his past appeared to be. Yes, he'd told her when he started that he'd come to her because she'd found the journal. But it wasn't true that she was without baggage, a neutral third party. She had a stake in this conversation, because of the tangled relationship between the Monroes and the Hammonds and because of Caleb.

Elizabeth was anguished by the honesty and painful insights Josiah was placing before her, like some sacrificial offering of atonement. These words should have been uttered to his mother, to his son. Perhaps Josiah recognized the pain would have been too much for them to bear. And it was too late to seek forgiveness from Mae. Would Josiah, after his revelations to Elizabeth, feel freed from his secrets and reach out to Caleb?

She glanced out at the bay, willing Caleb to stay away long enough for Josiah to finish.

"When I left Chappy, I was full of rage. My identity as a Wampanoag was tethered to the land, a fragile thread that was being eaten away over the years by a seed of doubt planted by my father's cousin Sadie."

"The bitter old woman who was at your house during the hurricane."

"That's the one. She'd been a fiery activist for the Chappaquiddick Wampanoag. When I was fourteen, I overheard her tell my father I wasn't a "true" Wampanoag, that I'd eventually deny my tribal roots and go to the dark side—my white mother's family."

"Which is what you did…"

"Yeah. When my mother sold Innisfree, she severed the thread that was holding me together, keeping those two sides of my identity intact."

"Because Innisfree was both originally tribal land *and* your mother's creation. Her legacy."

"Exactly. I blamed my mother, and wanted to punish her. So I left and turned to the family she'd run away from."

"But you came back. You raised Caleb here. And from what I gleaned when Matteo and I took shelter with you during the hurricane, you and Grace appear to be very much a part of the tribe."

"Thanks to Grace—and my father. He's still the sachem. Revered. I'm accepted, welcomed back as the prodigal son by those old enough to remember my rebellion, mainly out of respect for Tobias. I've made my peace with the tribe."

Elizabeth hesitated, but then spoke out loud the thought that had entered her head. Josiah had come to her, had revealed the edges of his past, a past that was generally known on the island. But Elizabeth guessed there was more, and felt emboldened to ask.

"But you haven't made peace with yourself, have you?"

Josiah studied her, then shook his head with a slight smile.

"My father warned me about you."

"What do you mean?"

"He said you were as direct as your grandmother."

"Direct?"

"Well, he actually used the word blunt. He told me that I should be prepared to tell the truth, because that is what you'd extract from me."

"You make us sound like torturers. Is that what this is for you, torture?"

"Not at all. You're a good listener. You hear between the words. And to answer your question, no, I haven't made peace with myself. This place has haunted my dreams for over forty years. Sitting here with you now, I see the shadow of the Boat House; I hear my mother's voice, humming as she baked her pies; I smell the wood fire; I taste the clams—both the raw ones we raked up and ate right down on the flats and the chowder simmering on the stove in the café."

"You are welcome here any time, Josiah. I hope you know that."

"To be welcomed is not the same as to belong. And I don't mean that Innisfree once belonged to me, to us. I mean that I once belonged to Innisfree. It claimed me."

Elizabeth did not diminish his pain by claiming she felt the same way about the land. Because she understood she couldn't fathom the depth of his connection. She let the silence settle between them.

A hummingbird swept across the lawn and hovered over the rugosa bush at the edge of the water.

"The hummingbirds still nest here." *But I do not.* Elizabeth heard the unspoken part of Josiah's observation.

"Would you like to walk around? With or without me, it's up to you."

"Thanks. Perhaps another time."

He got up and carried his coffee mug into the house. Elizabeth followed him into the kitchen, where she saw on his face the same fleeting expression she'd noticed on Caleb when he'd lit the gas lamp for her so many weeks ago. Longing. Loss. Regret.

Josiah reached out his hand to her, calloused, brown, firm.

"Thanks again."

"You're welcome. Please give my regards to Tobias. Tell him I take his warning to you about me as a compliment."

"That's how he meant it."

"I know."

And then he was gone, down to the dock and onto his boat. Elizabeth washed out the mugs and put them back on the shelf. She wasn't ready for Caleb to ask questions about who had been here.

Chapter Twenty-Eight

Peace Offering

Two hours later Caleb and the boys arrived back from the Gut lugging a cooler filled with stripers. They got to work immediately on the scarred and weathered table outside the kitchen, gutting and scaling the fish. Elizabeth watched from the window as her son deftly slipped the knife under the skin and pulled out the intestines. He'd learned to do that this summer, she realized, from the man standing next to him at the table now nodding encouragement.

Caleb looked up and exchanged a glance with Elizabeth that offered her reassurance. She smiled and turned away to peel potatoes and slice cucumbers for the supper she knew those fishermen would be hungry for.

Matt carried the platter of fish into the kitchen and presented it to her.

"A peace offering," he mumbled.

"For what?" A dangerous question, but she wanted to hear him say it. Wanted to talk about what had happened.

"For being a jerk this morning."

"I understood your reaction. It's not how I wanted you to find out. I'm sorry."

"When were you going to tell me? Were you ever going to tell me?" She heard the note of belligerence.

"I wasn't trying to hide it, Matteo. My friendship with Caleb changed quickly and I was just getting used to the change. Of course I planned to tell you."

"Did you think I'd be upset?"

"Weren't you?"

"Not because of why you think. You were worried about Babbo, weren't you? That I'd be angry because Caleb was taking his place."

"Caleb isn't taking Babbo's place. No one will ever take his place."

"I'm not a little boy, Mom. I was pissed this morning because I thought you were trying to protect me, keeping what was going on between you and Caleb a secret."

"Don't use the word pissed."

"It describes how I felt."

Elizabeth paused, attempting to rein the conversation back. Being the mother of an adolescent was exhausting.

"So you were upset when you found Caleb here because you thought I should have told you earlier, not let you discover it by accident." She thought by restating what she'd heard from Matt she'd better understand the tension simmering between them.

"Yeah. I felt stupid barging in on you. When I saw his truck in the driveway, I thought he'd stopped by at the end of his shift. I thought he'd come to take me fishing."

"If it helps, I felt pretty stupid, too. Embarrassed."

"I guess we're even then?"

"Even. And he did take you fishing. Now, thanks for gutting the stripers, but how about washing up, or better yet, going for a swim. You smell like a tuna canning factory." She wrinkled her nose.

He left, loping out of the kitchen and off the porch to collect his cousins and head for the beach.

Caleb stuck his head through the screen door as soon as the boys were on their way.

"Is the coast clear? Have the wounded been triaged and patched up?"

"What did you say to my son today that transformed him from a sullen teenager to a mature and sensitive young man?"

"I spent hours by his side, whipping a line into the water, saying nothing until he opened up."

"Did they train you to be an interrogator when you were in Special Forces?" She said it lightly, but realized she had come much too close to the truth when she saw Caleb stiffen, a shadow of pain flit across his face and then disappear. She recovered quickly and asked him, "What did he say when he was finally ready to talk?"

"He said, 'Didn't you trust me enough to tell me? I thought you were my friend.' And I decided to respond to him as an equal, not an adult talking down to a kid. I told him he was right, friends didn't withhold important information from one another, especially when it can have an impact on their friendship. I apologized."

"I did, too. I was so wrong about why he was upset."

"You thought he saw you betraying his father."

Elizabeth nodded and then turned back to her potatoes to blink away the tears welling up in her eyes.

"Is that because you *do* feel you're betraying Antonio?" Caleb's words were whispered, not accusing, not dismissive, but pained.

Elizabeth pushed the tears away with the palms of her hands and turned back to Caleb.

"I feel so much more alive, awakened and generous with you than I ever was with Antonio. That's the betrayal that I'm experiencing. And I can't go back to make amends."

Caleb moved toward her and took her in his arms.

"You gave him all that you were capable of then, Elizabeth. You were young. Inexperienced. And you cared for him devotedly. Don't say that you weren't generous. I can't think of any greater generosity than what you demonstrated in the final years of his life. You were a good wife, Elizabeth. You are a wonderful mother. Don't doubt yourself."

Elizabeth allowed herself to be enveloped in his embrace, but she found it challenging to embrace his praise. Like Caleb, many people had seen her as a saint in the final year of Antonio's life. But for her, life as his caregiver had been complicated, fraught with weariness, rage at the injustice of his disease and her awareness of her own imperfections and inadequacies. At the same time, she'd always been aware of Antonio's gratitude and love. *He* was the one who had been a saint.

"There was one more thing I told Matt," Caleb murmured in her ear. "I told him that I loved his mother."

Caleb stayed for dinner with the boys, but he and Elizabeth agreed that staying the night wasn't wise. She walked him to his truck while the boys finished cleaning up in the kitchen.

"I'm on duty again tomorrow, so I can't take the boys off your hands."

"No worries. They'll occupy themselves. Can you join us for supper?"

"I'll be here. Sleep well."

Elizabeth sat outside by the pond long after Caleb's headlights had swung onto the trail and disappeared toward Drunkard's Cove. When she saw the lantern lighting up Byzantium she stopped at the door to say goodnight to the boys. They were setting up a board game and had fortified themselves with the usual quantity of snacks and soft drinks.

"G'night, Mom. Don't bother fixing us breakfast. We'll probably play Risk till dawn and then sleep till noon. Isn't that what summer vacation is for?" He sounded like a typical teenage boy without a care beyond having enough Doritos to last the night. She left them to dominate the map of the world and climbed into a bed that suddenly felt very empty.

The next morning, after she returned from her swim on East Beach, she was sweeping out the sand that accumulated with unchanging regularity throughout the cottage when her phone rang. It was Izzy.

"Elizabeth, Tobias is having a good day and has asked to see you. Can you come?"

Chapter Twenty-Nine

"You have a story to tell"

Elizabeth taped a note to the refrigerator and left immediately for Cove Meadow. Caleb had done as she asked and spoken to Tobias.

When she got to the house, Izzy led her to Tobias' room. Neither Grace nor Josiah was there and Izzy asked no questions. She seemed unsurprised by her father's desire to see Elizabeth.

Elizabeth slipped into the room. It was awash with sunlight and a gentle breeze blowing off the bay lifted the curtains at the windows. Tobias was sitting up in a chair, his feet propped up on an ottoman.

He smiled and squeezed Elizabeth's hand when she greeted him.

"My grandson tells me you are adrift and need a beacon to guide you home."

Elizabeth smiled. "Are those Caleb's words or yours?"

"Those are the sentiments of a man who loves you."

"Is that why you called me here today, to tell me that Caleb loves me?"

"No. You already know that, Elizabeth. You do not need my words to understand that. I suspect you don't need any words at all."

"Which is good, since he has so few."

Now it was Tobias who smiled.

"I called for you because I can still hear the conversations going on in my kitchen. I know you are hurting and frustrated about the film."

"I didn't ask to come to you to make a plea for you to overrule your family and the tribe. I've accepted their answer."

"Good. I have no energy to listen to the arguments that have already been voiced."

"Then why…"

Tobias held up his hand. He turned away from her while a coughing spasm rose up out of his chest. With his other hand he clutched a handkerchief and brought it to his mouth. When his coughing subsided, Elizabeth saw that the handkerchief was spattered with blood.

She reached for the glass of water on the table next to him and handed it to him. He took a sip between lips she could see were parched and cracked.

"I should go. Let you rest."

"Not yet. Unlike my grandson, I do have words for you." His voice was hoarse, barely a whisper.

"Come closer," he gestured, and reached out for her hand.

"You have a story to tell," he said. "You have a gift in how you see the world, how you listen. The story is both all around you and in you. The story is Innisfree, Elizabeth. The story of the land, but also of our two families. Tell it."

Then he let go of her hand and leaned back in the chair, his eyes closed.

Elizabeth rose and bent to kiss his cheek.

"Thank you," she whispered, and then left the room.

Izzy was in the kitchen, chopping carrots and onions.

"Thank you for calling me."

"Would you like to stay for lunch?"

"No, thank you. I've got to get back to the boys. I'm so grateful that you've allowed me this visit. I know what it's like when someone you love is close to the end. The presence of others can be such an intrusion, a violation."

"You're not an intrusion, Lili. You are one of us. Even more so now."

"You mean Caleb."

Izzy smiled. "My nephew keeps his emotions as bottled up as my brother sometimes, but it's clear something happened to him on Tuckernuck, and that something is you."

Elizabeth longed to unburden herself with Izzy, to reveal the emotions that were shattering her perception of who she was and what she wanted. But she held back. This house, this family, had a far greater burden right now in saying farewell to Tobias and easing his journey.

She hugged Izzy and left before her tears overwhelmed her.

On the trip back to Innisfree she contemplated Tobias' words. Innisfree is the story. She felt as if she'd been smacked upside the head. Of course. There it was, all around her as Tobias had said, and she'd been blind to it.

When she returned to the cottage she dug out the albums Lydia had saved over the years and began as she always did. Absorbing images, unlocking memories, searching for patterns that would eventually coalesce around themes.

She was scribbling notes on a narrow-ruled pad when she heard the screen door slam and the hungry voices of three teenage boys foraging in the refrigerator.

"Mom, what's for lunch?"

Real life.

After the boys had eaten and left for the beach, she picked up where she'd left off, dimly aware that in a few hours she'd be feeding them again. A frittata would be quick, give her more time to work. She made a mental inventory of the contents of the fridge and decided to call Caleb to ask him to pick up a few items before he joined them for supper.

"I'll make a stop at Morning Glory Farm. Save me wrangling with tourists at Stop & Shop… How did your conversation with my grandfather go?"

"It was a precious gift from an incredibly generous spirit. I'll tell you about it tonight." She hesitated for a minute and then asked the question she knew would be hovering between them. "Can you stay the night? We'll find a way to be discreet."

"Yes." He answered without hesitation. Elizabeth could sense the smile, even though she couldn't see it.

Chapter Thirty

The Phone Call

The next morning her ringing phone woke Elizabeth at six. Caleb stirred and turned to hold her as she reached to answer it. She rubbed the sleep from her eyes to focus. Calls at this hour of the morning were rarely casual chats. As soon as she heard the voice at the other end of the line she stiffened and sat up. Caleb's arm slipped away.

"Ciao,cara. C'e Mama."

"Mama! Come e sta?" It was the first time her mother-in-law had initiated a call all summer. Elizabeth had been conscientious in calling every week, making sure that Matteo spoke to his grandparents. He had even sent a few postcards and Elizabeth had mailed a package filled with photographs. What now? Was Massimo ill?

"Lisa, we've decided to accept your invitation to visit. Instead of going to the mountains for Ferragosto, we will come to your island."

Elizabeth was speechless, until Adriana shouted into the phone. "Are you there? Have we lost the connection?" Elizabeth recovered and answered with as much graciousness as she could muster, lying in bed with her lover beside her.

"Mama, that's wonderful! When do you arrive?"

"We fly to Boston next week. Can you send a car to meet us?"

"We'll come ourselves. Let me get a pen and you can give me your flight details."

After she'd scratched out the information, she bid her mother-in-law a safe journey and hung up.

Caleb was propped on one elbow, waiting.

"Real life?" he asked, stroking the side of her face.

"Real life in spades. I have myself to blame. I offered them the opportunity to come when they protested I was taking Matteo away from them. I didn't really think they'd accept. This isn't exactly the Riviera, which is more their style. Even Antonio found Innisfree challenging. He called it *primitivo*."

"Do you think they'll want to stay out here? Why not get them a room at the Harbor View, or one of the resort hotels like that one on Beach Road."

"It may be the only solution. I can't imagine Adriana surviving even one night in the Linnet cottage, with the only bathroom at the other end of the back porch."

"The accommodations aren't the only thing worrying you right now, are they?"

"If you mean, am I concerned about how they will react to you, yes. But it's not just that. I've not spoken to you about my relationship with my mother-in-law. She's never accepted me, even after fifteen years. And since Antonio's death, her disapproval has only increased. She was furious with me for leaving Italy with Matteo. Frankly, I don't know how I found the courage to defy her. If it hadn't been for Lydia and her insistence that I needed to mourn where I could heal, I don't think I could have rescued myself."

"But you did."

"And now I'm afraid the peace I've been able to attain, the acceptance of my own needs, is all about to be lost. Adriana has the capacity to diminish me, suck me dry."

"Elizabeth, you're not the fragile, shattered woman I found here at the beginning of the summer. You've restored yourself as you restored Innisfree. And from what you told me last night about your conversation with Tobias, you've found a renewed purpose for your filmmaking. Don't give up on yourself. You were strong enough to walk out of the villa in June. You're much stronger now. Don't allow anyone to drag you back."

Elizabeth kissed him. "Thank you for that shot of confidence, Dr. Monroe. I know you're right. But I'm still scared."

"Being scared doesn't mean you're going to crumble when faced with whatever challenge your mother-in-law may throw in your path. That was a lesson Mae imprinted on me. Even when we are afraid, we can be brave."

"You seem to have learned a great deal from both your grandparents. I hear echoes of Tobias in you, calming me right now."

"I will do whatever you need to help you get through this visit. If you want me to disappear, I will."

Elizabeth shook her head.

"I'm not going to flaunt my newly awakened sexuality in front of my in-laws, but I'm also not going to make you hide out. You are a part of both Matteo's and my life here."

"Since I don't expect that will include sharing your bed while they are here, I suggest we make the most of the next couple of days," he smiled, taking her in his arms.

An hour later he was out the door and on patrol. Elizabeth used the time until the boys woke up to rough out more ideas for the Innisfree project, another worry that gnawed at her. How to accomplish the drafting of a script and filming while hosting guests who could hardly be expected to entertain themselves on the island with neither a car nor fluency in English. She'd figure it out.

Once the boys were up she informed Matteo of the impending arrival of his grandparents. Elizabeth began making phone calls—to Sam and Debbie, to the Harbor View, and, in a flash of genius, to her parents. She knew they'd barely arrived back from her father's Asian business trip and weren't planning to come to the Vineyard for at least two weeks. She decided the risk of waking them if they were still jet-lagged was overridden by her desperate need for reinforcements.

"Hi, Mom! It's Elizabeth. How was your trip?"

"Hi, honey. We had a fabulous time. Wait till you see what I brought you from Thailand. How is your summer going? We can't wait to see you and Matt."

"That's why I'm calling. Do you think you could push up your visit? Let me explain why."

Elizabeth launched into her news of the Innocentis unexpected decision to come to the Vineyard. Susan Todd was well aware of the strained relationship between Elizabeth and her mother-in-law, exacerbated to near breaking point by Antonio's death. It was Susan who had shared her concerns with Lydia and who had asked her mother to intervene by encouraging Elizabeth to spend the summer at Innisfree.

"Of course we can come early, honey. Why don't Dad and I pick up Adriana and Massimo at Logan? It makes more sense for us to do it, since it's on our way. No need for you to spend half a day getting off the island and up to Boston. And I think putting them up at the Harbor View is brilliant, rather than have them isolated at Cape Poge. They're not exactly the kind of people who can be content with the beauty and solitude of Innisfree. Edgartown can entertain them more effectively than digging for clams or casting a line for bluefish, I imagine."

Elizabeth hung up with a sigh of relief. Her fears were subsiding, knowing she wasn't going to be dealing with her in-laws alone.

She spent the rest of the day scrubbing the house and put the boys to work gathering the detritus three teenagers can spread over every flat surface in their surroundings.

"Round up the trash and recyclables. After we haul it to the dump we can grab some pizza and ice cream in Edgartown." She'd learned the fine art of bribery from her grandmother, who'd always rewarded chores at Innisfree with treats both edible and experiential.

When they returned to Cape Poge after sunset Elizabeth surveyed the house. While it would never meet the expectations of her mother-in-law, Elizabeth was proud of how far the state of the cottage had come since her arrival in June. It was, as Caleb had reminded her that morning, restored. Her fingertips grazed over the top of the cupboard in the living room, with its Melamine tray holding bottles of gin and Scotch and bourbon. Above it on a shelf were mismatched glasses—crystal wine glasses, highball and rocks glasses etched with sailboats, even a pair of gold-rimmed champagne flutes that had been a gift to her grandparents on their 50th wedding anniversary. Like the marks carved into the wall charting the growth of all the children who had summered at Innisfree, each of those glasses had held more than gin-and-tonics and Bloody Marys. The family's history was contained in this house, a history she feared was slipping away as the family dispersed far and wide beyond the island. Even her own parents, who in the past spent the entire summer on the island, now only came for a few days at the end of the season.

She took a deep breath. All the more reason to capture Innisfree on film. She hauled her notebook out of the cupboard and curled up on the couch, determined to eke out as much of the story as she could before her in-laws arrived.

The next day dawned gray and damp. A light drizzle coated the lawn and the bushes with beads of water, and the opposite side of Shear Pen was hidden behind a veil of mist. The familiar sounds of the pond were muffled. Occasionally the screech of an osprey or the splash of a cormorant diving for its breakfast broke the silence. Elizabeth rolled over, burrowing under the covers. She wasn't quite ready to emerge from the cocoon of her bed to face the day.

Caleb was still asleep. He'd arrived late in the night, pulling her away from her notebook and her contemplative sense of loss. They'd made love, aware that duty was once again tugging them away from one another. Elizabeth had known that Italy loomed for her at the end of the summer. That shadow had cast its chill over every aspect of her life on the island, not just her relationship with Caleb. But until Adriana's call, Italy had remained still in the distance. But now, Italy was coming to her, abruptly and invasively.

She wrapped her arms around Caleb's middle, pressing herself against his back, his bare skin against hers spreading a protective barrier between her and the world.

"Are you hiding?" he mumbled.

"I didn't mean to wake you. I'm not ready to get up."

He turned to face her.

"And I'm not ready to let you go."

She suspected that he was not only referring to this morning, or even the limitations imposed on them by

Massimo and Adriana's impending arrival. She felt herself pull back from the comfort and pleasure of his body, the undisguised hunger in his voice. She explored his face, inches from her own, his dark eyes questioning, seeking in her the longing she'd just heard him express.

"I'm not ready either—not for any of this. Not for my in-laws, not for Matteo's adolescence, not for making my film, not for returning to Italy. But I'm also not ready for us."

"You're not talking about our lovemaking, I take it. For which both of us appear to be ready."

She shook her head, but with a smile.

"Shall we talk about this now, or after?" he asked, kissing her neck.

"After," she murmured. As much as her "unreadiness" was gnawing at her, she wasn't about to lose what might be a last opportunity for them to have an intimate moment together. She couldn't deny either of them, although she feared the time would soon be upon them when she was going to deny him. She was returning to Italy. He had to know that. But this morning, she understood he was also not ready for that reality.

The time to talk after their lovemaking was cut short by Caleb's need to get to work and Elizabeth's wish that he not be in the house when the boys woke up. She walked with him down the drive to the pump, where he'd left his truck out of sight of the cottage.

"So what about us are you not ready for?"

She took a deep breath.

"I'm not ready to confront what my return to Italy will mean for us. I know for me it looms as pain, loss, guilt…"

"Why guilt?"

"Guilt that I've let this—us—grow so deeply connected that I'm going to cause pain."

"I'm not convinced that you are going back."

"That's exactly what I mean. You still have this hope, and I'm going to be the one to destroy it."

"It's not a zero-sum game, Elizabeth. You have options."

"Not that I see. I go back to Italy and I lose you. I stay here and I lose Matteo."

"That's not clear."

She shook her head. So much he didn't understand about her life—as a mother, as a widow.

"Wait until you meet Adriana and then tell me that."

"Are you still sure you want me to meet your in-laws? I ask only to spare you some of the disruption you seem to be anticipating. I mean it. If it will ease what are surely to be challenging days ahead with them, I'll stay away."

"I'll think about your offer."

He kissed her, tenderly at first, and then, the realization appeared to hit them both that this might be the last kiss for a while. He lifted her and she wrapped her legs around him as he leaned back against his truck.

"Don't leave me," he whispered.

"I don't want to," she assured him. *But I will.*

Chapter Thirty-One

Wisdom

Elizabeth wanted to see Lydia before her responsibilities to her in-laws consumed her attention. She knew the boys would rather not spend time in the oppressive confinement of the nursing home, but hesitated about leaving them alone for several hours at Innisfree. Geoff, the older of her nephews, reassured her.

"We'll be fine. We'll stick to Shear Pen if we take the boat out. And we'll dig up some clams for supper if you promise to bring back a pie from Morning Glory."

As she drove off, she reflected on her willingness to afford Matteo far more freedom here on Chappy than she'd ever been comfortable with in Florence. It had less to do with city versus country life, and more to do with how much both of them had changed over the summer. She wondered how Adriana would react, especially to the newly independent Matteo. He was so definitely not the little boy who'd left the villa in June. She smiled to herself.

Shady Knoll assaulted her with its usual smells of disinfectant and despair. But she found it even more disheartening than her earlier visits to her grandmother.

As she walked down the linoleum-covered hallway, she wondered how Lydia tolerated it. She knocked on Lydia's door. She hadn't called ahead, so Lydia wasn't expecting her. Elizabeth found her sitting by the window, staring listlessly. When she turned at Elizabeth's greeting, the face she presented to her granddaughter was strained and hollow.

Elizabeth was stunned, unprepared for what she saw in her grandmother's countenance. Perhaps her sojourn at Innisfree had given Elizabeth a different perspective from when she'd first visited Lydia at the beginning of the summer. Or maybe she'd been so exhausted by her own grief that she hadn't perceived then how much her grandmother had lost—of the beauty and freedom and energy of Innisfree—when she was forced to accept the limitations of her failing health.

"Granny, are you ill?" Elizabeth rushed to Lydia's side.

"Oh, Elizabeth, you dear girl. I'm just tired. Tired of these four walls and my own thoughts. I already feel better knowing I'll have your company for a little bit. Tell me what you've been up to. Did you talk to Tobias?"

"I did, which is one of the reasons I came to see you. Would you like me to wheel you down to the solarium?" She gripped the handles of Lydia's wheelchair, determined to change at least one set of walls for those of the glass-enclosed sun porch, where light and greenery permeated the space.

Lydia reached up to pat her hand as they rolled down the corridor.

"What are the other reasons you're here?" Despite her expressed fatigue, Lydia's mind was still sharp.

When they were settled in a quiet corner, although still watched longingly by other residents who had no visitors to distract them, Elizabeth brought her grandmother up-to-date on her news: Tobias' loving advice, the impending arrival of Adriana and Massimo, Matteo's transformation under the sun, wind and comradeship of his cousins at Innisfree.

In contrast to her listlessness when Elizabeth first arrived, Lydia listened to it all with eagerness, nodding when she heard about the film and shaking her head in sympathy about the Italians.

"Are you putting them up at Innisfree?"

"No. Mom and I agreed they'd be much happier at the Harbor View here in town. She and Dad are meeting them at Logan and bringing them out."

"How long do they intend to stay?"

"They didn't say. All of Italy shuts down in August, but I'm hoping they're not here for the whole month. Now that I've finally got a film project, I'm chafing at the intrusion."

Lydia reassured her. "Oh, honey, you've never let anything get in your way of filming before. You'll get it done. You've got Hammond blood in you, after all."

"Thanks for the confidence boost, Granny. You can always be counted on. Although I'm not sure everyone views my Hammond blood as a positive."

"Don't let 'them,' whoever they are, distract you. You have a gift and a passion. Don't bury your talent because you might disappoint someone, especially your in-laws. Is that what's eating at you? Because something is."

"You don't miss anything, do you, Granny. Especially when it's unspoken. I really didn't come here to burden you with my problems."

"Nonsense. I'd rather be listening to you and dishing out my wisdom than staring out the window at what I can no longer smell or touch or revel in. Spill the beans."

"There are too many to count, but before I fling my problems into your lap, I need to ask you if you'll let me film you talking about Innisfree."

"What about it?"

"Your history of it—how you came to own it, the early memories, things you cherish."

Elizabeth caught a fleeting glimpse of wariness on Lydia's face before she answered. But her reply was warm and unhesitating.

"Of course. Do I need to get dolled up? And where do you plan to shoot this epic interview?"

Elizabeth looked around at the false cheeriness in their surroundings, which could work as a counterpoint to Innisfree's wild expanses. But then an idea took root.

"I'd like to film you at Innisfree."

Her words hung in the air between them. Lydia took a sharp intake of breath, as if Elizabeth had unmasked her, exposing a need Lydia hadn't dared admit to herself.

Was she causing her grandmother pain to suggest she return to Innisfree? Was Elizabeth's idea so impossible, a risk Lydia's physician would forbid? Had she opened a Pandora's box of longing that her grandmother had tamped down, stifled, in order to survive in these diminished surroundings?"

"You argue before my parole board and get me out of this joint and I will sit on top of the flagpole if that's where you want to film me."

"The back patio will do just fine, Granny."

"Good. That's settled. What else is on you mind? Is it Caleb?"

"Yes."

"You've fallen in love with him, or he with you, and now your life is complicated at a time when you were looking for simplicity, a retreat from emotion after you were emotionally wrung out by your husband's illness and death."

"Have you ever considered a career in counseling? Or maybe the priesthood?"

"I did, actually. The priesthood. But no church was ordaining women then, so I turned my nursing into a vocation. Now, let's unravel this tangle you've got yourself wrapped in. Do you love him?"

"I do. But I can't. Not now."

"Why the hell not?"

"Because I have a son to raise in Italy. My life is in Italy."

"And what is it that you're living here and now? This isn't your life?"

"Not my real life. This is a dream. A bubble that is about to burst as soon as Adriana sets foot on Chappy."

"The Elizabeth I knew pursued her vision, crawled under a rose bush to photograph a hummingbird and gave up her familiar, comfortable life in America to step into the unknown with the man she loved. That Elizabeth, who I believe still resides in your heart and your spirit, is not going to be thwarted by the expectations of a woman who has no right to dictate how and where you live. Don't give her power, Elizabeth. Decide for yourself what's best for you and your son."

"That's it, Granny. What is best for Matteo."

"And hasn't he thrived here, surrounded by family who have been all but strangers most of his life?"

"Yes, but… it's summer vacation. He's supposed to start *liceo* in September. Remember, he's been in Italian schools all his life. His friends, his home, everything he knows is in Florence."

"Have you asked him what he wants?"

"He's fourteen. How does he know what he wants?"

"I'm not going to tell you this is easy. Lord knows, raising kids anywhere in the world is a challenging job. And your grandfather and I made our share of mistakes, as your parents did. As all parents do. I'm only suggesting that you not see this decision as simply black or white."

"That's what Caleb said."

"The more I hear about this man, the more I like him."

"That's because he agrees with you."

"Elizabeth, you came to me to hear my advice. I'm not going to tell you 'stay' or 'go.' Just think about why you came here this summer, and whether it was a good decision. And consider what you are going back to. Parenting is hard enough, especially for a single mother. But will you have support from Adriana, or will she undermine you?"

Elizabeth did not want to hear what Lydia was saying. She did not want to doubt herself or reconsider. She wanted to be safe. But she realized that she didn't know where she'd find that safety.

"You've worn me out," Lydia broke into Elizabeth's silent reverie. "I think I need to lie down."

Elizabeth brought her back to her room and helped her into bed. As she settled back against her pillow, Lydia touched the side of Elizabeth's face.

"Nobody's going to give you permission to do what you want, sweetheart, except you. Believe that you know what is right for your child at this moment. A year from now, you'll be making other decisions. Now, go get me my parole."

Chapter Thirty-Two

Homecoming

Once she'd suggested bringing Lydia back to Innisfree, Elizabeth knew she couldn't disappoint her grandmother, and began her quest to get her doctor's permission as well as instructions on how to care for Lydia in the isolation of Innisfree. The list of medical equipment was more extensive than she anticipated—wheelchair, oxygen, extra medication, a commode to put at her bedside because the distance to the toilet would be too far for her to safely navigate. Her physician was fine with an excursion of a few days, once he was reassured the house had both a generator and a motorboat that could transport Lydia to the hospital in an emergency.

"I more than approve," the geriatrician told Elizabeth. "Your grandmother's keen intellect is trapped by both her physical frailty and the confines of her surroundings. A few days away will be good for her spirit. Just don't overdo her activities. Make sure she rests, even if she protests."

"You sound as if you know her well."

"I enjoy Lydia immensely. She's one of my favorite patients, even when she's telling me how to do my job."

When Elizabeth arrived back at Innisfree, the Jeep packed to the roof with equipment, she enlisted the boys' help in unloading the car and setting up her own room for Lydia.

"Where will you sleep?" Matteo asked.

"I'm going to make up a bed for myself on the window seat in the alcove. I'm not comfortable leaving Granny alone in the house at night."

"When is she coming?"

"I'm going to pick her up tomorrow morning. I could use your help. An extra pair of hands and a strong back to keep your great-grandmother from falling and your mother from making a fool of herself for thinking this is a good idea."

"Sure. But it *is* a good idea, isn't it? She must miss Innisfree, especially living in that awful place."

"I know, honey. That's one of the reasons I wanted to bring her here. I just hope it isn't a mistake."

"Because once she's here, she won't want to go back. I sure wouldn't."

Elizabeth looked at her suddenly insightful son. Where was this understanding of his elderly great-grandmother coming from? And had he revealed something about his own feelings toward Innisfree? She let his comment simmer in her brain. Too much to think about and do before Lydia's arrival.

"What about supper? Did you guys have a successful hunt?"

In answer, Matteo pulled her out to the back porch and opened the refrigerator with a flourish.

"Ecco," he exclaimed, pointing to a bowl filled to the rim with shucked clams. Over the meal, Elizabeth and the boys planned Lydia's visit like a military campaign. By the time the last of the dishes had been washed and put away, Elizabeth felt more reassured that her spontaneous invitation had been neither crazy nor selfish. She wanted to give Lydia the gift of time here in this beloved place, but she also knew in her heart that Lydia's presence at Innisfree had been one of the missing pieces of the summer. She realized she couldn't recreate the magic of her childhood by restoring her grandmother to her role as matriarch of Innisfree, but she longed to recapture even a fragment of the security, warmth and effervescent energy that Lydia generated.

She had already remade her bed with fresh sheets, so she spent the night in the alcove, its two walls of windows affording her an expansive view of the night sky. She was nestled under a quilt when Caleb called, and she curled around the phone, staring at the Milky Way as she explained to him what she'd planned.

"You know, Tobias may want to see her. They've both been so ill, it's probably over a year since they've been together."

"I'll mention it to her once we're settled tomorrow. I'm not supposed to tax her physically. I'm actually a little nervous about this responsibility I've taken on. Too much acting and not enough thinking, is how my father used to characterize my spontaneity."

"I think you underestimate your capacity to handle challenges. You're an experienced caregiver, Elizabeth."

"I had a lot of help. And I wasn't alone then."

"You're not alone now."

Elizabeth was reminded of Izzy's words after the hurricane. Despite Innisfree's isolation—or perhaps because of it—Elizabeth's connection to the place made her part of a community. With the reassurance of Caleb's comments echoing in her brain, she drifted off to sleep.

She wanted to get an early start the next morning and roused the boys on her way back from the pump.

They groaned, but were as eager as she was to bring their great-grandmother to Innisfree. Lydia was beloved, and the boys had never become accustomed to seeing her confined in the nursing home.

After a quick breakfast of mammoth bowls of cold cereal, they piled into the Jeep for the journey into town.

Lydia was waiting in the lobby, the overnight bag in her lap clasped by hands that had been freshly manicured. She waved to them all as they trooped in, and the boys lined up for her exuberant embrace.

"Let's get the hell out of here before they realize I'm running away," she whispered, and Elizabeth heard a note of truth under the teasing playfulness her grandmother was known for.

They wheeled her down the ramp to the car. Geoff and Matteo were positioned on each side of her to lift her and get her settled in the front seat, but she batted them away.

"I'm not a cripple," she protested. "I can get in the car by myself. I may no longer waterski across Cape Poge Bay, but I can certainly walk two steps across the sidewalk."

So that's what the next few days will be like, Elizabeth thought. *I'm going to have a willful toddler on my hands in addition to three teenage boys with raging hormones.* She got in the car and drove back to Chappy, hoping she was doing the right thing.

As soon as they were underway on the ferry, Lydia had the window down and was beaming as the breeze lifted her hair. In addition to her polished nails, it appeared that Lydia had also had her hair done. Just like the old days, Elizabeth remembered. Her grandmother would get "dolled up," as she put it, whenever Grandpa Lou was scheduled to arrive from Philadelphia for the weekend. Lydia stayed at Innisfree all summer, but Lou was a cardiologist with a busy practice and only traveled to Innisfree intermittently.

Lydia was chatting with the crew as the ferry swung across the channel. The trip took no more than a few minutes, but she had managed to extract some island gossip and send her greetings to their families by the time they rolled off onto Chappaquiddick Road.

Lydia seemed to savor every step of the journey and would even have gotten out of the car at the Dike Bridge to help the boys deflate the tires if Elizabeth hadn't placed a gently restraining hand on hers as she reached to unhook her seatbelt.

"I taught Matteo how to do it on our first trip out, and he's done a great job all summer. Just like you made us learn the 'responsibilities' of living at Innisfree." Elizabeth figured if she framed it that way, as a tradition passed on to the next generation, Lydia would accept the restraint far better than if she'd said, "Granny, you're not strong enough to do that."

Lydia smiled. "You don't fool me for a minute, sweetheart. I hear you. I'm supposed to be a good girl if I want to last out here for more than an hour."

"I only want you to enjoy yourself and not wind up in the emergency room. I want you to be safe."

"Innisfree has never been about being safe, Elizabeth."

The boys clambered back into the car and Elizabeth backed out and turned to cross the bridge without responding to her grandmother. Although the weather was clear and it was low tide, she gripped the steering wheel tightly, concentrating as fiercely on the driving as if it were as treacherous as the morning of the hurricane.

When they arrived at Innisfree, her fingers were cramped and her mouth was dry.

The boys tumbled out. Matteo grabbed Lydia's bag from the trunk while Geoff retrieved the walker they had rented. Elizabeth had secured a wheelchair for inside the house, but the uneven terrain outside made that impractical. There also wasn't a ramp and Lydia would have to negotiate a couple of steps to get inside anyway.

Once again she waved away any assistance and pulled herself up out of the car with the hand rail above the door. She grasped the sides of the walker and stomped behind it. But instead of entering the house, she turned away and moved slowly toward the flagpole.

Elizabeth followed alongside, all her energy focused not only on preventing Lydia from falling, but also on keeping her own mouth shut. When Lydia reached the point overlooking the pond and the bay, she stopped, closed her eyes and basked in the sunlight pouring over the water. Elizabeth waited. This spot was where she, too, had come that first disastrous morning at Innisfree; where Josiah had stood when he had returned as well. The view was both expansive and intimate. From here you could see as far as the surf on East Beach in one direction and the shore of Edgartown beyond the Gut in the other. But you could also see the osprey feeding its nestlings on the opposite side of Shear Pen and the cormorants sunning themselves on the sandbar in the middle of the pond. On the beach below, tiny crabs scuttled sideways into the reeds. A breeze rippled the slack folds of the stars-and-stripes and Lydia released one hand from the walker to wipe tears away from her eyes.

Elizabeth put her arm around her grandmother.

"Welcome home."

Chapter Thirty-Three

Come Sit with Me

Elizabeth eventually convinced Lydia to sit, offering her the choice of the bench by the flagpole, an Adirondack chair on the lawn or the back patio, or the couch in the living room. She acquiesced and parked herself on the patio, where she had a good vantage point of the bay.

The boys clustered around her while Elizabeth made a pot of coffee. They filled her in on their summer exploits and she got to shower them with the unconditional acclaim that was the privilege of grandparents. By the time Elizabeth brought out the coffee, Lydia had challenged them to a game of poker after supper and banished them to the beach.

"I don't want you hovering over me every minute, so scoot and go do your wild-boy escapades out of sight of the grown-ups."

"Don't encourage them, Granny. Sam and Debbie are counting on me to make sure they behave."

"Sam, of all people, should understand the need for letting loose out here. It's not good for them or you for them to be constantly underfoot. Besides, I want some quiet time with you. Come sit with me."

Elizabeth sank into the slider. The intensity of the preparations for Lydia's visit had consumed her, and the stress of transporting her had demanded more than she'd anticipated. It was only eleven in the morning, but she was exhausted.

Lydia sipped her coffee with relish. "M-m-m, I see you learned how to make a good cup of coffee over there. When your grandfather and I traveled to Italy, that was one of my small pleasures—cappuccino, espresso, caffé latte. The coffee at my current abode is adequate, but not satisfying."

"Are you happy there?"

"Happiness is not an expectation when you reach my age and state of health. Let's say I'm content. I'm not in pain, rarely bored, and free of domestic burdens. I can leave the roof repairs to you while I sit here and enjoy the view. Works for me. The more important question is, are *you* happy?"

"I'm happy to be here, and especially happy to have you here with me. Innisfree hasn't been complete without you. Now it is."

"I'm flattered, sweetheart, but I don't think Innisfree needs me."

"*I* need you, Granny."

"Well, that's why I came. And not just for your film. I listen better out here, away from the sighs and mutterings and despair at the nursing home. I know you've got a lot of work to do in the next few weeks, and if I can be your sounding board, have at me. You've been much more agitated recently than you were at the beginning of the summer. You were never a placid child, and your calm when you first came to see me struck me as numbness. I'm relieved to see you're no longer frozen."

"No, I'm definitely in a heightened state of something. I careen from anxiety to euphoria."

"Let's start with euphoria. What a gift! What's the source?"

Elizabeth contemplated for a moment before answering.

"It has more than one source. This place, for one. I wake up every morning feeling blessed to be here. So thank you. I don't think I had any idea how profoundly it would affect me to be back. It's more than childhood memories. I feel connected, rooted."

Lydia smiled. "What else incites the euphoria?"

"My work. To be creating again fills me up. I was an empty vessel after Antonio died, and unable to replenish myself. Despite the setback with the Wampanoag project, I've found my bearings, thanks to Tobias."

"He has a way of providing that. He's a compass, a beacon."

"Would you like to see him? Caleb thought your presence here was an opportunity for both of you."

A flicker of emotion briefly lit up Lydia's face—agitation, doubt, discomfort, then hope followed one after another. Elizabeth was unsure how to read her grandmother's unspoken reaction to the proposed visit.

"Of course, if you think it's too much for you…"

"No. It's not too much. I'd like very much to see him, if he's able."

"I'll call Caleb later and check."

"And what about Caleb? Another reason for the euphoria?"

"Yes and no. That's where the anxiety comes in."

"You're still tortured about what to do about Italy."

"I can't think about it right now, not with the film and the imminent arrival of my in-laws."

"Understood. But don't put off the decision. Not deciding is also a decision."

"I know. I know."

"Enough of my probing. My blood sugar is dropping and if I don't eat soon, I'll be even crankier than usual. What's for lunch?"

"You're never cranky! Opinionated and outspoken, yes, but not cranky. Sit and enjoy the sunshine. It'll only take me a few minutes to pull lunch together."

After sandwiches, iced tea and homemade brownies, Elizabeth easily persuaded Lydia to take a nap. While she slept, Elizabeth reached Caleb and they arranged a visit at Cove Meadow for the next day.

"Tobias is pleased. I think it was weighing on him that he hasn't been able to say good-bye to her."

Elizabeth didn't share with him the range of emotions she'd seen on Lydia's face when she proposed the visit. Perhaps she'd misread what may have simply been fatigue.

After her nap, Lydia wandered through the house in her wheelchair, fingering the curtains; scanning the marks on the wall recording the heights of all her children, grandchildren and great-grandchildren; studying the family portrait taken on her 75th birthday.

"You've done a fabulous job bringing Innisfree back to life, Elizabeth. I made Sam tell me the truth after he came out here to open up the house before you arrived. I know it had started to succumb to neglect and the elements. That was the hardest part of the decision to move to Shady Knoll. In the end, it was either my health or the house, and I knew I wanted to stick around for a while longer. I especially wanted to make sure you got back on your feet."

"And I have, thanks to you, Granny. I admit, I was nearly undone by the state of the place when I first got here. If it hadn't been storming and so late when I arrived, I think I might have climbed back in the car that night and taken Sam up on his offer for me and Matteo to spend the summer in Oak Bluffs. But Innisfree held me here and confronted me. I realized it needed me as much as I needed it."

"Thank you, sweetheart. You were my last hope. No one else in the family has the passion or the imagination or the reverence to protect Innisfree that you do. Caring for this place is about more than ownership. Mae understood that, and I've tried to follow her lead. I've never 'owned' Innisfree. It never belonged to me."

"That's what Josiah told me. He said, on the contrary, that he belonged to Innisfree."

"Josiah was here?"

"Yes, a few days ago. Does that surprise you?"

"In all the years since I've been Innisfree's steward, Josiah never once set foot here. After Mae relinquished it to me, he turned his back on the land and his family. His reconciliation with Mae when he returned to Chappy with Grace and Caleb did not include returning to Innisfree. You must have done something extraordinary to bring him back."

"I found Mae's journal in the loft with a box of baby clothes. I returned it to him as soon as I realized what it was."

"Mae's box! She asked me to hold it in safekeeping until Josiah was ready to accept it. It broke my heart when she died that he hadn't been able to reach out across the gulf the loss of Innisfree represented to him in his relationship with his mother. I was tempted to hand it over to him after the funeral, but I couldn't justify it. I'd made a commitment to Mae."

"I thought the box had been forgotten; that somehow, out of neglect, we'd kept a vital piece of his history from Josiah."

"I hadn't forgotten that box at all. How did he react?"

"He showed up here a few days after I'd returned it. I was alone. Caleb had taken the boys fishing. The journal seemed to release him from the bonds that had kept him away from Innisfree and his feelings for it. I felt as if I were hearing his confession."

"You've always been a good listener, sweetheart. What it would have meant to Mae to know her boy had truly come back! Bless you, Elizabeth."

Once again, Elizabeth saw tears fill her grandmother's eyes, and wondered if the emotional toll of bringing her to Innisfree was evolving into something far more piercing than she had anticipated. Was she taxing Lydia's heart in damaging ways? They still had the visit with Tobias ahead of them, and Elizabeth had already suspected that the encounter would be fraught with turbulent memories.

Chapter Thirty-Four

Settling In

Lydia had a good night. The poker game with the boys had brightened her mood and she'd settled into bed with a large-print novel plucked from the bookcase in the living room.

"I'm something of a night owl, honey. I hope the light won't disturb you. Don't you want to have your privacy and sleep in the Linnet cottage?"

Elizabeth understood it was her own privacy that Lydia was concerned about, but there was no way she was leaving her alone in the house.

"I'm fine, Granny. I'm going to be up myself for a while working. I'm blocking out some scenes for the project. I'd like to film you tomorrow after we visit Tobias. I'd also like to ask the Monroes if I can borrow some photos and I want to organize my list."

"You're going to use the 'Ken Burns Effect' in your film? I have some photos here in the house you might want to include. They're in some shoe boxes in the cabinet behind the booze."

Elizabeth smiled to herself. *Why am I not surprised Lydia knows the panning technique Ken Burns developed for documentaries? My granny, interested enough in her grandchildren's work to educate herself on how they do it.* She turned back to that work. An hour later, when she glanced in on Lydia, she saw the book sprawled open on her chest, her eyes closed and her mouth open in a gentle snore.

Elizabeth gently lifted the novel and placed it on the bedside table with a scrap of paper stuck within its pages as a bookmark. She turned off the gas lamp, drew the curtain across the doorway and climbed into her own nest in the alcove. She knew first light would wake her without an alarm clock with the windows directly facing East Beach.

Even with the responsibility of Lydia under her roof, Elizabeth kept her early morning rituals. She slipped on her bikini in the bathroom and walked briskly down the path for a swim. The tide was high and the sky was clear. On the horizon she could see the outline of a couple of fishing boats, but otherwise she was alone. When she emerged from the water, she scanned the beach to the north for signs of fishermen returning from early-morning outings to the Gut, their SUVs mounted with rods and plastered with stickers allowing them access to the Refuge. But the beach was empty. She'd hoped she might see Caleb, either on his way back from a night of fishing or on his way out in a Trustee truck at the beginning of his shift. She wrapped her towel around her against the morning chill and made her way across the sand through the dune break and back up to the house, stopping as usual at the pump to fill the water tank.

After her shower she started a pot of coffee and toasted some bread in a cast-iron skillet on top of the stove. Without electricity, typical kitchen appliances like toasters were nonexistent at Innisfree.

Both Lydia and the boys were still asleep, so she took her coffee and toast out to the patio. She was close enough to hear if Lydia stirred, but still able to enjoy the solitude of early morning at Innisfree. The hummingbird was hovering above the beach roses, its iridescent wings mesmerizing in the morning light. Elizabeth stole quietly into the house and retrieved her video camera. The bird obliged by continuing to dance when she returned to the patio and began filming. The heft of the camera in her hand, the sureness of her eye as it tracked the movement of the bird, and the keenness of her sense of the light were all both reassuringly familiar and vividly unexpected in their power to reignite her passion for her craft.

She had just clicked off the camera when she heard Lydia's voice calling her. As seamlessly as the camera, she switched from artist to granddaughter and caregiver.

"Good morning, Granny!" she called as she entered the house.

It was after ten when Izzy called them with the green light for the visit to Tobias. By then, everyone was up, dressed and fed. The boys weren't accompanying them to Cove Meadow and spread out a game of Risk on the coffee table in the living room.

"Save a place for me," Lydia told them with her usual sparkle. "I can catch up when I get back."

Elizabeth was certain that she could.

They arrived at Cove Meadow in silence. Lydia, usually chatty and inquisitive, had drifted into wordlessness shortly after they'd left Innisfree, her head turned away from Elizabeth, staring out at the calm waters of the bay.

Elizabeth left her to her musing. She doubted that Lydia would share with her the reason for her hesitation about this visit. She understood that it was intensely personal, part of the warp and weft of the tangled relationship between the Hammonds and the Monroes. It was more than two fragile nonagenarians bidding one another farewell in the last days of their lives.

It was Josiah who greeted them when they arrived, opening Lydia's door and offering her his hand. Elizabeth was surprised to see her take it willingly. None of the fiercely expressed independence of the previous day.

"You dear boy! What a joy it is to see you!" Lydia stood and took his face in her hands. "If only your mother were here, my day would be complete."

"I imagine Elizabeth told you she gave me the box. Thank you for saving it for me."

"I knew one day you'd want it. I'm so glad it was now."

Josiah nodded toward Elizabeth. "She's something special, your granddaughter. I'm indebted to her."

"So am I. But we can pay our debt by appearing in her movie. You will, won't you, Jo?"

Josiah stiffened. He addressed Elizabeth directly. "I thought everyone had been clear that the Wampanoag story wasn't yours to tell."

Elizabeth started to explain, but Lydia interrupted. "She's given that up, Jo. Elizabeth is making a film about Innisfree, on the recommendation of your father. I thought you knew."

Elizabeth suspected that the topic of Innisfree was only slightly less charged for Josiah than the tribal story.

"I can see that you'd do a sensitive job." A glimmer of a smile accompanied his words. But he didn't commit to participating.

"Let me help you inside. Dad's eager to see you."

Lydia allowed Josiah to support her into the house. Elizabeth followed behind, watching her grandmother lean into Josiah as if she couldn't proceed on her own. Elizabeth thought his arm around her was offering emotional reassurance as well as physical strength.

Caleb, Izzy and Grace were waiting inside the kitchen. Lydia exclaimed over all of them, kissed Izzy and appraised Caleb with a discerning and ultimately approving eye.

"Take me to my friend," she said, when the greetings were completed. Izzy led the way as Josiah continued to serve as Lydia's crutch. Elizabeth had brought the walker, but saw that Lydia was fine with Josiah.

She and Caleb and Grace remained behind. As much as she wanted to be a fly on the wall, this visit belonged to Lydia and Tobias. Even Izzy and Josiah didn't stay in the room once they'd gotten Lydia settled.

"Coffee, anyone?" Grace lifted the pot. "Who knows how long they'll be in there."

Chapter Thirty-Five

The Visit
Lydia and Tobias

"Hello, my friend," Lydia spoke softly, leaning in close so that he could hear her. "We are a pair, aren't we? I have a heart that's barely pumping and you've got lungs that don't want to inflate. Maybe they should stick us both on a skiff and push us out to sea."

"Never at a loss for words, are you? Always with the joke. You don't have to perform for me, Lydia. And you don't have to be afraid of me."

He reached out and took one of her hands, hands that she held tightly together in her lap, as if to keep them from touching him.

His long brown fingers stroked her pale, blue-veined, gnarled ones.

"I've missed your voice and your straight talk. They're all so earnest, my children and my grandson."

"They take after you. Serious. Caring. Thoughtful. Caleb has been good to my granddaughter."

"He loves her."

"She loves him."

"Innisfree has brought them to one another. They've brought our families together."

"Innisfree has always been at the center of what unites us and tears us apart. I've always carried the burden of taking it away from you."

"Mae chose you."

"And never returned after that. Just like Jo. Until now. Did you know he came to Innisfree to see Elizabeth?"

"He told me. Came to me for forgiveness."

"What did you say to that?"

"I told him I forgave him long ago, before he returned to Chappy."

"Did he believe you?"

"Now, yes. He needed to read his mother's words, to understand that Innisfree is here." He tapped his heart as if it were a drum. "Not a physical place."

"Did you know Elizabeth has brought me back there? Convinced my prison warden of a physician that I'd survive a few days in my old home."

"It must bring you peace."

"Peace and distress. It's made me realize I have to make a decision. Soon."

"About what to do about Innisfree."

"Once upon a time I thought I could leave it to them all, let them share it the way they did when they were children."

"But now…"

"I understand that was wishful thinking—the hope that it would still mean something to them. But, unlike your family, they're scattered. All over the globe, actually. They've moved on; forgotten or abandoned Innisfree."

"Except for Elizabeth."

Lydia nodded. "Except for Elizabeth. I held out hope when I offered her the place for the summer. I knew she'd endured an almost unbearable loss and needed to heal. And also hide."

"And she has."

"Yes. And she knows it was because of Innisfree. She loves it as much as we do, Tobias."

"I know."

"So, I've made my decision. It's hers. I'm not waiting till I die so they can all squabble about how unfair it is and force a sale to divide up the bounty. I'm signing the papers when I get back to Edgartown. She'll be the steward Mae envisioned."

Chapter Thirty-Six

Legacy

Lydia and Elizabeth sat on the patio with glasses of iced tea after lunch watching the boys out on the bay in the Sunfish. The wind was brisk and the boat was skimming rapidly across the water.

"They should have a New England sleigh ride on the way back in. What a delight to see them having so much fun together. Thank you, sweetheart, once again, for making the effort to bring me here."

"Are you up to being filmed this afternoon, or was your time with Tobias too draining?"

Elizabeth longed to know what had gone on between them, but knew better than to intrude. If Lydia wanted to tell her, she would in her own time.

"I think this would be the perfect opportunity. I'm not tired and the sun is warming these old bones. Why don't you go ahead and set up your camera."

Elizabeth started with a simple prompt. "What do you love most about Innisfree?"

Lydia closed her eyes for a moment and then looked into the camera.

"Innisfree gave me the freedom to be vulnerable. I allowed me to admit that order and control, the tight rein I held over everything in my life—including myself—were simply not possible in a world as wild and isolated as this one. The wind, the sea, this quixotic house that seemed to have a life of its own—they all taught me to embrace uncertainty and the unknown. Innisfree led me to understand the futility of seeking safety. We are not safe. Life is not safe. Each time we choose safety, we lose a piece of ourselves. There were moments at Innisfree when I was terrified. But in addition to the terror, there was exhilaration, in the beauty and solitude and loneliness and awe."

Elizabeth listened with her own awe to her grandmother.

"If I were the Lydia of twenty years ago, or even ten, I'd get up right now and have you follow me around as we roamed from the clam flat to the meadow to the cedar wood. I'd open my arms to the expansiveness that is Innisfree. But Innisfree is also about stillness, which is where I am in my life right now. I am forced by the limitations of my body to be still. Once upon a time I chafed at inactivity, felt stagnant and restrained, like a becalmed sailboat. Now, I welcome the stillness. Here at Innisfree, I don't need to move to experience the teeming life all around me. I am surrounded by the drama of the natural world—the elegance of a diving bird; the transformation of the sea with the shifting of the tides or the wind; the splendor of the curtain of the Milky Way unmarred by the lights of civilization. Stillness has taught me how to see."

Lydia grew silent then. Her vision shifted away from Elizabeth's camera and she seemed to be seeing something in her mind's eye, not the natural beauty that encircled them.

"The Boat House Café used to stand over there. Did you know that? It's where I met Mae. We'd just arrived on Cape Poge and I'd been cooped up in a tiny cottage with your mother and your hellion uncles for three days of relentless rain. I was desperate for human contact and I'd heard about the café from the boatman who'd brought us over from Edgartown. I'll never forget that day, seared in all our memories because it was the day Izzy fell ill with polio. But it was also the day Mae entered my life. Everything I've gained from Innisfree had its source in Mae. She was the soul of Innisfree. I miss her."

Lydia dug in her pocket for a handkerchief. "Turn that thing off now, honey. I'm done."

Elizabeth did as Lydia requested and then approached her grandmother. She knelt in front of her and threw her arms around her, holding her as Lydia sobbed.

That evening after Lydia was settled in bed, she called Elizabeth to sit with her. She patted the edge of the bed.

"Come here. I want you close. I have something to tell you."

She told Elizabeth about her plans to deed Innisfree to her.

"You are the only one of my descendants who will know how to care for it. You are the only one I trust to carry on Mae's legacy."

Lydia's announcement stunned Elizabeth. She loved Innisfree, and her attachment to its magic had only deepened in the weeks she'd been here. But she wasn't alone among those in the family who cherished it. And why had Lydia skipped over her own children? Elizabeth's mother and two uncles were still young enough to take on the work a place like this required. She voiced her bewilderment to her grandmother.

Lydia waved away her questions as if they were a swarm of black flies plaguing her.

"My answer to that is 'Where have they been for the last several years?' Your mother and dad spend exactly two weeks on the Vineyard. The rest of the time they're gallivanting all over the globe for your father's business. Your Uncle Lewis has his own place on Catalina Island in California, with all the bells and whistles his surgeon's income can provide. As far as he sees it, Innisfree is slumming it. And your Uncle Richard is too busy developing property in Miami to be bothered with this spit of land. Besides, he'd knock it all down and build a McMansion if it were up to him. None of their kids took to this place after they hit adolescence. So don't go thinking you're taking something away from anybody, sweetheart. My bet is they're all going to be immensely relieved that it's no longer their problem."

Lydia wouldn't hear any more objections from Elizabeth.

"My mind is made up. Now let me get my beauty sleep on my last night of freedom."

Elizabeth turned down the gaslight and kissed Lydia goodnight.

In the living room, she poured herself a Scotch, wrapped a sweater around her shoulders, and went out to the bench by the flagpole, where she could hear the water lapping at the edge of Shear Pen below.

As grateful as she was for Lydia's gift, Elizabeth felt as if she'd been thrown into a maelstrom of conflicting desires. The exhilaration that Innisfree was *hers* was immediately subdued by her memories of conversations with Josiah and Caleb. No one *possessed* Innisfree, they'd told her. The responsibility of stewardship crowded out her excitement. She was honored that Lydia had chosen her and allowed herself the hope that Caleb would concur with Lydia's decision. But that responsibility complicated her life even more than her relationship with Caleb. It added another layer of duty to the decisions clamoring for her attention. How would she care for Innisfree when she was thousands of miles away in Italy?

She swallowed the last drops of whiskey, hoping the alcohol would knock her out enough to get a few hours of sleep before she brought Lydia back to Shady Knoll and awaited the arrival of her in-laws. She didn't want to face them bleary-eyed and sleep-deprived. She needed a carapace as sturdy and opaque as a horseshoe crab's shell to navigate the treacherous waters of Adriana's desperation and bitterness. As she returned to the house awash in moonlight, she realized Innisfree was her carapace, her armor. It struck her that it had, most likely, also been Mae's.

Chapter Thirty-Seven

Bonfire

Elizabeth had expected Lydia's departure from Innisfree and return to Shady Knoll to be distressing for her grandmother. It was unlikely she'd be able to make the trip again, and neither of them spoke of it as she packed Lydia's bag. Lydia was on the patio sipping a cup of coffee.

"Leave me for a few minutes to my solitude," she'd told Elizabeth.

Whatever memories had drifted across the water while she sat gently rocking, she didn't share them with Elizabeth. She'd given up whatever she was willing to part with during the filming the day before.

Abruptly she called inside. "Let's get this show on the road. I've got a meeting set up this afternoon with Henry Walker's granddaughter, who took over Henry's legal practice last summer. I want the paperwork done and filed before I kick the bucket."

"I didn't know you were planning on doing that any time soon—kicking the bucket." Elizabeth was trying too hard to inject some levity. Her ricocheting ambivalence about the gift could have used a few days of cooling off, but she knew her grandmother. Now the decision had been made, she'd be agitated until it was implemented. Elizabeth wondered when and how her grandmother intended to let the rest of the family know. If she understood Lydia at all, she'd only make the announcement after the deed had been transferred and no one could interfere.

With the boys' help, the car was packed and Lydia took her place in the passenger seat. As Elizabeth negotiated the turn away from Innisfree, she saw that her grandmother did not look back.

The staff at Shady Knoll welcomed Lydia enthusiastically. Elizabeth could understand why she was a favorite, with her wit and salty language. As Lydia put it, "I don't drool or wear diapers yet, so I'm way ahead of most of their charges."

It was lunch time, so Lydia said good-bye to Elizabeth in the dining room.

"Thank you, sweetheart. These last few days were a precious gift. Now you find your Caleb and spend a few hours in his arms before the Italians descend upon the island. Love you."

Elizabeth was tempted to follow Lydia's advice. But she had a list of errands to accomplish in town, not the least of which was grocery shopping. The day before, Lydia had raved about her cooking. "Here's a thought. Get the boys to haul in a mess of bluefish; smother them in butter and garlic; throw some potatoes in the oven with rosemary from the bush on the leeward side of the house. Distract your in-laws with your outstanding culinary skills and they won't notice the oilcloth on the table or the mismatched plates. If you don't think they'll appreciate Innisfree's wildness, astound them with how civilized we are—cocktails and canapés on the patio at sunset; after-dinner drinks and coffee by the fire. This is *your home*, Elizabeth. Be its mistress, not a servant."

Her grandmother's words echoing in her head, she mapped out her journey around the island, from the mundane and overcrowded aisles of the Stop & Shop to the artisanally arranged vegetable bins at Morning Glory Farm and the heady sweetness of Munson's Fudge Shop and Chilmark Chocolates. She stopped on the wharf at Menemsha to pick up lobsters at Larsen's Fish Market. She'd planned a four-course meal, with lobster mac-and-cheese for the pasta course.

She was on her way back to Innisfree when her phone rang. She was close to the Dike Bridge and pulled over on the sand to answer it.

"Honey, it's Mom. The Alitalia flight is delayed and it looks like it won't arrive until after 8 p.m., which means it could easily be midnight before we get to Edgartown. Dad and I agree, knowing Adriana and Massimo, that we should put them up in a hotel in Boston for the night and bring them out to the island tomorrow morning. So give yourself a night off. After coping with Granny you deserve it. Whatever possessed you to take it upon yourself to bring her out to Innisfree?"

Elizabeth knew her mother didn't have the best relationship with Lydia and she wasn't going to explain herself while sitting in the sun with a car full of perishable food.

"It went fine, Mom. She's safely back at Shady Knoll and I've got a cooler of groceries to get home and in the fridge. I think your idea is brilliant, as will Adriana, I'm sure. Thanks for the rescue. I'll see you tomorrow."

She ended the call and swung back on the road, her relief in her reprieve palpable.

She rewarded herself with a swim after she'd unpacked the groceries and hung on the line the bed sheets that she'd tossed in the washer before leaving for Edgartown.

The boys were nowhere in sight, but the Sunfish was also gone. The wind was light, so they'd be tacking their way back later in the afternoon. East Beach had a few scattered families strung along the sand, their SUVs parked above the high-tide mark and each group's spot punctuated by colorful beach umbrellas, floats and boogie boards, and sandcastles in varying state of construction. The laughter of small children and the thump of music from boom boxes filtered across the sand. High summer on Chappy. Elizabeth threw her beach towel on the sand midway between two groups of revelers and plunged into the water.

Swimming was a form of meditation for her. Concentrating on each stroke and breath, she emptied herself of the competing demands scrabbling for her attention. She gave herself up to the sea and the sun and the wind, smiling inwardly at the secret gift that was both immensely satisfying and dauntingly challenging in its complexity.

She turned on her back and floated after a strenuous swim, reveling in the blissful moments of peace before she returned to the house and everything that confronted her there. From the simple needs of hungry teenage boys to the impending visit of her in-laws, those were demands she knew how to meet with food and gracious hospitality. It was the more open-ended, undefined challenges that paralyzed her: her relationship with Caleb and where and whether it had a place in her life; the tension between her roles as mother, artist and lover; the responsibility of stewarding Innisfree now hovering over all the other questions she needed to answer. In resolving her own dilemma, Lydia had quite emphatically complicated Elizabeth's. But Elizabeth guessed that was exactly what her grandmother intended. A way to push Elizabeth to step off the edge, give up the illusion of safety, and define what she truly wanted.

As she approached the house she saw the green-and-white triangle of the Sunfish sail approaching the mouth of Shear Pen. The boys would be back soon, just enough time for her to shower off the salt and fatigue of a busy day. But as she rounded the curve of the drive, she caught sight of Caleb's battered truck parked on the grass near Byzantium.

She found him around back on the stone steps of the patio, lost in contemplation of the rippling water of the bay. He turned when he heard her gently call his name and she saw on his face that something was wrong.

Without a word she sat next to him and touched his hand.

"Tell me."

"Tobias."

That was all he needed to say. She took him in her arms.

When he was able to speak, he said, "It was as if the visit with Lydia was the last thing he needed to do, a closing of the circle before he could let go. Even knowing every day this summer might be his last, we are all stunned, bereft. His passing leaves such a hole in our lives—in the family, in the tribe. I can't imagine anyone being able to fill it."

Elizabeth knew she was in the presence of the man who *would* be able to fill the emptiness now confronting him and his people. But she recognized he wasn't ready to hear that, and certainly not from her. Her own tears were coursing down her cheeks. "I feel blessed to have had those precious moments with him this summer. Ever since I was a child, I've carried his words, his influence, in my heart. What can I do to help you, your family?"

"You have your hands full, don't you, with the Italians. Aren't they due tonight?"

"Plane delay. My parents made the executive decision to put them up in Boston tonight after they land. I'm yours till tomorrow afternoon. Tell me what you need."

"I've got to get back to Cove Meadow. Word will spread quickly and the house will be full."

"I've got two full fridges in anticipation of feeding my in-laws this evening. Let me cook up something easy for you to heat up. I'll drop it off later and stay to pass around coffee and do dishes."

"Just your presence is all I need, but thanks. I'm sure Izzy and my folks will appreciate having you there." He kissed her softly and got up just as the boys were skimming into Shear Pen. He drove off before they climbed up to the house, leaving her to tell them the news.

She put them to work in the kitchen after they'd cleaned up. They shelled the lobsters she'd steamed; grated cheese; chopped garlic and onions. Within an hour she had two casseroles of mac-and-cheese ready, one for them and one to take to Cove Meadow. She grabbed a berry pie she'd bought at Morning Glory. It wasn't the quality of Mae Keaney's legendary pies, but it would help to feed the many people she expected would show up at Cove Meadow to pay their respects.

She dashed under the shower, found a pair of dark slacks and a sweater, and headed off to Cove Meadow. In the morning she'd drive to Shady Knoll and tell her grandmother in person.

As she expected, the driveway at Cove Meadow was full. She parked along the road and juggled the Pyrex baking dish and pie box as she approached the house.

Caleb had seen her from the window and emerged from the kitchen to help her. He'd changed out of jeans and a sweatshirt into chinos and a dress shirt. His hair was loose.

On the bay side of the house, Elizabeth saw a group of men stacking driftwood. Caleb followed her gaze and explained.

"It's for a bonfire. An old tradition. I can't remember the last time one was lit, but it was the first thing my father wanted. It's a departure for Dad. For so long, he's removed himself from the tribe. Ever since you gave him the box, he's been a different man. I know I shouldn't expect too much, when he'd been so depressed and withdrawn. But he's engaged in a way I haven't experienced in all the months I've been home."

They brought the food into the house and then Caleb led her through the living room and out onto a terrace overlooking the bay and the piled driftwood. The fire was just beginning to catch as they stepped outside. Elizabeth saw that several people had gathered around the blaze. She heard a low chant mingled with the snap of dry wood as it caught and exploded into flame.

Caleb stood behind her, watching not just the bonfire but the face of his father, the words of the chant on his lips and a drum in his hands.

When the chant was finished, Caleb led her to Izzy and Grace and she murmured her condolences. Josiah was on the other side of the fire, now silently adding wood to it. Caleb had told her they'd continue to feed the fire until they buried Tobias. Elizabeth left Izzy and Grace, mindful of the others who were waiting to talk to them. She moved around the blaze to Josiah and stood by his side.

"Would it be all right if I put a log on the fire?"

"He would be honored. It's fitting. He once described you as a spark. You have certainly ignited this family since you arrived." He glanced across the flames at Caleb. "Not just my son. Me. I wouldn't have been able to stand here and sing my father's spirit home if you hadn't thrust my mother's journal on me."

"I wish I'd been able to light a fire for my husband when he died. I longed for some way to release my anger, to take everything I'd held inside me while he was dying and have it be consumed."

"We all take what we need from the fire."

Elizabeth stood with him until newcomers arrived to offer condolences and add a sliver of wood to the fire. Then she slipped back into the house; she'd come to be of help. Food was piling up on the counters and table in the kitchen. Someone had plugged in a large coffee urn that was percolating. Izzy and Grace were still outside, and Elizabeth hesitated in the doorway as she observed a bevy of middle-aged women bustling to organize cups and slice cakes.

"Does anyone know where they keep the napkins?" one woman asked as she opened cabinets and drawers.

Elizabeth's initial hesitation, thinking that she'd be in the way of these efficient women, gave way to her sense that she belonged here. She stepped across the threshold and retrieved the sought-after napkins.

"Thanks. Who are you?" The question was asked with kindness, not irritation.

"I'm Elizabeth Innocenti, a friend of the family. My brothers and I grew up with Caleb." She felt a need to establish her right to be there.

"You're not an islander now, though."

"I'm back for the summer."

"She's the one with the camera, Estelle, who wanted to film Mariah for some documentary." Elizabeth heard the sharp voice of Francine, the tribal member who had been so suspicious of Elizabeth the day she filmed Mariah painting the deerskin.

"You didn't bring your camera here tonight, did you? To film the natives and their primitive customs?"

Elizabeth was not going to give Francine the satisfaction of knowing she had given up her project. But she also wasn't going to allow herself to be treated as an outsider.

"I came, as I'm sure you all did, to pay my respects to a family I love, who've lost a man I adored and revered. Tobias was like a grandfather to me." She turned away from a speechless Francine, pulled a tray from a cupboard and filled it with plates of cake. Then she left the kitchen, trying to keep her hands steady as she balanced both the tray and her raw emotions.

One of the women who had witnessed Francine's confrontation followed Elizabeth out of the kitchen with insulated pitchers of coffee in each hand. She put them on the sideboard in the dining room and then helped Elizabeth unload the tray.

"Francine thinks she knows what's best for everyone—the tribe, the township. Good for you for standing your ground. You're Lydia Hammond's granddaughter, aren't you? I'm Sophie Butler. I work at Shady Knoll and I've seen you visiting her. We don't get too many family members as dutiful and committed as you. Did I understand correctly that you make documentaries?"

"I do."

"I've had this idea that we ought to capture the stories of the residents at Shady Knoll. I listen to them reminisce and I think it's such a waste that I'm the only one who hears them. Would you consider bringing your camera sometime to record them? Francine may have a bug up her ass about protecting the legacy and integrity of the tribe, but the residents at Shady Knoll are a diverse population. And I think it would delight them to have someone make a movie about them. What do you think? I have a small budget for activities. I can pay you."

Elizabeth was grateful to the woman for her kindness, but her suggestion was so unexpected that she didn't know how to respond. A litany of excuses ran through her head of why she couldn't do it—her unfinished Innisfree project, her visiting in-laws, her return to Italy in a few weeks. But something held her back from turning the woman down at that moment.

"I think it's a fabulous idea. I'm not sure I'd be the right person to do it, but I'd love to talk with you about it. I can't make any promises. But I might be able to advise you. I'm planning to visit Gran tomorrow. She and Tobias were good friends and I think it's best to tell her in person. Are you in tomorrow?"

Elizabeth surprised herself with her enthusiasm. What was she thinking! Another commitment in her already overwhelmed life. But she took the woman's name and agreed to meet her at eleven in the morning.

She spent the next hour ferrying cake to the dining room and retrieving dirty dishes and cups. The bonfire was visible through the living room windows, casting its light on the faces of the Monroes gathered around it, receiving the words and embraces of friends. Once, Caleb looked up and caught her eye, nodding with a half-smile.

Eventually the callers drifted away to a handful. Elizabeth was drying dishes when Caleb came back into the house, a tumbler of Scotch in each hand.

"Come sit with me down on the dock. You've done more than enough here."

She followed him outside. Two camp chairs were waiting for them at the water's edge and she sank into one, taking a long slog of whiskey from the glass.

"How are you holding up?"

He shrugged. "I'm talked out. My parents are handling most of the arrangements for the funeral, so my job is simply to be present, listen to people's stories of my grandfather, and run interference when anyone brings up tribal succession."

"You don't mean that tonight someone mentioned it? Who would be so insensitive?"

"Francine Everett. She was practically campaigning. She thought she was out of earshot of the family, but I overheard her. Sophie told me you had a run-in with her in the kitchen."

"Briefly. She considers me an outsider, but I know I belong here, Caleb."

He took her hand and brought it to his lips. "Yes, you do."

"I should get back to Innisfree and make sure the boys haven't stripped the cupboards bare. Are your parents and Izzy still up for me to say goodnight?" She rose from the chair. He stood with her and took her in his arms.

"Thank you for coming. It meant more to me than you can know, especially watching you with my father. I'm sure it's not easy for you, being reminded of Antonio's death."

"On the contrary. It was comforting to see how the community rallied around your family. I was happy to be a part of it." She didn't add what a contrast it was to the days immediately after Antonio died. The villa had seen a steady stream of mourners, as here at Cove Meadow, but it had been much more formal. Adriana had been at the center of the ritual, shrouded in a heavy black veil, receiving visitors in a stupor induced by the tranquilizers her doctor had prescribed to calm her hysteria. Elizabeth had sat numbly in the parlor, merely the grieving wife, not the mother. Many of the visitors didn't even know she spoke Italian and hadn't attempted more than a few formulaic words in English. It was just as well. She was exhausted from the final days of Antonio's life, when she hadn't left his side.

"I felt, more than anything, that people came here tonight to celebrate Tobias' life as well as to console you and your family."

They walked up to the house together. Elizabeth saw that a large pile of driftwood had been stacked on top of the fire for the night.

She said her goodnights to Izzy, Grace and Josiah and climbed into her car. Caleb insisted on following her in his truck to the Dike Bridge and deflated her tires.

"It's late. I don't like the idea of you alone at the pond outside your car. Call me when you get back to Innisfree."

She kissed him goodnight, knowing it was pointless to scoff at his caution. She'd never been nervous driving across the Refuge at night. Even in rough weather, the lighthouse had always kept her oriented, and the most she'd ever encountered on the trail had been a fox or an owl or a fisherman heading to the Gut.

As she expected, the drive was uneventful. As she drove along the water's edge toward Wheeler Point she could see the glow of Tobias' bonfire across the bay, and thought of Caleb and Josiah tending it during the night. The boys were still up, deep into a board game in the living room. She shooed them out to Byzantium.

"You can leave the board game set up and pick it up again tomorrow. I need to get some sleep before I go visit Granny and then meet Nonna and Nonno in Edgartown."

Grumbling, they picked up the remnants of their snacks and drinks and shuffled off to their cabin. She punched in Caleb's number as she collapsed into her bed.

"Home safe and sound," she reported.

Home, she thought again, as she drifted off to sleep.

Chapter Thirty-Eight

Arrival

Elizabeth roused the boys early. With the disruption caused by the delay of the Alitalia flight, she'd decided with Sam and Debbie to drop all three boys in Oak Bluffs until her parents arrived on the island with Adriana and Massimo. The plan was to have lunch at Sam and Debbie's, then get them settled in their hotel before taking them to Innisfree for an afternoon tour and then dinner before bringing them back to Edgartown. After leaving the boys at Sam's, Elizabeth sped to Shady Knoll and the sad task ahead of her.

Lydia was doing a crossword puzzle in the solarium when she arrived. "What's a ten-letter word for 'sodality,' honey? In my day, girls in the sodality were holier than thou in chapel and in front of the nuns, but they hiked up their skirts and snuck cigarettes just like the rest of us."

"Does 'fellowship' fit?"

"Bingo! Thanks. Now, what brings you here? I'd have thought you'd had enough of me for a while after my visit. And where are the Italians?"

"Not arriving till later this morning. And I'll never have enough of you, Granny. But I'm here with sad news.

Tobias passed away yesterday." She didn't know any way to make the news easier.

"Oh, the dear, dear man. At rest at last. Do you suppose the visit with me…?" She pulled her clenched fist to her mouth and sobbed.

Elizabeth sought to reassure her. "I think it was simply time, Gran. Don't blame yourself."

"Oh, honey, that's not what I meant. I think seeing me was perhaps the last box to tick. What is it those AA folks have to do—make amends to everyone you've hurt? Maybe we had to forgive each other for him to let go."

"Forgive? What did either of you have to forgive?"

As soon as she asked it, Elizabeth wished she could call the words back. It was none of her business, and she fully expected her grandmother to tell her that. Instead, Lydia answered her in a single word.

"Innisfree."

That is all she would say. Then, "When is the funeral?"

"Saturday."

"I want to go."

Elizabeth didn't argue with her, as taxing as she knew it would be for Lydia. She sat with her for a while, mostly in silence. Usually not at a loss for words, Lydia this time had nothing to say.

At eleven, Elizabeth left her to meet with Sophie Butler about filming the residents. She was subdued after her conversation with Lydia. She knew Innisfree loomed large in Lydia's relationship with Mae and Tobias, but she'd never considered it the source of anything requiring forgiveness. Was she now taking on that burden? Would Innisfree stand between her and Caleb? She shook off the questions prickling her consciousness. A lot more than Innisfree lay between her and Caleb: physically, an ocean; emotionally, her responsibility and love for her son.

During the meeting with Sophie, Elizabeth made no promises. She explained that her time was committed for the rest of the summer. But she offered to spend an afternoon training her on how to elicit the kinds of stories she hoped to capture. Sophie was disappointed, but asked Elizabeth to keep in touch. "If you should decide to stay longer on the island, please let me know."

Her phone rang as she was leaving. "Honey, it's Mom. We've just boarded the ferry at Woods Hole. We'll be in Oak Bluffs in 45 minutes."

Elizabeth took a deep breath and steered the car in the direction of OB.

She retrieved Matteo from Sam's house and together they waited at the dock for the passengers to disembark. It was impossible to miss Adriana when she emerged from the ship. In the midst of day-trippers in shorts and t-shirts with L.L. Bean backpacks slung over their shoulders, and mainlanders arriving for weekly rentals laden with strollers, bicycles, overexcited children and large dogs on leashes, Adriana appeared in a wide-brimmed black straw hat, designer sunglasses and a sleeveless red linen sheath. Her black, stiletto-heeled sandals clicked on the metal of the gangplank. She appeared to be scanning the faces of the waiting crowd, although it was hard to tell behind the enormous sunglasses. She looked absolutely stunning, and Elizabeth heard murmurs behind her speculating on who the celebrity was descending from the boat.

Matteo waved the bouquet of flowers Elizabeth had thought to pick up at one of the more elegant florists in Edgartown.

"Nonna! Nonno! Over here!"

Matteo ran up to his grandparents. Massimo enveloped the boy in a bear hug and Adriana beamed as Matteo kissed her on both cheeks. Elizabeth offered the same continental greeting, welcoming them in Italian. Her own parents were still on the ferry, retrieving the car from the hold. Massimo explained that Susan and Tom had encouraged them to disembark on foot so that they'd have a bird's-eye view of the island from the deck as the boat pulled into port.

Elizabeth escorted them along the dock to the street, where her father would pick them up. Matteo chattered away to them in Italian and Massimo exclaimed how much he'd grown. There was an ease about the two of them, grandfather and grandson, that calmed Elizabeth. She knew Massimo adored Matteo and she could see that he approved of the changes that a summer of fresh air, sunshine and the companionship of his cousins had wrought. Adriana walked along with Elizabeth, and she, too, remarked on Matteo's transformation.

"He's so full of energy! And so tall! Just like his father. We've missed him. The villa has been too quiet. We're looking forward to your coming home and everything returning to normal at the end of August."

Elizabeth did not trust herself to remain neutral in her conversations with her mother-in-law and so did not respond except with a smile and a nod. Adriana had lost no time in laying down the gauntlet. It was clear that the subtext of her comment was that Adriana had tolerated Elizabeth's moment of rebellion with her summer on Martha's Vineyard, but tolerance had its limits. It was time to come home.

Elizabeth's conflict about where home was couldn't be expressed to Adriana at this moment on the dock in Oak Bluffs. But Elizabeth knew that home had a very different meaning for her now.

Her father had pulled his car into a parking spot along Ocean Park and both he and her mother got out of the car for hugs all around. It had been over a year since she and Matteo had seen them, when they'd flown to Italy for Antonio's funeral. Elizabeth was glad they'd been busy with the car in the hold and hadn't witnessed Matteo's enthusiastic welcome of his Italian grandparents, whom he'd seen only six weeks earlier. He was warm but diffident with Susan and Tom, and it saddened Elizabeth that he didn't have an easy intimacy with them. They were strangers to him, after all. She hoped the next few weeks would remedy that. He'd grown close to Sam and Debbie and his cousins in the short time they'd been together.

Once the greetings were over, the group made its way to Sam and Debbie's. Matteo pulled Massimo across Ocean Park for the short walk. Elizabeth took Adriana in her car and Tom and Susan followed in theirs. As expected, the atmosphere at Sam's was raucous and informal. Twelve people crowded around the dining table for chili, beer, Back Door donuts and conversation in two languages, with Elizabeth and Matteo seated in the middle to handle the translation.

It was Susan who detected when it was time to rescue the Italians and deliver them to their hotel. Bags were transferred to Elizabeth's car, farewells were said, and she and Matteo escorted Adriana and Massimo to the Harbor View Hotel in Edgartown.

Adriana wanted a shower and a nap. Massimo wanted to wander around the town and Matteo was happy to accompany him. Elizabeth escaped into the Historical Society to do some research on Cape Poge for the Innisfree film. They all agreed to meet at the hotel in two hours for the trip out to Innisfree and dinner.

Elizabeth collapsed in a chair at one of the scarred wooden tables in the Historical Society library, trying to focus on a bound volume of eighteenth- and nineteenth-century deeds and census data, but her brain was fizzing with the dilemmas of managing two sets of grandparents, entertaining sophisticated Europeans in a hundred-year-old cottage with no electricity, and providing her lover solace in his grief. The larger questions about what to do about Innisfree or the rest of her life would have to wait.

She closed the dusty volume. Her film would also have to wait. She left the library and ducked into Espresso Love behind the courthouse for a strong cup of coffee. Her phone vibrated. It was Caleb.

"Just checking in to see how the arrival of the grandparents went."

"So far fine. No major incidents, and I've got a brief reprieve and grabbed some caffeine. But I'm the one who should be checking on you. How's everything at Cove Meadow?"

"Quiet. I've got a few days leave from the Refuge and most of the funeral plans are in place."

"You know I'll be there."

"I know. Thanks. And thanks again for last night. I'm not the only one who noticed."

"How's Josiah?"

"Holding it together. Spends a lot of time out by the bonfire."

"I've got to meet Adriana and Massimo. I'll talk to you tonight. It'll be late. I've got to bring them back to Edgartown after dinner."

"Right. No primitive accommodations for them. Till tonight."

Elizabeth finished the last of her coffee and headed down toward the hotel. On her way she met up with Massimo and Matteo. She was surprised to see her dapper father-in-law already kitted out with a bucket hat embroidered with "Martha's Vineyard" on the crown. She was sure Matteo would have him in a pair of Nantucket red pants, boat shoes and a Vineyard Vines bow tie within a week. She could imagine Adriana's eyes rolling as soon as she saw him.

At the hotel Massimo went to the room to get Adriana. It was close to four o'clock. It would be another hour, at least, before they reached Innisfree, and Elizabeth was beginning to question the wisdom of hauling her jet-lagged in-laws out there, only to turn around in a few hours to bring them back.

Fortunately, Adriana had reached the same conclusion. Massimo came back to them apologetic. "Nonna is exhausted and has a headache. She asks if we can postpone the visit to your Innisfree until tomorrow. We can eat something here in the hotel if we are hungry, but your sister-in-law's chili was very filling. You don't mind if we wait? Nonna will be grateful for the extra rest and enjoy the outing much more if we postpone."

Elizabeth kissed Massimo. "Of course we'll wait. We have plenty of time to show you the island. There's no rush."

As she and Matteo walked to the parking lot, Elizabeth had an idea.

"Let's see what Gran and Poppa are doing this evening. We could stay in town for a bit and spend some time with them."

She dialed her mother's number and over the tumult in the background at Sam's house heard the pleasure in her voice that they'd have some exclusive time together. She and Matteo headed back to OB.

Sam took his father, his sons and Matteo out in the Whaler to fish while Elizabeth settled on the front porch with her mother shucking corn and drinking gin and tonics. They caught up, but Elizabeth didn't mention Lydia's decision about Innisfree. That news had to come from Lydia herself.

After a dinner of the bluefish the boys had caught, everyone played a noisy game of Sorry. Sam and Debbie offered her and Matteo beds for the night. It was tempting, but there were things she needed to get done at the house. Matteo stayed, another opportunity to have some down time and get to know Susan and Tom better.

"Call us when you get back to Innisfree," her mother said.

As Elizabeth passed the turn off to Cove Meadow she wished she could ask Caleb to join her at Innisfree for the night. It was selfish. He was in mourning and his family needed him. Let it go, she cautioned herself.

When she got home, she made two calls. The first to her folks, reassuring them all was well and she'd spent many a night alone at Innisfree. Then she poured herself a Scotch, climbed into bed and dialed Caleb.

It took several rings before he answered. She thought they must still have visitors, although it was late.

"Everyone safely back in Edgartown?"

"They never made it out here. Jet lag. Matteo and I spent the evening in OB with my folks. It hit me today how little time they've spent together. He barely knows them. I want to change that. He's staying in town tonight. I know I can't force a relationship between them, but at least I can provide opportunities."

"So you're alone at Innisfree."

"Yeah, but I'm fine. My family worries about me, but the solitude nourishes me."

"Does that mean you'd rather be alone tonight?" He sounded disappointed.

"I told myself I wouldn't ask you to come here tonight. You belong with your family."

"I'm not with my family. Everyone was exhausted and made it an early night."

"Where are you?"

"At the Gut. I wanted some solitude myself and came to fish."

"Do you still want solitude, or can I offer you an alternative?"

"I'll be there in twenty minutes."

Chapter Thirty-Nine

Revelations

Elizabeth climbed out of bed and pulled another glass from the shelf above the liquor cabinet. She had the Scotch poured and ready for Caleb as soon as he entered the house.

"Drinking alone…was the first day with your in-laws that bad?" He asked as he took the glass.

"In retrospect, not really. I actually spent very little time alone with them. Massimo is a teddy bear, and Matteo entertained him for a few hours in Edgartown. And I can probably count on Adriana to take her afternoon siestas the whole time they're here. It's not the stress of their visit that's draining me and driving me to drink."

"Then what is?"

"You've got enough to deal with right now. I don't want to dump my burdens on you."

"Don't be a martyr. It's not who I know you to be." His voice cut through her indecisiveness and reluctance to share with him what was running through her brain on a continual loop.

"Lydia has signed over the deed to Innisfree to me."

"Tobias would have been happy to know that."

"Do you think so? That reassures me."

"I'm happy to know it. Of all the Hammond clan, I think you understand what Innisfree means, what it is."

"It's a moral commitment. I feel as if I've taken a vow. I'm bound to this place. I was already, even without Lydia conferring the deed. Your father said something to me the other day, that Innisfree doesn't 'belong' to anyone. We belong to it."

"It's an ancient concept, that we do not own the land or the water. We are its stewards, its caretakers. In a way, that disregard for the formalities of ownership, like deeds and bills of sale, is what led to our loss of the land. What will you do, now that you are Innisfree's guardian? Is that why you're sitting here staring into a glass of Scotch?"

"My response to Lydia's gift has lurched from gratitude to doubt that I can honor the obligation, and then back again to elation. I know I have to find a way. At first, I saw Lydia's decision as yet another complication in my already tangled life, and I was resentful. It's still very new. Lydia told me only two days ago. But a lot has happened since then to open my eyes and my heart."

"Tobias' death."

"Yes. It's had a profound impact—as he did in life—on how I look at the world and my place in it."

"Am I allowed to hope?"

"Don't." She put her hand up, palm out. "I need to sort this out for myself, and you're not exactly a neutral party here. Which brings me to ask a question also precipitated by Tobias' death. What now for you? You came back to care for him. I had the impression that the job at the Refuge was just marking time while you helped your family. I know grief has no sell-by date. It's impossible to anticipate how your family will rebuild itself around his absence. But have you thought at all about your own future? Or have you been avoiding it, drifting in the ease of the familiar?"

"Whoa! When did you become so insightful? Yes, I've got my own stuff to sort out. But you, especially, should understand that I'm still in the maw of grief. Any decisions I'd make right now would be deeply flawed, colored by the immediacy of loss. Not just of Tobias. I may be losing you. And that could drive me to do stupid, reckless things."

"So here we both are, hovering on the edge of life-changing decisions, and trying not to push each other in one direction or the other."

"Even if we kept away from one another, left each other in peace to find our own way, I have the feeling it's too late. We are already entangled. I know I want you in my life, Elizabeth, enough to leave here and follow you to Italy, if that is what you decide."

"I'm not going to be strong tonight, Caleb, and argue that you need to do what you are called to do here on Chappy—for your family and for the tribe. I'm not going to send you away. Come to bed. Make love to me. Let's leave the hard decisions until after the funeral."

Elizabeth woke first the next morning. Caleb lay next to her on his back, his dark hair fanned across the pillow and his breathing steady and untroubled. She turned carefully on her side to face him, unwilling to disturb him not only for his need for rest, but also because she wanted a moment to study him when he was unguarded.

How many times had she observed Antonio's face in repose? Antonio had been a beautiful man—his mother's son, with Adriana's thickly lashed blue eyes, black hair and sculpted cheek bones. Until the disease had slackened his muscles, he'd been lean and tall, vibrant in his movements. His face had always been easy to read, his emotions right on the surface in the curve of his lips or the piercing clarity of his eyes.

Caleb's face was more often a mask than an open invitation. And beautiful would not be a word she'd use to describe him. In his face she saw power, secrets, pain, compassion. Despite the intensity and intimacy of the past two months, she didn't know him at all. He remained hidden. And yet…a connection had been forged between them, an understanding that went beyond words, or touch, or unexpressed history. The Elizabeth who'd arrived at Innisfree in the beginning of the summer would not have trusted the connection, would have considered it dangerous. But she wasn't that woman anymore.

She slid out of bed with a smile on her face and let him sleep.

He found her later at the dining table, laptop open.

"There's a fresh pot of coffee on the stove. Help yourself to eggs in the fridge or the cereal on the counter."

He poured himself a cup of coffee and leaned over her shoulder, planting a kiss on her neck that made her lose focus.

"Not fair! I'm trying to grab an unexpected hour of work before I turn back into a pumpkin, aka a mother and a daughter-in-law."

He held up his hands. "I hear you. I'll leave you to it as soon as I finish my coffee."

She studied him, propping her chin in her hand.

"Will you appear on camera for my film? I'm making a list of potential speakers and you're at the top of the list."

"I'd be honored. Who else do you intend to ask?"

"Essentially, all the Monroes and all the Hammond descendants on the island. Do you think your father will agree? Lydia cajoled him the other day, but he didn't commit."

"I overheard her. I don't know what to tell you. With Tobias dying, his mind is somewhere else."

"I know. I don't want to disturb him in his grief. After Antonio died, I couldn't eat or sleep or speak. I was barely going through the motions of living, and only because of Matteo."

"It's never very far from you, is it? Antonio's death."

She looked up sharply.

"Is that a criticism? Do you think I dwell too much on it?" Her voice was unintentionally brittle.

"No. It's just an observation. I'm not a novice at grief, Elizabeth. I've lost loved ones. I know it can sneak up on you, muffle joy in the present, drag you back to that piercing moment when everything changed."

"You're not speaking about Mae or Tobias right now, are you?" Elizabeth closed her laptop.

"Tobias taught you well, didn't he, to see within the brambles where the hummingbird has hidden her nest."

Elizabeth sat quietly and waited.

"I lost someone I loved in Afghanistan. She was a journalist embedded with our unit. It wasn't an IED or an ambush, the usual precariousness of daily life that we pushed out of consciousness in order to make it through the day. She got sick. An acute infection that was resistant to antibiotics. She died of sepsis. I wasn't there; I was out on patrol. She died alone. She died before I could find the words to tell her I loved her."

"I'm sorry. All this time I've been pouring out my sorrow and guilt without a thought to what was locked away in your heart. How did you endure it? Why didn't you shut me up?" She reached out her hand and stroked his face.

"Because it was easier to listen to your lament than admit my own grief. I tried to tell myself that, even given the stupid, unnecessary, inexplicable cause of her death, we were in a war zone. Death was the norm. I packed it away. Like a piece of shrapnel too dangerous to remove, scar tissue grew over it."

"Why open that wound now?"

"Because of your openness and honesty, first of all. You've taught me to appreciate the messiness and squalor and sheet exhilaration of your raw emotions working through a problem. That day on the boat before the storm, when you laid out your Wampanoag film like a shaman around the fire in a long house, you poured yourself out, drained yourself. The second reason I'm speaking this now is because I want you to know who I am as you make your decisions. I don't want to conceal my past. I don't want you to feel betrayed by my silence."

"Oh, Calcb! This morning I wokc transfixed by the wonder of having you at my side and, even understanding that I knew so little about your past, I embraced and welcomed the bond we've formed."

He pulled her into his arms and wept.

She had told him the night before that their decisions could wait until after the funeral. But she knew in that moment she had resolved one question. She could not leave him. Now she had to figure out how, given the tentacles of need and expectation clutching at her.

Both their phones rang. They lingered for a moment before separating reluctantly. She lifted her hand and wiped the tears streaming down his cheek.

His mother. Her mother. Both gentle but insistent. They were needed elsewhere.

"I don't think I'll have another night free with the funeral tomorrow."

"I know. I have no idea what to expect today with Adriana and Massimo, but I'm sure it will be demanding. We'll talk, yes?"

"Yes. Don't be bullied."

"You sound like Lydia." She smiled.

He left first. She made a whirlwind attempt to tidy the house, scooping up the glasses of Scotch they'd left in the living room when they'd gone to bed. She saw that he'd made the bed. She scanned the room for signs of his presence. She wanted time to prepare her in-laws for him, not confront them with her lover. But only his scent remained in the room, inextricably bound with Innisfree.

She washed and replaced the glasses, closed up the house and drove away.

Adriana and Massimo were on the terrace at the Harbor View lingering over breakfast when she arrived. Her mother had offered to bring Matteo from Oak Bluffs, but they weren't there yet.

Massimo gestured to the waitress as Elizabeth sat down at the table. "You'll join us for some American breakfast?" He seemed to be relishing the abundant choices available, judging from the remnants on his plate. Adriana nibbled at a croissant.

"I've already eaten, but I'd love a cup of coffee," she beamed at the waitress, a middle-aged woman she'd seen at Cove Meadow the night Tobias died.

"How was your night? Feeling better adjusted to the time change?"

"I took a pill. It helped somewhat. Massimo likes to tough it out."

"I woke early and took a walk along the sea. It's a charming town."

"When Matteo arrives, we'll go out to Innisfree. He's eager to show you everything and take you for a sail."

Elizabeth sustained the veneer of polite conversation, catching up on family news and the state of disarray in the Italian government until Susan and Matteo rescued them.

"Are you still planning to have us for dinner, honey," Susan asked quietly as Matteo greeted his grandparents and Massimo pressed a glazed donut on him.

"Yes, if that's still going to work for you and Dad. I'm planning to attend Tobias' funeral tomorrow and haven't figured out yet how to occupy Adriana and Massimo while I'm at the service."

"Dad and I are going to the funeral as well. Granny seems bent on coming, so we'll take her. Why don't we book the Italians on the Mad Max cruise? They can walk to the dock from here and it will keep them busy for a few hours."

Elizabeth high-fived her mother. "You're a brilliant social secretary! Thanks."

"I'll take care of the reservation. See you this evening. Six o'clock?"

"Cocktails at sunset. See you then."

Organizing her in-laws for the trek to Innisfree took longer than expected, and the wait for the ferry had lengthened as day-trippers formed a long line of cars on Daggett Street. Friday in August on Martha's Vineyard.

"It might be more pleasant for you to cross over to Chappaquiddick as walk-on passengers and enjoy the fresh air on the other side. I'm afraid it's going to be a hot wait here in the car."

Matteo jumped at the chance to be tour guide to his grandparents.

"Nonna, Nonno, come with me! He opened the back door of the car with a flourish and led them to the ferry landing as the boat eased into the Edgartown slip. Elizabeth watched them as the ferry pulled away again,

Massimo at the railing listening intently to Matteo as he gestured at their surroundings. Of Adriana, Elizabeth saw only her black straw hat. She had sat on the bench facing away from the water, one hand clutching the hat to keep it from blowing away.

Once Elizabeth arrived with the Jeep, she lost no time in traversing the three miles to the Dike Bridge. As Matteo expertly deflated the tires, Massimo asked the question every visitor finds compelling.

"So this is it, Teddy Kennedy's Chappaquiddick bridge?"

In the parking lot, tourists were taking photos. Not of the birds for which the Refuge was a paradise, nor of the quintessential island landscape of pond and moor and sand dunes, but of the infamous bridge. So that they could tell their friends they'd seen it. Decades later, that bridge was still the object of a morbid fascination. Only Adriana remained devoid of curiosity, staring listlessly out the window of the car. Elizabeth was beginning to suspect that she was suffering from more than jet lag, and the "pill" she'd mentioned at breakfast was causing her to remain detached from her surroundings. Detached even from reality.

They crested the drive at Innisfree forty minutes later. Would Massimo and Adriana see the wild beauty of the place, or would they only notice the weathered buildings and shabby furniture? *Primitivo*, Antonio had labelled it. No flash or elegance.

As she parked the Jeep on the grass, it no longer mattered to Elizabeth what they thought. She loved Innisfree, and she wasn't going to make excuses for it. Matteo seemed equally oblivious to any disdain on the part of his grandparents. His energy, bouncing from the car to extoll his surroundings, seemed to overcome any reluctance, at least on Massimo's part, to share in his enthusiasm.

Elizabeth brought them to the front door and ushered them into the house.

"I'll give you a quick tour of the main house so you'll be familiar with where to find things. It's not very large, as you see." Her hand swept the expanse of the living room. The boys' unfinished board game was still spread out in front of the stone fireplace. The walls were covered with nautical maps, watercolors of various island scenes, and her own calligraphy of Yeats' "The Lake Isle of Innisfree" poem.

Adriana was drawn to the bookcase crammed with photos at the end of the room. She lifted the family portrait taken on Lydia's 75th birthday.

"Such a big family!" she exclaimed. And then she realized Antonio was in the photo, hoisting a two-year-old Matteo on his shoulders. She brought her fingertips to her lips and then pressed them to the image of her son.

Elizabeth imagined Innisfree was an unlikely place for Adriana to be reminded of Antonio, but was grateful for the photo. She wanted Adriana to know he had been here, however briefly. She wanted her to know that Innisfree was an important part of her life that she had tried to share with her husband.

"Would you like Matteo to take you for a walk around the property while I make lunch?" There was no Carmella in the kitchen at Innisfree.

Matteo was a natural. Elizabeth watched from the kitchen window as he led his grandparents down to Shear Pen. She had no doubt he'd have Massimo in the pond with his pants rolled up raking for clams before the end of the afternoon. She was busy arranging an antipasto platter filled with prosciutto, salami, mortadella, mozzarella, provolone, olives, tuna with capers, fresh tomatoes, and marinated artichoke hearts and mushrooms. Her parents had stopped in Boston's North End at her request and stocked up for her at an Italian market. She didn't hear the French doors open in the living room and was startled when Adriana spoke behind her.

"May I help you, *cara*? Believe it or not, I once knew my way around a country kitchen."

Elizabeth was surprised by Adriana's offer, but accepted it. She anticipated that her mother-in-law wanted to talk without Massimo and Matteo around. Elizabeth handed her a loaf of bread, a knife and a cutting board, and waited.

"Matteo appears to be thriving. The summer has been good for him, yes?"

"It has. Lots of time outdoors, the companionship of cousins, and a measure of independence and responsibility. Not so different from my own childhood summers."

"I apologize for objecting so strongly when you took him away."

Elizabeth wanted to clarify that her intention in coming to Chappy had not been to "take Matteo away," but rather to "bring him to" a place of healing. But she stopped herself. Adriana had just apologized—an extraordinary act in her history with Elizabeth.

"I understand how difficult it has been for you, Mama. I cannot imagine my grief if I were to lose Matteo."

"It's not right, not the order of things for a child to die before his mother." She wiped her eyes. "You would think I'm slicing onions, not bread…My nonna had a kitchen like this. It must be, what, nearly a hundred years old? I know you think I've spent my entire life in villas like Bellosguardo, but I grew up in a small village in the mountains south of Rome. Most of it was destroyed by the bombs during the war. My mother gave birth to me during the Battle of Monte Cassino. Those were hard years after the war. Not enough to eat. My father killed in the final days before the surrender. But what sustained me was my nonna's house. I would consider it a hovel now, but then it represented warmth, safety, food. This place," she waved the knife around the room, "awakened those memories. Thank you for inviting us. Thank you for giving Matteo this haven. He will hold it in his heart when you come home, I promise you."

Elizabeth didn't know what to make of Adriana's revelations. She'd never spoken of her early life to Elizabeth before. Elizabeth knew she'd won a modeling contest when she was eighteen, launching her career. But that is where her biography had begun, both for Elizabeth and the press. Elizabeth had studied Italian neo-realist films of the 1940s and 1950s—the time of Adriana's childhood and adolescence. Only now did she grasp that the deprivation and poverty depicted in those films had shaped her mother-in-law. For the first time, she recognized the fear that had fueled Adriana's fierce drive. It helped Elizabeth to understand her; but she was uneasy about why Adriana had chosen now to speak of her childhood. Was it simply the familiarity of Innisfree that had prompted the disclosure of her deeply hidden past, or did she have another motive? Or were the drugs she was on loosening the tight control she had always maintained over every aspect of her life?

Elizabeth wanted to feel empathy for Adriana, who had lost her only child to a devastating disease and who had endured a childhood in a war-ravaged country. But she was wary. Adriana had survived that childhood and had climbed to a pinnacle of success and wealth not on her beauty alone. Elizabeth steeled herself against

Adriana's manipulation. It was no mystery to her that Adriana and Massimo had come to Innisfree not to acquaint themselves with their daughter-in-law's homeland but to make sure that she and Matteo returned to Florence.

Elizabeth turned to Adriana. "It fills me with joy that Innisfree has kindled these memories for you, Mama. It is a special place and holds its own magic. Thank you for coming!" What else could she say? *I don't trust you?*

They finished the meal preparation together and carried the platters outside to the wooden picnic table overlooking Shear Pen. After lunch, Matteo insisted on taking both grandparents for a sail on the Sunfish, and Elizabeth was astounded when Adriana agreed. While they were gone, Elizabeth worked, her thoughts interrupted by Adriana's unexpected revelations. She banished her apprehension by deciding to ask Adriana if she would describe on film the memories sparked by Innisfree. The connection drawn between two widely disparate places was a dimension she hadn't considered.

When they all returned from the sail, Adriana retreated to the hammock for a nap and Massimo happily obliged his grandson by clamming, just as Elizabeth had anticipated.

She shut down her computer and retreated to the kitchen to cook. The chopping and sautéing eased her into a respite from the tension of managing Adriana.

The arrival of Elizabeth's parents lightened the atmosphere. The cocktails at sunset on the rear patio set the tone for the rest of the evening. Majestic beauty, good booze and delicious food—including baked, stuffed quahogs thanks to Massimo and Matteo's productive afternoon—contributed to a comfortable evening, where the language barriers were bridged by sighs of contentment and awe.

Susan and Tom brought the Italians back to their hotel. Elizabeth had explained the plan for them to cruise around the island on the charter trimaran docked in Edgartown while the Americans attended Tobias' funeral. After a spark of curiosity about Native American rites, Massimo was persuaded that it would be intrusive for him to attend, and he agreed to the adventure of the cruise. The prospect that they might see whales amused him, and he abandoned any more ideas about encroaching upon the mourning of the Monroes.

As soon as the lights of her parents' car disappeared toward Drunkard's Cove, Elizabeth felt her adrenaline level plummet. She hadn't been aware of how primed for battle she'd been all day. She thought about pouring herself another Scotch, but she'd already drunk more than enough that evening, and she didn't want to face the funeral with a hangover. Matteo helped her clean up the kitchen. Just before he retreated to Byzantium, she enveloped him in a hug.

"You were an amazing host today. I know both Nonna and Nonno appreciated learning about this place."

"Yeah, even Nonna seemed to enjoy herself. I always figured her for fancier digs, but she was more relaxed than I remember."

"Good work, Matteo. Now go crash. We've got to be at Cove Meadow at nine. Goodnight, sweetheart."

"G'night, Mom."

Chapter Forty

Requiem

Elizabeth could smell the smoke from Tobias' bonfire as she turned off Chappaquiddick Road. The Monroes had decided to hold the entire funeral outdoors at the Burial Ground, rather than splitting the service between the old Indian church up island and the graveyard here on Chappy.

Izzy explained, "The church won't hold all the people we expect. Tribal members and grandmother's family from off-island are coming, in addition to all the folks in the local community whose lives he touched."

Elizabeth had to park on the verge along Jeffers Lane and walk up to the house, where people had begun to gather in preparation for following the hearse up to the Burial Ground. Behind the house, she heard the murmur of chanting mingled with the occasional sharp snap of wood.

She knew her parents would already be at the Burial Ground. The walk was too much for Lydia and Elizabeth knew her grandmother had finally acquiesced to wait for the cortege on a chair near the grave that Caleb, Josiah and some of the other men of the tribe had dug the day before.

Elizabeth found her brother and Debbie, their kids as scrubbed and dressed as Matteo—the girls in matching sundresses and the boys in khaki pants, button-down shirts and Vineyard Vines bowties. She herself was in a black sleeveless sheath that she'd bought in Edgartown. When she'd left Italy, she hadn't planned on needing funeral clothes. Looking around at the crowd, she was glad she'd made the effort. Everyone was formally dressed; many of the older women with hats.

Caleb opened the door of the house and stood on the top step scanning the clusters of mourners until his eyes alighted on Elizabeth when she raised her hand in greeting. He came down from the porch, working his way through to her, shaking hands proffered in condolence and kissing the cheeks of the women elders.

Elizabeth heard scattered phrases as he moved in her direction. Not just words of sympathy, but words of urgency: "Give it thought;" "We need you;" "Don't abandon the work he began." From Caleb's face, the mask lowered, those speaking to him could detect no response. But Elizabeth watched as his expression hardened. He doesn't want to hear those words. Whatever they are asking, he does not even want to consider.

When he reached her, he offered her the same chaste kiss on the cheek he'd been bestowing on the others. But as he bent toward her, he whispered in her ear, "Walk with me in the procession."

She looked at him. "Are you sure?"

He nodded, then gave Matteo, Sam and his boys hugs. He bent down to the little girls holding Debbie's hands.

"Thank you for coming to help me say good-bye to my grandad."

As he stood up, a cadence began and Elizabeth saw the drummers appear from the back of the house and the bonfire. Following them were Josiah, Grace and Izzy, who had the arm of a spry, white-haired woman in a navy blue suit. A silver cross hung from her neck.

"Who's that with Izzy?" Elizabeth leaned over to Caleb.

"My Great-Aunt Mo. Grandma Mae's baby sister. She's the only Keaney left. A nun."

Before Caleb and Elizabeth took their places behind his family, he ran his finger over the streaks of soot on his cheeks and swept it across Elizabeth's, marking her.

The rest of the gathered mourners formed ranks. The hearse was at the head of the driveway and began to move slowly up the hill toward the Burial Ground.

Josiah took up a chant behind the drums. Elizabeth saw that his hair was bound with an osprey feather, and wampum earrings hung from his earlobes. A buckskin cloak, decorated with the designs Elizabeth had filmed Mariah painting, hung over his shoulders. His face, like Caleb's and now hers, was marked with bands of soot.

Elizabeth had never seen Josiah in Wampanoag regalia, not even with a simple wampum shell strung on a leather thong around his neck, as Caleb always wore. Grace and Izzy also bore symbols of their Wampanoag heritage, even though they weren't wearing buckskin. Grace wore a wampum necklace, the purple and white swirls on its many stones a striking contrast to the warm brown tone of her neck. Izzy had left her hair free, its natural curl forming a honey-colored halo around her face. A single feather hung from a loop in her ear. Caleb had bound his hair like his father's. His feather, however, was different, flashing with the iridescence of the hummingbird. Beside Caleb in her black dress, her blond hair piled on top of her head, Elizabeth felt exceptionally white.

Several older mourners were already at the Burial Ground. By the time everyone in the procession had arrived, the cemetery was full. A tent had been erected over the empty grave and several chairs were arranged under it. Elizabeth saw Lydia seated in the back row, her hands rigid in her lap. Elizabeth's parents stood behind her.

A shaman and a minister conducted the services, a blend of Christian and Wampanoag spirituality dominated by the drums, the chanting, and tobacco burning in a bowl. Izzy had carried a leather bag in the procession and placed it on top of the coffin as it was lowered into the grave. Elizabeth gestured to Caleb and quietly asked its purpose. He explained that it was a prayer bundle, filled with meaningful objects to accompany Tobias on his journey home.

Throughout the funeral, Caleb did not let go of her hand.

When the final prayers had been intoned, the last chants sung, each person in the cemetery stepped up to the grave to toss in a handful of soil.

Lydia made her way slowly to the front on Tom's arm. When she arrived at the edge of the grave, she knelt to scoop up some of the sandy earth. She murmured a prayer and strewed the earth over the wooden casket.

She pushed away the arms reaching out to help her up.

"Leave me be in peace for a moment with my friend."

When she was finally ready to rise, she grasped Mae's gravestone, the space for Tobias' name empty and waiting for nearly twenty years. Lydia kissed the stone and pulled herself to her feet.

"Take me home," she said hoarsely to Susan and Tom.

"Oh, no, you can't go yet," a voice spoke to her across the grave. It was the white-haired woman, Caleb's Great-Aunt Mo.

"You have to have at least one shot of whiskey with me. You and I appear to be the only ones left. Come, take my arm. If I'd remembered how far it was from the house I'd have brought a flask."

Lydia's face broke out in a broad grin. "Sister Mary Pain-in-the-Ass! Mo, give me a hug."

The two white-haired women embraced and started back to Cove Meadow, laughing like school girls as tears streamed down their cheeks. Izzy and Susan followed closely behind their two charges, their arms entwined around one another.

Mourners were drifting in pairs and threes back down the lane. Grace had gone back to the house, but Josiah was still in the cemetery. He had his back to the grave and was standing at the water's edge.

Elizabeth saw him and made a decision. She touched Caleb lightly on the chest with her free hand.

"I'd like to stay and talk with your father. Something I need to ask his advice on. Can I meet you back at Cove Meadow?"

Caleb glanced back at his father. "If anyone can pierce my father's solitude, it will be you."

She squeezed his hand and walked toward Josiah. When she reached his side, she stood with him silently for a few minutes, as she had the first night of the bonfire. The bay was alive, gulls cawing, ospreys shrieking and diving, the wind stirring the water to small white caps. Across the expanse of the water, clusters of brightly colored umbrellas punctuated the shore.

"Will you walk with me a bit? I need your advice."

Josiah studied her face and then shrugged.

"Lead on."

Together they descended to the beach below the burial ground. In the distance to the northeast, the tip of Innisfree was just visible.

Elizabeth slipped off her shoes, taking comfort in the sensation of her bare feet in the fine sand. And then she began, her vision unfolding as she spoke, casting a spell with her story. But this was no film she was describing. It was real life.

Chapter Forty-One

Announcement

By the time Elizabeth and Josiah returned to Cove Meadow, the crush of mourners had thinned. The bonfire was consuming the last of the driftwood, and the scent of sage hung over the back yard.

Caleb saw her and mouthed silently, "How did it go?"

She smiled. "Well."

Elizabeth saw that the only people remaining were members of the Monroe and Hammond clans. Great-Aunt Mo had apparently convinced Lydia to stay beyond one shot of whiskey. Elizabeth hadn't intended to make her announcement now, but the presence of everyone in one place seemed serendipitous. But there were three people she wanted to speak with individually first: Lydia, Matteo and Caleb. They would be affected most profoundly by her plan.

She approached Lydia first, sitting in an Adirondack chair next to Aunt Mo.

"Honey, come here and let me introduce you to Reverend Mother. Mo, this is my granddaughter Elizabeth, the filmmaker and now the mistress of Innisfree. Elizabeth, Mo is Mae's baby sister. After she and Mae reunited, she visited often in the summer. In addition to being a formidable drinking partner, she taught Mae and me how to forgive ourselves for our failings."

Elizabeth perched on the arm of Lydia's chair and listened to the two women. Aunt Mo radiated a straightforward goodness, full of humor and warmth. She then excused herself when she saw Josiah sitting by the fire.

"I'm going to go sit with my nephew for a bit. I've been keeping him in my prayers, and I understand that you, Elizabeth, had a role in those prayers being answered. Bless you, child, for knowing that he needed to read his mother's journal." She lifted herself from her chair and strode over to Josiah, whose face lit up like a child's at her approach.

Elizabeth slid into Mo's vacated seat and took her grandmother's hand.

"Remember how you told me when you gave me Innisfree that I would know what to do with it, how to care for it?"

"Of course, honey. It was only a few days ago. My mind is going, but not that fast."

"Let me tell you what I've decided."

Elizabeth bent toward her grandmother and spoke quietly as Lydia listened intently. If she was surprised by what Elizabeth told her, she didn't show it. When Elizabeth finished, Lydia took her face in her hands and kissed her.

Elizabeth repeated the conversation to Matteo, who seemed awe-struck.

"Wow, Mom. That's epic. And, yeah, I'm cool with it."

Her final words were with Caleb, who had wandered down to the dock.

"Thanks for taking care of Dad. You and Auntie Mo, the Josiah whisperers. Are you going to fill me in on what is going on?"

"I came down here to tell you what we talked about. I didn't know until the funeral that I'd be ready, but everything came together for me. Perhaps it was the combination of the drumming and chanting, the reverence and solemnity of the ritual, and the solidity of you beside me."

"Thank you for walking with me and staying at my side. It was important to me."

"That wasn't just for emotional support, was it? You were making a statement to the community that we are together. I was honored to be there. I also have to admit, it gave me some satisfaction to see the surprise on a few of those faces."

"Francine, for example."

She nodded, a smile on her face. "You weren't exhibiting a bit of defiance, were you?"

"Just following in my grandfather's footsteps. He approved of you, you know."

"I know."

"But what about my father? What was so important?"

"I'd made a decision about Innisfree, but I couldn't implement it without his agreement. I'm relinquishing Innisfree."

"Why? You love it! Are you turning it over to the Refuge? Is this because you can't care for it from Italy? Let us help. Don't give it up!"

"I don't want your help." Somehow, this conversation was going off the rails. None of the others had gotten so agitated when she described her intentions.

"I'm not selling it to the Refuge because it isn't mine to sell. The stories I grew up on—that you and Izzy and Josiah grew up on as well—were all about Cape Poge as once-upon-a-time sacred Wampanoag land. I'm returning it to its original purpose. Your father has agreed to accept responsibility for its care. I know I'm not supposed to use the term 'belong.' Innisfree hasn't *belonged* to any of us. But we've been entrusted with it."

"How did you arrive at this place in your thinking?"

"It's been evolving since I spoke to Tobias and began to explore Innisfree's meaning to everyone touched by it. But it all came together very quickly, as I said, at the funeral this morning. I knew very clearly what I had to do. Understanding that lifted an enormous burden."

"I can only imagine my father's reaction."

"He resisted initially. I think he doubted my commitment, especially when I told him it was my idea alone and I hadn't discussed it with anyone, not even Lydia. He was afraid the family would stop me."

"Aren't you concerned that they will? Anyone listening to you would call you crazy. The emotional and economic value of Innisfree is enormous. It's priceless."

"Exactly. It's priceless. And yes, I'm certainly feeling like I'm on the edge of a precipice here, about to step off into the unknown. But in my heart I know it's the right thing to do. And I have both Lydia and Matteo behind me. I think she knew exactly what she was doing when she signed Innisfree over to me."

"What about my father? You said he opposed the idea at first. Did he come around?"

"Oh, yes. With a kind of joy that affirmed what I am doing is right."

"It will give him purpose in ways that have been missing from his life. Did you know he was a bone marrow donor for my grandmother? He saved her life. And I don't think anything since then has given him the same satisfaction, the same sense of meaning. But Innisfree will. You are amazing. Insanely amazing."

He kissed her.

"I take it you support my decision, despite your earlier skepticism?"

"I do."

"Then please stand with me now when I announce it to everyone. Hold my hand, just as I held yours during the funeral. I don't think I'll have another opportunity to gather Hammonds and Monroes together in one place again this summer."

"Gladly." And he took her hand.

The fire was down to embers and everyone was collapsed on the odd assortment of chairs scattered around the yard. Sam's youngest was asleep in the hammock wrapped around one of Cove Meadow's cats. The older kids were tossing a Frisbee on the side lawn. Elizabeth asked Josiah to join her as she called for everyone's attention.

"As Granny has told Mom, Dad, Sam and Debbie, she signed over the deed to Innisfree to me this week. When she did, she reminded me that Innisfree was a legacy—Mae's legacy. I've been overwhelmed with gratitude for the gift. I think you all have recognized how much my love of Innisfree has been rekindled over the summer, and how well Innisfree has restored my spirit. Watching Matteo thrive there and spending time with the Monroes—especially Caleb—has shown me how precious it is to everyone who has been blessed to know it. I've been pondering how best not only to preserve Innisfree but also how to insure that it flourishes. Tobias has always helped me put things in perspective, and it seems that even in death he's been guiding me. Participating in the funeral, absorbing the chanting and the drumming and the smoke, taking it all in without thinking but simply being, my decision became clear to me. I sought Josiah's advice—and I apologize for taking him away earlier. Without Josiah, I couldn't do what I know Mae and Tobias would want.

"I have decided to relinquish Innisfree to the Chappaquiddick Wampanoag. My only request is that Josiah take on the stewardship of the land, and he has agreed."

Elizabeth heard the gasps of surprise spreading around the circle. Her mother tilted her head, ready to ask "Are you sure?" But Elizabeth anticipated her question.

"Yes, I know it sounds crazy, but this is what I know I have to do."

"And if any of you think I'm the crazy one, or that I'm upset with Elizabeth's decision, I ask you to consider how much responsibility you've taken for Innisfree in the last few years, or even how often you've been out there." Lydia looked defiantly around the circle at her family. "I thought so."

"My sister would have been pleased, Elizabeth. It's a very fitting legacy." Mo was the first to offer positive words.

"Thank you, Lili. I'm speechless with gratitude, for our family and for the tribe." Izzy rose from her seat and crossed the grass between them to hug her.

Grace had tears in her eyes. For her, Elizabeth knew it wasn't only about the land but also about her husband's renewal of purpose.

"I know it's a lot for everyone to absorb, so I'm going to take my leave right now. I've got in-laws waiting for me in Edgartown. Josiah and I can meet next week to start the paperwork and discuss with the tribal council the details of the handoff. I'd like to stay until the end of the summer."

Caleb had not let go of her hand, but had stood with her throughout her announcement and the reactions it triggered. But now she had to face the next hurdle alone.

"I'm off to pick up Adriana and Massimo for dinner. I'm exhausted, so I'm hoping to make it an early night with as little confrontation as possible. I'll call you later this evening when I'm back at Innisfree." She kissed him.

As she walked down the drive toward her car, calling to Matteo that it was time to go, her mother caught up to her.

"I didn't mean to question your decision, honey. I just wanted…" she didn't finish as Elizabeth completed the sentence for her.

"To make sure I hadn't acted in the intensity of the moment, without considering the consequences. I understand, Mom. Believe me, this has been simmering in my heart and my head for a while. The funeral pushed me to make the announcement, but the decision had already been made."

"OK. Dad and I will bring Granny to Shady Knoll. Are you on your way to the Harbor View? One thing before you go. I'm not sure you noticed from where you were standing at the cemetery, but a taxi brought Massimo and Adriana to the funeral. They were on the periphery and obviously didn't stay and come back to the house. But, honey, I'm pretty sure they saw you."

"You mean saw me with Caleb."

"Yes. You two made a statement today without a single word, by your position in the procession and at the graveside, even the soot on your cheeks. Your in-laws won't have missed that."

"Thanks, Mom. At least I know what I'll be walking into. I would have preferred to tell them on my own time, when I'm not so exhausted. I'll pull up my big-girl pants and get through it. But in addition to their seeing me connected to Caleb, I'm appalled that they violated such a sacred moment, especially after we made it clear it would be intrusive for them to attend. I thought Massimo understood that. But perhaps Adriana, for whatever reason, insisted, and Massimo conceded. I've had the feeling since they've been here that something is off, and Massimo seems to be making a great deal of effort to protect her and keep her calm."

She was reaching for the car door when Sam caught up with her.

"Sis! That was some brave thing you did back there. A watershed moment for both families."

"You're not angry with me or think I'm crazy?" Elizabeth was starting to fall apart.

"Hell, no! I told you at the beginning of the summer how far we've drifted from the old homestead. The more important question is, what's going on between you and Caleb? You two looked like the heir apparent and his consort up there at the cemetery."

"Later, Sam. I'm on my way to explain to my in-laws that, yes, there is another man in my life. Apparently they were there today. I can only imagine their sense of betrayal. There's no easy way to get through this. I'm anticipating a lot of yelling and screaming on Adriana's part. The word *putana* will probably cross her lips several times."

"You have a right to happiness, Elizabeth. The days of dressing in black and honoring the memory of your dead husband by remaining celibate for the rest of your life are long gone."

"Oh, I don't think they'd care if I took off with another man and disappeared from their lives. They just don't want me to take Matteo with me."

"What are you going to do? It seems to me your head is in a very different place than it was when we had our heart-to-heart earlier in the summer."

"My head and my heart. Honestly, I haven't figured it out yet. Matteo comes first. No matter what."

"Call me later, OK?"
"OK. I've got to go. Here comes Matteo."

Chapter Forty-Two

Disintegration

"Did you see Nonna and Nonno at the cemetery?" Elizabeth questioned Matteo as they waited in the ferry line to cross over to Edgartown.

"No. They were there? I thought they were taking the Mad Max out to whale watch. Why didn't they come back to the house?"

She shrugged. "Maybe they realized they shouldn't have been there at such a private and solemn moment." *Or maybe they were so furious they couldn't stand another minute of watching their daughter-in-law connected to another family, another man.*

When they arrived at the Harbor View, Elizabeth sent Matteo in while she parked. She'd planned to take them to Menemsha for the sunset and lobsters on the dock at Larsen's Fish Market. But the thought of driving all the way up island in her depleted state was crushing. And she and Matteo were still in their funeral clothes. Hardly comfortable for sitting on old lobster traps and cracking open steamed shellfish dripping in butter. One of the bistros on Water Street would have to do tonight. A quiet, elegant place that would keep the shouting to a minimum.

She checked her face in the mirror. She still had faint remnants of soot on her cheeks and pulled a Wet Ones from the container she kept on the console between the seats. She wiped her face. If only she could wipe away the guilt as well.

Lydia's voice admonished her. *You have nothing to be guilty about.*

She climbed the verandah into the hotel and smiled as she greeted her in-laws.

"How was your day?"

"We decided against the boat ride. Nonna was feeling a bit off and didn't want to risk seasickness. Another time, perhaps, when we can all go together."

Elizabeth took her cue from Massimo. If they weren't going to bring up their presence at the funeral, neither was she. After all, she hadn't seen them, nor had Matteo. *Let me just get through this day,* she silently prayed, *without a screaming match with my mother-in-law.*

Elizabeth suggested a simple meal in town and they had started walking to the bistro when her phone rang. It was Debbie. Elizabeth motioned the others to keep walking while she took the call.

"Elizabeth, Sam and I were talking on the drive back and we thought it might be helpful for you if we took Matt for the night. I'm sorry we didn't think of it before you left Cove Meadow. If you're about to have a knock-down, drag-out confrontation with your in-laws, it might be better if Matt's not there."

Elizabeth stood in the middle of the sidewalk rubbing the tension in the back of her neck as Edgartown's busy Saturday night pedestrian traffic streamed around her. She considered Deb's offer. She trusted neither herself nor Adriana to keep the conversation civil, even if Matteo were at the table. She'd hoped to have her plans for the future more thought out, a fait accompli presented to Adriana and Massimo. She still hadn't decided whether she and Matteo would return to Italy, but if they did, it would not be to the villa. If they were to have any life apart from the shadow of Antonio, it had to be in their own home. Elizabeth recognized now that the villa was a prison, for both her and her son.

She wanted desperately to be free of the weight of the difficult conversation ahead with her in-laws. Why not push it tonight?

"Thanks, Deb. I think that's a good idea. We're on our way to Atria on Main Street. Should Matteo eat with us, or do you want to pick him up now?"

"We're just driving off the ferry. Do you think you can make excuses to pull him away now, or should we come back? We're going to pick up some pizza."

"Not necessary to come back. He'd much rather have a pizza than eat at a fancy restaurant. I'll meet you on the corner."

The exchange was handled with a minimum of fuss. Matteo was more than happy to pile into his uncle's van with his cousins, and Adriana and Massimo were surprisingly gracious about their disappointment not to have his company.

"We'll do something fun together tomorrow. Matteo has been at the funeral all day. He needs to kick back with his own age and relax after behaving like a polite young man. You don't mind, do you?"

Adriana and Massimo smiled. "Boys need to work off their energy. No need to bore him with adult conversation for several more hours."

They had to wait at the bar before they could get a table in the crowded, popular restaurant. Adriana was on her third martini by the time they were seated. Elizabeth sipped her Scotch slowly. She needed to be in control.

After the waiter took their orders, she decided to take the offensive rather than wait for Adriana's accusations.

"I understand you came to the funeral today. I'm sorry I didn't see you. I would have introduced you to the Monroes. They are a wonderful family. Izzy and Mom have been friends since they were little girls. The Monroes owned Innisfree before my grandparents. Our family ties go back a long way. I've become especially close to Tobias' grandson this summer. We've renewed our own childhood friendship. Perhaps you saw him. He was standing next to me at the graveside."

She took a sip of Scotch, trying to keep her hand from trembling.

"Is he your lover? Your summer fling?"

"Adriana!" Massimo put his hand on his wife's arm. She was twisting her napkin. "It's not our business."

Adriana turned to her husband. "How can you say that? He could be replacing Antonio in our grandson's life. Keep him away from us."

"Mama, no one will replace Antonio for Matteo. He will always be Matteo's father. And you will always be his nonna and nonno. Matteo is my first concern. Every decision I make is in his best interests. No one else takes precedence."

"I saw how you looked at him, that Indian with the feather in his hair, hair like a woman's. I saw the lust in your eyes."

Elizabeth had expected vitriol from her mother-in-law, flailing for control. But she was stunned by the nastiness coming out of her mouth. She made herself breathe deeply before answering her.

"That wasn't lust, Mama. It was love. He's a good man, a man who cares for Matteo and me. But he doesn't come before Matteo."

"I knew. I knew if you left Italy something like this would happen, turn you away from us."

"Mama, you told me yesterday you understood how good this summer has been for Matteo. He's no longer a boy under the shadow of an immense grief. He's finding himself, as any teenager needs to do. He's had the freedom to be a carefree boy for a few months."

The waiter arrived with their appetizers and Adriana ordered another drink.

"Are you coming home?"

Elizabeth contemplated lying, saying yes to buy some peace. But she knew lying now would only complicate her final decision, possibly even thwart it. She didn't doubt that Adriana could do something dramatic, even threaten suicide, as a way to coerce Elizabeth into bending to her will.

"I don't know."

"I told you! I told you!" Adriana screamed at Massimo, and heads turned in the restaurant.

"Cara, she didn't say no. She's being honest with you. Would you rather she lie, get your hopes up, and then crush them when she decides to stay?"

Elizabeth listened to Massimo attempt to calm his wife and knew he must be feeling the same pain of loss.

"Mama, please know I will only do what is best for Matteo."

"Then let us take him. Go, become your Indian lover's squaw, or whatever they call it these days."

Elizabeth rose from the table. "I will never give up my son. You, of all people, should understand that. What you don't seem to understand is how offensive you are in your characterization of the man I love, his family, his culture. I'll pay the bill; I think you can find your way back to the hotel. I'm no longer willing to continue this conversation. If anything, it has only made my decision easier."

Adriana tried to grab her, clutching at her arm with her red-painted fingernails.

"That boy has an Italian passport. You can't keep him here. We have powerful friends." She was no longer the hysterical, desperate grandmother. She hissed her threat with conviction, as if she had already prepared for this.

Elizabeth left the restaurant shaken. She picked up her car at the Harbor View and drove straight to Sam's. She needed to be with her son.

Chapter Forty-Three

The Comfort of Family

The adults were out on the porch, comfortably sprawled on the wicker furniture. Pizza boxes still littered the table. The cousins were inside in front of the Xbox, finally out of their formal clothes. Elizabeth assured herself that Matteo was there, but didn't disturb him.

Thank God she'd accepted Debbie's offer.

Her mother picked up immediately on Elizabeth's agitation.

"Honey, come sit. You've had a day. Sam, get your sister a drink." Sam was already at the cooler, hauling out a beer.

"This OK?"

She nodded, took the dripping, ice cold can from him and swallowed several gulps. Her mouth had gone dry in the heated argument with Adriana.

"That was a quick dinner."

"I left. I'd had enough."

"Do you want to tell us about it?"

Elizabeth burst into tears. The hours of standing by Caleb's side, supporting him in his grief; the conversation with Josiah, convincing him of the sincerity of her intentions; the need to defend her decision to everyone; and the bitter, unhinged attack by her mother-in-law had finally undone her. She had no resources left.

Her mother held her while she sobbed.

When she was coherent, she described the conversation at the restaurant.

"I'm afraid they'll try to take Matteo back to Italy without my permission. And if they do, they have the influence to keep him there."

Her father weighed in. "Adriana is wrong about his passport. He has both. He's a dual citizen. I remember insisting on it to you when he was born. She must have forgotten. You're his mother, Elizabeth—a loving, competent, stable presence in his life. No court, Italian or American, would uphold her claim. You're overwrought. They can't hurt you."

She wanted to believe her father. But he hadn't witnessed Adriana's disintegration. "I think she's mentally unstable, Dad. And because of that she's unpredictable. She'll take risks. I never told her I'd gotten Matteo U.S. citizenship. She would have seen it as a betrayal; an indication that I didn't plan to stay in the marriage."

"But stay you did. Does she now expect you to remain married to a dead man?"

"What set her off was seeing me with Caleb at the funeral. Mom, thank you for warning me that they'd been there. At least I was prepared. I thought it would be better to bring it up directly, but in retrospect, that was a serious mistake. The abuse she threw at me was unbelievable. I can't even repeat it, it was so disgusting. I tried to go into the conversation with an open mind. I was honest with her when she asked if I was coming back to Italy. At the start of the evening I was still undecided, mainly because I haven't had a conversation with Matteo. I don't want to rip him away from his home, his friends.

The only thing I was sure of was that we needed to move out of the villa and have a place of our own. But now, I honestly think she's a danger to Matteo if we go back. She'll smother him, turn him against me. It's not a life I want for him or me."

She saw her parents exchange looks across the table. Looks of relief. She knew neither one of them would say, "I told you so," but she read the expressions on their faces.

Her phone rang. It was the Harbor View phone number.

"I can't talk to them right now." She was about to let it go to voice mail, but her father reached for the phone.

"I'll take it."

It was Massimo. She only heard her father's brief answers and waited for the call to end.

"He's distraught and apologetic. But he admitted that Adriana is not well. He had the hotel call a doctor to sedate her. He seems finally to have admitted that her behavior has gone beyond grief. He's making arrangements to fly home with her tomorrow and get her into a psychiatric hospital. He said to tell you that he will accept whatever you decide. But he also begs you to keep Matteo in their lives. He's a broken man, Elizabeth."

"He's been a wonderful grandfather to Matteo. He adores him. I just need some distance; I need to know that Matteo is safe."

"Will you stay here on the Vineyard?" Sam asked her gently.

"I can't uproot Matteo from here as well as Italy. At least he'll have his cousins. I'll need to find us a place to live."

"You won't be living at Cove Meadow?"

"That seems a bit premature. So much has happened so quickly that Caleb and I haven't discussed any of this.

As of a few hours ago, I still didn't know whether I would stay or go. And Caleb has to find his own path now that Tobias has died. That was the only reason he was on the island."

"Don't you think you should let him know?" Her mother suggested.

"I'm not leaving Matteo out of my sight until Adriana is out of the country."

"I wasn't suggesting you leave. You have a phone. Go take a walk on Ocean Park. Clear your head, and let the man you love know you've chosen him."

"I have to talk to Matteo first. I'll take him for that walk."

She called to her son through the screen door.

"Can you break away for a little while?"

"Give me five minutes, Mom."

She finished her beer, hugged her parents, her brother and Debbie, and waited for her son to extract himself from his game.

Together, they set off across the green expanse of Ocean Park toward the water and found an empty bench overlooking the harbor.

"I had a long and difficult conversation with Nonna and Nonno tonight."

"I heard you crying on the porch."

"Nonna is sick, Matteo. She's going to need care in a hospital and Nonno is taking her home tomorrow."

"Is it because of me?"

"Oh, honey, no! She's mentally ill, and she imagines terrible things because of her illness. Babbo's death made it even more difficult for her to cope."

"I had the feeling they came because they were afraid we weren't going back."

"You're right. Nonna felt that way from the very beginning, when I accepted Granny's invitation. She didn't trust that I would bring you back. I always intended that we would return, that this was just a summer visit."

"But you've changed your mind."

"Only tonight, and only because of how sick Nonna is right now. We're going to stay for a while. How do you feel about that?"

"Stay here on the Vineyard? You mean, go to school here with Geoff and Kyle?"

"Yes."

"But we can't live at Innisfree anymore."

"No. We'll find a house here in OB to rent while we figure everything out. Are you OK with all this? I know it's a big change."

"I like it here. I like being an American kid. Are you OK with it? You were crying so hard before."

"As long as we're together, I'm good. Really good."

She put her arm around him.

"What about Caleb? Does he know we're staying?"

"Not yet. I wanted to talk to you first."

"Do you love him?"

"Is this 20 questions?" She smiled. "Yes. I do love him. But we all have a lot to sort out about the future. Give it time, Matteo. If we're supposed to be together, all three of us, we'll find a way."

"When we get back to Innisfree, I'd like to do something."

"What's that?"

"Watch Babbo's film. I think I'm ready. It will be a way to keep him here with me, even if we don't return to Florence."

"We can do that. Anything else?"

"Yeah. I'm starved. Can we stop at Back Door Donuts on the way back to Uncle Sam's?"

"Sure. Let's get a couple dozen for breakfast."

"Are you staying in tonight?"

"Nothing could motivate me to drive back out to Innisfree tonight. I might even challenge you to a round on the Xbox."

"You're on, Mom."

When they returned to the house laden with the donuts they were surrounded, and it took Elizabeth several minutes to extract herself and find a quiet corner where she could call Caleb. It was late; she was spent. All she wanted to do was hear his voice. But sharing the troubling scene from dinner was not something she felt capable of. She still shook when she recalled Adriana's bitter, spiteful words.

His voice was sleepy, muffled.

"Did I wake you?"

"I must have dozed off. How did it go with the in-laws?"

"A scene. Not one I want to relive tonight. I just wanted to wish you good night."

"I can come out to Innisfree."

"I'm not there. Too weary to make the trek. Matteo and I are bunking at Sam's. I'd invite you, but we literally are in bunk beds. Get some rest. I'll see you in the morning. I can stop at Cove Meadow."

"I'll come to Innisfree. Call me when you're on your way and I'll meet you there. Good night, Elizabeth. I love you."

"I love you, too."

Chapter Forty-Four

Innisfree Abides in Me

The following morning, Massimo called again to ask Elizabeth if he could stop at Sam's with Adriana to say goodbye. He had ordered a cab to take them to the airport. They'd fly to Boston and were booked on the evening Alitalia flight to Milan. They wouldn't linger. Just enough time to calm Adriana and keep her from having another meltdown. Please, he implored.

She agreed. They waited on the porch and met the cab in front of the house. Adriana didn't get out of the car. She looked like an old woman, her skin nearly gray in its pallor, her eyes glazed from the tranquilizers. She wore no makeup. It was a shock to Elizabeth to see her in such disarray.

Matteo bent into the car to kiss his grandmother goodbye. She clutched at him, murmuring not in high Italian but in what Elizabeth realized must have been the dialect from the Roman hills of Adriana's childhood. Matteo freed himself after kissing her on both cheeks. Massimo stood on the sidewalk and hugged his grandson, as usual slipping money into his hand.

"It's not necessary, Nonno! But thank you."

Massimo had also seemed to age overnight. The weight of his losses pulled at him, dragged his robust confidence into the posture of a defeated boxer. Elizabeth kissed him.

"Please let me know when she's settled."

"I will. And you let me know where you will live, how the boy is doing. If you need anything, anything at all, you call."

"Yes, Papa. Take care. Not only of Mama, but of yourself."

She and Matteo waited and waved from the porch until the taxi was out of sight.

In the house, the usual chaos reigned. Her father escaped to play golf, her mother to brunch with friends. Elizabeth had been so wired for the past week that she truly didn't know what to do with herself. The boys traipsed off to the beach and Debbie was ferrying the girls to a playdate. Elizabeth wandered through the empty house with a trash bag, collecting the debris of the previous night that they'd all been too exhausted to deal with.

She felt a curious reluctance to call Caleb and revisit the cruelty she'd experienced the night before. The invective hurled at her by Adriana at dinner because of Caleb's race had horrified her, but it had also sent a ripple of doubt through her. She remembered how white she'd felt at the funeral surround by the Monroes and the Wampanoag mourners. Did Caleb's family see her as an outsider because of her white skin? She had an "a-ha" moment recognizing that this must be how people of color felt in white society. If she was to become a permanent part of Caleb's world, as she hoped she would, she resolved to be more conscious of those she'd perceived in the past as other.

Her hesitancy in calling also reflected her concern that her decision to stay on the Vineyard might interfere with whatever choices Caleb was considering now that his family no longer needed him.

Her resolve to stay away made her jumpy. She'd expected her decisions to lift a weight from her and bring her a measure of peace, but instead, she was reeling from the consequences—Adriana's breakdown, the bureaucracy and paperwork she faced to establish a life for Matteo and herself on the island as well as transfer Innisfree to the Wampanoag; even her grandmother's frailty. So much change in just a few days. She felt paralyzed when she had anticipated exhilaration.

Her phone rang and she saw it was Caleb. Instead of letting it go to voice mail, as she'd intended, she answered it with relief.

"Are you OK? You sounded on the verge of collapse last night."

"I'm still exhausted."

"Are you ready to leave for Innisfree? I was hoping I could stop by for lunch."

"I can be there in an hour."

"Thanks. I'll see you then."

She left a note for her family and drove back to Chappy.

Caleb's truck was already in the driveway when she arrived. She found him around back, his eyes closed as he swung back and forth on the glider.

"Sorry it took me so long. Ferry line was backed up again with beachgoers. How are you?"

"Wiped out. You?"

"The same."

"Where are the Italians today?"

She hesitated, but saw the futility of keeping the story from him. She recounted what had happened without repeating the more hurtful epithets.

"So they're on their way back to Florence. What now? Have you made your decision?"

She was sitting next to him on the glider, holding his hand.

"We're staying. Last night convinced me of the damage Adriana could do to Matteo. We're not going back."

She heard the sigh of relief escape from Caleb's lips and felt the tension in his body relax.

"But that's not the only reason. Even before that disastrous meal, I knew one thing for sure. I wanted to be with you. I hadn't resolved how, but it was the touchstone, the foundation upon which everything else had to be based. I love you, Caleb. I want to be by your side always, as I was yesterday at Tobias' funeral."

"And I want to be by yours. I was prepared to follow you to Italy if that was what you believed you needed to do."

"I was so lost when I arrived here in June. Literally lost, if you remember that night you found me wandering on the beach. After Antonio died, I no longer felt at home in the villa. I was a stranger. Italians have such a strong sense of family, of the clan. I'd often heard them refer to anyone who wasn't a blood relative as '*stranieri*.' It was only through the force of my marriage to Antonio that I was grudgingly accepted. But never embraced. After he was gone, I was isolated. I was seeking a haven when I came here, and I was utterly dismayed when I arrived to discover that the sanctuary I'd cherished as a child had fallen into neglect.

"It was only after I began to clean up the place that I realized how much I needed it to be home, to be where I belonged. But to my deep disappointment, Matteo didn't share my sense of refuge here. I remember vividly one night when he threw it back in my face. 'It's not home to me,' he had insisted. I was devastated."

"That's why you've felt so compelled to return to Italy."

"Italy was all he really knew. Of course, it was home to him."

"Then why the change of heart? Was it only Adriana's breakdown and your fears for Matt?"

"That was certainly part of it. But I also came to see that I'd allowed Matteo to lead a confined, narrow life. He's not only an Italian boy. I'd turned away from my American roots so thoroughly that I'd denied my son the opportunity to understand a whole side of his heritage, as well as experience the love and chaos of my family. He barely knew them when we arrived at the beginning of the summer. And I felt that loss acutely. I decided it's time for him to live an American life, be an American boy, for a while. He may very well decide that Italy is where he ultimately makes his home. But if he doesn't experience the 'real world' here, not just summer vacation, how can he make a thoughtful decision?"

"He, and you, may be in for some rough spots on the way."

"I fully expect so. He's an adolescent, with the roughest years ahead. But at least I'll have the support of my family as I navigate those turbulent waters."

"You'll also have me."

"I know."

She leaned her head on his shoulder.

"Can we sit here for a while? Just us. Pretend that no one needs us or has expectations for us to meet. No legacy to fulfill or heritage to maintain. We'll do all that—for our children, our parents, our people. But right now, I want to be here only for each other. Breathe in the sea air, listen to the birds, and watch the sun dance upon the water. Allow Innisfree to abide in us."

And it did.

Epilogue

The drums begin, a cadence in the distance, beyond the grove of cedars bent by a century of wind. Wafting in the air along with the music made by strong hands against taut deerskin, the aroma of sage drifts across the meadow—sage that has been gathered from the herb garden where Mae Keaney had once planted her beans and squash.

Elizabeth stands in the meadow, one hand on the shoulder of her older son, the other resting on her belly, where her younger son seems to be dancing to the rhythm of drums, his vigorous kicks reminding her of his presence inside her. She is surrounded by members of the tribe, gathered for the first powwow at Innisfree. She waits, as they do, for the drummers to make their way from the woods. At their head, her father in-law, Josiah, who in less than a year has transformed Innisfree into a tribal center. Inside the main house, on a video screen, Elizabeth's film unfolds the story of this sacred land and its meaning to all whose lives have been touched by it.

Beside Josiah, Elizabeth's husband, Caleb, clad in ceremonial deerskin rather than the blue-and-gray of the police uniform he now wears in his daily life. The lines of fatigue from studying at night for his law degree appear smoother, erased by the joy on his face as he accompanies his father.

He will officially take on the mantle of sachem today, elected by the scattered tribe and blessed by the elders, the matriarchs of the tribe, of whom his mother is one.

Elizabeth lifts her head to the sun and basks in its warmth and light on her face.

She is home.

Discussion Questions

1. How has Elizabeth's experience of the devastating effects of her husband's ALS disease changed her?
2. How does caring for and restoring Innisfree affect Elizabeth?
3. Caring for dying loved ones and coping with grief after their passing is a recurring theme in *Island Legacy*. How do the Monroes, the Hammonds and the Innocentis differ in their encounter with death in the family? How does your family and culture make the journey through the death of someone you love?
4. Do you relate to Elizabeth's sense of betrayal and guilt when she realizes that she is falling in love with Caleb? Why do you think she is so resistant and agitated when Caleb first enters her life?
5. How does Elizabeth's parenting evolve as she and Matteo are thrust into the challenges of adolescence away from their normal environment? Do you agree with how she handled Matteo's attitude during the hurricane?
6. Do you agree with Caleb's response when Matteo finds him and Elizabeth together?
7. Was the decision Elizabeth made about where to live the right one? Why or why not? Why do you think she decides to give Innisfree to the Wampanoag tribe? Do you agree with that decision?
8. Another powerful theme in the book is the search for home and community. What does "home" mean to Elizabeth, Caleb, Matteo and Josiah? What does it mean to you?

Acknowledgments

As I bring the First Light series to its conclusion, I am grateful, first of all, to the readers who have joined me on the journey through the lives of Mae Keaney, Tobias Monroe and their descendants. Your heartfelt connection to these characters has nourished and sustained me as I continued their stories. Thank you!

The making of a book takes many hands, and I am especially indebted to three individuals who helped to shape *Island Legacy*: Ann Brian Murphy, a literary scholar who brought her wisdom and knowledge to the text as its editor; Julie Winberg, who delved into the weeds and culled the words with a sharp pencil and equally sharp eye as its proofreader; and Daisy Miller, first reader, whose commitment to my work continues to make it better.

And finally, love and thanks to my husband, Stephan Platzer, who, after nine books, has not yet tired of listening to each new chapter as it was written and whose creative talent captures the essence of each story with his photographs.

About the Author

Linda Cardillo is the award-winning author of the critically acclaimed novels *Dancing on Sunday Afternoons, Across the Table* and *The Boat House Café*, as well as novellas and children's fiction.

Linda's First Light series includes Book One, *The Boat House Café*; Book Two, *The Uneven Road;* and the current Book Three, *Island Legacy*. She is also at work on a trilogy set in 16th century Italy focused on a dynamic group of literary women. The first book in the series, *The Poet*, is based on the life of the poet Vittoria Colonna, the only woman Michelangelo ever loved.

In an earlier life Linda worked as an editor of college textbooks before earning an MBA at Harvard Business School at a time when women made up only 15% of the class. Armed with her Harvard degree, she managed the circulation of *Inc.* magazine during its successful start-up, founded a catering business and then built a career as the author of several works of nonfiction, from articles in *The New York Times* to books on marketing and corporate policy. She later went on to teach creative writing before her debut novel, *Dancing on Sunday Afternoons*, launched Harlequin's Everlasting Love series.

With Ann DeFee, Linda is the co-founder of Bellastoria Press (www.bellastoriapress.com), an independent publisher of books about women with grit and gifts, who not only survive but flourish; and wildly imaginative and colorful children's picture books. Bellastoria Press books have been called everything from lyrical and sparkling to quirky and laugh-out-loud. Readers will find stories told from the heart, with an eye for vivid detail, an ear for snappy dialog and a funny bone that gets exercised regularly.

Linda loves to cook and is happiest when the twelve chairs around her dining room table are filled with people enjoying her food. She speaks four languages, some better than others. She plays the piano every night—sometimes by herself and sometimes in an improvisational duet with her younger son. She does *The New York Times* Sunday crossword puzzle in ink, a practice she learned from her mother. From her mother she also absorbed a love of opera, especially those of Puccini and Verdi, whose music filled her home when she was a child. She once climbed Mt. Kenya and has very curly hair.

Visit Linda's website at www.lindacardillo.com; follow her on Facebook at Linda Cardillo, Author; or write to her at linda@lindacardillo.com.

Made in the USA
Lexington, KY
16 August 2019